MY FRENCH WEDDING DATE

FROM ENEMIES TO LOVERS...

OLIVIA SPRING

HARTLEY PUBLISHING

1

____

MELODY

Being stuck in traffic or on hold (especially if I had to listen to rubbish music) ranked amongst my top three most boring things. Time always went *so* slowly.

But right now, I'd rather be crawling along the M25 in rush hour or be caller number one hundred in a telephone queue than here at work, which these days was my number one source of boredom.

As soon as I stepped into this dreary office, time stalled. Seconds felt like minutes. Minutes felt like hours. *Ugh.*

I looked at my watch again: 12.27.

See what I mean? I swear it was 12.24 half an hour ago.

Only thirty-three minutes until lunch.

First, I had to make another call. If I didn't hit my daily target, my boss would get his knickers in a twist. And I was already on his naughty list.

I took a deep breath and picked up the phone.

'Hello, is that Joseph? Great! How are you? It's Melody from Value Office Supplies. I'm calling because we have some exciting BOGOF deals on toilet roll and I… Sorry, the line isn't very clear. I said *BOGOF*. No! I'm not insulting you. It means *buy one get one free*. Joseph? Are you there?'

That went well…

If I'd known that the 'Customer Service Executive' role I'd accepted seven months ago involved flogging cheap loo roll, I wouldn't have applied.

Then again, who was I kidding? After getting laid off from the council, I'd struggled to find work and I had a teenage daughter to feed, so I'd taken the first job I could find that paid enough to cover the bills.

Every second I sat here, staring at the magnolia walls, I felt my life slipping away. But it wouldn't be forever. All I needed was to find a cushy nine-to-five office job that didn't involve sales or too much responsibility and every-thing would be better. As soon as I got back from my holi-day, I'd start looking.

Just thinking about my trip sent my mood from zero to a hundred. This time tomorrow I'd be on a plane to the sunny South of France for my best friend Cassie's wedding. I couldn't bloody wait.

I pulled up the invitation on my phone.

Melody and guest are invited to the wedding of Cassie and Nico…

As I read the first few words, I laughed. It was crazy that Cassie bothered to give me a plus-one when she knew my sixteen-year-old daughter, Andrea, couldn't make it. She'd had this Butlin's holiday planned with her tosser of a dad for months, and seeing as he rarely showed an interest in her, I didn't want to cancel it.

Cassie said she'd left the offer open in case I wanted to bring a date. But with less than twenty-four hours until I flew to Provence, there was more chance of me landing an all-expenses-paid trip to the moon.

It wasn't like I hadn't tried. Ever since Cassie announced her engagement, I'd doubled down on the dating apps, hoping to find someone, but nope.

I supposed it wouldn't hurt to have one last check on Tinder. Just in case.

A new notification!

My heart fluttered with excitement. I quickly opened the message.

Oh.

Seriously?

That was the third dick pic I'd received this month. What was with these blokes?

Not once had I seen a guy on a dating app and thought: *I know. Let me take my kit off, spread my legs and send him a snap of my fanny flaps.*

If I wanted to see a photo of a wrinkly little sausage, I'd go to the butcher's.

'Hello, Melody!'

I jumped out of my seat, causing my bangles to jangle loudly.

When I looked up, my colleague Norman was in front of my desk. I breathed a sigh of relief and quickly locked my phone screen. We weren't supposed to use our mobiles during working hours and my boss had already caught me scrolling on Tinder last Friday.

'Hi, Norman.' I tried my best not to look at the stain he had on his grey shirt. At least it looked more innocent than the wet patch I'd spotted in the crotch area of his trousers a few days ago. I didn't even want to think about what *that* was all about.

'Your hair looks nice today. And your dress is, um, certainly colourful.'

'Thanks.' I smiled.

My hair had come out much redder than I'd wanted when I'd dyed it at home last night, but there wasn't much I could do about it now considering I had my legs, bums and tums class straight after work, then had to finish making the jewellery for the bridesmaids.

Norman's mention of my outfit, a bright orange maxi dress, reminded me I had to finish packing too. Truth be told, I hadn't even started.

'Sheila said you're on holiday tomorrow until Monday, just like me.' Norman grinned, flashing his brownish-yellow teeth. 'Going anywhere nice?'

'Yeah. My friend's wedding in Provence.'

'How marvellous!' Norman ran his fingers through his greasy brown hair. I was surprised his hand didn't get stuck. 'I've always wanted to go there.'

'Really…?' A brainwave flashed into my head. 'Actually, I was wondering. Would you…?'

I paused.

No.

It was a stupid idea. Although this was my last chance to find someone, I couldn't seriously be contemplating inviting *Norman* to be my date.

He was fifty-one and still lived at home with his mum. A five-minute conversation with him would make a chronic insomniac fall asleep, so imagine spending four whole days together.

No way. I'd rather go on my own. It wasn't like I hadn't flown solo at events before.

Anyway, like my other bestie Bella had said months ago when I was fretting about finding a plus-one, being free and single at a wedding had its advantages. She reckoned that if I didn't get a date here, it was because I was meant to meet a tall, dark and handsome Frenchman at the wedding who'd sweep me off my feet. I liked the sound of that a lot more.

As I saw Norman's eyes sparkling with excitement, blood drained from my face. He'd worked out that I was thinking about inviting him. *Bollocks*. I had to shut this down.

'Would you… do you know if they eat frogs' legs in Provence?' I added quickly, groaning inside at how stupid it sounded. What can I say? It was the first thing that came into my mind.

'Oh.' Norman scowled. '*That's* all you wanted to ask?'

'Yeah. Don't worry. I'll google it.'

'Fine,' he snarled. 'And it's not frogs' legs you should be worried about. There's going to be heavy rain here and in France over the next few days, so the wedding will be a washout anyway.' Norman walked off.

What a prick.

I'd definitely had a lucky escape.

~

'Cheers, Mel!' Arlo, my neighbour, beamed as she rifled through the bag of shopping I'd stopped off to buy for her after my exercise class.

She'd twisted her ankle and couldn't get to the super-market, so I'd picked up a few bits to tide her over.

'Pleasure!'

'And have fun at the wedding! Can't wait to hear all about it!'

After we said our goodbyes, I opened my flat door.

'I'm home!' I shouted out. First things first, I needed water.

As I glanced around the yellow kitchen, I groaned. The dishes were piled up in the sink from breakfast and the potatoes I'd left on the counter for Andrea hadn't been peeled like I'd asked.

I stormed into the lilac-painted living room to find her in front of the TV, eyes fixated on the screen. Andrea's long brown hair was tied in a messy ponytail, and she was in her favourite purple pyjama top and shorts. I wondered if she'd even showered.

'You've been at home all sodding day! Would it have killed you to wash the dishes or peel the potatoes?' I huffed, hands on my hips. 'Especially seeing as you're the one who'll be eating them!'

My dinner was already sorted: bean and vegetable soup with steamed broccoli. I couldn't wait until this wedding was over and I could go back to eating proper meals.

'This is nearly finished! I *have* to find out what happens to Jake. He's so dreamy!'

'Last week it was Callum, now it's Jake?' I sighed, struggling to keep up with Andrea's infatuation with reality TV stars. A topless bronzed twenty-something guy who resembled a Ken doll filled the screen. 'Guys like him may look *dreamy*, but like most men, he's got trouble written all over him. And the good-looking ones are the worst.'

'It's not like I'm going to actually date him.' Andrea rolled her brown eyes. True. With any luck, she'd wait until uni in a few years before she started going out with a boy. 'Anyway, you can talk!'

'What?' I frowned as I caught sight of my jewellery bench in the corner of the living room, which was covered with chains, clasps, beads, dozens of tiny ziplock bags and tools, plus the different necklaces I'd worked on last night.

If I had any hope of finishing everything in time for the wedding, I needed to organise it all. Yet another task to add to this evening's growing to-do list.

'You say men are bad, but we both know you're hoping to meet a rich Frenchman, like Aunty Cassie. That's why you're so excited about going to this wedding.'

How the hell did she know that?

My mouth fell open and I quickly closed it.

'N-no!' I protested. 'You make me sound like a gold digger! I've got no interest in the size of a man's wallet.'

Cassie's hubby-to-be was a billionaire, so there were bound to be lots of rich guys at the wedding, but what I said was true: I wasn't bothered about their money. Yeah, I was only human, so given the choice, I wouldn't say no to dating someone loaded if he treated me right (chance would be a fine thing), but as long as he could support himself, that was enough.

As for the other part of Andrea's comment, even

though there was no way I was going to admit it, she wasn't entirely wrong. Ever since it had become obvious that I wasn't going to find someone in London, I *had* been secretly hoping I'd find a hot French wedding date in Provence.

Maybe that was where I'd been going wrong all these years. I'd always dated British guys and it'd always ended in disaster, so perhaps it was time to cast my net further afield. After all, like me, Cassie had been unlucky in love for ages, but her luck had changed when she'd met Nico.

Same for her sister, Lily. She'd found love with a Spaniard. And Bella's friend Sophia had shacked up with a gorgeous Italian chef.

All their romantic fortunes had transformed when they'd met someone from abroad, so the same might happen to me too.

Anyway, *whatever*. Experience had taught me not to hold my breath. Having expectations from men only led to disappointment. As long as Cassie had the perfect day, that was the most important thing.

'It's also why you haven't bothered to find a plus-one.' Andrea raised her eyebrow.

'Rubbish! I *have* tried!'

'*Yeah, yeah.*' Andrea rolled her eyes again. 'If you say so.'

'Oi! Less of the lip!' I crossed my arms. 'And we're talking about *you*, not me. Stay away from boys. You're starting college in September, so focus on your education and then your career. You don't want to end up in a shitty job like me.'

'Mum…' She shook her head. 'We both know you hate where you work because you always pick rubbish jobs that you're overqualified for because you're too scared of trying to do something cool and creative that'll actually make you happy.'

'Excuse me?' My cheeks burned. 'You think it's so bloody simple! When you're an adult with responsibilities, *enjoyment* doesn't come into it. I have to do whatever job will pay the bills and put food in your ungrateful belly. I'd love to do something that'd make me happy, but all the *cool* jobs are given to graduates, not a single mother in her forties like me.'

Ever since Andrea was born, I didn't have the luxury of being choosy. I had to take what I could get, which was usually admin jobs I could do with my eyes closed.

Whenever I'd tried to go for something more stimulating, either I didn't get a sniff of an interview, or if I did, they'd always turn me down. I'd had enough rejection in my life. It was easier and less painful to go for the positions I actually stood a chance of getting.

'Frankie's mum is forty-one and a single mum and *she's* got her own cool salon. With staff and everything!'

'*Whoopee-bloody-do for Frankie's mum!* I don't have time to argue with you, missy. I'm going in the shower. And make sure you've peeled those potatoes by the time I get out!'

I loved Andrea dearly, but she really knew how to push my buttons. I'd always put her and her needs first and *this* was the thanks I got. Listening to *her* tell *me* I should get a 'cool job' and basically calling me a loser because I wasn't like Frankie's mum. *Bloody cheek.*

After a few days with her wanker of a dad, hopefully she'd appreciate me more. And Lord knows I needed a break to let my hair down.

This time tomorrow I'd be in France, hundreds of miles away from my shitty life. Hopefully with a double vodka and Coke in my hand, and with any luck, a dreamy Frenchman by my side.

Yep. This wedding couldn't come quickly enough.

2

____

NATE

'Push your hips back,' I commanded.

'Like this?'

'Yeah.'

'Should I open my legs more? If you want, I can spread them wider…' She looked up at me and bit her lip.

Jesus.

I knew agreeing to an after-hours session with a new client was a bad idea. We'd just started and she'd already turned the flirtation dial up to max.

'I'll let you know if you need to change your stance. But right now, just slide your butt backwards—like you're sitting down on a low chair.'

'I don't know how to do that.' She cocked her head to the side and adjusted her pink designer crop top. 'Maybe you could help? Feel free to touch me if you need to…' She slid her hand slowly over her arse, raking her eyes over my biceps and chest before fixing her gaze on my dick.

I sighed. Just like I'd thought: another rich, bored

housewife who was more interested in checking me out than actually working out.

It didn't matter that I was wearing a loose white vest and a pair of black shorts. I knew that look. To her, I might as well be butt naked.

'Nah.' I bit my tongue, resisting the temptation to tell her point-blank that I wasn't interested. 'I'm sure you can manage just fine on your own. Watch.'

As I guided her through how to do squats, I questioned what the fuck I was doing with my life.

Don't get me wrong. I loved my job, but these past few weeks I wasn't getting the same buzz.

Normally, after training a client, I felt hyped knowing that I'd taken them a step closer to reaching their fitness goals. But lately, I'd had way too many sessions where I couldn't wait to bail.

It was because I was tired and pushing myself too hard. Loads of clients had wanted extra sessions before they went on holiday, so I'd worked sixteen days straight. And now I was *this* close to burning out.

I'd only planned to work this morning, then catch a flight to France this afternoon, but then another client had recommended this woman, Harmony, who'd said she'd pay triple if I could train her after nine tonight. So here I was, at her fancy townhouse in Chelsea, trying to teach her how to do fucking squats, knowing full well that all she wanted to do was squat on my face.

I knew what I needed, though: a proper holiday. Two weeks somewhere hot, chilling in the sun during the day and partying hard at night. Just like me and my best mate Carlos used to do.

In the meantime, I just had to keep horny Harmony

under control for forty-five more minutes. Then tomorrow I'd be off and could cut loose.

I had a four-day trip to Provence for my sister Cassie's wedding, which was this Friday. I'd need to focus on making sure she had the best day, that everything went to plan and my family were taken care of, so it wouldn't be a relaxing break. But at least it'd be a change of scenery. I missed the days when I used to travel a lot for work. I needed to get back to that.

The rest of my family had flown to the South of France earlier this afternoon. Dad was pissed that I wasn't coming early like them, but when you're self-employed, you gotta take the work when you can get it, and catching the flight tomorrow meant I'd still arrive a few hours before the rehearsal dinner and get a sweet pay cheque for this session.

Even though I was doing well, I couldn't take that success for granted. If everything went to shit tomorrow, I didn't want to be stressing about how to pay the bills. I had to plan for the future, now.

When the session finally finished, I quickly took a leak in Harmony's gold-and-marble bathroom, got changed, called an Uber, then headed to the hallway.

'Laters. Enjoy the rest of your evening.' I walked towards the door.

'Wait! There's no need to rush off.' She ran her palm down my chest. 'My husband won't be back until the morning, so we've got the place to ourselves. Maybe we can try *another* kind of workout…'

I stepped back and her hand fell. Some guys might be up for screwing their clients, but I wasn't one of them.

'Look, I appreciate the offer, but I'm done for today.' I reached for the handle and opened the door.

'But I paid you extra!' she folded her arms like a bratty kid. I exhaled loudly, then turned to face her.

'Listen: you paid extra for me training you outside of my normal working hours. That's it. My sessions are always strictly professional. I don't do extras. Good night.'

As I walked to the cab, I shook my head. That was the first and last time I'd be working with her.

Don't shit where you eat, was my motto. No point risking my career just for a fuck. Work was for work. If I wanted some pussy, I'd just go to a bar or a club. It wasn't difficult.

I didn't use dating apps anymore. It'd been ages since I'd been on them. I couldn't be arsed with all the messaging.

For a second, I contemplated hitting a bar. A couple of drinks and a quick bang with a stranger would help burn off some steam.

Nah. That'd have to wait until *after* I'd got to France. I needed a clear head. There was no way I was rocking up to the rehearsal dinner hung-over. Cassie needed me and I wasn't gonna let her down.

I looked at my watch and nodded. Almost eleven. Yeah. This time tomorrow, I'd be chilling in the fancy chateau her billionaire fiancé had hired for their wedding with a rum and Coke in my hand and a hot Frenchwoman on my dick and everything would be right in my world again.

3

MELODY

I wasn't the tidiest person in the world.

I didn't always make my bed and I had jewellery-making supplies scattered in every nook and cranny. But Andrea took the word *untidy* to a whole different level.

As I stood at the doorway to her purple bedroom, I wondered if a bomb had exploded whilst I was in the shower.

There were clothes *everywhere*. On her bed, draped over her tiny red desk in the corner and on the floor. And don't even get me started about the empty glasses. It was like she was running a competition to see how many she could collect before eventually taking them to the kitchen.

But somewhere in this junkyard was my pink jumper and I needed to find it in the next two minutes, otherwise I'd be late to catch my flight.

She'd borrowed it two days ago but hadn't worn it, so it had to be here. I lifted things off the bed before tackling the table. But as I moved a white T-shirt, I froze.

WTF.

Andrea rushed into the room and picked up her rucksack.

'Dad's around the corner, so I'm leaving.'

'What the hell is this?' I thrust the packet of pills I'd just discovered in her face. I knew what they were for, but I wanted to hear her say it.

My cheeks burned and beads of sweat pooled on my forehead. Despite it being a rainy Thursday in July, it felt like I was standing directly beneath the sun.

'Have you been going through my stuff?' Andrea spat.

'No!' I snapped back. My parents used to do that and I always swore that if I became a mum, I'd give my kids their privacy. 'I was looking for my jumper. *So?*' I put my hands on my hips.

'It's obvious what it is.' She rolled her eyes.

'But why do you…' I stopped myself. 'Have you been? Are you…?'

My brain raced at a hundred miles an hour.

My little girl was on the pill. Which meant she was having sex, or at least thinking about it. I'd always thought I'd know when she did the deed or was close to it. But I hadn't had a bloody clue.

The alarm sounded on my phone, reminding me I needed to leave. Of all the times to discover Andrea was sexually active, it had to be now.

I was already running late and now I'd been hit with this bombshell.

'Tell me straight!' I shouted. 'Are you having sex?'

'Mum! I don't know why you're making such a big deal out of this! I thought you'd be happy that I'm being responsible.'

'So you *are*? *Jesus!* I didn't even know you had a bloody boyfriend! How long has this been going on?'

'I don't want to talk about it now! I told you, I have to go. And don't *you* have a plane to catch?' She folded her arms.

Smart-arse.

The flat buzzer sounded, announcing that her dickhead dad had arrived. He always complained if he had to wait, and I couldn't deal with the headache.

'You'd better go, but this conversation isn't over, young lady! We'll speak about this when I land.'

'*Whatever.*' She shoved her phone and the pills in her pocket and barged past me.

When had my sweet, innocent little girl turned into a teenager who had a boyfriend and went to the doctor's to get the pill behind my back?

Last night when she was going on about that reality TV guy, I'd hoped she wouldn't start dating until she was at uni. Now I felt like a right prat.

What else didn't I know about her? Was she taking drugs? Hanging out with criminals? My stomach twisted.

The door slammed shut. I looked out the window at the dark, gloomy sky and sighed.

I'd been looking forward to this wedding for ages, but maybe I should stay to keep an eye on her. The last thing I wanted was for her to end up pregnant and go through a load of crap like I had.

No. I needed to be there for Cassie. She'd helped me so much and I promised I'd be a bridesmaid for her big day. I wasn't going to let her down.

I headed to my bedroom to find another top. The rain

was hammering down, so I needed something with long sleeves.

After grabbing a vest, a loose multicoloured blouse and pink jeans, I got dressed. Thank God these jeans were stretchy. I glanced at my bum in the mirror and shook my head. I'd been going to legs, bums and tums for months and subjected myself to this godawful green diet for the last three weeks and it hadn't made a blind bit of difference.

My arse still looked huge. I turned sideways. I didn't know how it was possible, but maybe it'd got even bigger.

That reminded me. I needed to pack my control pants. There was no way I'd fit into my dress for the rehearsal dinner tonight otherwise.

What else?

I ran through my mental checklist.

Make-up? Check.

Jewellery including the headdress I'd made for Cassie and the hair clips and bracelets for the bridesmaids? Check. I'd finished them at two thirty this morning and put them inside my giant red handbag.

Even though Cassie said she didn't want gifts, I couldn't turn up empty-handed. So I'd stayed up late every night for weeks, making sure every piece I'd created was perfect. Although I couldn't afford the materials and would be paying my credit card off for months, it'd be worth it to see Cassie smile.

On the subject of jewellery, I needed my bangles.

Some women never left the house without wearing mascara or high heels. For me, it was my jewellery.

My bangles were like armour and confidence boosters

in one. Whenever I wore them, I instantly felt better. It was like sprinkling myself with magical fairy dust.

I swiped a huge handful of my favourites from my dressing table. I was about to slide them on, then remembered I'd be going through airport security. I'd feel naked without them, but it'd only be for a few hours. I shoved them into a red velvet jewellery bag, then tossed it into my handbag.

Heels? Check.

Vibrator? Check. As much as I was hoping that one of Nico's hot friends would sweep me off my feet, there was no guarantee, so my Rampant Rabbit was tucked away in my case. I might get some weird looks when it went through the security scanner, but a girl's gotta do what a girl's gotta do.

That was everything. I just needed my passport, which I'd get in a second.

My alarm sounded again. I was really running late now. I'd have to sort out my hair and make-up on the way. After zipping up my case, I grabbed my passport, jacket and umbrella, then flew out the door.

Yesterday when Norman had made that comment about it raining a lot, I'd thought he was being bitchy. But on the radio this morning, the weather forecaster had been banging on about a big storm coming tonight. Luckily, though, I'd be in France by then.

Once I was on the bus, I swiped on some mascara and my favourite red lipstick, then tossed my hair into a beehive.

Time to check my phone. Loads of messages had come through earlier. There was an email from my mobile phone company letting me know they were increasing my monthly tariff. *Great.*

The next message was a bill from my energy supplier. *How much?* The weather had been mild, so I'd barely had the heating on in the past few months. Why was it so expensive?

I didn't know how I'd manage it all. After paying for the ticket to France and buying materials for the jewellery and some new clothes, I was maxed out until payday in a couple of weeks.

Cassie had offered to cover the cost of my ticket, but she'd already loaned me some money a few months ago when my fridge-freezer had broken down. The least I could do was pay my own way to her wedding.

As the bus pulled outside the station, I lugged my case off, hotfooted it to the platform and jumped on the train just before the doors closed.

My phone pinged. After I'd put my suitcase in the rack and found a seat, I glanced at the screen. It was Lily— Cassie's sister.

Lily

Hey! You on your way? Weather's looking rubbish and Cassie's worried about everyone getting here in time for the rehearsal dinner. She's fretting about it raining tomorrow and ruining the wedding too.

Me

Hiya! Yep, I'm on the train to Gatwick.

Me

Weather's crap here too. It's been pouring all morning, but fingers crossed it'll clear up over there soon.

Me

If not, I'm sure they can arrange a marquee or something or do the ceremony inside the castle? It'll be fine.

Lily

Yeah, the wedding planning team are on it. Cass just wants everything to be perfect, so having us all there will calm her down.

A wild hen do might've helped loosen her up, but Cassie didn't want one. She said she preferred us all to have a good time at the rehearsal dinner. So that was exactly what we'd do.

Me

Don't worry. We'll get her nice and relaxed tonight!

Lily

Yeah, hopefully! See you in a few hours xxx

I signed off with kisses, then jumped as the loud sound of thunder crackled through the air. My heart thudded against my chest.

Keep calm. It's just a bit of thunder. It'll clear before the flight. I'll be safe.

After taking a few long deep breaths, I tried thinking positive thoughts, hoping that'd help my heart rate return to normal.

Despite the Andrea pill thing, I still had lots to be happy about. I was on my way to France for a long weekend filled with fun and fab friends, and nothing, including this shitty weather, was going to ruin it.

4

NATE

What the...?

I leapt out of bed. I'd slept through my alarm. I was more tired than I'd thought. Fuck.

After jumping in the shower, I creamed my skin, brushed my beard and ran some products through my short jet-black curls. I'd had the back and sides shaved yesterday so I'd look sharp for the wedding.

The clothes I'd planned to wear were hanging up neatly on the chrome wardrobe handle, but it was pissing down outside, so I quickly unzipped my suitcase and swapped the shorts for jeans.

Once I'd pulled on a T-shirt, I grabbed my shit and flew out the door. I still had time. Luckily, I'd packed before I trained that damn woman last night.

After I arrived at the station, I checked the platform, then headed to the stairs. A woman at the bottom was struggling with a pushchair and a toddler.

'Need some help?'

'Y-yes, please!' Her eyes widened.

I lifted the pushchair up the stairs, making funny faces to the baby inside, then went back down to get my case.

'You're so strong!' She blushed, twirling her long brown hair around her finger. 'Thanks.'

'Happy to help.' I shrugged. She looked like she wanted to chat—well, probably do more than just chat, but I wasn't going there. 'Have a good day.'

Just as I got to the top of the stairs, the train pulled in. The rain was coming down harder, so as soon as the doors opened I flew inside, found a seat and took out my phone.

Fuck. Twelve WhatsApp messages and most of them had come through just before midnight, which was when I'd last checked. This was why I always put my phone on do not disturb before I hit the sack.

Penny

Hey, want to come round to my place?

Penny. That name rang a bell, but I couldn't place her. I clicked on her profile photo. Oh yeah. *Her*. The underwear model with the long braids. We'd met at a club last month and hooked up once. It was okay. But, nah. Pass.

Tina

Hi! Wanna meet? x

Who the fuck was Tina? She didn't have a profile photo, so I couldn't check. But I must know her, otherwise I wouldn't have saved her name.

Tina, Tina, Tina…

Oh… *Tina*. Now I remembered. The blonde swimwear model. She'd chatted me up in a bar a couple of months ago. She was weird. When we were fucking, she kept asking if she looked okay, then wanted to take a picture of my dick. As soon as I was done, I was out of there.

I dragged my hand over my face. There were messages from a few other women, but I'd look at them later. Mum had just messaged.

Mum

Hello, son, are you on your way? We're all here. The weather is awful. We have a meeting with Cassie and her wedding planner later. You didn't let her know if you're bringing a lady with you? Last chance to add a plus-one…

I loved my mother dearly, but *damn*. She had to let all this *settling down* BS go. Ever since Cassie had announced the engagement, she kept asking if I was bringing someone. *Hell no*. That'd cramp my style. Like I kept telling her, I was good on my own.

Mum thought that because I was thirty-nine I should get tied down. Especially since Carlos had started dating my youngest sister, Lily. I still couldn't get my head around the fact that those two were together. As long as he kept treating her right, we wouldn't have a problem, though.

But I liked being free. I planned to be a bachelor for as long as possible. George Clooney had the right idea. Stay single until your fifties. By then *maybe* I'd be ready to settle.

Then again, eleven more years of freedom might not be enough. I didn't know if I'd ever find a woman that I could deal with for more than a few hours.

Maybe it was because I was getting older, but I hadn't

been dating as much lately, and when I did, it was almost always a one-night thing. Any longer and I just tuned out. Most dates were just so fucking boring.

I looked at the next two messages and sighed.

Cheyenne

Hey… dinner was fun last week. Want to meet up this weekend?

Cheyenne

Maybe this time if you play your cards right, you could have dessert…

Exactly what I was just talking about. My last date was with Cheyenne. She was fine as hell. But man, that date was painful.

First she'd bored the shit out of me talking about whether or not she should paint her bedroom bubblegum pink or warm rose. They looked exactly the same.

Then she only ate vegetables because she was on some stupid faddy diet to prepare for a photo shoot. She'd ordered the stuffed peppers, but freaked out after the first few bites because she'd swallowed some seeds and was worried that if she drank water, peppers might start growing in her stomach.

I kid you not.

At first I laughed because I thought she was joking. But when she asked if I thought she should go to the hospital to get her stomach pumped, I realised she was being serious.

After I paid for dinner, she invited me back to her place, but I said I was tired. There was no way I'd be able to get my dick up after hearing that foolishness. I liked my women pretty, but they needed to have something between their ears. Even if we were only going to fuck once.

I'd reply to the messages later and let them all down gently. I didn't do ghosting. Over the years I'd seen my sisters driving themselves crazy too many times about whether a guy liked them, if a man was going to call or not, what this cryptic message meant and whether he actually meant X when he said Y, so I tried to be honest.

I was always upfront that I didn't do relationships, just sex. That way no one got hurt or disappointed. But women thought they'd be the one to change me. Never gonna happen. *Catch flights, not feelings.* That was my motto. Life was easier that way.

When I saw that Carlos had messaged, I skipped straight to it. He was already at the castle with Lily.

The driver announced that Gatwick was the next stop. I picked up my case, walked to the doors, then, once the train pulled into the station, stepped outside, trying to dodge the heavy rain.

Before checking in, I needed to piss. Should've gone on the train but was too busy looking at all those texts.

I headed along the platform, then swallowed hard, stopping in my tracks.

Damn.

That is one fine arse.

I licked my lips as I took in the glorious sight of the beautiful backside straining against the fabric of those fitted pink jeans. Man, I'd love to tap that.

She was curvier than the women I normally went for, but the way my dick twitched with approval told me all I needed to know.

It'd been way too long since I'd had sex. Two weeks.

Wait. No. Maybe four? I definitely needed to get some this weekend.

Weddings were always rich pickings. Lots of horny single women dreaming of getting their cheesy happily-ever-after. I couldn't offer them a fairy tale, but I knew how to rock their world.

As I got closer, I was captivated by her bright red hair. I wondered if she was fiery and a freak in the sheets. I'd like to find out.

And maybe now I'll get a chance.

A green silky scarf that was wrapped around her handbag strap loosened and fell to the floor.

'Excuse me, miss!' I called out. She didn't hear me, so I quickened my pace, scooped up the wet scarf, then tapped her on the shoulder. I couldn't wait to see if the front matched the beauty of that butt. If she had boobs as well as back, I'd have to fight to keep my cool. 'Excuse me, you dropped…'

Ms Hot Arse span around and…

What the fuck?

'Nate?' Her eyes widened. 'What are you doing here?'

Fuck.

Just when I thought I was about to score, I had to see the woman that was on the top of my *hell no* list. My sisters' friend Melody who hated my guts. And trust me, the feeling was mutual.

All the thoughts I'd just had about spinning her around, bending her over and doing her doggy style so I could slap that arse, evaporated.

'It's an airport, so I'm here to catch a plane. That's kinda obvious.'

'And your sisters wonder why I think you're a twat.' She glared at me.

'*I'm* the twat?' I ground my jaw. 'You're the one asking a stupid question. We both know my sister's getting married in Provence tomorrow. I'm here at an airport—you know, where they have planes and shit—holding a suitcase, and you've just asked me what I'm doing here. But if that's not crystal enough for you, sweetheart, maybe I should paint you a picture.'

Melody's jaw dropped.

'I just meant, ob-obviously, I know you're going to Cass's wedding, but I meant, I-I thought you'd already be there,' she stuttered.

'I had to work last night. Anyway, as much as I'd love to stay and chit-chat, I'd better go. Here. Take your scarf.'

Melody snatched it from my hand. She looked like she wanted to say something else, but I didn't have time to hang around. Now my dick had discovered who the owner of that arse was, not only had it deflated, it reminded me that I needed to piss.

'See you in France, Captain Obvious.' I smirked.

5

MELODY

*P**lease God, if you're listening, I beg you not to put me on the same flight as that giant arsehole.***

I heaved my suitcase up the escalator, my blood boiling hotter than molten lava.

Was it really so necessary for him to always be so rude? What was his fucking problem?

When I asked what he was doing here, obvs I knew that he was on the way to the wedding. *Duh.* I was just shocked, so the words came out wrong. He didn't have to make me feel like a prat.

Cassie and Lily always stuck up for Nate and said he was a good guy deep down, but how deep are we talking? Five billion metres beneath the earth?

Every single time I saw him, I thought he deserved to be crowned wanker of the year, but today, I was elevating his status to wanker of the *century*. And that was saying something, considering what I thought of Andrea's chocolate teapot of a dad.

Numpty Nate clearly thought that just because he was

wearing that fitted white T-shirt which accentuated his pecs and biceps and those jeans which showed his rock-solid thighs and huge muscular legs, he could just swan around acting like a wanker.

Well, he's wrong. A hot body could only get you so far. Like my nan always used to say, manners cost nothing. Someone should remind him of that once in a while.

I mean, who even wore just a T-shirt when it was pissing down with rain? He just loved the attention.

And he couldn't get away quick enough. He didn't even offer to take my suitcase. Not that I needed him to, because the escalator was right there, but would it have hurt him to ask? Yeah, he gave me my scarf, which was a relief because it was one of my favourites, but, anyway. Enough about him. I had a plane to catch.

Once I'd gone through the ticket gates and walked through to the airport concourse, I squinted at the announcement screen, crossing my fingers that everything was okay with the flight. The rain was coming down harder and there'd been more thunder and lightning when I was on the train, so I'd had to put my headphones on to try and drown it out. I really hoped it stopped before the plane took off.

Yes! The flight was on time. I breathed a sigh of relief and headed to check-in.

After seeing that Nate wasn't in the queue, I did another mental fist pump. He must be flying with another airline. Probably WankerJet or Arrogant Airlines. Good riddance.

The travel gods were looking after me today. Despite a stressful morning, I'd made it here easily, my flight was on time and my journey wasn't going to be ruined by some grumpy sod making me feel like shit.

Once I got on the flight, I'd put my feet up, order a vodka and Coke, then sit back and relax. At some point I'd need to figure out how best to handle the whole Andrea thing too. I'd speak to Bella, Cassie and Lily about it tonight and see what they thought.

The queue moved a few metres. There were now only three people in front of me. Whilst I waited, I'd get my ticket and passport ready.

I loaded the ticket on my phone screen, then took my passport out. I'd checked the expiry date when Cassie sent the invite, hadn't I? I was paranoid it had expired. As long as there were six months, it'd be fine. Wouldn't hurt to check again, though.

When I flicked through it, my jaw crashed to the floor.

'Fuck!' I screamed loudly. 'Fuck, fuckity fuck!!'

The woman in front shielded her daughter's ears.

'I thought you would've checked in already?' a deep voice came from behind me.

Great.

I squeezed my eyes shut with dread, knowing exactly who'd spoken without even turning around.

'Were all the seats on WankerJet full?' I snapped.

'Is that supposed to be a joke? Don't give up your day job, darling.' He smirked, flashing his annoyingly white, perfect teeth.

Everything about Nate's face was frustratingly flawless. His neatly shaped beard, his gorgeous light brown skin, his hair with the ridiculously cute curls on top. *Ugh.* How could someone with such an ugly personality look like *that*?

'It wasn't *supposed* to be funny. I was serious.'

'Move up, then. You're next.'

'What?!' I shouted in horror. 'How did the queue go down so quickly? Y-you go ahead of me.' My heart pounded.

'No, no. You were here before me. *Ladies first.*' He ushered me forward.

'Er, no. I need to… I've got to go to the toilet,' I lied. My eyes fell to the floor and heat flooded my cheeks. This was so embarrassing.

Earlier Nate had thought I was stupid, and I wasn't about to fess up to the fact that I'd bloody proved him right by picking up the wrong sodding passport. Because I was rushing, I'd taken Andrea's instead of mine.

Bollocks.

I knew people said we looked alike, but after staying up late last night to finish the gifts, I had bigger bags under my eyes than Kim Kardashian's luggage for a two-month trip. Even if our names weren't different, there was no way I could pass for a sixteen-year-old.

I had to get my passport. But it'd take at least an hour to get back home, then I'd miss the flight, and the ticket was non-refundable.

Tears pricked my eyes. I pushed past Nate, dragging my suitcase out of the queue, and headed towards the train station, wondering how I'd pay for another ticket to get to France in time for the wedding.

6

———

NATE

I watched Melody drag her case away from the check-in desk and across the concourse.

Something wasn't right.

If she was going to the toilet, why had she just walked in the opposite direction?

She was lying. As soon as I'd seen her eyes drop to the floor, I'd known she was hiding something. I'd grown up with three sisters who were just as shit at it as Melody was. I knew the signs.

Anyway. Not my problem. She was a grown woman. If she wanted to piss off somewhere, that was up to her.

After pulling my ticket up on my phone and taking out my passport, ready to check in, I paused. Melody was heading in the direction of the train station. That meant she was leaving. I didn't know where the hell she thought she was going, but check-in closed soon and if she didn't catch this plane, there was a chance she'd miss the rehearsal dinner.

Personally, I didn't give a fuck whether she was there

or not, but Cassie would. And there was no way I was letting Melody upset my sister.

I ducked out of the queue and ran towards the station, cursing under my breath.

Apart from waking up a bit later than I should've, my morning was going to plan. I'd arrived at Gatwick more or less on time. Everything was cool. And then I'd seen *her*.

That arse of hers had a lot to answer for. If I'd known who owned it, I'd have kept on walking.

We hated each other. I'd always found her loud and annoying. I couldn't remember when things had gone sour, but I knew she'd started it.

She was always so cold and whenever I saw her, Melody glared at me like I was a cockroach she wanted to crush.

Things had escalated over time. At first it was just dirty looks, but in the past couple of years she'd become more vocal. Saying things that rubbed me up the wrong way or disagreeing with advice I gave my sisters, like she knew better.

As I got to the ticket gates, I saw Melody walking towards the escalator, wiping her eyes.

Fuck. That was all I needed. If there was one thing I couldn't stomach, it was seeing a woman cry. It was my kryptonite. It pulled on every damn protective heartstring.

Whenever I saw a lady weep, I thought about my sisters and my instinct to always want to keep them safe. Even though Melody wasn't blood, I couldn't shake off the need to try and help her. Shit.

After going through the ticket barrier, I ran down the escalator.

When I got to the platform, there were trains on both

sides. I looked left, then right, but there was no sign of Melody. And because I didn't have a clue where she was going, it was impossible to know which train she'd be on.

I quickly walked along the wet platform, doing my best to scan the inside of the train on the left, but it was hard to see with the rain thrashing against the windows.

The guard blew his whistle and the doors closing alarm sounded. Before I could give it a second thought, I jumped on the train.

As I stormed through the carriages, I ground my jaw. If I didn't find her by the time we reached the next station, I was bailing. I was already arriving at the wedding venue a day later than my family. The last thing I needed was to miss the rehearsal dinner. I'd never hear the end of it.

A sharp pain filled my chest as I pictured the disappointment on Cassie's face when Melody didn't arrive, then her anger when she found out I could've helped but didn't.

Then I heard Dad's voice in my head. Growing up, he'd always said I had to take care of the women in our family. Not because they weren't capable of taking care of themselves, but because it was what a real man did.

Nah. I wasn't gonna bail. As much as I couldn't stand Melody, there was no way I could just leave knowing she was upset. Something serious could've happened to her kid. I had to put my feelings to one side and help her out.

I continued searching. She must be on the other train. Just as I was about to walk to the next carriage, I saw a flash of red hair poking out from one of the seats in the corner.

That's her.

'Where are you going?' I growled, towering over the seat beside her.

'Wh-what are you...? You *followed* me?' She wiped her red-rimmed eyes and the sharp pain returned to my chest.

'Answer the damn question. What happened? Why'd you leave? And tell the truth this time.'

Melody hung her head. Fuck. This must be worse than I'd thought.

'I... I... my passport... well. That's the thing. It's not *my* passport. I kind of, sort of, picked up the wrong one. It's my daughter's.' She winced.

'You're shitting me?' I shook my head with disbelief. 'Didn't you think to check it before you left?'

'I left in a hurry!' she snapped. 'It's been a stressful morning and... anyway. I don't have to explain to you. I know I've cocked up, so I need to work out how I'm going to dig myself out of this.'

'Well, you have to go home and get the right passport.'

'No shit, Sherlock!' She clapped her hands together in mock applause. 'Ten out of ten for pointing out the obvious.'

'Well, you know, *you* were the one who asked me what I was doing at an airport earlier, so I just assumed you had a problem with seeing things that are obvious...'

There was so much more I could say about her fuck-up. And I should definitely get off this train right now and check in whilst I still could. But if Cassie, Lily or Flo were at an airport, less than an hour away from catching an important flight, and realised they didn't have their passport, what would I want my mates to do? Laugh and leave them to it? *Hell no.* I'd expect them to help. So that was what needed to happen. Even though I'd rather sit in an ice bath for a week than spend another second with her, helping Melody was the right thing to do.

And no offence, after the foolishness that had come out of that woman's mouth today, if I left her to her own devices, she'd forget something else important, like her suitcase, or wouldn't make it at all.

Cassie deserved a happy wedding with zero logistical problems and I wasn't going to let her flighty friend ruin her big day.

'I've got no idea why you bloody followed me, other than to annoy me, but you can go now,' Melody hissed. 'I'll work out how to get to France by myself.'

'Sorry, sweetheart, no can do. I'm not letting you screw up this wedding by not showing up or letting you stress Cassie out by arriving five minutes before it starts, so I'm coming with you.'

That way I could make sure she was in and out of her place with the right passport, then we could catch the next flight.

'I don't need you to bloody babysit me!'

'Too bad. I'm coming with you, whether you like it or not. End of.'

'I can't be arsed to argue right now,' Melody huffed, wiping her eyes again.

'It won't work anyway. I'm not changing my mind. Here.' I took a fresh tissue from my wallet and offered it to her.

'You keep tissues in your wallet?' She frowned.

'Congratulations!' I imitated the same sarcastic tone and round of applause she gave me earlier. 'You've correctly stated the obvious. Keep it up, darling.'

'I'm not your *darling*!'

'Another obvious observation! Do you want the damn tissue or not?'

'Thanks.' She snatched it out of my hand and wiped her eyes.

'So where do you live?'

'West Croydon.'

'This train goes to East Croydon, though, right?' I'd heard the announcement on the tannoy at the last station.

'Yeah. I'm getting the train there, then the bus.'

'Right.'

I moved my suitcase from the aisle and put it in the overhead rack, then sat back down. Maybe I should sit behind her instead. The four-seater we were in right now wasn't a good idea because I was right opposite her and I preferred not to make eye contact.

It wasn't that she wasn't nice to look at. Melody was pretty, with big chocolate-brown eyes and full lips. The kind that I'd love to have wrapped around my... damn. Why was I even thinking about *that*? There was no way I'd ever go there with *her*.

The women I normally dated had a pretty face and a body like a supermodel. That was why I was surprised about how my dick had reacted when I'd seen Melody today.

Although her physique didn't match my usual type, she had curves in all the right places and her arse looked like it was carved by angels. But even that beautiful backside wasn't enough to convince me to fuck her.

It wasn't just that we didn't like each other. She was also my sisters' friend. And after all the stick I gave Lily about getting together with my best mate, I'd look like a hypocrite.

And I knew Melody's type. She wanted all the whole hearts, flowers and relationship bull, and I was definitely *not* down for that.

Oh, and she had a kid. I wasn't about to start playing daddy to another man's child. No way. Shit like that always ended badly.

'So what happened this morning?' I asked. Melody's eyes were fixed to her phone screen. At least she'd stopped crying.

'What?'

'You said you had a stressful morning.'

Her head darted upwards and shock was written all over her face.

'I'd rather not talk about it.'

'Whatever.'

'I'm sure this is already painful enough for you, so don't bother pretending to be interested in talking or making awkward conversation on my account. Feel free to just stare at your reflection, get back to picking up women on Tinder and whatever else you do.'

My eyes widened. *That* was what she thought of me?

I should've taken that damn plane and left Melody and her smart mouth to find her own way to France.

7

MELODY

Never have I regretted not doing something more.

If only I'd double-checked I had the right passport, I wouldn't be sitting here with this giant prick scowling at me.

I still had no idea why he'd decided to follow, then bloody babysit me, and I wasn't going to ask. After staying up so late to finish the jewellery, the Andrea confrontation this morning, the passport bollocks and now the stress of not knowing how I was going to get to France, I was exhausted. The way I saw it, the less we spoke, the less chance there was of me wanting to scream at him.

Yeah, I supposed he'd done a nice thing by coming with me, but it was probably so he could brag to Cassie and Lily later about how he'd swooped in like a hero and saved me.

Well, I didn't need bloody saving. I'd brought up my daughter single-handedly after Rodney, her muppet dad, let me down time after time. I may have screwed up today by bringing the wrong passport, but I'd find a way to drag myself out of this crap. I always did.

'It's the next stop.' I slid my phone into my pocket.

Nate nodded and got up. As he pulled our cases down from the rack, his bicep flexed and I swallowed hard. This was the first time I'd seen them so close. In real life, anyway. I may or may not have accidentally zoomed in on his photos several times when his profile had come up on Tinder last year.

And I may have also swiped right. Of course, he'd ignored me, which was exactly what I would've expected from someone who exclusively dated supermodels.

In my defence, I'd only swiped because I was having a weak moment and was going through a particularly dry spell. *Story of my life.* I had more dry spells than the Sahara desert in a heat wave.

And although Nate was a twat, even I had to admit, he was fit as fuck. He was six foot three with a solid chest and arms that would give The Rock a run for his money. So of course, when I saw those photos of him with his top off on Tinder, flexing his muscles and staring at the camera with those come-to-bed eyes, my fingers couldn't help themselves, and before I'd even registered what I was doing, they'd moved right.

Dating was hard enough, but when you were a single mum, sometimes it felt like trying to climb an icy mountain in ten-inch stilettos.

Most guys couldn't handle the 'baggage' of getting involved with a woman with a kid. So as soon as they found out about Andrea, I rarely heard from them again.

I'd learnt over the years that all I could expect was a

one-night thing. If I was 'lucky' they'd stick around for a couple of months and keep me as a regular fuck buddy.

But as far as relationships went, forget it. I was too loud and brash for them. I was just a fanny filler: the woman men liked to shag for fun when they were bored or horny or whilst they waited to find a woman who was *wife material*.

As much as I'd been holding out hope that I'd meet someone decent at the wedding, if my track record was anything to go by, my chances weren't looking great.

We stepped off the train and out of the station. The rain was tipping it down. Crikey. What happened to the great British summer?

'It's this way to the bus stop.' I pointed.

'Forget the bus. I'm not standing around in this weather. I'll call an Uber. No, wait—there's a cab station there.'

I was already into my overdraft and panicking about how I was going to pay for another flight. I couldn't start shelling out for taxis.

'But, I don't have any—'

'Let's go.'

Nate tilted his head in the direction of the cab station and ran towards it. Reluctantly, I followed.

Thankfully a driver had just pulled up. I gave him my address. As he loaded our cases in the boot, Nate got in on the left-hand side of the car, whilst I slid in on the right.

I seriously contemplated getting my case and putting it on the seat between us. The last thing I needed was his muscular thighs rubbing against me.

The scent of Nate's woody aftershave was already

flooding my nostrils. If the rain wasn't coming down so hard I would've opened the window.

It wasn't that he didn't smell nice. He really did. And that was the problem. It was the type of fragrance I loved on a man. Rich and intoxicating. The kind that lingered on your pillow and sheets the morning after a night of hot sex.

Not that I could remember the last time I'd had a night like that, but, y'know…

So yeah, it was best that I kept as far away from this delicious-smelling arsehole as possible. I didn't want to catch myself closing my eyes and inhaling his hypnotic scent. The man's ego was already bigger than several continents. There was no way I wanted him to think I liked him, which, for the record, I absolutely did not.

The driver switched the windscreen wipers on full blast, but even then, he struggled to see. Blimey. This was the kind of weather I expected in a tropical storm or during a bad case of April showers.

Thankfully, the driver turned up the radio, which masked the awkward silence. Never had I wanted to get home so quickly.

Once we'd pulled outside my building, Nate said he'd wait in the cab so we could get it back to the station, which was a relief. The flat was a tip, so didn't want him to come up and start judging me even more.

I ran into the flat, grabbed the passport from the drawer, making sure that this time it had my name and photo and was in date, then put Andrea's back in its place.

After a quick wee, I washed my hands and glanced in the bathroom mirror. Before I even realised it, I'd pulled out my lipstick, swiped on a fresh coat and started fixing my hair.

What are you doing? my brain screamed. *You've got a plane to catch and you're wasting valuable seconds tarting yourself up to impress a guy you don't even like and who has zero interest in you.*

There was nothing wrong with looking presentable. And anyway, I wasn't doing it for him. It was for *me*, I protested in my head as I locked up and returned to the car.

'Change of plan,' Nate said as I quickly shut the door and put on my seat belt. His scent hit me like a truck. Him sitting inside this tiny car for all of five minutes whilst I went upstairs had only made it even more intense and intoxicating than before. I pushed myself against the door, hoping that creating a few extra millimetres of distance would make things better.

'What change?' I turned to face him. His eyes dropped to my lips, then he looked away. *Weird.*

'I've checked online and the flight we were supposed to get was delayed before it took off and the next one is cancelled.'

'Sodding hell. And after that?'

'That one's cancelled too.'

'This storm's gonna get worse. There's no point going back to Gatwick.'

Nate rubbed his hand against his jaw and for a split second I wondered how it felt. His beard always looked so soft and it was ridiculously neat. I bet the vain bastard woke up an hour early every morning so that he could preen himself and brush every strand of hair into place. I wouldn't be surprised if he even used hairspray afterwards.

'The weather forecast said the storm wasn't due until this evening,' I said, snapping out of my thoughts. I had no business looking at his beard.

'Well, we all know how reliable the weather forecasts are,' Nate said sarcastically. 'In case you can't tell from, y'know, the torrential rain and high-speed winds, it's already started.'

I bit my tongue so hard, I was surprised I didn't draw blood.

'What about Heathrow? I know it's a bitch to get there from here, but maybe it's worth a try?'

'Already checked. Same cancellations and delays there and at Stanstead. Our best bet is the Eurostar. There's a train still scheduled to leave in an hour and a half. If we're quick, we might just make it.'

'Maybe if we speak to Cassie, Nico can arrange something. Like charter a plane or whatever billionaires do.' I hated the thought of having to ask, but I really didn't want to miss Cassie's rehearsal dinner tonight or worse: the wedding tomorrow.

'The guy's a billionaire, but even *he* can't control the weather. Trust me. This is much better. They're saying the storm could last until at least tomorrow night. The most important thing is that we get to France. Once we're in the country, we'll have more options.'

'Well, you never know, maybe when we get to the airport, the planes will be up and running again.'

'You don't travel much, do you?'

'Why do you say that?' I folded my arms.

'Do you *really* want me to answer that?' He glared at me and I waited for the inevitable comment about my passport. *I walked right into that one.*

'You two remind me of me and my wife,' the taxi driver chuckled. 'How long have you been courting?'

'What?' we both replied.

'I'd never be stupid enough to date someone like *him*!' I spat.

'In your dreams, darling.' Nate turned to me and grinned.

'Oh, I'm sorry,' the taxi driver replied. 'I just thought… even when we first got together, me and my missus argued like cat and dog, but the making up afterwards, well… it's always fireworks. And you two have the same kind of…'

'What?' we both repeated again.

'*Tension.*'

'Yeah,' I added. 'You're right about that. In case you haven't already guessed, we can't stand each other.'

'Oh, no.' The driver shook his head. 'I didn't mean tension, as in anger. I meant…' He cleared his throat nervously. '*Sexual* tension…'

'No way!' Nate laughed.

'Rude!' I snapped. 'You don't have to sound so disgusted.' My stomach twisted. Hearing him say that out loud again brought back the memory of when he'd rejected me the first time, years ago. Twat.

'I'm sure you feel the same, darling.'

'Too bloody right!' I folded my arms and huffed. 'I wouldn't touch you if you were the last man on earth. Even if I had a hundred-foot bargepole.'

'Sorry, I must have got the wrong end of the stick.' The taxi driver turned to face us, looking mortified.

'Yeah.' Nate grinned again. 'Anyway, like I was saying, storms like this don't just pass in an hour. This is some epic shit. I can't see any flights leaving today, so there's no point going to another airport. Trust me.' He leant forward. 'Take us to St Pancras, please, mate.'

8

NATE

I didn't even have to look at Melody to know she was pissed off. I could feel the steam coming out of her ears.

As soon as she'd got into the taxi, Melody had made sure she was as far away from me as possible.

Normally women wanted to get closer. But not this one. Melody acted like a skunk had just pissed on my lap. If she could've put a concrete screen between us, she would've.

And what she said about never coming near me if I was the last man on earth was harsh. I must be losing my touch. If she wasn't my sister's friend, I'd change her mind. Just for the thrill of it. But I didn't care how good her mouth looked or what she might be able to do with it, I wasn't going there.

I turned to face her. Melody's eyes narrowed and her perfect red lips pouted. She was still fuming and it was messing with my vibe. The driver was right about the tension. Not about it being sexual, though. He was *way* off base. But there definitely was an atmosphere. It'd take at least forty-five minutes to get to St Pancras and I didn't want this awkwardness hanging in the air.

'Out with it,' I huffed.

'What?'

'I said *out with it*. What's your problem now?'

'You just told the driver to go to St Pancras without even waiting for me to agree!' she snapped.

'Seriously?' I shook my head with disbelief. 'In case you haven't noticed, we're in a hurry. In a few hours, this storm's gonna shut down every form of transport: not just the planes, but the trains and the buses too. So excuse me if I don't waste another ten minutes sitting in this car creating a fucking PowerPoint presentation listing our travel options so you feel like I've considered your precious feelings.'

Melody opened her mouth to talk, then closed it again. She knew I was right.

I'd travelled enough to know that flying in this weather was dangerous. It was borderline bad when we were at the airport earlier, but now it'd blown up into a full-blown storm. I doubted any airline would risk flying in these conditions.

'Fine,' she spat. 'Let's go to St Pancras.'

Thank fuck for that.

I checked the availability again for the Eurostar. It was still scheduled to run on time, but we were only in Streatham and the traffic was crawling.

As I looked through the seating options, I wasn't surprised that most of them were taken. The only avail-ability was first class, which would cost a pretty packet, but I couldn't put a price on Cassie's happiness. She'd already be shitting bricks about the weather. The last thing I needed was her worrying about whether her brother and one of her besties would make it to her wedding.

I clicked on the two seats, pressed confirm, then took my card out of my wallet.

'What are you doing?' Melody frowned.

'Booking the tickets.'

'Now? Shouldn't we wait until we get there?'

'Too risky,' I sighed. Did she have to fight me on everything? 'They're almost sold out. It's done.'

'I-I'll pay you back.'

Damn right. The way she'd scowled at me all day, she didn't deserve this ticket, but it was for Cassie, not her.

A loud rumble of thunder sounded and I glared out of the window. The wind howled loudly and the car shook. Melody gripped the seat.

'You okay?' Her face was pale and sweat trickled down her forehead. My hand almost reached out to her, but I caught it just in time.

I couldn't believe I was just about to try and calm her down. She'd done nothing but snipe at me since we'd bumped into each other. Even though all I'd tried to do was help.

She hated me so much that if my hand got anywhere near hers, she'd pull out something sharp from that ridiculously huge handbag and cut it off.

From the corner of my eye, I saw that she was still clinging to the seat. I hadn't noticed that she'd taken off her jacket and rolled up the sleeves of her blouse. Her arms were smooth, with a light smattering of light brown hair.

I didn't remember seeing her arms so clearly before. Something about them was different.

That's it.

'Where are your bangle things?'

Every time I'd seen her, Melody was always wearing a hundred bangles. You always heard her before you saw her. Jangling like a prison guard clutching a shitload of keys. But today her arms were bare. If she'd worn her jewellery this morning, I would've instantly known it was her. And I could've avoided this whole damn journey.

'I don't wear them when I'm travelling. Sometimes it sets off the alarms when I go through security. Not worth the hassle of taking them all off, so I just wait until I've checked in and put them on afterwards.'

'Right.' I nodded. 'Makes sense.'

A bolt of lightning flashed through the sky and Melody jumped.

'It's okay.' I reached for her hand before even realising. *Fuck it.* If she wanted to chop it off, then she could give it her best shot. I couldn't just see her scared without trying to help. 'We're safe in here.'

Her hand was soft and warm. I was a sucker for a woman with soft hands. They always felt so damn good on my skin. Especially when they were wrapped around my cock…

Jesus. I really needed to get some pussy at this wedding. My mind had no business thinking about my sister's annoying friend like that.

Melody looked at me, those pretty chocolate eyes wide with surprise.

Oh shit.

'Sorry.' I pulled away. 'My bad. I should've asked you first if it was okay to touch your hand. It's just, you seemed upset and—'

'It's fine,' she jumped in. Her voice was soft, which made a change. Normally her tone was spikier than barbed wire. 'Thanks. I just, I'm just not a fan of thunder and lightning.'

'Flo's the same. She might be the eldest sister, but she was always the first to hide behind the sofa when the storms came.' I glanced out of the window. This wasn't looking good.

After checking my watch, I winced. We were now approaching Brixton and the traffic was getting thicker.

'What's wrong?' Melody asked.

'At this rate, we won't make it on time. We should get the Tube to St Pancras.' I quickly pulled up the live timetables. Everything seemed to be running fine. 'Sorry, mate,' I called out. 'Can you drop us off at the Tube?'

'Okay.' He nodded.

'You understand why we need to get the Tube, right?' I faced Melody.

'You're not about to mansplain, are you?' She rolled her eyes.

'Jeez.' I dragged my hand over my face. 'I can't win. When I *don't* consult you about our journey plans, you complain. When I *do*, you still complain.'

'Getting the Tube is fine. As long as we don't get struck by lightning when we're crossing the road...' Her face went pale.

'I can't promise, but if I see a bolt heading your way, I'll push you to safety. That cool with you?'

'It's something, I suppose.' She smirked.

'Wait...' I raised my eyebrow. 'Did you just *smile* at me, Melody?'

'No!' The corner of her mouth twitched. '*In your dreams!*'

'Quoting my own words back to me, I like it,' I said, remembering that was what I'd said to her earlier.

She definitely smiled, though. Maybe the ice queen was thawing.

The driver pulled over and we got out. After handing him the cash, I put on the jumper I'd taken out of my case when Melody was in her flat.

'Thanks. And enjoy your trip together.' He gripped his cap firmly with one hand to stop it from blowing off and opened the boot with the other.

'Not likely,' Melody hissed, putting on her jacket as I quickly lifted out our cases.

So much for the ice queen thawing.

This was going to be a *long* journey.

9

———

MELODY

As we crossed the main road to the Tube station, Nate stood in front of me.

'Stay close,' he said, rain streaming down his cheeks. He'd put on a fitted blue jumper, but it wasn't any less distracting. It clung to every muscle in his arms and chest. 'If the lightning strikes again, it should get me first.'

My traitorous heart fluttered. He was acting like a shield because he knew I was scared. Even though he held the title for London's biggest knob, that was kind of sweet.

And when I say *knob*, I was referring to the *annoying idiot* meaning of the word, not *knob* as in *penis*.

I'd heard that he was well hung (one of the bimbos he was dating decided to share this information with me when we were in the toilets at a family party a few years ago). But I wasn't thinking about the size of his man meat right now.

My eyes darted to his jeans before I warned them to behave.

Okay, maybe calling him a knob was a bit harsh. If it

wasn't for me, he'd be halfway to Provence by now. He hadn't had to follow me on the train, or pay for the taxi. But he had. Why, I still didn't know, but the least I could do was try to be nice to him.

Well, maybe *grateful* was more manageable than *nice*. He just rubbed me up the wrong way.

I picked up the pace, my body just a few inches behind his. When he'd said to *stay close*, how close was he talking? Like, should I wrap my arms around his solid waist? Considering we'd spent the last few hours bickering, it'd seem a bit weird.

Another rumble of thunder vibrated in the air, but somehow I felt a bit calmer than I had before. If I was going to have someone act as a personal shield, Nate was definitely the man for the job.

Since he was a personal trainer, I knew his body was as hard as steel, so I'd be well protected. That was the only reason I'd wanted to get close to him. Just to stay safe. That was all. He was exactly the kind of guy I'd been talking about last night when I'd told Andrea that good-looking blokes were nothing but trouble.

Before I had a chance to decide what to do, we arrived at the station and dived inside. Nate carried my case down the stairs.

'Please tell me you've got your Oyster card?' He wiped the rain from his eyes.

'Yep.' I waved it in front of his face.

'Thank fuck for that. I was worried you'd either forgotten it or brought your daughter's,' he laughed, tapping his card on the reader and going through the ticket barrier.

I froze and opened up the card holder. *Phew.* For a

second I wondered if I had. Andrea and I had almost identical ones, so it *may* have happened before…

Whilst I stood on the escalator, Nate charged down it.

'Chop-chop!' He paused on the step below and looked up at me. 'No time to stand. The next Tube's leaving in one minute!'

We quickly moved down the escalator, then shot through the doors just before they closed. The Tube was packed. The only free space was next to Nate or in the corner on the opposite side, next to another man.

No brainer. There was no way I was travelling for several stops pressed up against Nate's hot, hard body. I squeezed over to the other side. As I approached, the man's eyes widened and he licked his lips. I hoped he was just moisturising them.

It was bloody hot in here. And the odour definitely matched. As I got closer, I realised it was coming from the man next to me. Why did some people on the Tube hate their shower or have an aversion to deodorant? The stench was so strong I wanted to gag.

I looked over at Nate, who was grinding his jaw. What was his problem?

The Tube jerked and the man fell onto me, his sticky skin pressing against mine. Ugh. I wished I had some of those bloody disinfectant wipes from work in my bag. And now the creepy guy was smiling. My stomach twisted.

'Melody,' Nate called out, his face like thunder. 'Come here. That man doesn't seem right.'

I looked up at the stinky guy, who glared at Nate. He wasn't wrong. The Tube stopped and a few people got off. I headed over to Nate before another load of passengers squeezed on.

'You need to be careful,' Nate said, his warm breath tickling the back of my neck. 'There's weirdos on public transport who like to take advantage of pretty women. Creep.' He scowled at the man.

Had Nate just called me pretty? My body tingled before I told it to calm down. He was talking generally. Not specifically about me.

As Nate moved to get a better look at the Tube map above the seats, his gorgeous scent flooded my nostrils. It was a massive upgrade from the smell of stale fried onions and bad BO that I'd been subjected to two minutes ago. I closed my eyes and breathed in, inhaling the delicious aroma.

'You okay?' Nate said. I looked up and saw him frowning.

'Y-yeah. Fine.' I composed myself. It wasn't Nate that was delicious, just his aftershave. It was just a nice contrast to the normal sweaty Tube odour, that was all.

When we got to Oxford Circus station, more passengers piled into the carriage, causing me to fall back onto him.

'Sorry,' I said as my back hit his chest. It was just as solid as I thought. It was like I'd been pushed onto a brick wall. I swallowed hard.

Ordinarily, I wouldn't give a second thought about being so close to someone in a carriage. It was almost second nature. But being pressed up against your best friend's brother, the guy you famously hated, brought the awkwardness to a whole different level.

The heat from Nate's body radiated onto me. He was so close I could feel his heart vibrating against my back.

'H-how many stops are there?' I stuttered. 'I can't see.'

The tall guy in front was blocking my view.

'We're almost at Euston, so it's the stop after that.'

'Good,' I said, desperate to get out of this carriage.

'How fit are you?'

'Why?'

'Because, when we get off, we're gonna have to leg it to the Eurostar.'

'What, you assume that because I don't have a body like one of your Victoria's Secret girlfriends, I can't run?'

'What?' Nate screwed up his face. 'No! I was just—'

'I can run just fine,' I snapped.

It was like being back in the school playground again. With no one wanting to pick me to be part of their relay team because they thought the chubby girl couldn't run. And just like that, Nate was back to being King of Knobs.

When we arrived at the station, even though I felt like I was going to pass out, I made a point of keeping up with Nate as he weaved through the crowds, then raced up the escalator, clutching our suitcases like he was carrying two feathers.

Yeah. I get it. You're strong. Big deal.

I hadn't been busting my gut at legs, bums and tums and sticking to my diet for some musclehead to try and make me look like a lard arse.

I quickly followed him. Admittedly, I regretted the pace I'd set about a third of the way. As fit as I was, I was no match for him. I wasn't giving him the satisfaction of knowing that, though. I'd haul my backside to the top of the escalator even if it killed me.

'It's this way,' he said as I reached him. We ran across the concourse to the Eurostar entrance. 'Over here.'

'No,' I cried out, short of breath. 'That's the wrong

entrance. That's first class. We're on this side. We've got to join the queue.'

'Nope.' Nate shook his head. 'We're in first class.'

'Huh?' My eyes bulged and my stomach dropped. Those tickets must've cost an arm and a leg. 'Nate, I can't afford this. That taxi already cost a lot and I—'

'Don't stress about the money,' he interrupted. 'I've got it.'

My blood ran cold. The last thing I needed was more debt.

'I'll pay back every penny.' It might take a while—years at this rate, but the last thing I wanted was to owe him anything.

'Come on.' He grabbed my arm and the heat from his huge palms charged through me like electricity.

Just like it had when he'd held on to my hand in the car to try and calm me down.

Thankfully, Nate let go once we reached the gates. He took out his phone to scan the ticket barcodes.

Just as we'd finished going through security, Nate put his phone to his ear.

''Sup, sis?' he said as I wondered whether that was Cassie, Lily or Flo. 'It's Cassie,' he mouthed, reading my mind. 'Chill. Like I said in my message to Lil, we missed our flight, but it's all good. Our Eurostar leaves soon and once we're in France, we'll get a train to Marseille or something. Don't stress. Yep.' Nate nodded. 'We'll message straight away. Melody sends her love. No, I'm… okay…'

Nate rolled his eyes, then pressed the speaker button on the phone.

'Mel?' Cassie called out.

'Hey, Cass!'

'You okay?'

'Yeah! I'm fine!'

'It's just, you're with *Nate* and I know how much you guys can't stand each other. Are you sure you're both still in one piece? Do I need to call the United Nations and send some peacekeepers to keep you two from murdering each other? Seriously, I'm not joking!'

'Don't worry. Your brother is still a giant tit, but he's been on his best behaviour—well, most of the time—and I took an extra dose of patience this morning with my breakfast. We'll be fine. Honestly, don't worry.'

The word *breakfast* made my stomach rumble. I'd been running late and couldn't stand the thought of having another green juice, so I'd skipped it. I was starving. I had been ever since I'd started that bloody diet.

'I can't help it.' Cassie's voice cracked and my heart sank. 'Everything's a disaster. Some of Dad's side of the family are struggling to get here because the weather in Scotland is pants and there are no flights. Nico's been trying to see if anything can be done from our end, like getting a private jet, but no one's flying out. It's too dangerous to be in the air and safety has to come first.'

'I know it's not great now, but I'm sure it'll be glorious sunshine by tomorrow! Anyway, love, we don't want to miss this train, so we'd better go. Like Nate said, we'll let you know as soon as we get to France, okay?'

'Okay. Can't wait to see you.'

'You too. Bye.'

'Laters,' said Nate as I handed back his phone. 'Come on.' He gestured to the platform. 'Let's go. We've got a wedding to get to.'

10

———

NATE

Melody's face was a picture. We'd just sat in the first-class carriage and she looked like a child who'd been given a VIP Disneyland pass.

I was tempted to tell her to forget about paying me back for the ticket. Her smile seemed like a big enough reward, but when she caught me staring and gave me her trademark scowl, I remembered how much she hated me and pushed those thoughts clean out my head.

Our seats faced each other. Which meant over two hours of trying to avoid eye contact. Great.

For a while, we both just stared at our phones. Then Melody pulled out a velvet bag and started sliding on her bangles. One after the other. Six… ten… fifteen…

'Damn. You like your bangles…' I raised my eyebrow.

'And?' she snapped.

'Nothing.' I held my hands up in surrender. 'Just an observation.'

They were… sparkly. If she visited someone's house,

she wouldn't need to ring the bell. That jangling would tell half the street she'd arrived.

I wondered if she wore them to bed. And imagine the noise they'd make during sex. My dick twitched.

Wait, why was I thinking about Melody fucking?

'I feel naked without them.' She pouted again and the sight of her hot red lips made my dick twitch. Her mentioning being naked wasn't helping.

That was it. As soon as we got to that castle, I'd find myself a hot Frenchwoman to fuck. I needed to get laid— that was the only logical reason why I was thinking about banging a woman I didn't even like.

The steward brought over our drinks, then food.

'The way I feel about being without my bangles is probably like how you'd feel without your beard.' Melody poured her vodka into the glass, topped it up with Coke, then took a big gulp.

'Huh?'

'Your beard. You touch it a lot.'

I hadn't noticed, but the fact that Melody mentioned it was interesting.

'You must've been looking at me a *lot* to know that, *Bangles*?'

Her cheeks flushed pink.

'N-no,' she stuttered. 'You're right there, in front of me, so…'

'I think you like my beard,' I teased. She was getting flustered and after the shit she'd given me today, I liked winding her up.

'No! Guys with beards aren't my type. I prefer clean-shaven.'

'Really? Darling, that's only because you haven't

experienced the sensation of having a bearded man between your thighs…'

Melody had been blushing before, but now her porcelain skin had turned bright red. This was fun.

'Have, actually,' she snapped back. 'And he gave me a pussy rash. Exactly why beards are bad.'

'That's because you went with the wrong man, sweetheart. I've never had any complaints about my beard. Women can't get enough of it. That's because I take care of myself. I brush it and use beard oil so it's always nice and soft.'

Melody almost choked on her vodka.

'Sorry. Did you just say you use *beard oil* and *brush* your beard? Crikey. I knew you were vain, but that's a whole new level of vanity! I can just see you in the mirror every morning, primping and preening yourself like a peacock, telling yourself how gorgeous you are,' she cackled.

'So you think I'm gorgeous, do you?' The corner of my mouth turned up into a smile. 'Cheers, darling.'

'I never said that *I* thought you were gorgeous.' She rolled her eyes. 'I said that *you* think you are!'

'So you *don't* find me attractive?'

'Ye-n—' she stuttered, fiddling with the bread on the tray. 'I find you vain, arrogant and annoying. *That's* what I think of you.'

Melody always seemed to get some kind of sick pleasure from winding me up and dissing me in front of my sisters, so knowing I was making her tongue-tied was pretty satisfying. I could push her more, but I'd leave it. For now.

'Tell me, Bangles: why do you think I'm vain?' I said

calmly. If she thought she'd make me feel bad for taking pride in my appearance, she was wrong. 'How is using beard oil and brushing my beard different to women using face masks or wearing make-up? It's called *grooming*. What's wrong with wanting to look good?'

'Nothing, I suppose.'

She shrugged her shoulders, tore off a piece of bread, put in her mouth and groaned like it was the most delicious thing she'd ever eaten. Hearing a woman moan with pleasure was the sweetest sound. I planned to hear more of that this weekend. From other women. Not Melody.

A few minutes after we came out of the tunnel and onto French soil, a vibrating sound made us both jump. 'Bollocks!' Melody glared at her phone.

'Who is it?'

'The sperm donor,' she sighed.

Huh? Was she trying to have another kid?

'Yeah,' Melody answered the phone in a disinterested tone. 'No, I didn't give her any fucking money. That's the point of this trip, isn't it? You stepping up and being a father for a change? Newsflash, *dickweed*. Being a father means you have to pay for things. Kids don't survive on fresh air. They need food and clothes. You'd know that if you ever pulled your useless finger out of your backside and paid maintenance, like you're supposed to!'

Ah. So she's talking to her kid's dad.

The other passengers in the carriage glared at Melody, but she couldn't care less.

I'd heard from my sisters that the dad was a loser. Sounded like he deserved the earbashing. I couldn't stand men that didn't step up and take responsibility for their child.

'What do you mean you have *two* of them to feed? What?' The blood drained from her face. 'No! Absolutely not. You *cannot* let him stay over. Because I said so! H-hello?'

Steam hissed from Melody's ears.

'You okay?'

'That little fucker!'

A passenger cleared their throat dramatically. Melody turned to face him.

'What's your problem?' she snapped. 'Never heard a woman swear before?'

The corner of my mouth twitched. This woman was a firework. I loved how she tells it like it is. Most of the women I dated wouldn't say boo to a goose. But Melody was strong and feisty. At least now I knew that her venom wasn't just directed at me. Then again, she couldn't think *I* was like her arsehole baby father. I'd never disrespect the mother of my child like that. Not that I was even sure I wanted children, but y'know.

'Commoner,' hissed the passenger.

'What did you just say?' I span my head around and looked him in the eye, my face like thunder.

'I… nothing,' he stuttered.

'That's what I thought. Can't you see that the woman has shit to deal with? Read your damn paper, pull your stuck-up head out your arse and mind your business.'

Melody's jaw dropped.

'Er, th-thanks. I don't normally swear so loudly in public, it's just my…'

She had a pained expression on her face, like she was debating whether to tell me about her conversation.

'I get it. You don't have to explain. Like I said to our

friend over there, we all have shit to deal with. Is it sorted?'

'No. But I can't deal with it now. I'll wait until we get to Paris.'

The train shook, and as several bolts of lightning flashed in the jet-black sky, I wondered if we'd be getting as far as Paris today.

11

MELODY

*S**hut the front door.**

I did not expect Knobhead Nate to stick up for me. In my forty-four years of being on this earth, I couldn't remember a man ever defending me.

Not my useless excuse of a father. Not my boyfriends, and definitely not the man whose sperm helped create my daughter. Which was the only useful thing that fucker had done in his life.

I couldn't believe the arse had called to ask why *I* hadn't given Andrea any money for the trip that was supposed to be about father–daughter bonding. What a joke.

And then he'd said that Andrea's boyfriend was staying with them too. I mean, what the actual fuck. Was he crazy? I was in no hurry to become a granny.

Anyway, the way Nate glared at that toffee-nosed twat was brilliant. The snob had looked so worried I'd thought he was going to piss his pants. Calling me a commoner. Bloody cheek.

Yeah, I get that swearing in first class wasn't exactly sophisticated, but needs must and all that. When you were dealing with someone like Rodney, a few profanities were needed.

I was surprised, though. I thought that Nate would be shocked. The women he dated were meek and perfectly poised. Whilst I was the kind of woman to stomp into a room and snort with laughter, they glided across the floor in their ten-inch heels and giggled softly.

But yet he'd still stuck up for me. It was kind of… sweet. Hot even. It gave me a mild case of the fanny flutters. Another sign that I needed to dust off my coochie cobwebs and get my leg over soon.

I hadn't had sex in six months, or was it seven? Might even be eight. The last time was with some selfish prick I'd met on a dating app who'd lasted all of sixty seconds.

I'd been tiding myself over by using my vibrator and watching porn on an ethical site Cassie had recommended. But a woman could only do that for so long. Hard plastic was no substitute for a hard man.

Not that I was thinking of Nate in that way. *God no.* I mean, had I ever thought about him fucking me? Yes, guilty as charged. But that was during one of my weak moments. When I'd fantasised about how it would be to have hot, angry sex with him lifting me up in those huge muscular arms, throwing me on the bed and pounding into me until I passed out from multiple orgasms. Yeah, I'd thought about it. Sometimes a lot.

But I was stronger now. I was sure there would be other hot men at the wedding. With any luck I'd find someone nice who wasn't a loser or a player. Anyone other than *him*.

The train shook and lightning flashed repeatedly through the sky. I gripped the table and my heart thudded.

'Ladies and gentlemen, I am very sorry to announce that due to the adverse weather conditions, we will need to terminate this train at the next available station. Our passengers' safety is the highest priority, and therefore this is the best option. Members of our team will direct you to nearby hotels and…'

'Fuck!' I shouted. 'I mean, fiddlesticks! Where will they stop? We look like we're in the middle of bloody nowhere! Where are we going to stay?'

'Chill.' Nate tapped away on his phone. 'I'm on it. The main thing is we're in France. We're going to miss the rehearsal dinner tonight, but first thing tomorrow we can explore our options and see whether we can get a train or plane and still make it in time for the wedding. Like the man said, it's better to be safe.'

'Yeah,' I said as the train shook again. The journey had been bumpy. Nothing like when I'd visited Cassie in Paris before, so the conditions had to be really bad for them to take such drastic action.

After pulling into a station whose name I couldn't read, Nate grabbed our cases and we got off the train.

'Do you think they have a loo round here?'

'Why didn't you go on the train, woman?'

'I didn't know they were going to stop the train in bumfuck nowhere, did I? And by the time they'd made the announcement, the queue to the loo was longer than the January sales.'

'Come on.' Nate signalled to a sign in French. 'It's over here.'

After waiting to use the loo at the station, we set off to the hotel Nate had found.

As we stepped into reception, there was another long queue. Seemed like everyone from the train had arrived before us.

When we finally got to the front, Nate greeted the receptionist.

'Alright, mate? Do you speak English? My French is a little rusty.'

'*Oui*—yes, sir.'

'Cool, cool. So can we get one room, please, with two separate beds?'

'Two rooms would be better,' I jumped in. 'Then again, yeah, sharing will be cheaper. But definitely two separate beds.'

'I am sorry, *madame* and *monsieur*, but we have no more rooms available.'

'What, none at all?' Nate frowned.

'No, you misunderstand. We have no more rooms with two beds available. We have just one room left now. With one bed.'

'No way!' I shook my head. 'There's no way we're sharing a bed. Can you recommend another hotel?'

'I am sorry, *madame*, but I believe everywhere else is fully booked. You are welcome to leave and try to find something, but as you can see, there are several people behind you, and by this time I will give the last room to one of them.'

'We'll take it!' Nate handed over his credit card.

'What do you think you're doing?' I hissed.

'Bangles, you really do have a problem with not seeing the obvious, don't you? I'm paying for the damn room.

Unless you want to sleep in the station tonight, this is the best option.'

'But there's only one bed!'

'I'm sure they'll be a sofa or something.'

But as we opened the door to the poky room, my face fell. There was no sofa. Just one small double bed.

If we both slept on it, we'd literally be on top of each other.

Sleeping in a bed with the guy I hated, who also was a hottie.

It had disaster written all over it…

12

———

NATE

Fuck.

I dragged my hand over my face as I scanned the room, taking in the surroundings. There was no sofa, and that sorry excuse for a bed was barely big enough for a child, let alone two grown adults.

Normally, if I'd come to a hotel with a woman, having one bed wouldn't be a problem. But not tonight.

Of course, I'd let Melody sleep on the bed. A woman should never have to sleep on the floor, and I didn't want her to feel uncomfortable. But that damn carpet looked stickier than the seats in a strip club.

I cursed myself for the thousandth time for following Melody out of the airport. Right now, I should be relaxing in a fancy chateau, sipping a rum and Coke, checking out the women before the rehearsal dinner started. But instead, I was in this flea-infested minus-five-hundred-fucking-stars hotel with a woman I couldn't stand.

'So much for the room having a sofa,' Melody huffed.

'Like I said earlier, it was either this or sleeping in the

station, and seeing as you're not a fan of the weather right now, you should be happy. I didn't see you offering a solution.'

Melody went to speak, then decided against it.

Yeah. Thought so.

'I'll take the floor.'

'You can't!' She shook her head. 'The floor is disgusting. You'll catch something.'

'Awww.' I tilted my head playfully. 'Thanks, sweetheart. I didn't know you cared.'

'I don't!' Melody seethed. She looked cute when she was annoyed. Her face flushed and her eyes were hot and fiery. That was until she opened her mouth and reminded me why I didn't like her.

'So what d'you suggest? Top and tail?'

'What, so I get your smelly feet in my face?' She grimaced. 'No, ta.'

'My feet don't smell.'

'*All* men's feet smell.'

'Sexist.'

'Sorry. Look, we're adults. We can both sleep in the bed, but no funny business.' Melody raised her eyebrow.

'Don't flatter yourself, darling.'

'Oh yeah, I forgot, you only date *models*.'

The way she said it made me sound so shallow. I'd been with women who weren't models before.

There was the American girl a few months ago who was a dancer. Wait. Maybe she did some modelling too.

I didn't remember the name of the Jamaican lady I'd met on holiday last summer, but she ran her own lingerie business. Or was it swimwear? Yeah, she modelled her own creations too, but…

Maybe Melody had a point. But I couldn't help who I was attracted to. And what was so wrong with wanting to be with someone who looked good?

At school, I'd never got the pretty girls. I swallowed hard, thinking about the school dance, when I was sixteen.

Every girl I asked blanked me. Back then I was a tall, gangly teenager. I had no style. No swagger. All the boys in my class said I'd never be able to get a pretty girl. And they might've been right for that dance. But in the summer holidays, I got a part-time job at a sports shop which gave me money to join the gym, get a decent haircut and buy new clothes.

By the time I started college a few months later, girls paid more attention. And ever since then, knowing that I could date models, the kind of women a lot of men dreamt of being with, was a badge of honour. A kind of fuck-you to those classmates who teased me.

'Last time I checked, dating hot women wasn't a crime.'

'You're so shallow!' She dragged her case into the corner of the room.

'Am I, though? Be honest. If Henry Cavill rocked up right now, shirtless, muscles glistening with baby oil, and offered to take you home, are you telling me you'd refuse and screw Kevin from accounts who has a beer gut hanging over his badly fitted nylon trousers instead?'

'Well, I...'

'*Exactly*. Remember, it's not a *settling down, rest of your life* situation. When I date, it's just casual. So why wouldn't I want to go for the sexiest option? It's human nature. Take those romance novels. What would you rather read about? The woman hooking up with the average guy, or her getting with the hot guy in the office that every woman wants to fuck, who's way out of her league? I rest my case. We all want to punch above our weight, sweetheart. You like to act like you're all high and mighty, but you and I really aren't so different.'

'I'm nothing like you!'

'*Whatever*. You call me shallow, but you're the one who said earlier that you didn't date men with beards because they gave you pussy rash or some shit like that. Judging a guy by how much hair they have on their face sounds pretty shallow to me.'

Melody pouted, threw her jacket on the bed, then walked off, giving me a prime view of that delicious arse.

That backside should come with a damn warning.

Beware: looking at these peaches for more than ten seconds will cause any sane man to make stupid decisions, like missing their flight and getting stuck in a hotel room in the middle of fucking nowhere.

My dick twitched as it realised that sharing a bed meant there was a high probability that arse would be pressed up against my cock all night. As much as I hated the owner, that butt of hers was what wet dreams were made of.

Shit.

If I'd known I'd be in this situation, I would've gone to a bar last night and hooked up or at least wanked this morning. Doing it in that bathroom was a no-go. The walls looked flimsier than tissue paper.

'I'm going to the bathroom,' she snapped.

As the door shut behind her, I sat on the bed and squeezed my eyes shut.

This was going to be a long and very *hard* night…

13

———

MELODY

I closed the bathroom door, then leant against it.

It was so annoying. I didn't know what was wrong with me today, but every time I was around Nate, I'd got tongue-tied. Either I said something stupid or my mind went blank. I wasn't usually shy—far from it, but yet, when he spoke, sometimes I felt like a timid little snail who wanted to crawl back into its shell.

And why did he have to be right so often? I couldn't argue with what he'd said about there being nothing wrong with him liking pretty women. Deep down I knew that it was because I was just pissed off that he didn't think *I* was pretty enough to date someone like him. I mean, yeah, he'd said I was pretty on the Tube. But he meant pretty for a creep like that pervert, not his kind of pretty.

This was stupid. I didn't even want anything to do with a womaniser like Nate. I was done with players. It was just that when you'd been rejected by men as many times as I had, sometimes it was nice not to feel like you looked like the back end of a bus.

If you asked Bella, Cassie and Lily, they'd all say they were unlucky in love once, just like me. But although that was true once upon a time, they'd always attracted a lot more interest than I did.

Guys never went for women like me. And Nate was right. There was nothing criminal about that. I just wasn't most men's cup of tea.

My stomach rumbled. Thankfully they'd served food on the Eurostar, but I was still starving. I thought I'd died and gone to heaven when I'd bitten into that bread. It'd been so long since I'd eaten proper carbs.

The diet I'd been following was torture. I was only allowed to eat green things. Green juice for breakfast which tasted like vomit, green salad for lunch and boring soup with either salad, broccoli or kale for dinner.

Right now, all I wanted was to stuff my face with pizza. Or toast. Oooh… cheese on toast would taste divine. I'd missed bread *so* much. Once the wedding was over, I was going to eat every carb under the sun.

I needed a shower. Especially if I'd be getting up close and personal with the King of Knobs. Ha! I just realised, the acronym for that was KOK, like cock. Which was exactly what Nate was.

A tingle of excitement erupted between my legs. Jesus. Just the mention of the word *cock* gave me the fanny flutters and made me think about Nate and his bloody dick. I had to sort myself out.

Maybe it'd be safer if we did top and tail like he'd suggested. I wasn't worried about him doing anything. I could lie on that bed naked, covered in chocolate sauce and sprinkles, and Nate wouldn't bat an eyelid. I was worried about *me*.

What if he brushed his cock against me and I jumped him? It'd been so long, and for some reason, I was horny, so I couldn't trust myself.

I had my vibrator, but it wasn't one of those silent ones, so he'd hear it buzzing. Plus, I'd have to smuggle it out of my case into the bathroom. If Nate saw me, I'd never hear the end of it.

My eyes darted to the showerhead and I wondered if I could use that to get myself off. It wouldn't be the first time…

No, I'd be fine. All I had to remember was how annoying Nate was. And how much he'd got on my nerves today. Like when he'd followed me out of the airport and made me feel bad about picking up the wrong passport.

I suppose it was kind of him to come with me, pay for the taxi, the Eurostar tickets and the hotel. And he'd offered to sleep on the floor…

Okay, okay. Maybe he hadn't been a complete pain in the arse, but anyone could be nice for a few hours.

'You hungry?' Nate shouted. I opened the door and stepped into the bedroom. 'This place does room service. Probably frozen pizzas or some shit like that, but we need to eat. What kind of things do you like?'

'Er, um, I-I don't suppose they have broccoli or spinach or…?'

'What?' Nate's face crumpled. 'You want to eat *broccoli*? And what else?'

'I think I'm allowed some steamed fish or grilled chicken. No, that's only on Saturdays…' I unzipped my case and pulled out my wash bag.

'What the fuck are you talking about? *Allowed?* You're

a grown woman. Who's telling you what you should or shouldn't eat?'

'It's just a—' God, this was embarrassing. I didn't want to discuss my dietary habits with him. Then again, seeing as he was a personal trainer, maybe he'd understand better than most. 'I'm on a special food regime thingy. You know. For the wedding.'

'You mean a *diet*?'

Busted. I'd hoped that using nice words would make it sound better.

'Kind of.'

'Why?'

'*Seriously?*' I put my hands on my hips. 'The guy that dates models is asking *me* why I'm dieting?'

'But you look…' He paused. I imagined he was trying to find a polite word to describe me, which wasn't easy seeing as I clearly wasn't his type. 'You look… there's nothing wrong with how you look. And diets don't work. It's all about healthy eating balanced with exercise. When you deprive or starve yourself, it only makes you crave food more and any weight you lose piles back on again.'

'As long as it happens after this weekend, it's fine. I'm only doing it for the wedding. A lot of women watch what they eat before an event. It's normal.'

I'd never had the body shape that society said was desirable. I'd taken the *chubby* jibes on the chin as a kid and got used to guys picking other women. I'd accepted my figure and had been comfortable in my skin. Well, mostly.

But the past few years, I'd noticed I'd been putting on more weight and it'd been harder to shift.

It didn't help that the last couple of blokes I'd been with had joked and commented about the size of my 'fat arse' and wobbly stomach. And as much as I'd tried to brush it off and tell myself I didn't give a toss about what they thought, the truth was, I'd found myself feeling more self-conscious.

Some days, I'd even thought about not wearing my jewellery because I didn't want to draw attention to myself, but I loved wearing my bangles and bracelets. After decades of putting them on, they'd become a part of my identity. I felt invisible and naked without them. So I decided to try and get myself in better shape.

I wasn't ashamed to admit I wanted a relationship. It wasn't a crime. I liked having fun, but I was tired of being taken advantage of. I wanted to find someone nice who wanted me for more than just a quick shag.

But I had to face facts: I wasn't getting any younger and at my age, it was harder to find someone decent.

The women I'd seen in Nico's circles when I'd visited Cassie in Paris before were all slim, pretty and chic. There were going to be loads of gorgeous people like that there this weekend. Even though I'd never been one to conform and didn't want to change my style too much, to give myself the best chance of finding someone at this wedding, I had to up my game. That meant making myself more appealing by at least trying to lose some of the weight I'd put on these past years.

And that was why, as much as I hated it, I needed to stick to this diet.

'It's *not* normal.' Nate shook his head. 'It's unhealthy. And stupid. How many men do you think are just eating broccoli for dinner to prepare for this wedding? Yeah, some guys worry about their weight too, but most of us just come as we are.'

'Says Action Man with the big muscles.'

It was easy for him to say. Men weren't judged for their weight and looks as much as women were.

'I like working out. And it's my job. Forget about whatever outfit you're trying to squeeze into for the wedding. If you could eat anything right now, what would it be?'

My traitorous stomach rumbled loudly.

'*Anything?*'

'Yep.'

'Well, you mentioned pizza—that sounds good. Or anything with bread, and some butter.' I closed my eyes and licked my lips, fantasising about the dough sliding into my mouth. 'Or chips. I haven't them for ages.'

'So basically anything with carbs.' Nate smiled.

God, he had a nice smile. His teeth were perfectly straight, those lips looked so juicy and that beard. It *did* look really soft. I reckoned he was right. I doubted I'd get a rash afterwards if he went down on me. Maybe the friction would feel pretty amazing.

Wait. Why was I thinking about Nate's head between my thighs? The man was asking what I wanted to eat and somehow my filthy mind had taken that as a cue to think about him eating me out.

Bloody hell. I needed to have that shower. And make it a cold one.

'Carbs sound perfect!' I'd regret it tomorrow, I knew I would, but right now, I was so hungry I could eat a horse. And if I was going to sleep next to He-Man, I needed to keep my strength up. The last thing I wanted was to get all light-headed and do something to embarrass myself.

'You going in the shower?' Nate glanced down at my wash bag.

'Yeah.'

'Okay. Whilst you're in there, I'll call down and order it, so you shouldn't have to wait too long to eat.'

My heart fluttered. He said it like he actually cared. Which was sweet.

I definitely needed to eat. My hunger was making me think all kinds of stupid things, like the fact that Mr KOK might not be a total knob after all.

14

NATE

If there was one thing I couldn't stand, it was when women starved themselves voluntarily.

I'd lost count of the amount of times I'd taken a woman out to dinner and she'd pushed her food around her plate without actually eating anything, or nibbled on a damn lettuce leaf.

Food was fuel. Yo-yo dieting was bullshit. That was what I tried to explain to clients. Yeah, eating junk all day every day obviously wasn't healthy, but neither was starvation.

I scanned the limited menu and decided on pizza. If Melody wanted carbs, she'd get them. And for balance, I'd order a side of vegetables and a bottle of water. Fuck it. We were on holiday. A little alcohol wouldn't hurt.

'You want wine?' I called out. The music was playing loudly on her phone, so she probably didn't hear me. I'd go ahead and get it. If she didn't want any, I'd drink some. Today had been stressful. I'd earned it.

As I heard the water from the shower, I pictured

Melody naked, drops of water trickling down her skin. Along the curves of her big breasts, down her back and over that delicious arse of hers. *God, that arse.* I'd love to bend her over this bed, bury my dick in her and fuck her doggy style.

These thoughts of doing something with her were getting way too frequent. I must be hungry. For food. Not for putting my head between her thighs and tasting her. No. I definitely wasn't thinking about that.

Room service. Yeah, that was what I was supposed to be doing. Ordering dinner.

Once I'd placed the order, I called Lily. I needed to focus on something important.

'Hey, sis, how's it going? How's Cass?' She hadn't replied to the text I'd sent whilst Melody was going to the toilet at the station to let her know we'd arrived in France.

'Hey, bro! We're just having something to eat. Well, Cassie doesn't want to eat or drink because she's stressed.'

'The rehearsal dinner has started already?'

'No. Cassie and Nico decided to postpone it and the wedding by a day.'

'Shit.'

'Yeah. Too many people couldn't get here in time, so it's for the best.'

'I hear you.' Guilt flashed through me. 'Tell Cassie I'm sorry. I should be there. Helping her.'

'Don't worry. Me, Mum, Dad, Flo and Bella have it handled. And there's nothing anyone could've done to avoid this. We couldn't control the weather.'

'True.' The pain in my chest eased a little.

At least with Nico's money, Cassie wouldn't have to stress about the cost of changing the wedding date at short notice, like normal people would. And I couldn't lie. I was relieved that now I had a better chance of making it there for both the dinner and the ceremony.

'How about you? Where are you now?'

'Still in some town in the north of France. We'll find a way to get to the chateau tomorrow and…'

As Melody walked into the room with a towel wrapped around her, I lost my train of thought. I swallowed hard, taking in her smooth shoulders. Her skin looked so soft and the towel was tied in the centre above her chest. It would be so easy for that to fall to the floor…

My dick twitched as I pictured her naked. If she gave herself to me, I wouldn't even know where to start first. Sucking those tits or pulling her down on top of me so I could grip that arse.

And that mouth. The mouth that'd said how much she hated me all day would be screaming my name when I made her come. Begging me to fuck her again and…

'Nate? You still there?'

Shit. I'd done it again.

'Yeah, sorry, Lil. Melody just came…' *Yeah. In my fantasies I'd make her come so hard. Multiple times.* 'Into the room.' I finished my sentence and officially warned my dick to pipe the fuck down and behave.

'Hi, Lil!' Melody shouted, then sat on the bed beside me. The scent of her made my mouth water. Had it suddenly got hot in here?

'I'm going to have a shower.' I got up quickly, my back to her. I wasn't fully hard, but if I sat here any longer I would be. 'Here.' I put the phone on speaker, handed it to her, then went to get my stuff out of my suitcase.

'How's Cass?' Melody asked.

'I was just saying to Nate that she's stressed and they've decided to push the rehearsal dinner and wedding back because of the weather.'

'That's pants. She must be gutted. Maybe try getting a few drinks down her to take her mind off it.'

'We've tried,' Lily added, 'but she's refusing. Says she needs a clear head to think of what to do if the weather doesn't get better.'

'I thought they were just going to get a marquee or something?' Melody added.

I really wanted to go in the bathroom to cool myself off and leave them to talk between themselves, but leaving my phone with Melody wasn't a good idea.

'Yeah,' Lily replied. 'But if the weather's still bad, I'm not sure that'll be good. And it's not what she's pictured. Cassie deliberately chose to have the wedding in July so that the lavender would be in full bloom and she's dreamt about taking pretty photos in the grounds, so…'

'Is that Mel?' Cassie's voice boomed from the phone.

'Hey, Cass!' Melody replied.

'Did Lily tell you we're delaying things?'

'Yeah. I'm so sorry, love.'

'Thanks. Best that I don't talk about it too much. It'll just upset me even more. Are you still with Nate? What's happening? Where are you?'

'Chill, sis.' I stood in front of Melody with my wash bag in front of me to conceal the growth in my jeans, deliberately avoiding eye contact. Scrap that. It wasn't looking into her eyes that I was avoiding. More like trying not to notice the fact that her towel had lowered a couple of inches, giving me an even better view of the tops of her breasts.

Don't look. Don't look.

'We're fine. I texted you earlier to say we're in France,' I said quickly.

'Send me your location. I'm definitely sending a car to collect you from the airport. Or wherever you want. No arguments!'

'We'll keep you posted. We've gotta go now.' I signalled to Melody to let her know I wanted to end the call. The longer we spoke to Cassie, the more questions she'd ask and the more she'd worry.

'Remember, bro,' Cassie warned, 'behave yourself. Don't go causing trouble and upsetting my friend! I've got enough to worry about right now.'

'*Moi?*' I shouted. 'Your friend is the one who hates my guts. Why, I don't know.'

'You'd have to ask her that! Be nice. Okay? Love you guys!'

'Love you too!' me and Melody said together. Melody looked up at me and smiled. My dick twitched again.

Wow. Pretty sure that was the second time she'd smiled at me today. And it was everything.

She had cute dimples, and those chocolate-brown eyes sparkled. Angry Melody was cute. But smiling Melody was even better.

I'd like to do something to make her smile again, but I knew I wouldn't get the chance, because like I'd said to Cass, she couldn't stand me.

As she ended the call, I went back to my suitcase but then turned back to look at Melody. Her eyes were focused on me, more specifically on my backside, and she was biting her lip.

Wait. Was she just checking me out?

'So Cassie had a point. I should ask you. Not that I care or anything, but remind me again why you don't like me?'

Her eyes widened and she quickly looked away, fixing her gaze to the floor.

'I don't want to talk about it right now. How long before the food comes?'

'Probably another twenty minutes.'

'Well, you'd better hurry up and go in the shower, then. Give me a chance to get dressed in here.'

'Cool.' I nodded, taking my stuff into the bathroom.

Just twenty minutes to shower and find a way to wash the thoughts of this annoyingly sexy woman out of my mind for good.

15

———

MELODY

As I heard the shower turn on, I lay back on the bed and squeezed my eyes shut.

Nate was in the bathroom right now, naked. Rubbing shower gel over those big muscular arms, along his rock-solid chest and down every inch of his cock. And I wished that I could open that door right now and get a bird's-eye view.

Talking of views and cocks, my willpower had been stretched to the limit when he'd come and stood in front of me when I was just speaking to Lily and Cassie. He didn't realise it, but when he moved his wash bag, his dick was right at my eye level, just inches away from my face. And if the outline I saw straining against those jeans was anything to go by, then what that bimbo he was dating said about him being hung like a donkey was definitely true.

Ugh.

Why couldn't I push these thoughts out of my bloody head? Getting horny with him around wasn't part of the plan. I'd tried to use the showerhead between my legs earlier, but just as I was getting going, Nate called out to ask me something and I lost my nerve.

There was no lock on the door, and even though I was sure he'd respect my privacy, I'd turned the volume up for the music playing on my phone to mask my moans when I came, which meant if he did come in, I wouldn't hear. So that was that. I still felt like a dog on heat.

The sound of the water grew heavier. He was definitely still in the shower, so maybe I could try and get myself off quickly now? *No. Bad idea.* I'd get so caught up, I wouldn't realise when he turned the shower off, and could you imagine how much he'd tease me if he walked in on me with my hands between my thighs? He'd instantly assume that it was because I fancied him, and even if that was a little bit true, there was no way I was giving that smug KOK the satisfaction.

Satisfaction… cock…

For fuck's sake.

I pulled out my velvet jewellery bag. I'd put my bangles inside before showering. Once I was wearing them, I'd feel better.

A school friend had given me my first bangle for Christmas when I was thirteen. It was rose-gold-plated with multicoloured cubic zirconia stones. It couldn't have cost more than a few pounds, but it was so pretty and sparkly. Whenever I wore it, I felt like a million dollars and got so many compliments.

After that, I was hooked. When I got a paper round, Mum and Dad took most of what I earned, but I always spent some of the money I was allowed to keep on a new bangle.

Over the years, my collection grew. My friends never

needed to ask what to get me for a gift. A bangle or bracelet was always the answer.

When I went to college and uni, I realised that wearing an armful of colourful bracelets was always a great conversation starter. Strangers were always amazed by how many I wore. They'd say how nice they were, which boosted my self-esteem (God knows I needed it), and ask whether each one had a specific meaning or where I got them from.

Wearing jewellery made me more visible. I was suddenly more interesting and fashionable. I didn't have money to buy fancy clothes, but it was easier to afford a cheap bracelet and use it to dress up an outfit.

I hadn't really thought much about making my own jewellery until I was in my early thirties.

At the time I was failing at everything. I was a single parent, with no job, no boyfriend, no money and living in a shithole.

But then Bella had sent me a jewellery-making kit and I'd bloody loved it. Suddenly I had something to look forward to when I woke up. The feeling of transforming the materials into something I could actually wear was life-changing. I finally felt like I was good at something.

When Bella moved to Vietnam and let me and Cassie stay in her flat, I got back on my feet again. Once I found a job, I finally had some money to invest in myself, so I went on some courses, bought some tools and equipment and started creating some designs in my spare time.

When I started getting compliments on those too, Bella and Cassie, who were my biggest supporters, encouraged me to sell them online.

I also started selling them at a local market on Saturdays, but I heard a few people comment that they 'weren't worth the money', even though I'd reduced the price so low that I was barely covering my costs. Then a woman who bought a necklace came back the following week to complain about it breaking, which really knocked my confidence.

And because I did everything in my spare time, it was hard trying to juggle a full-time job and looking after Andrea with making jewellery, sorting out deliveries, customer liaison, marketing and all the other business stuff, so I gave up.

Over the years I still made bits and bobs, but for myself, Andrea or my besties. It was safer that way. No risk of being told I wasn't good enough.

I'd be lying if I said I hadn't thought about selling my pieces again. But it'd be a lot of work to get it up and running. Maybe I'd try in a couple of years when Andrea was working or at uni.

Once I finished sliding my bangles up both arms, I jumped off the bed and flipped open my suitcase. The shower turned off. Shit. I'd better get dressed before Nate came out. I quickly slid on my underwear, then looked for something casual to wear. T-shirt and leggings would do.

I stood up and pulled the T-shirt over my head.

'Oh, sorry!'

I span around and saw Nate standing at the bathroom door with just a towel wrapped around his waist.

Holy crap.

I swallowed hard. I'd seen pictures of Nate's bare chest several times on his Tinder dating profile (yeah, he was one of those guys who included topless photos of himself flexing his muscles. Told you he was a knob). But nothing, I repeat, *nothing* compared to seeing it in real life.

His skin glistened. He must have just creamed himself or put on body oil. His shoulders were broad and strong, his chest was perfectly sculpted and those abs. Jesus Christ. He had more than a six-pack... I was about to start counting when Nate spoke.

'You should take a picture.' He flashed a smile. 'It'll last longer.'

Busted.

I gulped like I was swallowing concrete. I knew I was staring and I'd told my brain at least twenty times to look away, but I couldn't.

'You...' My mind went blank. 'Maybe I should...'

What? *Nooooo!* I shouldn't have said that. Now his ego would expand so much, there'd be no space left in this room.

'Do you need more time to, er, get dressed?' His eyes dropped to my arse.

OMG. I was standing in front of Nate, Mr Body-Like-a-God, with my enormous wobbly bottom on display. I had knickers on, but they barely covered my flabby cheeks. Christ knows what he must think. He was probably planning a whole fitness regime in his head which involved me doing at least five thousand squats a day to get it in better shape.

I grabbed the towel and wrapped it around the lower half of my body.

'Um, yeah. If you could... I'll only be five minutes. And maybe you should...' I pointed at his chest and bit my lip. 'Cover this situation up too.'

'*Situation?*' He raised his eyebrow.

'Yeah, you know…'

'You want me to cover my chest?'

'Mmm-hmm.' I nodded, my eyes fixated on his pecs, wondering how smooth they'd be.

'So you don't like it?'

'Um…' *Lie*, my head screamed. *Tell him you hate it. Like you hate him.* 'Whether I like it or not is irrelevant,' I stuttered. 'It's just… inappropriate, that's all.'

'Oh!' Nate's face fell. 'Shit. I'm sorry. I didn't mean to make you uncomfortable. And sorry for… I'm going now.'

He picked up the set of fresh clothes resting on top of his suitcase, then darted into the bathroom.

My stomach twisted. I'd just freaked him out. He thought that I was trying to say that he was making me uncomfortable. It was true, but not in the way that he thought.

I was uncomfortable because I was doing everything I could to not want him. I didn't want to be attracted to him. I didn't want to keep having these fantasies about him pushing me down on the bed and fucking me.

This wasn't part of the plan. I was supposed to hate Nate. I was supposed to avoid the love 'em and leave 'em playboys like him. I was supposed to be looking for a proper relationship, with a decent man.

I didn't want to think about how amazing it would be to run my hands over Nate's hard, firm body.

I didn't want to keep getting fanny flutters every time I looked at him.

But yet, my mind and body didn't care what I wanted because it was making all of that happen anyway.

As I dragged on my leggings, I noticed that my

knickers were soaked. Thank God they were black. Otherwise he would've seen the effect he'd had on me.

If just looking at him made me wet, imagine what would happen if he touched me.

It was a good thing I'd never get the chance to find out.

16
———

NATE

S weet Jesus.

I closed the bathroom door and squeezed my eyes shut. It made fuck all difference, though. The image of Melody's almost bare backside was still ingrained in my brain. And it looked even more fuckable than I'd imagined.

Thinking about the long night ahead of us was some kind of torture. Maybe it was punishment. To balance the scales.

After I'd started college, when it came to women, things were easy for me. I could probably count on one hand the number of times a lady *wasn't* interested. As cocky as it sounded, if I was interested in a woman, nine times out of ten, the feeling was mutual. But with Melody, it was different. She blew hot and cold like the damn British weather. One minute she hated my guts, the next she was checking out my chest.

Yeah. She might not like me as a person, but I knew when a woman appreciated my body. And normally right now, I'd be feeling pretty good about that. But when she said that things felt *inappropriate*, I had to leave.

When I was with a woman, everything had to be one hundred per cent consensual. With three sisters, that was important to me. I hated the idea of a man ever taking advantage of them. So the last thing I'd want is to make a woman feel uncomfortable.

Just because I fancied Melody and I'd seen her looking at my chest, I couldn't make assumptions. I had to be careful.

That's right, I said it. I fancied her.

Given half the chance, I'd fuck her all night. But it was never gonna happen. It couldn't. Even if she *was* interested, it was a bad idea. It was too messy. If we banged tonight, imagine how awkward it'd be at the wedding.

She'd want the whole hearts and flowers shit afterwards and I wasn't down for that. *At all.*

When she realised she couldn't change me, she'd feel hurt and bitch about me to my sisters. Then they'd be pissed off and disappointed and I'd feel guilty.

Nah. I needed to hold it together. It was only for one night. By this time tomorrow, we'd be in Provence and I could find a stranger to fuck all thoughts of Melody out of my system. Then once the wedding was over, I'd return to normal life. No mess, no stress, no hurt feelings or awkwardness. That was the smart thing to do. And exactly what needed to happen.

Shame my dick wasn't getting the message.

I glared down at the tent in my towel. Jesus.

I'd only just got out of the shower and at this rate I'd need to take another one. I'd almost wanked in there but couldn't be sure that Melody wouldn't hear me groan when I busted my load. I should've brought my phone in the bathroom like she had and played music to drown it out.

Wait. Did she...? For a second, I wondered if she'd done the same.

Get over yourself.

'Dinner's here!' Melody called out.

'I'm coming.'

I wish.

As soon as my dick deflated, I'd go and have a civilised meal with the woman I disliked. No inappropriate thoughts, no fantasies whatsoever.

I wasn't some horny teenage virgin who couldn't control his urges. I knew how to manage my dick. I'd hated the woman for years and never thought about her sexually before, so I'd be fine. How hard could it be?

Melody bit into the pizza and squeezed her eyes shut.

'Mmm,' she groaned with pleasure, and I ordered my mind not to think about the sounds she'd make when she came. 'This tastes sooo good!'

It was nice to see her eating.

'How long has it been since you last had it?'

'Had what?' Melody's eyes widened.

'Pizza. Why? What did you think I meant?' My mouth twitched.

'A long time. Too long.'

'The pizza or are you talking about something else?'

'Maybe both.' She smirked before taking a large gulp of wine.

'Really? Interesting…' My voice trailed off.

There was something there. Between us. The way her eyes sparkled. Her body language. The room was warm, but her nipples were showing in her T-shirt. I reminded myself again that I needed to keep my thoughts PG.

'These days, apparently my daughter is getting more action than me.' She downed her wine.

'Wait, *what*? How old is your kid?'

'Sixteen.'

'Oh, right. Pretty standard these days. How do you know she's fucking?'

'Please…' She winced. 'As much as I use that word, I hate hearing it in the same sentence as my daughter's name. She's still my little girl. I can't believe she's… *ugh*. I need more wine.' Melody topped up her glass. 'That's why my head was all over the place this morning. Just as I was getting ready to leave, I found the pill packet in her room.'

'At least she's taking precautions.'

'That's all you have to say?'

'Well, it's true, isn't it?' I bit into the pizza, then took a sip of wine. 'Would you rather she didn't?'

'I'd rather she didn't have sex at all. She's too young.'

'Why? What age did you lose your virginity?' I asked. Melody slapped my arm playfully.

'You can't ask me that!'

'I just did, sweetheart.'

'Well, you shouldn't.'

'What's the big deal? I don't care how old you were. I'm not asking to get in your business. I'm just saying that if she wants to do it, she'll find a way. You can't stop that.'

'Just don't want her to end up like me.' She hung her head.

'What? Strong, confident and badass?'

Melody's head shot up. Her eyes were like saucers. She dropped the rest of the pizza on the plate.

'What?' I frowned.

'You think I'm *strong* and *confident*? Pff! More like single, broke, in a dead-end job with no prospects.'

That was what she thought of herself? That wasn't what I saw. Yeah, she was mouthy and annoying, but on the flip side, that meant she knew her own mind. And I'd take that over women who tiptoed around me, agreed with everything I said and didn't have an opinion on anything other than whether they liked what a celebrity wore on the red carpet.

'You're wrong. You're not afraid to tell it like it is and you don't take shit from anyone. That makes you confident. You've raised your daughter single-handedly. Put a roof over your heads, fed and clothed her. You do all that *and* work full-time. That makes you strong and badass. Who made you feel this way about yourself? Your kid's baby father?'

'Yeah, and every man after him. Oh, and reality. Everything I said is true. I *am* single. I *am* broke and I *do* hate my job. I tried to make my jewellery business take off, but—'

'Wait, hold up. Your *jewellery business*?'

'Yeah…' She hung her head. 'I used to make my own stuff and sell it online.'

'Whoa. I didn't know that. So did you do all of those?' I pointed to her arms. She nodded. 'Do you make other things too?'

'Yeah. Necklaces, earrings, headpieces… I made a load of stuff for the wedding. For Cassie and something for each of the bridesmaids.'

'That's cool.' I loved hearing about people who created stuff. 'Do you have photos?'

'Wh-what? Why?'

'I'd like to see.'

'Is this some kind of trick?'

'Why would it be a trick?' This woman had to fight me on everything. It was so damn annoying.

'Okay. I'll show you. I've got them here.' She downed her wine, reached in her handbag, took out a box, opened it, then put it on the bed.

'Fuck!' I said.

I didn't know what I expected. Sparkly shit, I guess, but it looked better than I'd thought. I wasn't into jewellery, but even I knew it was good.

'This is Cassie's headpiece.' Melody pointed. 'She didn't want a traditional tiara, so I made this. These are tiny crystals and pearls which I entwined between these rose gold crystal-encrusted oval embellishments, to make it look like a fancy hair vine. I thought that'd fit nicely with her dress and, y'know, the outdoor vibe of the wedding.'

There were some other bracelets and what looked like hair clips in a separate section of the box too. It looked so good I wanted to pick it up and have a closer look, but I didn't want to risk breaking something.

'You've got talent, Bangles. Cassie's gonna love it. Nice one.'

Melody just stared at me, her mouth open wide. I didn't know why she looked so surprised. I couldn't be the first person to tell her that her jewellery was good. It was obvious.

'Th-thanks.'

'You should sell your jewellery again. You'd make a lot of money. What made you stop?'

'I just found it hard to juggle being a single mum, working full-time, making the jewellery and trying to do the business side too.' Melody poured some more wine, then took a large gulp. 'I love Andrea to bits, but it's been a struggle, raising her with no financial support from her useless dad, always trying to make ends meet. I had to focus on work that paid the bills.'

'I hear you. Maybe it wasn't the right time before. I don't think you give yourself enough credit, though. You've raised your daughter to the age of sixteen. That's a big deal. And, yeah, I know it must be hard to see her growing up and having sex, but at least you've taught her to be responsible and take precautions. So many kids her age don't. And even with the challenges you faced, you still ran your own business for a while. That takes guts. So like I said before, you're *strong, confident and badass.* And I reckon, if Andrea turns out anything like you, then she'd be lucky.'

'Th-thanks.' Melody's eyes watered.

I meant what I said. Yeah, we didn't get on, but she'd clearly been through a lot of shit and was hard on herself. I believed in giving credit where credit was due. That was all. No big deal.

'Maybe you're not such a KOK after all.' Her gaze met mine and those chocolate-brown eyes made my chest do a weird fluttery thing.

'You think I'm a cock?'

'Yeah: K-O-K.' Melody drained her glass, then slammed it on the bedside table.

'What does that stand for?'

'King of Knobs!' A laugh escaped her lips. It was loud and infectious.

'King of Knobs?' I repeated, then burst out laughing. 'Thank you! I should put that on my CV. Anyway, how'd you know about my knob? Did you just check me out in the shower?' I smirked.

'No!' Melody slapped my chest. She'd made a lot of physical contact in the last five minutes. First touching my arm and now my chest. Must be the alcohol. 'Knob as in *idiot*. Not as in your cock. Although, if the rumours are true, you're packing a *lot* down there.'

'Rumours?' I raised my eyebrow. 'What rumours?'

'That'd be telling…' She dropped her gaze between my legs. 'Shall we have more wine?' she slurred.

'You've finished the bottle. Maybe you should have some water. And then we should sleep. It's late and we need to get up early.'

'Oooh, Big Knob Nate is taking me to bed!'

I shook my head. She was pissed, so I couldn't trust what she'd said.

Melody was in no condition to make any decisions. So sleeping was the only thing we'd be doing tonight.

17

—————

MELODY

'I'm going to the loo.' I got up from the bed and stumbled.

'Easy…' Nate grabbed my arm and a bolt of electricity shot through me.

'My hero!' I giggled as I straightened up and did my best to walk to the bathroom.

After closing the door, I pulled down my leggings and knickers, then plonked myself on the toilet.

My head buzzed. I couldn't believe I'd drunk almost all of the wine. It wasn't just my head that was buzzing. My whole body tingled. I might be pissed, but I was alert enough to remember what Nate had just said.

Nate had called me *strong, confident and badass*. And he'd complimented my jewellery designs. No man had ever been interested in listening to me talk about them, let alone asked to see them.

Never in a million years would I've believed he'd say such nice things about me. At first I'd thought he was joking. I'd always thought he saw me as a hot mess. So even if I wasn't half drunk, you could've knocked me over with a feather when those words and compliments escaped his lips.

Talking of lips, I couldn't take my eyes off his. The places that they'd roamed in my fantasies were crazy.

I flushed the toilet, washed my hands, brushed my teeth, then splashed water over my face. I needed to sober up. When I went back out there, we'd be going to bed. *Together*. With his hard body pressed against mine. All night. I had to hold it together.

Just because he'd said those nice things, it didn't mean that he fancied me. There were lots of people I thought were confident and strong. Didn't mean I wanted to shag them. I couldn't get confused.

When I came out of the bathroom, Nate was standing up with his toothbrush in his hand. I swallowed hard.

'You done?'

'Y-yeah,' I said, trying to look anywhere but his bulging biceps, muscular chest and definitely not between his legs. He was wearing clothes, but I could still see the outline of *everything*.

'Cool. I'm gonna brush my teeth. I thought, maybe you can get in the bed whilst I'm in the bathroom, then I'll put two pillows behind you and sleep on top of the covers with a separate sheet over me. That good for you?'

I nodded.

'Okay. I'll call out before I open the door, so… you know. To avoid taking you by surprise again.'

'Thanks.'

As soon as he went into the bathroom, I opened my suitcase and pulled out my nightdress.

Normally I slept in an oversized T-shirt. But because

Cassie's wedding was a special occasion and I was hoping to get lucky with a hot Frenchman, I'd packed a silky red fitted nightdress that was low-cut at the front and hugged me in all the right places. Well, that was what I'd thought when I tried it on and was having a rare moment of self-confidence. But now I was with Nate, I felt more self-conscious. Looking half decent by my standards couldn't compare to what he was used to.

I thought about wearing a T-shirt over it, but then I'd be too hot. Actually, did it really matter? Like he'd said, the plan was that I'd get under the covers and he'd only come out once I'd confirmed that the coast was clear. So he wouldn't see what I was wearing anyway. It'd be fine.

After taking off my clothes, I slipped into the nightdress, then dived under the covers.

'Ready?' Nate called out.

'Yep!'

'Okay.'

He strutted into the room and I bit my lip.

Holy macaroni.

He headed over to the other side of the bed. I heard the zip on his jeans go and my mind raced as I imagined him peeling them down his firm, strong thighs.

The mattress moved as he sat down. Even though he must've been several inches away, I felt the heat from his body and the hairs on my arms stood up.

Next, I felt something soft behind my back.

'Just putting the pillows there as a divider,' he confirmed. 'I'm turning off the light now. Night.'

'Night,' I replied, praying that I had the strength to survive it.

~

My eyes flicked open. I wondered what the time was. A glimmer of daylight peeked through the ugly beige curtains. I went to move, then felt something tight around my waist.

I glanced down and saw big muscular arms wrapped around it.

Oh. My. God.

Nate had his arms around me.

My heart raced at a million miles an hour.

Nate was *spooning* me. Annoyingly, it felt so good. And that wasn't the only thing that I felt. Something long and very hard was poking into me. If I thought I had the fanny flutters before, the situation going on right now between my legs was out of control.

I didn't know what to do. I knew what I *wanted* to do. Spin around, pull him on top of me and ask him to give me a good seeing-to. But that wasn't going to happen. One thing was for sure, I didn't want to move. It'd been ages since a man had held me.

I loved feeling his heartbeat against me, his body heat sent my temperature through the roof, and like I said, feeling that big bulge pressed against me was divine. Yep. Even though I was bursting for the loo, I was staying right here.

Just as I closed my eyes, I felt Nate stir. Suddenly he jumped up.

'Shit! Sorry about th-the spooning. I must've been cold or something.'

I wondered what the *or something* could be.

'Judging by what I can feel poking me, I wouldn't have

thought you were cold…' I teased. Pretty sure cocks shrank when it was chilly, not expanded…

'Sorry. I didn't mean to make you uncomfortable. I put the pillows between us, so I don't know what happened.'

'I couldn't sleep with just one pillow,' I said, still facing away from him. 'It was too flat, so I had to use the others.'

'Right. Cool. I-I should get up.' He climbed out of the bed and I instantly missed his body heat.

Before I realised what I was doing, I whipped my head around in his direction to get a better look. Oops, I mean I turned around to ask him a question. I hadn't thought of what that question was yet, though, because…

Jesus, Mary and Joseph.

He was stretching up to the ceiling giving me a prime view of every ab and pec and his raging hard-on, which was straining from his black Calvin Klein boxer shorts.

My eyes popped so far out of my head I was sure they landed in Australia.

I swallowed hard. Nate caught my gaze and his eyes darkened. Shit. I had to play it cool. Couldn't let him think I was ogling him.

Too late.

'Are you checking me out, Bangles?' He raised his eyebrow. My cheeks heated.

'No, I—' He *so* knew that I was. Maybe I should just own it. 'It's hard not to look when you're standing right in front of me half naked!'

'You were facing the other way. I didn't know you were gonna turn around. And just for the record, this…' He pointed to his dick. 'It's not, *y'know*. It's just a bit of morning wood. All guys get it. I hope it doesn't make you uncomfortable.' He reached for a towel and wrapped it around his waist. And I admit, I was disappointed. I was enjoying the view.

It was for the best, though. Looking at that hot body was going to give me a heart attack. His muscles, his solid thighs and, Jesus, the size of his cock. Never mind my eyes popping out as far as Australia. He could poke someone's eye out in outer space with a weapon like that.

'*Yeah, yeah*, "morning wood". I believe you!' I teased. 'And don't worry, I'm a big girl. You're not making me uncomfortable. I've seen men in their underwear before. No big deal.'

'Cool. Good to know.' His shoulders relaxed.

Just as Nate went to walk away, the knot on his towel loosened and it fell to the floor, giving me another glorious glimpse of his body. My eyes flew from my sockets.

'So, what time do you th—what should we have for br —are you hungry?' I stuttered, trying to compose myself.

'You're asking me if I'm *hungry*?' Nate's mouth twitched. 'Hungry for *what* exactly?'

Yep. He definitely knew I was checking him out and was appreciating the fact that he hadn't picked the towel up.

'F-food, of course. Breakfast. What else would I be talking about?'

'Breakfast, eh? And what do you like to *eat* for breakfast?' He stood with his hands on his hips, which only accentuated the shape of his biceps. I clenched my thighs and bit my lip.

'Well, if I'm staying off the carbs, maybe I should have some protein.'

'So you'd like some meat?'

'Yeah, *meat* sounds good.' My mouth watered and I don't think it was because of the food. 'Maybe a big sausage…' My eyes dropped to the bulge in his boxers. Dammit. I quickly move my gaze back up to his face.

I will not look at his fit body.

I will not look at his ginormous cock.

'You like a big sausage, do you?'

'I do.' I nodded enthusiastically. He had no idea how much I wanted *sausage* right now.

'Good to know, Bangles.' He smirked as he picked up the towel, wrapped it around his waist and strolled to the bathroom, leaving me feeling hot and hornier than ever.

18

NATE

If I'd ever doubted my levels of self-control, the last ten minutes had proven that my willpower was stronger than steel.

I unwrapped the towel from my waist and glanced down at my cock, which was as hard as rock. I wasn't sure if Melody believed the whole morning wood bullshit, but it was the only reason I could think of to excuse my massive boner.

The spooning thing was a genuine mistake. I must've forgot myself when I was sleeping and the heat radiating from Melody's body had drawn me towards her. I'd thought I was dreaming.

But even though it was true that I did wake up hard most mornings, seeing her in bed with that tight red night-dress was enough to make a monk's dick swell.

Melody's beautiful tits literally spilled out of the front and it took every ounce of strength not to jump on that bed and ask if I could suck on the nipples that were poking through the silky fabric. Jesus.

And that was *before* she'd checked out my dick. I wasn't sure at first. Then I saw the way her eyes bulged and caught her licking her lips.

But I wanted to hear her say it.

Of course, I was flattered if a woman looked at me like that. But somehow, knowing that Melody was eyeing me up felt even sweeter, because of how much she hated me.

Then there was all that stuff about wanting a *sausage* for breakfast. Under different circumstances, I would've been happy to give her a taste of mine.

Yeah. The attraction was strong. And it was mutual. But as much as I wanted to, I wasn't going there.

Just a few more hours, I muttered to my dick. Talking to it wasn't something I normally did, but desperate times and all that. By tonight I'd find someone else to hook up with and I could feel better again.

Once I'd finished in the bathroom and got dressed, I told Melody I was going downstairs for breakfast.

After what happened this morning, that room was too small for the two of us. I needed to create some distance. And the last thing I wanted was to watch her get out of bed and see the way that nightdress clung to her arse. My balls were already aching. I didn't need to make the situation any worse.

I went to the hotel entrance and glared out the large window. It was still raining heavily and the wind howled through the glass. This wasn't looking good.

I opened the weather app. Seemed like it was going to

be bad until at least this afternoon and then hopefully the storm would start to pass.

Next I checked flights and trains. Some were scheduled to run later but were subject to delays and cancellations. It was hard to know what to do. We still had a few hours until checkout, so I'd eat, then think about it.

I went to the hotel dining room, where there was a shitty buffet. Not the five-star food I thought I'd be eating this morning, but it'd do.

I headed to the hot food. The fried eggs looked like vomit. Better to stick with the croissants.

'Any sausage for me?' I felt someone's warm breath on my neck and when I span around, I saw Melody with a big grin on her face.

She looked fit as fuck, dressed in a red-and-white striped top, which accentuated her boobs. I could tell that they were all natural. Each to their own and shit—if a woman wanted to have implants that was her choice, but personally I loved the feel of natural breasts. Forget eggs, sausages or croissants. Right now, I'd love to suck on her for breakfast.

'There's some small ones in that tray, but something tells me you're the kind of woman who likes your sausages long and thick. Something that's gonna fill you up and leave you feeling satisfied, am I right?'

Melody's cheeks flushed pink. I was playing with fire and I knew it, but I couldn't help myself.

'We've only spent twenty-four hours together and you already know me so well.' She smirked. 'Long, thick and hard is *exactly* how I like it. Any idea where I can find a sausage like that?'

'Matter of fact, I do.' I held her gaze and her lips parted. 'I'm gonna get coffee.' As I walked off, Melody's mouth dropped.

I knew she wasn't expecting me to leave.

I knew she wanted more. More flirting. More of *everything*. If I suggested we go back to the hotel room right now and fuck, I had a feeling she'd agree. But *just because you can, doesn't mean you should*.

The coffee was just as shit as the food, but we had a long day ahead, so I drank every drop. Melody joined me at the table, her face like thunder. Looked like we were back to being enemies again.

My phone rang.

'Nico, mate, everything okay with Cassie?' I put the phone on speaker.

'*Salut. Oui.* Cassie is fine. Well, she is very worried that you will not make it in time.'

'We'll be there, don't worry. I was looking at flights and trains earlier.'

'The flights are still uncertain. My assistant is trying to get the jet, but…'

'I know private jets are expensive, so it could be a worst-case scenario option,' Melody jumped in. 'Maybe we can just try and get a train or hire a car first?'

'The money is not a problem, but *oui*. Understood,' Nico replied. 'I will send a car for you.'

'Cool, we'll let you know when we get to Marseille,' I said.

'*Non.* I will send a car to where you are now. I do not like you waiting to see when and if a plane will take off or a train will run. I will send a car with a driver—that way we have more control and Cassie will feel better knowing that you are on your way.'

'Good point.'

'Send me your location and I will organise everything straight away.'

'Okay,' I said. 'I'll send it now. Laters.'

19
—————

MELODY

It never ceased to amaze me what was possible when you had money.

Nate and I had just stepped out of the hotel, where a huge fully pimped-up car was waiting for us along with a man who was suited and booted and wearing a chauffeur cap.

Actually, I'm not sure the word *car* was an accurate description. I had no idea what make or model this was, but imagine a Range Rover and limo on steroids. It was so high up, I'd need a ladder to get inside.

Turned out there was no need because as I stepped forward, an electronic set of steps appeared from nowhere, allowing me to climb up and slide onto the seats with ease.

The inside was nuts. It was like the interior of those swanky limos celebrities used. There were large leather seats, a table, a TV, a little fridge, a stack of warm fluffy blankets, pillows… my eyes darted from left to right, trying to take everything in. I felt posh when I took a bloody Uber, but this was on a whole different level.

'Would you like me to show you how everything works?' The driver poked his head inside just as Nate climbed on the long seat opposite me. I tried not to be distracted by his scent.

'Cheers, but I'm sure we can work it out.'

'Very good, sir. If you need to speak to me, press the button. I will keep you updated with our progress. I hope that if the weather is good, we can arrive in about eleven hours. But if it becomes worse, Monsieur Chevalier has instructed me that we must stop and find a place to rest.'

'Cool.' Nate nodded.

'Okay, thank you,' I added.

'This is a sweet ride.' I saw Nate grinning from the corner of my eye, but I wasn't going to look at him. I'd had enough rejection for one morning.

It was like history repeating itself. I'd practically laid myself on a silver platter, just like I'd done before. My stomach twisted at the memory.

After speaking to Cassie last night, I'd been surprised when he'd asked why I didn't like him. Did he really not remember? I knew it had happened years ago, but still. I hadn't forgotten.

Even if I put what had happened in the past to one side and focused on the present, Nate knew I fancied him. He'd seen me staring at his cock, for God's sake. He knew exactly what I'd meant when I'd said I wanted a *sausage*. He went along with it. Flirting with me.

For a few brief, crazy moments, I'd thought that this time the feeling was mutual, but nope. Instead of acting on it, he'd just teased me and walked away.

It was all a big joke to him. Just another way to boost his ego.

Eleven hours. Stuck in this car with Nate. *Great.*

I took out my phone to check whether Andrea had replied to the text I'd sent at breakfast. Nothing. I fired off another message asking how she was and letting her know we'd be driving to Provence.

'*Yes*, Nico!' Nate's grin widened as he picked up the thin stack of books.

'What's that?' I huffed.

'Crossword puzzles.'

'*Crosswords?*' My face contorted. 'Don't tell me *you* do crosswords.'

'Yeah? Why's that so hard to believe?'

'So you want me to believe that Knobhead Nate, *Mr Loverman* himself, sits at home in the evening with a bloody crossword? *Yeah, right!* I bet the kind of stuff you get up to in the evenings at home doesn't involve a lot of words. Well, other than *bend over, bitch,* or *suck me harder.*'

Nate sighed and shook his head. 'You have a really low opinion of me, don't you?'

'If the shoe fits…'

'I would never call a woman a bitch if I was fucking her. Nothing wrong with asking her to bend over or suck harder, though, if she wanted to change positions or if she asked me how I liked it.' He winked.

'Unbelievable!' My jaw dropped.

'Bangles… you're so easy to wind up!' He threw his head back, laughing. 'In all seriousness, though, going back to your question, it's true, I like doing crosswords. It helps me switch off. It's a good way to pass the time if I'm travelling and it keeps my mind active. I always have one by my bed too if I can't sleep.'

I stared at him, trying to work out whether he was pulling my leg.

'I'm serious!' he added, reading my mind. 'Don't knock it until you try it! Nico knows I like them, that's why he arranged some for the journey. Same for the cards.'

'Cards?'

Nate pointed to the table, where there was a stack of playing cards.

'Yep. Me and Nico played cards together.'

'Listen to you! *Me and Nico played cards together.* You've changed your tune. From what Cassie told me, you weren't a fan of his when she first told you guys about him.'

'That was before I knew him. Nico's a top guy.'

'So are you any good?'

'At what? Are we back to talking about sausages again, Bangles?' He smirked and my cheeks heated with embarrassment. And anger.

'No! *Cards*, you numpty!'

'Wow. First I'm a knob—no, sorry, KOK. Now I'm a numpty. It's a good thing I have thick skin with all the insults you're throwing at me. Yeah, I'm pretty good at cards. I used to stay up until all hours at uni playing blackjack with my mates. The non-casino version. Some people call it knock knock or crazy eights.'

'I know what bloody blackjack is!' I rolled my eyes. 'A black jack makes the next player pick up five cards but is cancelled by a red jack, eights make them miss a go, king reverses the direction, ace changes suit, two means pick up two cards unless you also play a two… should I go on?'

'Whoa, do you play?'

'*Do I play?*' I raised my eyebrow. 'I bloody *love*

playing cards, especially blackjack. And I'm good at it too. Buckle up, big boy. Today you've met your match!'

I groaned inwardly, wondering why my bloody brain had decided to tell my mouth to call him a *big boy*.

'I was happy enough with King of Knobs, but you're really spoiling me with the *Big Boy* nickname too. I think someone has developed an obsession with my dick. If you want me that badly, sweetheart, you only have to ask…' He winked and I cringed.

'You won't be smiling when I wipe the floor with you.'

'You reckon?' Nate said. 'In that case, I challenge you to a game of blackjack. We've got a long journey ahead of us. Let's see just how good you are.'

20

___

NATE

'Last cards!' Melody called, letting me know she had a winning hand and was ready to end the game.

'Bullshit!' I glanced at my hand. It wasn't looking good. The annoying thing was I had a black jack. If I could put that down, she'd be forced to pick up five cards, but the card on the table was a six of hearts, so I couldn't use it. Having a three of diamonds plus a five and a seven of clubs was crap. I had no chance of beating her now.

I sighed as I picked up an eight of diamonds. At least that'd make her miss a go. But at this rate, I wouldn't get to use it.

Melody grinned as she dropped a two of hearts.

'You little…'

'Careful,' she warned. 'Definitely last cards now. Or should that be last *card*?' She grinned, kissing the single one she had left.

I huffed, picking up two more cards from the pile.

'Go on, then, do your worst.'

'And I win, *again*!' She slammed her three of hearts triumphantly on the table.

'I let you win.' I chucked my useless hand of cards down.

'*Yeah, right!* And did you *let me win* the last four games too?'

Never had someone beaten me so badly before. Yeah, I might lose the occasional game, I was only human, but five in a row? This was a new kind of thrashing.

And it was the first time that I'd played a woman too. The women I'd dated before had no interest in it. The only cards they ever wanted were the ones that let them go shopping at my expense. Meeting a woman who shared one of my interests was… weird and kind of… *nice*.

'I'll admit: you're actually pretty good, Bangles.'

'Thank you!' She beamed. Seeing her face light up like that was worth the embarrassment of being beaten. 'Another round?'

'How about we take a break?'

'Worried I'm going to whoop your arse again?'

'*You wish!*' I laughed. 'We can play more later. Want something to eat?'

'Yeah. I can't believe we've been driving for almost four hours and haven't checked out what's in the fridge.'

She was right. The time was going a lot quicker than I thought. When Clément, the driver, had said it was an eleven-hour journey, I was worried that time would drag, but so far four hours had felt like forty minutes.

We'd stopped a couple of times to go to the bathroom and stretch our legs, but apart from that we'd just been chatting and playing cards.

As Melody got up, the car shook. A gust of wind

howled through the air. I looked out of the tinted window and saw that the sky had turned black.

She steadied herself, then continued to the fridge. The car shook again.

'Sit down. I'll get it. The storm's picking up again.' Fear flashed over Melody's face and she stumbled back onto the seat. I opened the fridge and looked at the rows of bottles neatly lined up. 'Fancy some champagne?'

Melody shook her head. That was when I knew something was wrong. Although I was still getting to know her, from what I could tell, Melody liked to drink. Whenever I'd seen her at family get-togethers, by the end of the night she was always wasted. And she'd knocked that wine back pretty fast last night too. So for her to turn down alcohol seemed out of character.

'If I drink that right now, I'll throw up.'

'Why? You don't get travel sickness, do you?' If she did, she would've been ill by now.

The sky rumbled and the sound of thunder boomed around us. Melody jumped. There was a flash of lightning and then another. Melody lifted her knees to her chest and her face went pale.

'You okay?' My face creased with concern. She shook her head again and started shaking. 'Is it the thunder?' I went to sit beside her and squeezed her hand. 'It's okay. It'll pass soon.'

As soon as those words left my mouth, the sky erupted and it thundered angrily. The blood drained from her face. It looked like she was going to pass out. This wasn't normal. My sisters never liked thunder when they were younger, but they were never as bad as this.

Melody now had tears in her eyes. That was the last straw.

'Come here.' I pulled her into me. She rested her head on my chest. She was physically shaking and her heart was beating way too fast. 'It's okay.' I rubbed her back gently. 'It's gonna be okay. Just breathe. I've got you.'

I kept stroking her back as the sky continued to erupt. She sobbed, her chest quickly rising and falling.

Seeing someone as strong as Melody so scared and vulnerable made my heart want to fucking break. I wrapped my arms around her tightly, willing the weather to behave.

After releasing one of my hands, I brushed away the strands of hair that had fallen into her face.

I wanted to reach for a tissue to wipe away her tears, but I could feel her heart rate slowing. She was calmer, so I didn't want to disrupt that. Hell, if she needed to cry herself to sleep on my chest to feel better, that was exactly what I'd let her do.

Thankfully, the storm seemed to be passing, because several minutes went by without a sound. I closed my eyes and rested my chin on the top of her head. Melody stirred a little.

'Thank you,' she said softly.

'You feeling a bit better?'

She uncurled herself from my chest and sat up slowly, her eyes red-rimmed.

'Yeah. Sorry about that. You must think I'm a big baby. Crying because of a stupid bit of lightning.'

'Hey.' I held my hands up in surrender. 'No judgement. I know a grown man who cries when he sees strawberries.'

'What? As in, the little red fruit?'

'Yep. The *hairs* on them freak him out, apparently. Everyone has their thing. And a lot of people are afraid of thunder and lightning. It can be scary and dangerous, so it's understandable.'

'If only my dad had felt the same way…' She hung her head.

'Your dad?'

'Yeah. He's the reason I'm so afraid of it.'

'I don't get it.'

Melody grabbed one of the blankets and covered herself.

'When I was younger, I think around six, whenever Mum went to work at the weekend, he used to invite a "friend" to the house and I'd have to play in the garden. We didn't have much money, so it was barely big enough to swing a cat. Anyway, one day our neighbour, Juliet, came round. The weather was awful. There was thunder and lightning. Like most kids I was scared of it, but Dad told me to stop being such a weakling. That it was just a bit of light in the sky and was harmless. Then he sent me to the garden.'

'What?' I frowned. 'He forced you to go out when it was thundering?'

'Yep. He said that I wasn't allowed to come back inside for an hour. That it'd make me stronger and staying out there would show me I didn't need to be afraid. That it'd prove nothing bad would happen to me.'

'That's fucked up!' I shouted. 'That's fucking child cruelty!'

'Welcome to my childhood. The stories I could tell you…' She sucked in a breath. 'He let me take my coat to wear outside. He couldn't find an umbrella, though, so I just had to stand there. Hoping I wouldn't get struck.'

Melody's eyes watered and my chest ached.

'Come here.' I pulled her into me and she started sobbing again. 'No wonder you're upset. When shit like that happens when you're a child, it doesn't just go away. I'm sorry you had to go through that.'

'Thanks.'

'I know he's your dad, but the motherfucker shouldn't have treated you that way. Why didn't he just send you to your room?'

'I didn't realise at the time, but he was obviously shagging our neighbour and didn't want me to see or hear anything in case I told Mum. So sending me to the garden was his way of getting me out the house.'

'Jesus. Some people shouldn't be allowed to have kids.'

'Too right. So, yeah. There's something else you can tease me about. Grown woman in her forties who's scared of thunder.'

'It's nothing to be ashamed of. And I'd never make fun of someone's phobias. That's just cruel.'

'Well… thanks—for listening and being… nice.' She sat up.

Our eyes locked and I swallowed hard. God, she looked beautiful. Even with her tear-stained cheeks and red-rimmed eyes, somehow she just glowed. And I wanted to kiss her.

Fuck.

Her face edged closer. She wanted it too. We definitely shouldn't. Especially not after she'd shared something so personal. But something was drawing me to her. Something stronger than logic and my willpower.

I moved forward an inch and so did she.

This was happening.

The high-pitched ring of a mobile phone made us both jump.

Shit. What in the hell was I playing at?

Whoever was calling had good timing. They'd saved me from a lot of aggro. Kissing Melody wasn't a good idea.

'Hey, Lil!' Melody put the phone on speaker.

'Hi! Where are you? Are you close?'

'Not sure, love. We've been on the road for a few hours, so still several more to go.'

'Oh, okay. Well, I think you'll be very happy when you get here!'

'Why's that?'

'Well, more guests have started to arrive and let's just say that there's some hot French bachelors here for you.'

I froze and started grinding my jaw. *What the fuck?*

'Oooh, really!' Melody's eyes widened.

'So, you never know, you might get lucky! You might just find a hot wedding date after all or maybe even meet the man of your dreams.'

I wanted to take Melody's damn phone and toss it out the window.

'That'd be fab!' Melody replied. I cleared my throat loudly, reminding her I was still there. One little mention of other men and it was like I didn't exist. They were probably all loaded. I made good money, but it couldn't compare to the millionaires and maybe even *billionaires* that'd be there.

'Oh, hey, bro!' Lily said. 'I reckon you'll be happy with the women too. There's some French models here—you know, that Nico works with for his hair shoots and stuff. Mum's been going around showing them your photo and they're *very* excited to meet you. She even asked how soon they'd like to settle down and have babies. At this rate, not only will you have a wedding date, but you'll be the next one getting married!' She laughed.

Not funny.

I dragged my hand over my face. I loved my mother, but she really needed to cool it on the whole settling down shit.

'Tell Mum I don't need her to set me up with anyone. I can find my own damn women.'

'You know she won't listen. She's desperate for a grandchild. She cornered Carlos last night and told him. And you're the eldest, so…'

A bell rang in the car.

'I think that's the driver buzzing us,' Melody said.

'Yeah,' I said, relieved we'd been interrupted. The sooner this call ended, the better.

'Okay, I'll let you go. Keep us posted on when you hope to arrive.'

'Will do.' Melody hung up and I pressed the intercom button.

'Hey. What's up?'

'Yes, hello, sir and madam. Would you like to stop again shortly to get something to eat and use the bathroom?'

'I wouldn't mind having a little sleep first and then hopefully by the time we stop, the weather will be calmer. Nate?'

'Cool with me.'

'*Bien*. Tell me whenever you are ready and I will pull over at the next service station.'

Yeah. Melody going to sleep, then stopping at a service station was a good idea.

That'd give me time to figure out why the idea of her hooking up with another guy was making me feel so pissed off.

21

———

MELODY

After flushing the toilet at the service station, I washed my hands and then glared at myself in the mirror. I'd ended up sleeping for over three hours. My eye make-up looked shocking. And I couldn't believe that I'd blubbed like a baby in front of Nate. So embarrassing.

What shocked me the most wasn't the fact that I'd broken down—I always got a bit emotional when it thundered. It was his reaction. I'd been ready for him to tease me, to tell me to grow up and stop being so stupid, but instead he was so sweet. He'd even held me and, God, if I hadn't been so upset, I would've jumped his bones there and then.

I was so conflicted. I'd hated him for so long, so discovering this other side of him was annoying because it didn't matter how much I told myself not to be, I was attracted to him.

Actually, might be my imagination, but I thought we'd had a moment. Just before the phone rang, our eyes kind of locked and somehow, before I knew it, my face was inching closer to his. I was pretty sure that he had leant in too, like he was ready to kiss me, but now we'd never know.

Especially not since Lily had confirmed that there were a string of top models ready and waiting to greet him.

I could see it now. Them fawning all over him and him lapping up the attention. He might be being nice to me now, but that was only because we'd been forced together.

Any attraction I thought might've been there earlier was probably because he was horny. A guy like Nate probably had sex at least once a day, so he was going cold turkey. And with slim pickings in the last twenty-four hours he was willing to sleep with anyone. Including me. But as soon as we reached our destination, that'd change.

Once he was at the castle, he'd be back on familiar hunting ground. Surrounded by his favourite prey, he wouldn't give me a second thought.

Lily had said there were some eligible bachelors there, so there might still be hope for me. Then again, if the place was crawling with babes, I'd get pushed to the bottom of the pecking list. I was used to it. I'd come to France knowing that finding a wedding date wasn't guaranteed, so I'd just have to deal with whatever happened, like I always did.

I wet a tissue and dabbed it under my eye and down my cheeks to remove the mascara smudges. Then I pulled out my make-up bag and tried to make myself look more presentable—reapplying my lipstick, fixing my hair, straightening my top. I knew nothing was going to happen with Nate, but there was no harm with making myself look half decent.

'Ready?' Nate said as I stepped out of the bathroom.

He'd stayed in the service station restaurant but must've wondered why I was taking so long.

'Yep.'

'Clément said we're only about three hours away now.'

'Great!' My stomach sank a little.

Sounded stupid because the last day had been a travel disaster, but I'd kind of enjoyed the time I'd spent with Nate. Eating dinner with him last night in the hotel room. Waking up with his arms wrapped around me this morning.

Yeah, he'd pissed me off at breakfast, but I'd be lying if I said I hadn't had fun playing cards in the car with him. Who knew he loved cards as much as me? And beating him was the cherry on top. I got the feeling that didn't happen often and I was glad to be the one to do it.

And there was the way he'd comforted me. He'd definitely earned himself a shedload of redemption points by doing that.

My heart fluttered as I relived the feeling of my head resting on his beautiful broad chest. His delicious scent was out of this world. It was one thing having the aroma in the car and in the hotel room. But nothing compared to it flooding my nostrils up close. I didn't want to move. I could've kept my head there all day.

Then when he'd rubbed my back. Holy macaroni. It was like I'd been tasered. But in the most beautiful way. At the time I was too upset to process it properly. But now, just thinking about his hands making contact with my body gave me a serious case of the fanny flutters. Denying it was pointless. I'd give anything to feel his touch again.

Yeah, I'd said it.

As wrong as I knew it was, as much as I was supposed to hate him and as embarrassing as it was to admit it, the truth was that I wanted Nate. Even if it was for a quick shag. Just to get it out of my system. One last hurrah before I went back to searching for something serious.

We got into the car and Clément set off on the motorway.

'So what do you want to do now?' I turned to face Nate.

'Dunno. What do *you* want to do?' He smirked and a shot of electricity raced through me. I knew *exactly* what I'd *like* to do, but there was no way I was telling him that.

'Maybe we could play a game.'

'What, cards?' Nate asked.

'No. Like a question game or something.'

If I only had a few hours of having Nate to myself, it could be a good way to find out more about him. Okay, full disclosure. I wasn't that fussed about finding out whether green or blue was his favourite colour or if he'd ever told a lie or not, but more if he'd ever dated someone normal like me or if he'd consider us getting hot and heavy together, and games like this sometimes helped you find out people's feelings.

'Cool, cool. Hold up…' He reached for his phone and started tapping away. 'Got it. Let's play *never have I ever*.'

'Okay.' I got up and opened the fridge door. 'Let's have that champagne you suggested earlier. I'm feeling better now.'

'You sure?' Nate's face creased with concern.

'Yeah.' I laid two glasses on the table. 'So if you've done the thing, you drink.'

'Okay. You wanna go first? I've found some questions online which we can use if you want?'

'Yeah, I'll start.' I opened the bottle of champagne in preparation and glanced down the list. I'd start with something simple. 'So: never have I ever edited my selfies.'

'Nope.' He shook his head.

'*Yeah, right!*' I scoffed. The ones of him on Tinder were so perfect they had to be doctored. The way his muscles glistened, his flawless skin and that bulge between his legs. I remembered those images *very* well…

'Darling, have you seen *this*?' He gestured to himself from head to toe. 'What part of *this* needs editing?'

'Bloody hell!' I gasped. 'You love yourself so much! I'm surprised there's room for me and Clément in this car with the size of your ego.'

'It's not ego, Bangles. It's confidence. *Swagger*. If I don't love myself, who will? I work hard to look this good and I'm damn proud of it.'

It was hard not to argue. He *did* look good. *Arsehole*.

'Lucky you! Like a lot of women, I edit my pics.' There was no way I'd post a photo online without tweaking it first. If guys saw the real me on a dating app, I'd never get a sniff of a date.

'You don't need to. You look good, just the way you are.' Nate raked his eyes over me and my stomach flipped.

I clutched the glass, trying to process what he'd just said. Did he mean it or was he just turning on the charm for fun? I downed my drink, hoping I'd find some clarity at the bottom of the glass.

'Th-thanks,' I stuttered, still lost for words.

'Okay, my turn,' Nate said, completely oblivious to the

effect his words had on me. 'Never have I ever had a one-night stand.'

'I think we'll both be drinking for that one.'

'Yep.' He knocked back his champagne.

'Never have I ever said the wrong name in bed,' I asked.

'*Nope*. I have rules. I never invite women to my house. Can't risk them turning up uninvited. And I never use names in bed. It's easier.'

'What—because you sleep with so many women you'd get confused?'

'Something like that… you?'

'No, never.' If a man actually did something in bed that made me happy enough to want to scream his name, then maybe it'd be an issue, but not so far. Most if not all of my sexual dalliances had been disappointing.

'Next!' Technically it was Nate's turn, but whatever. 'Never have I ever been engaged.' I was about to laugh because this question clearly wasn't created for playboys like Nate, but when I looked at him, he was staring at his feet and had gone quiet. *Weird*. 'Earth to Nate! So—have you ever been engaged?'

'*Come. On!*' He rolled his eyes. 'I'm never getting hitched. You can't seriously ask a guy like me a question like that!'

'True. Obviously I haven't either. Your turn.'

'Ha!' his face lit up and he burst out laughing.

'What?'

'The next question is: never have I ever missed a flight! I think we both know the answer to that one…'

'Moving on…' I stifled a giggle. At least I was able to laugh about it now that we were closer to our destination.

I looked at the next question and gulped.

'Never have I ever had sex in a car.'

'I have.' Nate sipped his drink. 'You?'

'Not since uni.' I thought back to that time with some pleb whose name I couldn't even remember. 'It was awful.'

'It doesn't have to be.' Nate licked his lips. 'Maybe it's time you tried it again. It can be hot. Just like sex in a public place.'

I was tempted to ask whether he was offering, because I was deffo up for doing it again, like, right now…

I bit my lip and focused on the second part of his comment instead.

'Like where? Actually, we've only got a few hours left, so probably not enough time to list the millions of places you've got your leg over!'

'You really want to know?'

'Course!' The word flew out of my mouth before I thought it through..

My mind and my heart didn't want to know. But based on the tingles that were going wild between my legs, my vag definitely did.

'Plane, toilet, beach, field, swimming pool, sea, concert, mountain…'

'Mountain?'

'Not many people around, so it was cool. Anyway, enough about me. How about you? You a fan of fucking in forbidden places?'

'Hardly!' I snorted. Whereas Nate could probably reel off about another two dozen places, I could count my daring dalliances on one hand. 'Not many. Probably just in the bog and the car.'

Those locations weren't some kind of fantasy, though. At the time it was because the guys didn't think I was worth taking home, so it was that or nothing. And as always, I just took what crumbs they offered.

'You should try it sometime. It's a buzz.'

'Don't you ever worry about getting caught?'

'That's part of the thrill. Hasn't ever happened, though.'

I wouldn't mind trying it. Cassie and Nico had done a lot of al fresco fucking, and even Lily confessed that she and Carlos had got busy on a beach. I'd have to find a willing participant, though. And that was the problem.

'You're lucky. Maybe I will one day. There's no point asking you the next question'—I skimmed the list—'or the next!'

'Ask anyway.'

'Never have I ever had a threesome and never have I ever fallen in love.'

'Yeah,' Nate laughed. 'No point asking me that.'

'In case it wasn't obvious, I haven't had a threesome and—'

'Would you like one, Bangles?'

'Nate!' I slapped his arm. God, it was so firm. I'd be happy to have one night with him. I wouldn't want to share. Which was stupid because even if Nate did sleep with me, he'd be onto the next woman faster than you could say *one-night stand*. His dating strategy was sharing himself with as many women as possible. Which was exactly why I should stay away.

'And you've fallen in love?' he asked.

'Too many times,' I sighed. Hard to believe it now, but

once upon a time I loved Andrea's dad. I thought the fucker was *the one*.

We met in a pub in London. He'd come down from Coventry, which was where he was from. After spending a few wild weekends together, I fell pregnant. Obviously it wasn't planned, but we said we'd make a go of it.

When Rodney said I should move to Coventry, I gave up my job in London, which was a mistake.

I'd never known what I wanted to do for a career. I'd mainly gone to uni to escape my parents and have fun. I chose English because I thought it would be a safer bet for getting a job later on than doing art, which was what I really wanted to study.

I hoped that once I'd graduated I'd have more of an idea what direction to go in, but nope. So I went travelling for a year. When I came back I tried teacher training like Bella had done, but it wasn't for me.

After that, I drifted from job to job for years, mainly working in offices or shops. Then a few months before I met Rodney, I was offered the opportunity to train to be a window dresser. I loved it. For the first time I was excited about going to work, so I was gutted about leaving.

At the time, though, I was giddy with excitement and madly in love. I thought we were going to be a family, so I wanted to put my baby and the man I thought was my Mr Right, first.

But a few months after Andrea was born, Rodney left me. I was alone in a strange city with no friends and no money. He said that being with me was only supposed to be 'a bit of fun' and he never wanted anything serious.

Funny that, because a few months later, he shacked up with another woman who he'd got pregnant. But instead of running, he stayed with her and their son. Clearly he wanted a family. Just not with me. I was just the filler before he found someone he wanted to settle with.

Dating with a child wasn't easy. It wasn't just me I had to think about. There was also Andrea to consider. I didn't want to bring a man to the house and have her get attached, only for them to leave like her dad had done. I had to protect her and my heart.

The minute any man showed me attention, I was so starved of affection that I thought they were going to be the one. So I'd fall hard. And when it inevitably crumbled soon afterwards, I'd be a mess. Which was exactly why I was skipping the next question: never have I ever eaten a pint or more of ice cream by myself.

I'd eaten so much ice cream to drown my sorrows over men over the years that I should be bloody sponsored by Ben and Jerry's.

'Is it my turn?' Nate asked.

'I think so?' My head was getting fuzzy with all this champagne.

'Cool. Next question: never have I faked an orgasm.'

'All the bloody time!' I snorted.

'What?' Nate's mouth fell open. 'You're shitting me. Why?'

'Because men are selfish fuckers and don't care about satisfying a woman in bed.'

'I don't know what men you've slept with, sweetheart, but trust me, I never leave a woman's bed without making sure she's a hundred per cent satisfied.'

His eyes darkened and tingles erupted between my legs. I wondered if Nate really was a stallion between the sheets. From what I'd felt pressed into me this morning and what I'd seen when he'd stood in front of me, he was hung like a donkey and I definitely wouldn't say no to having a ride or ten on him.

I took another gulp of champagne to try and push the illicit thoughts out of my head.

'Never have I ever had a sex dream about someone in this room. Well, that's what it says here, but in this case, it's obviously this car…' My cheeks heated as I looked at him, keen to see his reaction.

'Hmm…' He fixed his eyes on mine. 'Have I ever had a sex dream about someone in this car? Well, Clément isn't really my type, which only leaves you, doesn't it?'

Nate licked his lips and my heart thudded. Silence filled the air and my nipples tightened. I wanted to scream, 'Do you fantasise about me or not?' This time yesterday I would've put money on the answer being a hard no, but now I wasn't so sure. There was that almost moment we'd had in the car earlier. And then him saying I looked good just the way I was.

'Well…?'

'I think I'm gonna need some more champagne.' He took the bottle, filled his glass right up to the top, then turned to face me as he downed the whole lot in one. 'And you, Bangles? Aren't *you* drinking for that question?'

I might be a bit slow on the uptake here, but we did both agree that if something was true, then we drank, right? So the fact that he'd just necked a whole glass of champers confirmed he was interested. Didn't it?

Holy crap.

I picked up my glass and drained it dry.

Nate liked me.

Fuck.

'This is a fun one.' Nate broke the silence and picked up his phone. 'Never have I ever kissed a friend's sibling.'

I swallowed hard.

'You just made that up!'

'It's right here!' Nate smirked, pointing at the screen. It was. Someone was really fucking with me.

'Never,' I muttered.

'There's a first time for everything…' His eyes darkened. 'Your turn.'

My cheeks burned. So he fancied me and said that there was a first time for me kissing a friend's sibling. *He* was my friend's sibling, so what was he waiting for? Why didn't he act on it? He wasn't shy. I didn't get it.

But the objective of this game was to work out if he liked me. And now that I knew he did, at least a little bit, I'd achieved my goal.

Now I just had to find a way to move things to the next level…

22

———

NATE

I was playing with damn fire and I knew it.

When I'd agreed to play this game, I hadn't realised it would lead to me admitting I had feelings for Melody.

Nah, scrap that. *Feelings* sounded too deep. Yeah, I wanted to fuck her, but that was all. It was a primal need. Pure and simple. It'd been too long since I'd had some and all that talk about having sex in cars and screwing outdoors was making me horny.

At least I hadn't confirmed outright that I'd fantasised about her. Yeah, I'd drunk, but I hadn't said yes or no.

It wasn't like I'd fessed up about the fact that ever since I'd seen her at the airport, I'd thought about how it'd feel to bend her over. Or how when she came out of the bathroom at the service station, wearing a fresh coat of that fire-engine-red lipstick, then got in the car and asked me what I thought we should do, I'd wanted her to drop to her knees, wrap those lips around my hard cock and suck me off.

Shit.

My dick jerked as I relived the fantasies all over again. They kept playing on a loop in my head.

Melody had drunk for that question, so maybe she'd fantasised about me too.

She'd said she'd never fucked in a public place before, but the way Melody had bit her lip and crossed her legs made me think she might be open to it. And if she was, I'd be up for helping her out.

When it came to the question about whether she'd kissed a friend's sibling, I almost asked if she wanted to rectify that. But common sense ruled and I'd kept my damn mouth shut.

And man, when she said she faked her orgasms, I wanted to take her right there and then and show her how a *real* man got to work.

If Melody gave me the chance, I'd fuck her so good, she'd see stars and would never want another guy to touch her again.

Which was exactly why we couldn't. I wasn't a happily-ever-after kinda guy. Not anymore. All that love BS was for suckers.

I was relieved I'd avoided answering those questions about whether I'd ever been engaged or in love before. That was too close to the bone. There was no way in hell I was gonna open up to her about shit like that. Even after all these years, it was still too painful.

After whipping the glass of champagne off the table, I guzzled it down, trying to ease the ache in my chest.

'We're gonna need another bottle…' I got up and opened the fridge. My head was buzzing. I needed to slow down before I said or did something stupid.

Knowing that Melody was into me and not acting on it was hard. Thank fuck we weren't far away from the chateau.

'A new bottle of bubbly calls for a new game, don't you think?' Melody slurred.

'Maybe I shouldn't open another bottle. You okay?'

'I'm fine! I know my limits and I'm just warming up.'

'What do you wanna play?'

'Strip poker! Well, not poker, but strip cards. Strip war or… no! *Strip blackjack.* You take off something every time you lose.'

'Seriously?' My cock twitched again. She wasn't wearing much, so it wouldn't take long before I got to see her body again.

'Yep!'

'So, you'd be happy stripping naked, in this car, with me?' My pulse raced at the thought of it.

'I wouldn't be so cocky if I were you. Considering I wiped the floor with you before, I think the question is whether *you'd* be happy sitting here in the buff with me.'

'Never gonna happen, sweetheart. I was off my game before, but something tells me that my winning streak is about to return.'

I just needed the right motivation and this was definitely it.

'In your dreams, sunshine!' She crossed her arms over her beautiful chest. 'I'll have you sitting there naked in no time.'

'You think so?' I cocked my head. 'Tell you what: I'll do you a favour. To give you a head start, I'll take my top off right now. *That's* how confident I am.'

'Okay…' Melody gulped as I lifted my T-shirt over my head, slowly.

That was *exactly* the reaction I was hoping for. I never would've suggested this game. It wouldn't be appropriate, but she wanted to see my body, so I wasn't gonna refuse.

Soon we'd be at the chateau with a shitload of eligible bachelors all trying to get into her knickers. I might not be able to match the size of their wallets, but I knew I could beat them in other areas.

When Melody met them, I wanted to make sure she had the image of my body etched on her brain.

I wanted her to be thinking of me. Fantasising about me. The way I'd been thinking about running my mouth over every inch of her.

'Ready?' I deliberately scratched my neck so I could flex my bicep.

'Yeah.' She bit her lip.

'Good. Game on.'

23

MELODY

Strip blackjack wouldn't have been my game of choice. But Nate wasn't making a move and it was the only way I could think of to subtly hurry things along with him before we got to the castle.

There was no way I was going to ask outright if he wanted to get busy in the back seat. But if we were both wearing less clothes it might help…

The idea of getting naked in front of him was terrifying. But I'd thought about it. Nate was good at cards, but I was confident I could beat him.

Secondly, he'd been calling me *Bangles* for the last twenty-four hours. And the guy was so excited to show me his chest (no complaints from me) that he hadn't even thought about clarifying the rules.

I'd only said that I'd take *something* off. I hadn't said *what*. I was wearing at least thirty bangles, earrings and other accessories. He only had on a pair of jeans and boxer shorts. It didn't take a mathematician to work out who was most likely to get naked first…

After dealing the cards, I picked up my hand. Shit. It was crap. I looked up at Nate, whose smile was bigger than the Joker's. Within minutes he'd slammed down a black jack.

Not content with me picking up five more rubbish cards, he hit me with a two of spades, making me pick up another two. Then he called last cards and threw down a two of hearts.

Nate: 1. Me: 0.

'Come on, then, sweetheart. What you taking off?' He smirked.

Cocky git.

I held eye contact and smiled as I slipped the shoulder of my T-shirt down an inch. Nate's eyes widened. He was transfixed and I liked it.

'Are you excited to see me take something off?' I teased.

'Maybe…' He licked his lips.

After slipping it down an extra inch, I stopped, slid off one of my bangles and put it on the table.

'There you go! One item removed!'

'Nah, nah, nah!' Nate shook his head. 'Not cool! You can't include jewellery. That's cheating!'

'Is it, though?'

'You're too smart not to know the rules. Players have to wear an equal amount of *clothing*. Jewellery doesn't count. Here I am being the good guy, giving you a head start by taking off my top and you repay me by cheating. If that's how you're going to play, then I'm out.'

Bollocks. That hadn't quite gone as planned.

Nate reached for his T-shirt and my traitorous vagina screamed in protest. I'd been enjoying the view of his broad shoulders, solid chest and row upon row of rock hard abs. And if he threw in the towel now, there was no way I'd get a chance to run my hands over that eight-pack. Or was it ten?

My eyes dropped to his stomach and I salivated as I began counting each one. Back at the hotel I'd wanted to do the same but was interrupted.

Two-pack, four-pack, six-pack, eight…

'Hey!' He held his T-shirt up against his chest. 'No perving. Only honest players can look and that's not you.'

'Okay, okay!' I huffed. 'You win. Equal clothing.'

'Good. So, what are you wearing?'

'Mind your own business!'

'How am I gonna know whether we're equal or not unless you tell me what you're wearing? Have you got knickers on?'

'Course I have!'

'Well, I don't know. Some women prefer not to. I go commando sometimes. It's freeing.'

I swallowed hard. So there was a chance that under his jeans, he was *bare*? So if he went to the loo and forgot to do up his zip, I'd get a glimpse of his knob? My mouth watered at the thought.

'So are you… do you have pants on *now*?' I bit my lip.

'Let's see, shall we?' Nate smirked, undid his button slowly, then pulled his zip down a centimetre, then another…

I didn't need a mirror to know that my eyes were like saucers. Saliva pooled inside my mouth. And let's not even talk about what was going on between my legs.

'Yep!' He quickly zipped himself up. 'Looks like

today's a boxers day. Lucky for me, but not so much for you.' He winked.

God, this guy was so cocky, but there was something so hot about it.

'Well, uh, um…' *For fuck's sake, get it together, Mel,* my brain shouted. 'I'm wearing underwear, so a bra and knickers, this top and my jeans obviously, so that makes four items.'

'And I'm wearing just jeans and boxers, so that means you need to lose two items…'

'No! Just put on your T-shirt and…' I reached into my bag. 'Here! Take this scarf.'

'I don't need your damn scarf. I'm gonna win.' He threw the scarf on the seat beside him. 'For someone who suggested playing this game, you're suddenly very shy about stripping. Or were you just hoping to get me naked?'

My cheeks heated. How was he always able to read my mind so easily?

'No, I…'

'Just deal the cards, Bangles.'

I'd bitten off more than I could chew. Nate won the next game in record time. Beads of sweat trickled down my back as I wondered what to take off first. If I took off my T-shirt, he'd see my belly fat. If I took off my jeans, I'd be showing him the cellulite on my thighs and my ginormous arse.

Bloody champagne.

I really shouldn't drink so much. If I wasn't tipsy, I wouldn't have thought of such a stupid idea.

There was only one option—remove my bra. At least then, my body would still be covered.

After sliding down the straps, I unhooked it from the

back, pulled it out from under my T-shirt, then dropped the red lacy bra beside me.

Nate froze, his eyes dark. His Adam's apple bobbed and he shifted in his seat before picking up my scarf and dropping it on his lap.

Was he… *hard*?

Fuck. I'd turned him on just by removing my bra. That was… that was good. No. It was bloody amazing. The plan was working.

I took another gulp of champagne. I knew I shouldn't, but I needed some Dutch courage.

'Like what you see?' I teased.

'Yeah, I do…' He licked his lips. 'A *lot*.'

Blimey. Nate had actually answered properly this time. He'd admitted he liked me. Well, my breasts anyway.

Typical man. My tits were always the first thing they made a beeline for. It was what they always liked the most about me. I supposed I couldn't expect Nate to be any different.

If I had a pound for every guy who wanted to take pictures, come all over them, or suggested I do topless modelling, I'd be a millionaire by now.

But then I had a brainwave. If Nate liked them so much, I could use this to my advantage. And right then, I decided that that was the last game I was going to lose.

Throughout the next round, I deliberately leant forward a few times, accidentally on purpose brushed my hand against my nipples, which thanks to looking at Nate's half-naked body were rock hard, or squeezed my boobs together with the inside of my arms… and it worked. It completely threw Nate off kilter.

He lost the game and his jeans. He was now sat in just

his black boxer shorts and I had a prime view of his solid thighs. And that wasn't the only thing that was solid. He'd been trying to disguise it, but I knew he had a boner and that gave me more confidence.

I was *this* close to going to sit on his lap. But I had one more game to win first. My hand was good. I reckoned in just a few short minutes, Nate would lose and have to remove the last item of clothing: his boxer shorts. I bet he wished he'd taken up the offer to wear my scarf.

'Last cards!' I said triumphantly, rubbing my chest.

'What?' Nate's eyes widened as the realisation hit him. 'Nah, you can't win!'

'No?' I pushed my inner arms against my chest, squeezing my boobs together again. 'Just watch me!'

As I dropped the two cards on the pile, Nate shook his head and laughed.

'Okay, Bangles, you win. You think I care about taking my clothes off? I don't. If you're lucky, I might even do it *nice and slow*, so you can have a better look.'

Nate placed his hands at the side of his boxers and tugged them down oh so slowly.

Oh. My. God.

My heart thudded and my pulse raced at a million miles an hour. Forget the fanny flutters, it was like a tsunami down there. I was so wet for him and he still had clothes on.

I wasn't sure if my body could handle the excitement of seeing the guy I'd hated but lusted over in equal measures for years butt naked.

As he moved the boxers down a millimetre and then another, I gasped. His ginormous cock was straining against the fabric and as I imagined it springing out like a jack in the box, I gasped with anticipation.

'You ready?' he said, confidence oozing from every pore.

I nodded, squeezing my thighs together.

'Are you sure you want this, Bangles? I won't do it if it'll make you uncomfortable.'

'Yes,' I said, dribble practically rolling down my chin. 'Show me.'

'Okay. You asked for it…'

Just as I caught a glimpse of the trail of dark hair leading to what I was sure was the King of Knobs in the best possible way, the intercom sounded.

'*Monsieur, madame!* We have arrived at the chateau safely!'

'What?' I called out. '*Already?* You said we were three hours away!'

'*Oui*, and it is exactly three hours, *madame*.'

I glanced at my watch and groaned. He was right. Fuck. Talk about shitty timing. All I needed was one more minute. If he'd buzzed just sixty seconds later, I could've got a glorious view of Nate's delicious dick.

And who knows? If it had been longer, I might've got to feel it.

Where was a bloody traffic jam when you needed it?

'Oh well!' Nate pulled his boxers up and reached for his jeans. 'Saved by the bell. Bad luck, Bangles.'

24

———

NATE

That was close.

One minute later and I would've had my cock out in front of my sisters' friend. What the fuck was I thinking?

Scrap that. I knew *exactly* what I was thinking. I was salivating over those beautiful tits. When Melody had taken off that sexy red lacy bra I'd nearly lost my damn mind.

I could see the curve of her breasts through the fabric and those nipples. Damn. The way they poked through her T-shirt made me fantasise about sucking them. If she'd taken her top off, I would've got down on my knees and begged her to let me do it.

Instead of focusing on my hand and winning the game, all I could think about was how it would feel to bury my head between them. For her to straddle me and dangle them in my face.

Jesus.

I pulled up my boxers and stepped into my jeans. Since

yesterday I'd been hoping we'd get to this chateau as fast as possible. But even though I knew it was for the best that we'd arrived before things got out of hand, part of me was disappointed.

Now the attraction between us was obvious. I'd told her I liked her. She felt the same. Once I'd taken off my boxers, I didn't think it would've been long until we'd started fucking on the back seat. It would've been hot, angry sex. Both of us still pretending to hate each other's guts but enjoying every second. We could've got it out of our system.

Now I'd have to go to my room and use my hands. I wouldn't last until dinner. I was too far gone. I needed to release. Now. Unless I invited Melody to my room…

The car door opened, just as I'd finished zipping up my flies. Melody quickly stuffed her bra in her bag, swiped the scarf from the seat, then wrapped it around her shoulders and part of her chest.

My eyes were still locked on her nipples, which were poking out underneath, and I told my dick to calm the fuck down. I couldn't get out of the car with a hard-on.

'Mel! Nate! You're here!!!' Cassie poked her head inside.

'We are!' Melody got out and they started that loud squealing thing that women did when they were excited before throwing their arms around each other and jumping up and down.

I wasn't complaining. I needed a minute to sort out the *situation* in my boxers.

Hearing my mum and dad's voices did the trick. I stepped out.

'There he is!' Mum chirped. 'My baby boy!'

She was dressed in a cream blouse with a knee-length navy skirt. Her brown skin was glowing and her short silver hair was even neater than usual. Looked like she'd been given the pro hair and beauty treatment.

'Mum! I'm almost forty. I'm not a *baby* or a damn *boy*, I'm a grown man. Don't embarrass me with shit like that in front of people this weekend.'

'I'm your mother!' she scolded in her St Lucian accent. 'I can call you whatever I want. And watch your mouth, boy.'

I rolled my eyes, walking over to give Dad a hug.

He was suited and booted and his salt-and-pepper hair had been freshly cut. He must've just shaved too as his white skin was slightly red at the jawline.

'Dad: you know the wedding isn't this evening, right?'

'Gotta look sharp, son.' He patted me on the back. 'Can't have Nico's rich mates thinking we don't know how to carry ourselves.'

Before they'd retired, Dad worked as a builder and Mum was a nurse and a cleaner. I knew they thought dressing up would help them feel better about mixing in these fancy circles.

'Hey, sis!' Whilst Melody was busy greeting my parents, I gave Cassie a hug. Her long brown curly hair was shiny and on point as usual and I could tell the floaty blue dress she was wearing cost a pretty packet. But even with make-up on she didn't have her normal glow. She looked tired. Must be the stress. 'How you doing, Cheeks?' I said, using her childhood nickname.

'Much better now you're both here. Come on.' She took mine and Melody's hands. 'Let me show you the chateau.'

I'd been so busy thinking about Melody that I hadn't even looked at the surroundings.

Damn.

So *this* was how you did things when you were loaded.

It was like something out of a film.

Although the sun had set, thanks to the outdoor lights, I could still see how fancy it was.

The stone chateau was massive. It had four towers— one on each corner. There was a large illuminated fountain in the massive courtyard in front of the building and it looked like there were acres of fields surrounding the property. I'd have to check it out properly in daylight tomorrow.

The scent of lavender hit me. You didn't get fresh air like this in London. It was all car fumes, smoke and pollution. I inhaled, then exhaled, feeling my lungs expand. I was gonna enjoy going for a run here every morning.

As we stepped into the grand entrance, I saw Carlos with his arm around Lily. Still wasn't used to seeing my best friend with my sister.

He looked dapper in a smart white shirt and dark shorts and Lily had on an orange sleeveless dress and her dark curly hair hung loosely above her shoulders. They both looked good.

'Carlitos! *Hombre!*' I called out. His face broke into a smile.

'*Qué pasa, colega?!*' Carlos held out his arms and pulled me in for a hug. 'We were worried you were not going to make it!'

'C'mon, bro! You know even if I had to swim across the Channel I wouldn't miss my sister's wedding.'

'Hey, what about me?' Lily folded her arms. 'Where's my hug?'

'You know I've got mad love for my favourite sister. Come here.' I released myself from Carlos and gave Lily a squeeze.

'Did I just hear you call Lily your favourite?' Flo shouted. She was dressed in a black suit with her hair pulled back.

'*Moi?* No. You're getting old, sis. Your hearing must be going!' I winked at Lily and laughed.

My chest expanded. I was finally here. With my family. I loved my sisters so much. What I'd said to Carlos was true. If I'd had to swim here I would've. I was happy it hadn't come to that, though.

'Glad to see you and Mel are still in one piece!' said Lily. I looked over at Mel, and she was staring at me, those nipples still standing to attention.

For a moment I'd forgotten all about what had happened in the car, but now looking at her, it all came flooding back.

My dick swelled, begging for relief.

If I could get off, I'd be more relaxed. Time to make things happen.

'Yeah. Just about…' I said, thinking if I had to spend more than a few minutes in the same room with Melody, that wouldn't be true. My balls were ready to explode. 'Listen, it's been a long journey. I need to sort myself out in my room.'

Literally.

'Course!' Lily said. 'The reception is over there. Someone will take you to your room. Cassie would probably do it, but she looks busy.' I glanced over and saw her chatting to Mum and Mel.

'I'm good. Catch you later.' I smiled at Lily, Carlos and Flo, then headed to get my key.

Once I got up to my room I'd work out my next move.

Use my hands or dance with the devil and ask Melody if she wanted to help me with the *problem* inside my pants instead…

25

MELODY

As Lucy, Cassie's friend from Paris, came over to chat to us, I moved slightly to the right so I could get a better view of Nate.

He was at the reception desk and all I wanted to do was follow him to his room.

My knickers were still sodden from the car, where I'd fantasised about him taking me on the back seat, and my nipples were harder than stone. I knew the plan was to try and find a decent Frenchman who'd treat me right, not another bad boy Brit like Nate. And I knew that hooking up with a player was a distraction from that goal, but never in my life had I wanted someone to fuck me so badly.

Nate looked over, smiled, then waved. I did the same, wondering if that was an invitation to join him.

I knew from the ginormous bulge in his boxers earlier that he was up for it just as much as I was. So maybe if I slipped away, we could continue what we'd started in the car.

Although I'd just arrived and should socialise, Cassie

had so many friends and family around her that we wouldn't be missed for half an hour. People would just assume we were checking into our room, organising our suitcase or having a shower to freshen up after the long journey, which was understandable. The last thing they'd suspect was that Nate and I would be getting it on. Everyone knew we hated each other.

It was the perfect plan. But the window for this to be plausible was short. The longer I hung around here, the more the effects of the fireworks between me and Nate would wear off. And the more likely he'd be to get with the women Lily had mentioned earlier.

Nate nodded at the receptionist and the woman beside him, who I think was his aunt, and one of the porters signalled to Nate to follow him.

It was now or never.

'Hey, Cass, I'm just gonna take my case up to my room, sort myself out and give Andrea a quick call. I'll be back down soon, okay?'

'Oh, no! Can you hold on a sec? Bella and the others are having cocktails in the piano room. You've got to see it! It's *amazing*. And I know Nico wants to say hi too. Don't worry about your case: we'll get the porter to take it up for you.'

I looked at her face and she was so excited. So happy to see me. So eager to show me the rooms around the castle. As much as I wanted to get my leg over with Nate, I couldn't choose sex over my bestie's happiness. Friends before fucks and all that.

'Sounds great!' I said enthusiastically. 'Lead the way.'

Cassie took my hand and led me along the black-and-white chequered tiles down the grand hallway. This place was amazing. It was like an updated version of something you saw in films like *The Princess Diaries* or TV shows like *Bridgerton*.

Although you could tell it was centuries old from the period furniture, antique tables and chairs along the hallway and chandeliers hanging from the tall ceilings, it also had a modern vibe. Instead of being dark and deep like I'd seen in photos of old castles, the stone walls were bright white with contemporary art hung on them.

Who would've thought that my friend from South-East London would be marrying a billionaire in a place like this? It was like a real-life fairy tale. Cassie was practically royalty. Wow.

And the whole place smelt of lavender. I definitely needed to take some soaps, candles and creams home as souvenirs.

As we stepped inside the room, there was a grand white piano with a pianist dressed in a white tux playing 'What's Going On' by Marvin Gaye.

A bartender was mixing a colourful cocktail at the sparkly gold bar in the far corner, and in the centre was one large circular stone table with plush rich lavender velvet chairs around it.

I waved at some family members I'd met before and instantly recognised Doris, Cassie and Lily's glam eighty-eight-year-old friend. She looked like an old-school Holly-wood actress with her chic silver hair, smoky eyes and red lips. I'd heard so much about her and couldn't wait to be introduced.

Bella caught my eye. She jumped out of her seat, then rushed over. Her curly hair had been styled into an elegant

French plait and as always her black eyeliner flick was done to perfection.

'Mel!' She threw her arms around me.

'Hey, Bella-boo! How's it going?'

'All good! Even better now you're here. Come on, I've saved you a seat!'

The bartender brought over a tray of red cocktails which looked like cosmopolitans. We all dived in, grabbing a glass.

Cassie sat down next to Lily and Flo.

'To Cassie and her soon-to-be hubby, Nico!' Bella raised her glass.

'To Cassie and Nico!' we all repeated, clinking our glasses against one another's.

'Thanks, ladies!' Cassie beamed. I'd never seen her so happy. 'And shout-out to my friend Melody! We're so glad you made it. Sounds like you had a shitty journey.'

'It was my own bloody fault. I picked up Andrea's passport by mistake, so had to go home and get the right one, and by the time I got it I missed my flight, and because the weather was so awful, all the later ones were cancelled.'

'What a nightmare!' Bella said. 'We're so lucky that we got here a day early. Otherwise we might've been in the same situation. I know some of the family are still trying to get flights here tonight.'

Cassie's family from St Lucia had arrived too, but her dad's Scottish relatives hadn't all managed to get here yet.

'Well, you're here now, and you're still in one piece,' said Cassie. 'It was sweet of Nate to go with you.'

'Yeah,' added Lily. 'When we heard you were travelling together, we all thought we'd need to check the news in case one of you murdered the other! How was the journey with him? Did you argue like cat and dog?'

'Yep! Your brother can be a right knob at times, but we survived...' My voice trailed off.

It was true. In the beginning, we had rubbed each other up the wrong way, but now I just wanted Nate to rub me up any way he felt like it. I wasn't going to tell his sisters that part, though.

'I'm glad,' Cassie said. 'Hopefully it'll mean you two won't be going at each other whilst you're here.'

Cassie meant *going at each other* as in arguing, but my filthy mind couldn't help thinking about the other definition: going at it, as in having sex.

'Don't worry.' I stroked her shoulder. 'I'm sure we can control ourselves...' Sexually, probably not, but in the way that Cassie meant, yes. I was confident that Nate and I wouldn't argue anymore or cause a scene. I'd do my best to avoid it anyway. I wanted to put her mind at ease. It was important that her special day was everything she'd dreamt of and more.

'Glad to hear it!'

'What time's the rehearsal dinner tonight?' I took a sip of my cosmo. God, it was delicious. I'd be ordering another one shortly.

'So...' Cassie paused. 'There's been another change of plan...'

'Melody!'

I looked up and saw Nico strolling into the room with a big smile across his face. As you'd expect from a billionaire, everything about him was flawless. His dark hair looked like it had been cut two seconds ago, his crisp white shirt and tailored trousers were probably fresh from some posh designer shop, and his black shoes were so shiny I could do my make-up in them.

'*Bonjour!*' I said as Nico greeted me with a kiss on both cheeks. '*Ça va?* And that's my limit with French, so go easy with your reply!' I cackled.

'*Très bien!*' He gave me a thumbs up. 'I am good. Very happy to see you have arrived safely. Did Cassie update you about the wedding?'

'She was just about to.'

'Now we will have the rehearsal dinner tomorrow on Saturday, then the wedding on Sunday. Just to make sure that the weather is better. Do you think that you will be fine to take extra time away from work?'

'Um…' I paused.

I was due back on Monday because with the wedding originally scheduled to take place on Friday and my return flight booked for late Sunday afternoon, I'd thought that'd be fine.

Although I was running low on holiday dates, because I hadn't been at the company that long and had taken time off earlier this year when Andrea had fallen off her bike and broken her leg, I'd find a way to make it work.

'I wouldn't miss celebrating your special day for the world!'

'I will of course pay your wages if your boss tells you that you must take unpaid leave if you do not have enough holiday left. The most important thing is that Cassie gets the wedding of her dreams. So if we have to wait longer to do that, then that is how it must be.'

'This guy's a keeper!' My heart fluttered. 'I love that! This is going to be the best wedding *ever*!'

'I hope so,' Cassie said. '*There* you are!' She looked over at the door.

Before I even had a chance to follow her gaze, I felt the air in the room change. The hairs on my arms stood up and I got goose pimples.

'Hey, sis! Had to go and sort out my room and stuff.'

Even if he hadn't mentioned the word *sis* I would've known it was *him*. Something about Nate made the air pulse with electricity and an intensity I'd never experienced before. He just radiated *hot man* vibes from every pore.

I resisted the temptation to turn around and just waited for him to come to the table.

'And who are *you*?' Doris sat up straighter in her chair.

'This is our brother, Nate,' Cassie said.

Doris gasped dramatically, her hand flying to her mouth.

'Cassie, Lily!' She looked at them. 'You didn't tell me your brother was *buff*! Did I say it right this time, dear?'

The whole table burst out laughing.

'Yes, Doris!' Lily grinned. 'You said it perfectly!'

Everyone's eyes were fixated on Nate as he walked around to greet Doris. As he passed me, my nostrils were flooded with his intoxicating scent and I wanted to stand up, pull him into me and bury my head in his chest to have a good sniff. Just like I had when he'd comforted me in the car.

Nate held out his hand.

'We're not in a business meeting, darling. We're in France, which means you need to kiss me!' Doris winked. Nate's eyes widened. 'On the cheeks, dear. Although, I don't mind if you want to kiss me somewhere else...' She smiled mischievously and the whole table erupted into laughter again.

Nate leant forward and pecked each cheek gently. A pang of jealousy flashed through me as I wished his lips were brushing against my skin.

'Now, tell me.' Doris touched Nate's hand. 'Which of these lovely ladies are you with?'

'Me?' Nate rested his hand on Doris's shoulder. 'I'm free and single and ready to mingle…' Nate shot a quick glance in my direction and my stomach fluttered. Just as the wetness in my knickers was starting to dry, he caused the horny floodgates to fly open again.

A group of women who were no doubt the models Lily had referred to earlier perked up, grins spread across their faces.

'You are?' Doris beamed. 'Excellent! I'm single too. Fancy being husband number eight?'

Everyone burst into a fit of giggles. It was like Doris was doing her own stand-up comedy show and we were all here for it.

'If I ever think about getting hitched, sweetheart, I'll keep you in mind. How's that?'

'That sounds wonderful, darling. But don't wait too long. With all of these yummy Frenchmen, I might get taken off the market this weekend.'

'True.' Nate nodded. 'I bet a fine woman like you will be beating them off with a stick.'

God, the man was such a charmer. He even flirted with women in their eighties.

'Sorry, Doris,' Nico interrupted. 'I must steal Nate away now, but I am sure you two will have time to speak later.'

'See you soon, gorgeous.' He winked at Doris before stealing another quick glance at me.

I wondered if he'd be with Nico for long and whether he'd be going up to his room after that.

Now that I'd socialised a bit and Cassie seemed more relaxed, it could be a good time to check in. Once I was sorted, I'd call down to reception and see if I could find out Nate's room number to pay him a visit…

After Nico and Nate left the room, I finished my drink, then went to Cassie.

'You okay? Can I get you a drink?' She didn't have a glass in front of her.

'I'm great! No, thanks. I'm going easy on the drinking. I want a clear head this weekend so I can take in every single moment.'

'And so you should! I'm so happy for you, Cass!' I gave her a quick hug. 'Do you need help with anything? If not, I think I'm gonna go to my room for a bit. Sort myself out. It's been a long journey.'

'No, I'm fine. We're going to have dinner in the dining room in about an hour. Will that give you enough time?'

'Yep!' Sixty minutes would be more than enough to check in, go to my room and with any luck enjoy a roll around on the bed with Nate before showering and changing for dinner.

'Okay, great! See you soon. And, Mel, thanks again for coming.'

'You don't have to thank me, you big ninny! I'm happy to be here!'

I waved goodbye to the other ladies, then headed to reception.

A helpful girl, who couldn't have been that much older

than Andrea, offered to show me to my room.

'You are so lucky, *madame*!' She smiled.

'Lucky? Why?' I said as I reached the top of the staircase and followed her down a brightly lit hall.

'You are staying in the room next to the brother of the bride.' She swooned, her eyes twinkling.

'I-I am?' I stuttered.

'*Oui*. He told us that you will be working on something together for the wedding and requested that your rooms be next door to each other.'

My heart almost flew from my chest.

OMG. Nate wanted this to happen just as much as I did. So much so he'd even arranged for our rooms to be together.

Holy crap. The sex gods were looking down on me and smiling today. This was definitely a sign. I was going to get some of that *good, good loving* tonight!

'Er, yeah. We have very, very urgent and important business to get down to. And we might be up all night.' Tingles erupted between my legs. 'So, you know, it makes sense to be next to each other.'

'Well,' she said, handing me the key, 'you are very lucky. Everyone has been waiting for him to arrive. His mother has shown all of the women his photograph and said he is looking for a wedding date. It is a shame that I am working. Otherwise I would gladly offer.' She grinned.

Back off, girlie, I wanted to shout. *He's mine.*

'Anyway, thank you for showing me to my room.' I smiled sweetly.

'My pleasure,' she replied politely. 'Enjoy your stay.'

'I will.' I grinned, imagining all the different ways Nate could fuck me tonight. 'I *definitely* will…'

26

———

NATE

I sat back on the sofa in the library, where all the other guys were chilling.

Just as the waiter brought over another round of drinks, I saw Melody walk past and wondered whether she was going to get her room key.

Earlier, when I'd checked in, my aunt had been at the desk asking if she could change her room. She'd just arrived and found out hers was next to her in-laws.

Aunt Agnes had leant forward and whispered to the receptionist. 'The kids are staying with friends back in Scotland and I don't get away with my husband often, so I was hoping to make the most of it, if you know what I mean…' The receptionist frowned. 'So being next to my nosey mother-in-law with an interconnecting door is just asking for interruptions…'

The receptionist finally caught on, and when I heard the words 'interconnecting doors', I had a brainwave.

'We could swap rooms,' I jumped in. 'Could you swap mine and my friend's room for theirs?' I asked the receptionist. 'We've got important stuff to work on... for the wedding, and having rooms next door would be helpful.'

My dick had twitched with excitement. It'd been straining against my jeans, begging for *help*, since I'd arrived.

'Thanks, Nathaniel,' Aunty Agnes said. 'That sounds like it would work out well. For both of us...' She smiled. My reputation preceded me.

'Perhaps I should check with Madame Melody first,' the receptionist said. 'To be sure she is happy with this arrangement?'

'I'm sure she will be. Look.' I caught Melody's eye and smiled and waved at her whilst she was chatting to Cassie.

Thankfully Melody beamed and waved back enthusiastically.

'Okay,' the receptionist said. 'I will make the changes now.'

'Perfect!' my aunt said. 'Please make it quick. My mother-in-law will be here any minute.'

This couldn't have worked out better if I'd planned it, I said to myself as I stepped into the grand room.

The bed was ginormous and my brain, or should I say, my dick, went wild thinking about the fun I could have rolling around on that.

It was a four-poster bed too. I imagined Melody gripping the pole as I bent her over at the edge of the mattress and pounded into her from behind, gripping onto that delicious arse.

And the interconnecting door was like a gift from the gods. We could spend the whole weekend fucking without the risk of anyone seeing us sneaking in and out of each other's rooms. When my aunt had said the room swap was perfect, she was right.

So, yeah. Everything was set. Dinner wasn't for another hour, so I had time to see if Melody wanted to continue what we'd started.

Just as I was about to leave, my mum came in with a tall brunette beside her.

'There you are, son!' she said. 'Cassie said I'd find you here. I wanted to introduce you to Amélie. She's single and doesn't have a date for the wedding, so she's excited to meet you!'

I groaned inside and rubbed the back of my neck. I seriously needed to have another chat with Mum and tell her again to butt out of my love life. Well, not *love*—I didn't do the L-word. But my *dating* life. I could choose my own damn women.

'Mum,' I said, putting on my best fake smile and gritting my teeth, 'thanks, but like I told you before, I don't need help finding a date. I reckon I'm already sorted.'

I hadn't asked Melody yet and I wasn't even sure if it was a good idea, but I wasn't going with *this* woman.

Don't get me wrong. She was pretty. Long legs, short skirt, nice face. In many ways, Mum was spot on. If I had a type, this woman would've been it. But as I looked at her, I felt nothing.

'But Amélie is a *model*,' Mum insisted. 'I know how much you like them. And she's just about to star in an underwear campaign—that's right, isn't it?' She turned to look at Amélie, who nodded. 'And I know how much you like women's underwear…' She grinned.

'Fuck's sake,' I muttered.

'I'll leave you lovebirds to it…' She winked and left.

Jesus Christ.

'Your mother is adorable,' Amélie said in a thick French accent. 'And you seem very nice too.' She stroked my arm and I flinched.

'Look, sweetheart, I don't know what she's told you, but like I said, I'm good. I don't need my mum to set up dates. I'm not looking for a girlfriend.'

'Who said anything about me being your *girlfriend*?' She tilted her head suggestively. 'We can just fuck, no?'

I had to hand it to her. She was a woman who knew what she wanted and was going for it. I liked when women made the first move—although usually they at least waited five minutes.

But I wasn't feeling it, which didn't make sense. Earlier today I'd told myself that as soon as I arrived, I'd look for a stranger to screw without strings or complications. That was the plan. So now I had a pretty woman offering herself on a silver platter, why was I still thinking about Melody? The woman who wasn't my usual type and would make my life complicated?

With Amélie, I knew that once we'd banged, I could leave, no questions asked. Then after the wedding, we'd go our separate ways and that'd be the end of it.

But with Melody, even with the benefit of interconnecting rooms, we'd still need to be careful that people didn't find out. I didn't need the questions or headache. And then she'd want more. She'd said herself that she fell in love easily.

She'd also said that men left her unsatisfied in bed. Not to blow my own trumpet, but I knew for damn sure that wouldn't happen with me. Once she experienced what it was like to be fucked by a real man, there'd be no going back. She'd want more than I could give her. It was messy and complicated. And yet, getting with her was all I could think about.

I must be a fucking sadist.

'So?' Amélie stroked my arm again, then whispered in my ear. 'I am very adventurous in the bedroom. I can do many things with my mouth that you will enjoy…' She ran her palm over my chest. This time I caught her hand and removed it.

'Listen, darling, I'm sure that's true, but like I said, I'm good.'

Her eyes bulged. This was probably the first time a guy had turned her down.

She muttered some shit in French before storming off.

At first, I wondered if I needed my head tested. I was horny as fuck and I'd just turned down an opportunity to screw a woman who'd probably be the next Kendall Jenner. What the hell was wrong with me?

But as I watched her strut towards another guy, swinging her hips, my dick confirmed I'd made the right decision. It was softer than a damn marshmallow. If Melody walked away like that, the sight of that beautiful butt would get my cock rock hard faster than you could say *boner*.

Yeah. Even though I knew it was a mistake, I was going to find her. And if she was willing, I'd give Melody the best fuck of her life.

27

———

MELODY

How could I be so bloody stupid?

As I stood at the doorway watching Nate getting up close and personal with a gorgeous model who'd give one of the youngest Kardashian/Jenner sisters a run for their money, my stomach plummeted.

There she was stroking his arm, then his chest, and—oh God, now she was whispering in his ear.

I couldn't look. I headed back to find the girls.

Earlier, after I'd gone to my room, I'd tried calling Andrea, who hadn't answered but texted to say she was *fine*, then I'd quickly showered and squeezed into my yellow maxi dress, putting on my bangles and a necklace I'd recently made before going down to find Nate.

The plan was to bring him upstairs ASAP and, once he'd given me a good seeing-to, go down to dinner. Clearly that wasn't going to happen now.

Nate was back on his familiar hunting ground. Going after his favourite type of woman. The kind that was nothing like me.

Well, screw him.

Oh, bollocks. I groaned. I just realised—if Nate hooked up with that woman, I'd have to listen to them going at it all night. Why the hell had he arranged for our rooms to be next door to each other?

Because he was an evil knob, that was why. He'd probably done it so that I'd get the message that he wasn't interested. To make it clear that nothing was going to happen. Or to taunt me. So I could hear the woman screaming his name and he could feel like *da man* because he'd given her multiple orgasms. *Prick.*

Anyway, I didn't care anymore. I'd had a momentary lapse of judgement. I'd never liked him and I couldn't just change my opinion because we'd managed to spend twenty-four hours together without killing each other.

As far as I was concerned, Nate could take a long walk off a short bridge. If he wanted to have a threesome in his room, I couldn't care less. I had my noise-cancelling head-phones, so I wouldn't hear a thing.

I strode back into the piano room, my head held high. Lily rushed over.

'Oh good! You're back! See that cute guy over there talking to Carlos?'

'Yeah?' I looked over.

'That's one of the men I was talking about earlier, when we spoke on the phone. He's French, single and really nice! Do you want me to introduce you?'

Lily was right. He was cute, but he wasn't a patch on Nate. He was an inch or two taller than me, had dark slicked-back hair and a strong jaw.

Looks-wise, he was exactly the kind of guy I'd hoped to meet at the wedding. Ordinarily I would've been chomping at the bit to speak to him, but yet, my stupid body was screaming, *He's not Nate!*

Well, Nate had clearly had a change of heart, and if he was going to flirt with other women, then I could flirt with another man.

I followed Lily over to Carlos and the other guy, putting on my brightest smile.

'Carlos, I was thinking we could introduce Melody to—'

'Toby,' he interjected, turning to face me before leaning forward to kiss my cheeks.

As he did, I got a whiff of his musky aftershave. God, had he bathed in it? It was so strong. But not good strong. Overpowering strong. It wasn't like Nate's scent. His was strong but delicious. The kind that made you want to bury your head in his chest and sniff it all night.

'Nice to meet you,' I said politely.

'I'll leave you both to it,' said Lily.

'I think everyone is going to the dining room now,' Carlos added, nodding towards the doorway where a crowd was filtering out of the room.

'Oh, right,' I replied.

'Perhaps we can sit together and get to know each other better?'

'Y-yeah!' I said as enthusiastically as I could. I wasn't really feeling any attraction, but the last thing I wanted was to be sat on my own at the table whilst Nate was flirting with Miss Universe.

'Shall we?' Toby lifted his arm for me to link mine with his.

'Yeah, let's go.'

As we walked past the library, I saw Nate and our eyes

locked. His gaze darted between me and Toby and then he scowled. *Good.* I couldn't see that woman beside him, but she'd probably gone to touch up her make-up.

The dining room was just as stunning as every other room in this castle. There was a huge fireplace at one end and the long solid wood table spanned from one end of the room to the other. It was decorated with tall silver candle-holders and multiple fancy silver plates and cutlery.

Cassie said there wasn't a formal seating plan tonight, so I gestured towards the seats opposite Carlos and Lily. At least then I wouldn't be stuck with making polite conversation with Toby if we didn't hit it off.

About five minutes later, Nate pulled out the chair next to Carlos and sat down.

Great. So now I'd have to look at him snuggling up with another woman all night. It didn't matter anyway. I wasn't interested anymore and I had Toby. I'd come here to find a nice Frenchman and the universe had delivered.

He might not be giving me the fanny flutters right now, but once I had a few drinks, I might feel differently, and if I was still in the mood, maybe I'd think about taking it further.

As much as I'd come here hoping to find a relationship, this was bound to be something casual—just like it would've been with Nate, so it didn't really matter who I slept with. Going from past experience, he'd probably only last a few minutes anyway and Toby was nice to look at. I'd certainly been with guys who had a lot less to offer.

'So, you are a friend of Lily and Cassie, yes?' Toby poured wine into my glass as I eyed up the bread on the table.

'Yeah. I'm the bride-to-be's bestie. I know Lily

through Cassie. And I know Cassie through Bella, who's Cassie's cousin.' God, why was I rambling?

Although I should be focusing on Toby, out of the corner of my eye I saw Nate smiling and chatting to yet another bloody woman. She was as pretty as the other one if not even prettier. *What happened to her?*

Earlier I'd been half joking about Nate having a three-some, but now it seemed like more of a reality. The woman pulled up a chair, sat down and rested her hand on Nate's shoulders as she gazed into his eyes.

The volume of chatter around the room meant I couldn't hear what was being said between them, but a big smile spread across Nate's face.

Knob.

'That is a very nice necklace,' Toby said.

'Thanks!' My heart swelled.

'Where did you buy this from?'

'I-I made it myself.' I'd always had imposter syndrome about my designs, but when people complimented me, it was like validation. Toby asking where I'd bought it meant he thought it was good enough to be sold in the shops and be sat alongside real jewellery designers' work. *A girl can dream.*

'Really? That is fantastic! My family has a department store in Paris. And they sell a lot of beautiful jewellery like this.'

'Oh, wow!' My eyes popped out of my head. 'That's fab! Do you work for them too?'

The size of the enormous watch on Toby's wrist and the cut of his suit told me he didn't work on the shop floor. Those two items combined were probably the equivalent of five years' salary.

'*Oui*. I am the head of finance.'

Knew he'd be loaded.

'Impressive.'

'So have you been to France before?'

'Just to Paris. To see Cassie.'

'If you are ever in the South again, perhaps you can come on my yacht.'

'Oh, thanks.'

The guy has a yacht? This was a totally different league. The men I knew that were doing well owned their own homes and a decent car. Toby here had a bloody yacht.

As I listened to Toby talk about his recent trip to Monaco, I found myself looking over at Nate again.

He caught my eye, glared at me like I was the most hated woman on earth and then turned his attention back to the model.

Fine.

Throughout eating the meal, which included this delicious fish and seafood stew called bouillabaisse which Toby said was a traditional dish from this region, I did my best to avoid looking at Nate, but it was hard.

I tried to focus on what Toby was saying, but the more we talked, the more I realised we had very little in common. We came from totally different worlds.

Sometimes that didn't matter. Even though Nico was a billionaire, Cassie still had a fantastic connection with him because they had similar interests. But it was clear pretty quickly that I didn't feel that with Toby.

For example, my idea of a good night out was having a pizza and drink with friends and then going out dancing, whereas for Toby it was fine dining followed by an evening at the opera.

Toby started talking about some famous artist called Paul Cézanne who was born in Aix-en-Provence and asked if I wanted to visit the Granet Museum with him tomorrow. But I wasn't really a museum kind of girl…

I subtly slid my phone out of my clutch bag to look at the time. Seriously? We'd only been talking for an hour. It felt like ten.

Maybe some women would be interested in him prattling on about his yacht, skiing trips and fancy nights out, but I was getting bored pretty quickly.

As I looked around the table, once again trying to ignore Nate, Lily was staring into Carlos's eyes. Cassie was talking to a guest and Bella was deep in conversation with her hubby, Mike.

And me? It'd been a long day and I hadn't slept much last night, knowing Nate was in the bed with me, so I was tired. The alcohol I'd drunk in the past twenty-four hours probably hadn't helped either.

I polished off the delicious lavender ice cream, then decided to call it a night. If I stayed any longer, I'd drink more and end up saying something stupid to Nate or telling Toby I thought he was a bore. Better to quit now.

'Toby, it was lovely to meet you. I've had a long day, though, so I'm going to my room now.' I stood up.

'That is a shame. Would you like me to walk you there? Perhaps then we could chat about the possibility of stocking some of your jewellery.' He smiled, his gaze dropping to my chest.

I froze, my eyes wide as I processed what he'd just

said. Basically, if I let him walk me to his room, he might *try* and help me with my jewellery.

But the way he was looking at me, eyes sparkling, lips parted, I wasn't sure that he wanted to just walk me to my door. I had a feeling he'd expect an invite inside my room and then into my bed.

Although I was hornier than a dog on heat and I'd love nothing more to be stocked in a Parisian department store, I wasn't willing to sleep with him. Which was odd because over the years, I'd shagged guys without getting anything decent in return.

Sometimes they hadn't even bought me a drink and a packet of crisps. But, if I ever decided to make a go of the jewellery thing again, I didn't want to feel like it had happened because I'd spread my legs.

And as for us getting jiggy, I just wasn't feeling it.

I knew that I'd been secretly hoping to meet a Frenchman here, but even with all of his money and connections, I didn't fancy him.

If Toby was Nate, I would've jumped on his cock so fast I would've got whiplash.

Well, that was before I'd seen him getting cosy with Miss Universe.

'Thanks, but it's okay. I can go by myself.'

'Right. I see.' His face fell.

'But if you are interested in my designs, then I can give you my number and maybe you can contact me once I'm back in London?'

'Of course.' He handed me his phone. 'Put your number here.'

I doubted he'd get in touch, but I had nothing to lose.

'Here you go.' I handed it back. 'Enjoy the rest of your evening.'

As I went to say bye to Cassie, I subtly looked over at Nate one last time. He didn't see me staring this time, so I took full advantage, using the opportunity to get a good look at those biceps, which were bulging as he stretched and put his hands behind his head.

Whilst I waited for Cassie to finish her conversation with a Scottish woman who I think was a relative from her dad's side of the family, my eyes darted back to Nate.

God. As much as I hated him, he looked so good. I couldn't blame those women for swarming around him.

His broad chest strained against the white short-sleeved shirt he was wearing and his beard was impossibly neat as usual.

My thoughts turned to what he'd said yesterday about the sensation of a beard between a woman's legs and the fact that he'd never given a woman pussy rash. As I pictured his face buried between my thighs, my body tingled.

'You okay?' said Cassie, causing me to break my gaze.

'Yeah—well, no. I'm going to my room.'

'Oh no! Why?'

'I'm not feeling great.'

'What's wrong?'

Two minutes ago, I would've sworn I was tired and bored, but right now, I was feeling sexually frustrated and horny. Of course I couldn't tell her that.

'Just, I'm… going to lie down.'

'Can I get you anything?' Cassie's face creased with concern.

A good seeing-to from your brother would make me feel a whole lot better…

'Thanks, but I'll be fine. I'll guzzle a load of water and I'll be right as rain. Don't worry.'

'Okay. If you're sure. But call if you need anything.'

'Will do.'

I quickly left the dining room. It wasn't water I needed. I needed a bloody orgasm. I'd feel much better afterwards. And seeing as getting one from Nate was off the table now, I'd need to do what I normally did in life: get the job done myself.

As soon as I stepped inside, I switched on the bedside lamp. This room was bloody gorgeous. It had sky-blue walls, huge windows draped with tall lavender curtains, a deep purple sofa and a four-poster bed decorated with lots of lavender and white cushions and bed linen. I'd feel like a princess sleeping in here.

But right now, I didn't want to be a princess. My inner wanton was calling me. I went to my suitcase and rooted around until I found my vibrator.

I took off my dress and knickers, then lay down on the bed.

Phone. I needed my phone. I'd watch something from the ethical porn site I used. That'd get me going. I'd use my headphones, though. The last thing I wanted was someone to overhear what I was watching.

Once I had my earphones in and the video up on the screen, I spread my legs and got to work.

I wasn't sure why, but the video wasn't doing it for me. I didn't want to see other people going at it. I wanted something *real*. More personal.

As I rubbed the rabbit-shaped stimulator against my

clit, I thought about Nate again and fireworks sparked all over my body.

That's it.

That was all I needed. Not the video. Just thinking about Nate's body and what he could do to me was enough.

Wetness pooled between my legs instantly. I squeezed my eyes shut and pictured the way he'd pulled off his T-shirt in the car. *Oh God.* My body bucked against the vibrator. I lowered the speed. I didn't want to come too quickly. I wanted to savour the sweet memories. Those rippling abs, that solid chest…

And when he was in just his boxers and he'd started to pull them down, *oh-so slowly*. If we'd had just a few more minutes, I could imagine him picking me up and throwing me down on the back seat.

Then he would've peeled down my jeans and ripped my underwear because he was so desperate to get me off. That was what he'd said, right? That he never left a woman's bed without them being satisfied.

Maybe he'd even consider going down on me. Nate would spread my legs, part my lips and lick me slowly.

'Oh God!' I moaned. 'Oh, oh…'

And he'd be right—the delicious friction of his soft beard rubbing between my legs would set off a grenade inside of me.

My heart raced and my clit throbbed as I hurtled towards the edge. I turned up the speed on the vibrator, picturing Nate slamming his hard cock into me.

I screamed with ecstasy as the hard plastic vibrated at full speed against my sensitive bud.

I thrust the vibrator inside of me, imagining it was Nate filling me up.

'Oh Nate… that's right, fuck me. Harder! Yes—oh, Nate! Yes! Give me your big, thick knob. Right there. *Ohhhhhhhh!*'

I cried out as my body jerked against the vibrator, over and over again. Heat flooded my cheeks and my whole body was on fire.

Another satisfied groan escaped my lips and just as I was coming to my senses, I heard a noise. It couldn't be the video. I'd switched that off. It must be someone in the hallway outside my room.

The voice grew louder. It was like someone was calling my name.

My eyes flicked open and…

No.

God no.

Please. I beg you.

Tell me I'm dreaming.

I quickly grasped at the bedsheet, dragging it over my body, tugged the headphones from my ears, then squinted.

It *wasn't* a dream. It was a fucking nightmare.

Standing at the foot of my bed was Nate, his eyes wide and a mischievous smirk on his face.

He'd seen me masturbating.

And judging by the smug look on his face, he'd bloody heard me calling his name whilst I did it.

Mortified didn't even cover it.

28

NATE

'What the hell are you doing in here?' Melody screamed.

I froze. My head was replaying the delicious sight of her on the bed, her legs spread wide, fucking herself and screaming my name.

At first I'd thought it was a mistake, but when she'd said it a second time, I'd nearly come in my boxers. She was thinking of me as she got herself off and it was so fucking sexy.

'Cassie said you weren't feeling well, so I came to check on you and I heard you screaming, so I thought something was wrong. I knocked and you didn't answer and I was banging really hard'—*bad choice of words* —'the door, I mean. I knocked a few times and your screams got louder, so I tried the interconnecting door and luckily, it was open. If I'd known you were... *y'know*, taking care of *personal* business, I wouldn't have come.' *Jeez*. Every word was loaded with innuendo. 'I mean, I wouldn't have entered...' I slapped my forehead. That word wasn't any better. 'Now that you've had a little warm-up, if you want the real thing, I could help you out…'

Melody glared at me, her face like thunder. In hindsight, that wasn't the smartest thing to say.

'Get out!' she screamed, throwing a pillow at me.

'Okay, okay, I'm sorry!' I held my hands up in surrender and slipped back through the door.

I sat on my bed. Fuck.

How had everything gone so wrong? One minute I was planning to find her to see if she wanted to bang, and the next, she was getting up close and personal with some slick-looking French dude. Laughing at his jokes, smiling, touching his arm.

When I'd seen her with that guy, a strange feeling had taken over my body. Like I'd been punched in the gut. It couldn't be jealousy. It'd been years since that'd happened. Normally if I wanted a woman, she wanted me too, and if she didn't, it was no big deal. I'd just move onto the next one.

But tonight, when I'd seen Melody touching that guy, a fire had risen within me. I'd managed to ditch that Amélie woman, but as soon as I spotted the competition, I knew I had to think quickly.

Carlos had already invited me to sit with him and Lily and there was no way I was going to sit opposite Melody on my Jack Jones. So when Mum sent over another woman she thought would be marriage material, I didn't refuse.

Like Amélie, chatting to this chick was about as exciting as being stuck in traffic. But I suffered the conversation about the fashion shoot she'd had in New York, just so Melody knew that if she was gonna hook up with someone else tonight, I could too.

Watching him with her made me so pissed. I couldn't believe that some slimy twat was going to get to touch her. To feel the softness of her skin, breathe in that sweet perfume and grip that fine arse.

I cursed myself for not acting on how I felt sooner. I thought I'd missed my chance for good. But when I saw Melody leave the table without him, I saw an opportunity.

I'd waited several minutes, in case she'd gone to the toilet. Then I'd excused myself from whatever her name was and asked Cassie if she knew where Melody had gone. And when Cassie said Melody wasn't feeling well, I went into my default protective mode. Just like I did for my sisters. I had a need. It wasn't sexual. It was a need to make Melody feel better.

So that was when I went, knocked on her door and heard Melody's screams. Now that I thought about it, I'd been with enough women to know that they sounded sexual. But at the time, I thought she was ill, so the last thing I would've thought was that she was getting herself off. I thought she was just in so much pain she was crying out for help. She needed me. And I wasn't going to let her down. Except... well, we all know how the shit hit the fan when I burst into her room.

An image of Melody with her legs spread open, calling my name, flashed into my head again and my dick throbbed. Fuck. She wasn't the only one who needed to release.

I jumped off the bed and headed to the shower. After taking off my clothes, I stepped inside and turned the temperature to cold. As the icy water hit my skin, I winced. But it was necessary. A few minutes of this and I'd freeze all thoughts of her out of my brain.

But it didn't work. Every time I closed my eyes all I saw was her. Not just the vision of her on the bed, but Melody in the shower with me as I pinned her against the tiles and fucked her senseless. Then as I laid her on the rug and licked between her legs.

Fuck it.

I grabbed my cock, sliding my hand up and down, back and forth, like my life depended on it. And it felt like it did. If I didn't come now, my whole body was gonna self-destruct.

As I fisted harder, I imagined it was Melody's hands on my dick. Then I pictured her fire-engine-red lips sucking my hard length. Sliding my thick cock to the back of her throat as I fucked her mouth.

That's right.

I grunted loudly. That was all I needed. I gripped the wall as I exploded in my hand. Fuck.

I jerked once, then twice, and squeezed out the last of my cum before sliding down to the base of the shower.

My chest rose and fell as I caught my breath.

Did I feel better? Kinda. But I knew straight away that wasn't going to be enough. It would tide me over for now, but the only way I was going to be satisfied was if I had the real thing. And as rich as the pickings were at this wedding, I wasn't interested in hooking up with a stranger anymore.

The only woman that could satisfy my appetite was Melody. Problem was, she was back to hating my guts.

It'd take a damn miracle to make her like me again.

Lucky for me, I wasn't afraid of a challenge.

29

———————

MELODY

As daylight streamed through a gap in the curtains, I slowly opened my eyes.

Had it all been a dream?

A groan escaped my lips as I realised it wasn't.

Nate had seen me masturbating and heard me screaming his name.

I dragged my arse to the shower, wondering how I'd face him. There was no way he wasn't going to tease me about this. He'd already started last night by offering to give me the real thing. A couple of hours earlier, I would've jumped at the chance, but now I was too embarrassed.

Bollocks.

After drying, then creaming myself, I returned to the bedroom and drew the curtains. Wow. The views were incredible. I opened the huge windows and the room was flooded with natural light.

The sky was bright blue and in the distance I could see rows upon rows of purple lavender fields. There were also landscaped gardens and olive groves. Apparently this place also had a vineyard. The fields stretched towards the mountains, giving me an amazing view of Provence.

No wonder Cassie and Nico wanted to have their wedding here. I hoped the weather was as beautiful as this on her wedding day tomorrow. The photos would look amazing in the sunshine.

I walked back towards my bed and flipped open the top of my suitcase. Tonight I planned to wear a bold red low-cut dress to the rehearsal dinner, but I was worried about it fitting.

It was already verging on the tight side when I'd tried it on again last week, but after I'd stuffed my face with pizza that first night with Nate, the food we'd eaten for breakfast and lunch yesterday, plus the three-course dinner last night, it was bound to be worse. And I'd drunk enough alcohol these past forty-eight hours to sink the *Titanic*.

I stepped into the dress. As I pulled it up to my thighs, everything got tighter. I just about dragged it all the way up to my waist, but when I tried to do up the zip, it struggled as if to say, *Are you having a laugh?*

Then I remembered. I wasn't wearing my control pants. Once I put those bad boys on, I'd be fine. After tugging off the dress, I forced myself into the control pants. They were so tight I thought I was going to pass out. How the hell did women wear corsets in the olden days and still breathe?

No pain, no gain, though, right?

I held my breath and tried wriggling into the dress again. Although it wasn't as tight, the zip still wouldn't budge. Shit.

If that didn't fit, there was a good chance my bridesmaid's dress wouldn't fit either. I had to try again. I didn't have any other options in my suitcase. I sucked in my stomach and attempted to drag the zip up again.

'Noooo!!!' I screamed. 'Fuck! Shit! Bollocks!!'

'Melody?' A deep voice called my name. 'You okay?'

It was Nate. I plonked myself on the bed without replying. This shapewear was limiting my ability to breathe.

There was another knock at the door.

'Melody. You're not answering. I'm worried. I'm gonna count to ten and then I'm coming in, okay? Are you dressed?'

'Yes,' I huffed.

'Okay if I come in?'

'Whatever.' I was past the point of caring. I might as well get the awkwardness over with. I didn't know what was worse—Nate catching me calling his name whilst I wanked or the idea of going to the wedding dressed in a bedsheet because it'd be the only thing that'd fit me.

I'd spent money I didn't have on that dress to try and look nice and now it didn't fit. Fuck's sake.

The door cracked open and Nate creeped in.

'Fuck!' He rushed over. 'What's happened? Did you collapse?'

'No,' I sighed. 'I'm… forget it.' I sat up slowly, hoping being upright would make it easier to breathe. Nope. I had to take off this sodding dress.

'Tell me.' He softened his voice and looked into my eyes. My stomach attempted to flutter but was restricted by the thick band of elastic.

'You'll laugh.'

'No, I won't.'

'It's this dress. It doesn't fit. I've got nothing to wear

for the dinner tonight. And now my bridesmaid's dress probably won't fit either.'

'Why? Didn't you try it on before you came?'

'Of course I bloody did! Cassie sent the bridesmaid's dress over for the last fitting three weeks ago and this dress sort of fitted last week. But then I ate pizza for dinner instead of broccoli and croissants and bread for breakfast instead of just coffee and now I can't do it up. Not even when I wear these godawful control pants. I'm screwed!'

I immediately wished I'd used another word considering Nate had caught me screwing myself last night.

'Melody.' Nate took my hand. Electricity sparked around my body. Well, the bits where I still had circulation. 'Have you ever considered that it's not your body that is the problem, it's the size of the dress? You did nothing wrong by eating a couple of slices of pizza and you had one tiny croissant and two pieces of wholemeal bread. That wasn't even a lot. Like I said before, extreme dieting doesn't work. Your body needs food, not starvation.'

'Trust a man not to understand! Eating carbs isn't going to help me get into my clothes!'

'We can get new clothes. There's still time.'

'I told you! I'm skint! I don't have any money.'

'Don't worry about that.'

'I'm not some hotshot personal trainer who charges hundreds of pounds to show rich people how to do sit-ups! I have bills coming out of my arse and I already owe you a shitload of money for the ticket and—'

'Breathe.' Nate rested his hands on my shoulders.

'I can't! This bloody thing has cut off my circulation!'

'Take it off, then.'

'Haven't you seen enough of my naked body?'

'No…' Nate winced, probably reliving the sight of me in the buff. 'I didn't mean take it off in front of me. I'll leave. But before I do, I want to apologise for last night. I didn't mean to… *y'know*. I wasn't trying to invade your personal space. I was worried. I'm sorry. It won't happen again.'

'Whatever,' I huffed. There wasn't much more I could say. I just wanted to forget about it.

'Let me make it up to you. Let me take you shopping and help you find an outfit. I'm good at knowing what will suit a woman. Trust me.'

'I thought you preferred taking women's clothes *off*, not giving them advice on what to put on.'

'Well, what can I say? I'm multitalented.' Nate smirked. 'But seriously, let's meet in an hour. We'll go shopping and I'll speak to Miriam, Nico's assistant, to arrange an urgent fitting with a seamstress for your brides-maid's dress. Just in case.'

'That'd be… thanks.'

'Put your number in my phone.' He handed me his mobile. After I typed in my details, I gave it back to him. 'Cool. I'm sending you a text so you have mine too. Got it?'

'Yep.' I glanced at the message on the screen, then saved his number.

'Good. Now go and have breakfast. And I mean a *proper* breakfast. Not carrot sticks or broccoli. Okay?'

'Okay.' My voice softened. That was really kind of him. I hoped they had a Primark nearby as that was about all I could stretch to. 'Now if you don't mind, I need to extricate myself from this tube of torture.'

~

After putting some fresh fruit salad in a small bowl and picking up a yoghurt, I found an empty seat at the dining table and sat down.

It was like I was a Billy No Mates. Cassie wasn't feeling well, so was resting. Lily was having a *lie-in* with Carlos, which I reckoned was code for shagging, and Bella had already eaten and gone for a walk with Mike.

Seeing as my friends were going to be tied up this morning, going shopping with Nate seemed like an okay idea. I needed something to wear and God knows how, but he seemed pretty confident about being able to help. But cockiness seemed to be his default setting, so time would tell.

Once I'd polished off the last spoonful of yoghurt, I walked past the buffet, doing my best not to look at the baskets of bread rolls and buttery croissants. I knew Nate said I should have a proper breakfast, but he wasn't the one who needed to find clothes to fit into. I only needed to watch what I ate for a couple more days and then once the wedding was over, I could go back to eating normally.

After leaving the dining room, I wandered through one of the exits. I looked at the time. Ten thirty. I wasn't sure whether Andrea would be awake, but I needed to speak to her. The brief replies she'd sent when I'd texted on Thursday night to check she'd arrived safely and again yesterday to see how she was weren't enough.

The phone rang several times before she answered.

'Yeah?' she said. Her voice sounded croakier than someone who'd smoked twenty cigarettes before break-fast. Oh God. I hoped she wasn't smoking.

'Is that any way to greet your mother?' I snapped, my stomach twisting with worry.

'Hello, *Mum*,' she added robotically. 'What is it?'

'How are you?'

'Fine.' *Standard teenage response.*

'And are you alone? In the bed?'

'Mum!'

'Andrea, love, you're too young to be in a sexual relationship. You should take things slowly.'

'Mum, I'm not talking about this with you right now. It's nine thirty in the morning. On a Saturday!'

I was about to correct her, then remembered France was an hour ahead.

'I know you think I'm being a spoilsport, but you don't want to ruin your future by having a baby when you're not ready. I'm speaking from experience.'

'What? So you're saying I ruined your life? Nice one, Mum. Enjoy your wedding!'

'Andrea, I didn't mean—'

Too late. She'd already hung up. Shit.

Being a parent was so bloody hard. I constantly felt like I was failing. I seemed to have a knack of always saying or doing the wrong thing. Now my daughter thought I hated her because she'd ruined my life.

I tried calling back, but her phone was switched off. There was no point going via Rodney. I'd leave it a few hours and then try again later.

In the meantime, maybe shopping with Nate could take my mind off things.

30

———

MELODY

Only a few minutes after I'd got back to the room, my phone chimed. I hoped it was Andrea, but it was Nate. My traitorous heart fluttered and I told it to calm down.

Although I was happy to have the chance to find a new outfit, my stomach was in knots, worrying about the awkwardness of being in a car for God knows how long with Nate.

Nate

I'm in a black Mercedes parked in the driveway.

Nate

Come down now.

So bossy.

After stepping out of the castle's door, I walked through the courtyard and down the long gravel driveway, my heart hammering against my chest. I'd been so distracted when we'd arrived last night that I hadn't noticed it was lined with beautiful, tall cypress trees.

I spotted the car and looked around before opening the door and sliding onto the black leather seats. *Fancy.*

As I caught sight of Nate, I swallowed hard. Did this man ever look bad? The curls on the top of his head looked so defined, like he'd applied serum to each individual hair strand. Like always, his beard was groomed to perfection, and that scent—good Lord.

'Hey.' His dark brown eyes locked on mine and I reminded myself that I was here to go shopping, not to imagine him naked.

'Alright,' I said in acknowledgement. 'Ashamed to be seen with me?'

'What?' Nate frowned.

'Parking as far away from the entrance as possible.'

'Nah, it's not like that. I don't know about you, but I don't have the energy to start answering questions from my family about why we're going somewhere together.'

The driver started the engine and set off at a gentle speed.

'True.' Cassie, Lily and Bella would think I'd had a personality transplant. It was one thing to be forced to spend time with Nate because we were stranded in bad weather trying to make it to the wedding. But today the skies were clear blue and the sun was shining brightly, so there was no reason for us to be together.

'There aren't many shops nearby, so I thought we'd go to Aix-en-Provence. They'll have a bigger selection.'

'Okay.' I nodded. 'Out of interest, how come you reckon you're such an expert on women's clothes?'

'I grew up with four women in the house. That on its

own was an education. But I know a few people in fashion, so you kind of pick things up. And I spend all day looking at women's bodies.'

'I bet you do!'

'For *work*.' Nate rolled his eyes. 'My job is about fitness and helping mostly women enhance their body shape and strength, so it's related.'

'What made you get into the whole personal training thing?'

'A few reasons: I've always been interested in fitness. When I was younger, I couldn't wait to join a gym. And I lift weights so I'm strong enough to protect my family.'

'From what?'

'From whatever I need to.'

'No offence, but don't you think you're a bit OTT with the whole protective big brother stuff?'

Nate's face fell. I felt bad about upsetting him, but it was true. Sometimes he treated Cassie and Lily like kids. That was one of the reasons I'd hated him for so long.

When Lily had started dating his best friend, Carlos, I heard Nate had hit the roof. Later it turned out that he had a good reason for being wary of his friends getting with his sister, but even so, if you asked me, he still fussed over them too much. Big brother or not, he had no right telling a grown woman who she should or shouldn't date.

'Maybe.' His head hung low. I raised my eyebrow, questioning his response. 'Okay, yeah. I'm working on it. I'm trying hard to butt out of my sisters' lives more. And not to worry about them so much.'

'Glad to hear it!'

'It's hard, though. Anyway, going back to why I got into personal training… growing up, Dad always drummed it into me that it was our job to take care of Mum and my sisters. I knew it was important, but one night when I was at a bar, I must've been around eighteen, I saw this guy hitting on another man's lady. The woman's boyfriend caught him and tried to get the guy to stop, but he refused, then ended up beating the boyfriend to a pulp before security stepped in. That man was so weak he couldn't even protect his own damn girlfriend. I saw that and knew that I never wanted to be like him. I'm not condoning violence— but I never wanted to be in a position where I couldn't defend my family or friends if I needed to.'

'Oh.' I swallowed hard. 'I just thought you did it to— y'know, for an aesthetic thing.' I chose my words carefully.

'Nah. I mean, yeah, I like to look good, but like I said, there were lots of reasons. Having a strong, healthy body also means a better and hopefully longer life so I can be around for as long as possible to protect my family.'

'I think you put too much pressure on yourself with this whole being the strong protective, dependable man stuff.'

'Probably.' He shrugged. 'I never said I was perfect.'

'Maybe cut yourself some slack.'

'Don't feel sorry for me. I enjoy staying in shape. That's why I work out every day.' Nate's eyes lit up. You could tell he was passionate about it. And not just because of his amazing physique or the whole overprotective stuff.

'Don't worry, I wasn't!' I cackled. 'But seriously? You work out *every* day?'

'Almost. I didn't the past forty-eight hours or on Christmas and New Year's Day because I was probably hung-over.' He laughed and my heart fluttered again. I liked his laugh. It was deep, hearty and infectious. Like how I'd imagine a big friendly bear sounded if you tickled his tummy.

'Wow, so excluding the last couple of days, you only normally work out three hundred and sixty-three days of the year. Such a slacker!'

'I know, right?' He chuckled again. 'But I went for a run and did a longer workout this morning to make up for it. Anyway, like I was saying, I started off doing it for personal reasons. I didn't intend for it to be my career. I did a physiotherapy degree and followed that route for a bit after graduating. But then I was travelling around the States and in LA I met a guy at a club who turned out to be a big PT who trained lots of celebs. He had his own gym and invited me down the next day and he kind of became my mentor. I ended up staying there for a while and he showed me the ropes.'

'So you lived in America?'

'Yeah. It wasn't easy getting a visa, but he helped me out.'

'So that's why you talk with American phrases sometimes?'

'Do I?' He frowned.

'Yep.' I couldn't think of any off the top of my head right now, but next time he said something, I'd make a note to point it out. 'Go on.'

'Yeah, so when I showed him what I could do, he started giving me some opportunities with some of his smaller clients. I was lucky. One of them was Nina Rose.'

'The actress?'

'Yup.'

'She was one of his *smaller* clients? But she's huge!'

'At the time she wasn't. I started working with her just before *She-Warrior* came out. And then she blew up. After that, everyone wanted to know who got her in shape for that film and then once she told them I helped, things took off for me.'

Crikey. I knew from Cassie and Lily that Nate worked with rich and famous people, but I didn't know about Nina bloody Rose. That woman was a goddess.

'So did you two, *y'know*…?'

'No, I don't know…' His mouth twitched. 'Wanna elaborate?'

He knew exactly what I was asking him. Me and my bloody mouth. I didn't even know why I asked.

Liar, my brain shouted.

Okay. I'd asked because if Nate hooked up with someone like Nina Rose, it would confirm that he wouldn't enjoy slumming it with a normie like me.

'Did you two… hook up?'

'Nope. I've learnt that you shouldn't shit where you eat. I've worked damn hard to build my career. No pussy is worth sacrificing that. No hooking up with clients or women who are too close to my circle outside of work.'

'Like friends of family members?'

'Right.'

My heart sank and my vagina wept.

'Avoids problems later on. It's less messy.'

Given what Nate had just said, now was probably a good time to address the elephant in the room. Even though he'd apologised this morning, there was still stuff that'd gone unsaid. And I'd rather get it out of the way instead of dreading him teasing me about it later.

'So… about last night, what you saw and *heard…*' My cheeks heated.

'Forget it.' He waved his hand. 'Like I said before, I shouldn't have come in your room. Period. Let's not talk about it. Today's a fresh start. I'm waving the white flag. I'm just here to help you. As a friend. Okay?'

'Okay.'

Friend. Right. It was more than we were a couple of days ago, I supposed.

I couldn't lie. Knowing that romance with Nate was off the cards was gutting. We'd come so close to things happening. Probably better in the long term, though.

My body disagreed, but what could I do? I wasn't going to throw myself at him and get rejected. *Again.*

Ever since I'd first met Nate at a family gathering Cassie had invited me to, I'd fancied him. But he was always with a woman. I'd heard Nate was a man whore, but I couldn't keep my eyes off him. So when he was flying solo at Cassie's thirtieth birthday party, I thought maybe I'd be in with a chance.

I'd taken a deep breath, gone over to where he was pouring himself a drink and said hi. Nate had grunted a hello.

'So I see you're alone,' I'd said, playing with my hair. 'If you need some *company* tonight, I'd be happy to help out.' I licked my lips, putting on my best seductress move.

Rather than grab my hand and lead me somewhere for a shag, which given his reputation was what I'd hoped, Nate glared at me, said, 'I'm not interested,' and walked off.

Although I knew he had a thing for models, Cassie and Lily also made out that Nate bonked every woman with a pulse who was up for it, so him rejecting me was a kick in the stomach. He'd fuck anyone, except me.

Naturally, I was embarrassed. But then when I'd heard him joking with his friends later saying only a fool would get involved with a woman with kids, that embarrassment had turned to hatred. And I'd avoided talking to him ever since. Well, up until we'd met again at the airport.

The sharp sound of a ringtone vibrated through the car. Nate took out his phone and started talking. From what I could overhear, it was a woman wanting to book him for a job somewhere abroad, because Nate had mentioned that his travel costs would need to be covered.

His life sounded so glam. Travel, parties and women.

He assured her that he was the right man to get her into shape.

I'd hate to imagine what he thought of my body. Thinking about that made me realise what I'd agreed to. When Nate had suggested we go shopping, I'd focused on finding a new outfit, instead of the fact that he'd be looking at every inch of my body and judging me.

Ice ran through my veins. I wasn't Nina Rose or the babes he was used to training. I was a middle-aged woman with stretch marks, cellulite, wobbly bits and a huge arse. Probably the kind of woman he used as an example of why people needed his services.

What had I got myself into?

The driver pulled up outside a boutique.

'Nice chatting to you. I'll be in touch.' Nate ended the call. 'Come on, Bangles.' He turned to face me. 'We're here.'

I followed him out of the car, my knees like jelly. We stepped into the boutique. This was *not* a bargain store. All the clothes were neatly arranged by colour and hung on expensive-looking hangers.

'Actually, if you want, you can just walk around the town whilst I find something,' I said nervously, surveying the racks.

'And tell me how I'm going to help you find something to wear if I'm not even in the shop?'

'Well, that's what I'm saying. You don't need to help me. I know how much men hate shopping, so I don't want to make you suffer.'

'Melody.' He placed his hands on my shoulders, sending shock waves around my body. I loved how he said my name. All deep and commanding. 'I'm here to help you. I'm not going anywhere. So why don't you see if there's stuff that you like and I'll look for things that I think would look good on you, then you can try them on. Cool?'

'Okay.' There was no escaping the scrutiny, so the quicker I found something, the quicker we could leave.

Nate was deep in concentration as he rifled through the rails. I'd never have believed this was his thing.

Ten minutes later he'd lined up a row of clothes on a rail that the shop assistant had wheeled to the large plush changing room, which even had a gold armchair. I headed over with my own pile, added them to the rail, then started looking at what Nate had selected.

I was surprised. I'd have thought a guy like him would pick out a load of low-cut tops and short skirts. My selection had loads of revealing stuff.

I tried on the first thing. A tight, sparkly purple dress with a generous amount of boob on show. Exactly the kind of thing men liked. I pulled the curtain open and walked towards Nate, who was seated on the cream sofa just outside the changing room.

'Nah.' He shook his head and my stomach plummeted. 'Too tight.'

'That's because I've eaten too much.'

'Somehow I doubt that. It's not your body. The size you picked is too small. And how are you going to eat, dance or breathe in that? It doesn't look comfortable. Is it comfortable?'

'Women don't dress for comfort when they go out. If we did, we'd wear our bloody pyjamas!'

'Try on one of my outfits next,' Nate said, ignoring my comment. 'You'll see the difference.'

I resisted the temptation to roll my eyes. I'd known my body for more than four decades. Apart from drooling over my boobs during our game of strip blackjack and obvs last night when he'd seen me with my hands between my legs, he'd barely even looked at my figure, so how did he think that he could choose something better?

As I did up the zip of the bold pink dress Nate had picked out, my jaw fell to my feet.

How did he know?

Firstly, I hadn't even given him my dress size, so how did this fit me? And not only did it fit, it hugged me in all the right places without restricting my breathing.

This dress clung to my arse, giving it a nice peachy shape, and there was only the slightest hint of boob. And it was bright and colourful. It was like it was made for me.

'You okay in there? You need help? Not from me,' Nate added quickly. 'From the shop assistant.'

Without saying a word, I stepped out of the changing room and stood in front of him.

Nate's eyes widened and his mouth turned up into a smile.

'Wow. That's… *fire*.' His gaze travelled from my head down to my toes and he licked his lips. It didn't seem like he was disgusted at the sight of my body. It was the opposite. There was something in his eyes. Was it… *desire*? 'You can try the other stuff, but I don't know what's going to look better than *that*. How does it feel?'

'Pretty amazing, actually.' I was still gobsmacked.

'And can you move?'

'What do you mean?'

'Like dance and bend over…?' He winced. 'Not like that—I mean, if you drop something, you need to know that if you pick it up, the dress won't rip. Trust me. I've seen that happen.'

'Good point.'

I turned away from him so he wouldn't get an eyeful of boob and bent down to touch my toes.

'Yep. I can bend down. And hold on…' I swung my hips and dropped down low like I was shaking it on the dance floor. 'All good on the dancing front too.'

When I turned around, Nate was in a trance.

'Er, *hello*?' I raised my voice. '*Anybody there?*'

'Yeah, s-sorry,' he stuttered. 'It looks… y-you look good.'

'Like what you see, do you?' I teased. Given his past rejection I wouldn't have normally asked, but this dress made me feel confident.

'I *do*.' His eyes darkened. 'That dress should come with a warning.'

'Yeah?' I tilted my head. 'Like what?'

'Like: this dress is dangerous… it can cause…' He paused. 'Nothing. Don't worry about it.'

'Hmmm…' I raised my eyebrow. 'I like that. I love this dress and the idea of being *dangerous* for one night.'

I held his gaze. Nate's eyes were the colour of onyx and his lips were still parted. He might not have been interested all those years ago, but the way Nate looked at me in this dress, I had the feeling that might've changed.

'Excuse me,' I called to the sales assistant. 'This is perfect. I'll take it.'

31

———

NATE

As I watched Melody turn and walk into the changing room, I thought about calling the French emergency service.

Hot. Damn.

The sight of her in that dress was just… I had no words. The way the fabric clung to every inch of her. The way it accentuated her curves and the shape of her chest. And don't even get me started on how good her arse looked in it.

I wasn't lying when I said that dress was dangerous. It made me want her. And that was bad on my part. The woman should be able to wear whatever she damn well pleased without me fantasising about what I wanted to do to her. I needed to get a grip on my feelings and my dick, which hadn't stopped twitching since we'd arrived.

Seeing how fucking amazing she looked just confirmed exactly what I needed to do tonight and for the rest of my time here in France: stay the hell away from her. It was the only way.

For some reason when I was around Melody, I wanted her, and I had no business doing that. Like I'd said in the car and a million times since I'd seen her at the airport, it was too messy. There were billions of women in the world and at least a dozen single ones at this wedding. If I needed to bang so badly, I should just choose someone else.

The next half an hour was torture. Watching Melody in all the different outfits. Seconds after saying she wanted the pink dress, Melody decided she should try on everything else first, just to be sure.

It wasn't torture because I hated shopping with her. It was torture because every time she tried something on, I couldn't stop thinking about how badly I wanted to peel those clothes right back off her.

If I had my way, I'd go in that changing room, pin her against the wall, push that dress up around her waist and fuck her.

Jesus. I was like an animal.

'Okay, you win,' she shouted from the changing room. 'As much as it hurts me to say it, you really *do* know how to choose clothes. You're like that fashion stylist Gok Wan, or what were those other two women called who used to do those TV makeovers in the noughties?'

'Trinny and Susannah,' I shouted back.

Yeah. I used to watch that. Like I said, I grew up with four women in the house. Dad and I were outnumbered when it came to deciding what to watch as a family.

'I'm not trying on anything else from my selection. I'm just going with yours now. Don't worry. I only have two more dresses to try on, so I'll put you out of your misery soon.'

There's only one thing that'd put me out of my misery, sweetheart, and that would be burying my cock inside you.

Fuck. This was out of hand.

As Melody skipped out of the dressing room, I dragged my thoughts out of the gutter and smiled. She beamed with confidence. The woman who'd walked out in the first outfit was unsure of herself and looked awkward. But less than an hour later, she'd totally transformed. I was glad Melody was starting to realise that she didn't have to squeeze into outfits two sizes too small and have every-thing on show to look good. That made me happy.

What *didn't* make me happy, though, was the thoughts that had been racing around my head. I needed to put a stop to them. It was wrong for me to think of her like that. She was a woman. Not an object there for my sexual desire.

'That one is hot too.' I nodded, fighting a losing battle to keep my thoughts PG rated.

'You're right. *Ugh.*' She winced. 'That's two compli-ments I've given you today. You better not let your head get big after this.'

The head on my shoulders was the same size, but the head in my boxers was growing by the second.

Now Melody was wearing a baby-blue dress which was more conservative than the others. More structured and less cleavage, but still so fucking sexy.

'I'm gonna sort out the bill.' I needed to remove myself from the delicious sight in front of me. 'I'll put these back.' I grabbed the two random tops resting on my lap, placed them in front of me, then stood up.

When Melody was getting changed, I knew I'd need

something to hide my hard-on, so had taken them from a nearby rack.

'Oh yeah.' Her face fell and she returned to the dressing room. 'I'll just try on the pink one again to be sure, then I'll hand it to you so the lady can ring it up. I'll call you when it's safe!' She pulled the curtain shut. 'OMG! How much? Nate, I can't afford this.'

She must've looked at the price tag. I was glad she did that after she tried it on and not before.

'Don't worry. Nico's covering it,' I lied. Although I'd spoken to him to organise the car and bridesmaid's dress fitting and got advice from his assistant about where best to shop, there was no way I'd expect him to pay. I'd take care of the cost. It was worth it to see Melody smile and look so confident.

As much as she tried to put on a brave front and could be loud and mouthy at times, I could see that underneath, she was sensitive. Life had given her a lot of knocks, so it was only natural that it had affected her self-esteem. But she still soldiered on. Like I'd said that night at the hotel, the woman was badass.

'Really? Oh wow. That's generous of him. Too generous. I mean, I know the cost of this to him is probably the equivalent of me buying a can of Coke, but even so. Here you go.' She slid her arm out of the changing room curtain. A hanger with the dress hung from her fingers. I stepped forward and took it from her.

Our hands brushed against one another's and even though it was only for a couple of seconds, it was long enough to cause my body to jolt with excitement.

Jeez.

I walked quickly to the cash register and handed over my credit card.

A few minutes later, Melody came out of the changing room, still beaming. I handed over the bag and she literally exploded with excitement.

'Thank you for helping me!' She threw her arms around my neck.

Fuck.

Fuck. Fuck. Fuck.

A rush of blood shot straight to my dick and I sent an emergency message to my brain to think of everything and anything that was not sexy to calm it down. I tried to move the lower half of my body back so it didn't make contact with her.

Shit. This was hard.

Bad word choice.

My face was buried in her hair and it smelt so good. Like sherbet. And coconut. I didn't know what shampoo she used, but I fucking loved it. Too much.

'You're welcome.' I pulled away quickly. Her face fell, but it was a price I had to pay. It was bad enough that I'd been imagining her naked. I wasn't about to become the ultimate pervert and rub my hard dick against her. Those were the kind of men I told my sisters to stay away from. 'Come on, let's go.'

After thanking the shop assistant, we headed outside and into the car. Melody's phone rang.

'It's Bella,' she mouthed. Thank fuck. The longer they talked, the less time I'd get to interact with Melody and the calmer I'd be.

To kill time, I took out my phone. Mum had messaged

to say that there was a woman she'd like me to meet this evening.

Just as I was about to curse her for interfering, I had a brainwave. Maybe meeting this woman wasn't such a bad idea after all.

Taking Melody to choose those dresses today was a mistake. It'd made me like her more. And now because I'd helped her, she thought I was a nice guy. Things had been easier when she'd thought I was the King of Knobs.

Yeah. She wasn't interested in me when she thought I was an arsehole. So the best way to pour cold water over this attraction between us was to do something to show I was.

It was settled.

By the end of tonight, Melody would want nothing more to do with me.

32

____

MELODY

I couldn't stop staring at myself in the mirror and smiling. Champagne bubbles popped in my stomach and my insides were warm, fluffy and light. I felt good. And I *looked* good. The last time I'd said that about myself was… I couldn't remember. Maybe when the dinosaurs walked the earth.

But tonight I was happy with my reflection. Nate was right. This dress was *fire*.

The flutters in my stomach intensified as I pictured the look on his face when I'd stepped out of the changing room. This time I was certain. There really *was* desire in his eyes. Nate, the guy that every single woman in this castle was lusting after, had shown a hint of liking *me*.

He'd been so kind taking me shopping, not taking the piss after last night and arranging that emergency bridesmaid's dress fitting.

Thank God he had. When I'd tried it on again, I couldn't even get the zip past my arse. But thankfully the seamstress assured me that everything would be fine for tomorrow.

And it was so sweet of Nate to ask Nico to pay for the dress, which was way out of my budget. I must find Nico later and thank him.

I smoothed down the front of the dress and admired myself again. This was definitely the last time, though. Didn't want to get a big head.

The other amazing thing about this dress was that I didn't even need to wear those horrible control pants to suck me in. Somehow the magical fabric made my curves look *good*. And I could actually breathe. I didn't know how I could thank Nate for today. Well, I could think of a few ways he might like… I cackled.

On the way back to the castle, I spoke to Bella and then Rodney called to say they'd be staying an extra day, which was a relief considering I wasn't coming back on Sunday night as planned.

He said Andrea was fine and that the boyfriend wasn't there. I didn't believe him, but what could I do? Like Nate had said during that first night at the hotel, I just had to hope that I'd raised Andrea right and she was sensible.

So anyway, with all of those calls, Nate and I didn't get to do anything in the car. Apart from him giving me Nico's assistant's number for the bridesmaid's dress fitting, we'd barely even talked.

Once we'd arrived back, Nate had suggested I get out of the car first. I'd thanked him again and said I'd see him tonight. I really hoped something would happen.

After applying my lipstick and spritzing on some perfume, I put in the sparkly long gold earrings I'd made along with one of my gold necklaces and a handful of bangles.

When I'd made this jewellery last year, I hadn't known when or where I'd get a chance to wear it, but it was perfect for tonight.

I slid into a pair of strappy gold heels and was good to go.

There was already a big crowd in the dining hall we'd eaten in last night when I got downstairs. Everyone was dressed up to the nines. I was so glad I had something decent to wear.

Because it was a warm evening, they'd opened up the French doors and people were sipping from champagne flutes outside too.

Cassie waved from across the room and I headed over.

'Look at you!' I pulled her into a hug. 'You look gorgeous!' She was wearing a floaty cream dress and her hair and make-up had been done to perfection.

'So do you! I love that dress! You look *hot*, my friend! You're definitely going to pull tonight!'

'Thanks! Here's hoping.' I smiled, doing a quick scan of the room to see if I could spot Nate. No sign of him yet. 'Feeling better now?'

'Much!' She nodded. 'Well, apart from the nerves about tomorrow, worrying if the weather will hold out. I just want everything to go smoothly.'

'It will. And whatever happens, you're going to have the most magical day. You're marrying the love of your life and you'll be surrounded by your nearest and dearest, so that's what matters.'

'Yeah, you're right. What did you get up to today, then?' Cassie asked, taking a sip of what looked like orange juice. *Smart move*. The last thing she needed was a hangover on her wedding day.

'Oh, I-I—nothing much…' I was going to mention that I'd had an emergency bridesmaid's dress fitting when I'd got back from shopping, but didn't want to worry her.

'Anyway, don't waste your gorgeousness speaking to me. Go and mingle. I can already see a few guys checking you out.'

'Yeah?'

'Yep. Especially him at the bar. He's one of Nico's people. I can't remember his name, but he can't take his eyes off you.' I span around, curious to see who it was, and my body deflated as I saw Toby smile and raise his glass at me. 'Well, go on, then! Go talk to him!'

'Right. Yeah. See you later.'

Cassie was so excited at the idea of playing Cupid that I didn't want to disappoint her.

Just as I started walking towards Toby, the hairs on my arms stood up and goosebumps spread across my skin— just like they had yesterday. I knew exactly why. A quick glance at the door confirmed it. Nate had just entered the room. Even from several metres away, he still affected me.

Christ almighty.

As I took him in, I struggled to keep my jaw closed.

Give me strength. And a bucket of ice water. The man looked bloody incredible. Even if you put two dozen chocolate fudge cakes in front of me I wouldn't salivate half as much as I was now.

He was wearing a cream suit. The top buttons of his silver shirt were undone, showing just a hint of his glorious chest. Just the sight of him sent my body into a tizz. The floodgates opened in my knickers, and my lips, both the ones on my face and between my legs parted with anticipation.

Looking that good should be a crime punishable by me handcuffing him to the bed and not letting him leave until he'd given me multiple orgasms.

Actually, I'd rather he handcuffed *me* to the bed. That way his hands would be free to roam across my whole body. I hoped his mouth would join in too. And don't even get me started on the things I would like to do with his knob. Given half the chance, I'd ride that like I was a jockey competing in the Grand National.

Our eyes locked for a few seconds before his gaze travelled from my feet to my legs, then up to my stomach and chest, where it lingered, before finally reaching my face.

Nate nodded with approval and licked his lips.

Seeing that tongue and imagining it between my legs made the dam burst in my knickers.

He wanted me. And it was time I went to get him.

I pivoted, ready to head straight over to him.

'There you are!' Toby stood in front of me.

Noooo!

I wanted to ask him to move because he was blocking my view of the hottest guy in the room, but then I remembered my manners.

'Toby! Hi! Fancy seeing you here!' I joked.

'I was hoping I would see you again,' he said enthusiastically.

'Well, here I am!' I quickly swiped a glass of champagne from the waiter who'd just appeared with a tray beside us. I needed alcohol to get through this conversation.

As Toby spoke about the fact that Provence was the

main producer of rosé wine in France and what he recommended I try, my mind drifted.

It was crazy. I had a handsome, intelligent, nice and financially stable guy standing right here who was interested in me. And who knows? Maybe he'd want more than a quick shag. Yeah, he lived in another country, but something told me Toby would be the type who'd find solutions to little hurdles like a few hundred miles of distance.

For years, that was what I'd wanted. A decent man. That was exactly the kind of bloke I'd hoped to meet here. But yet, who was I thinking about right now? The bloody player, the brother of my best friend, who was emotionally unavailable and would only want a quick fuck before he moved on to the next woman. The one who'd told me earlier we could only be 'friends'.

Why did I always want the bad boy? The kind of guy who'd have me reaching for a tub of ice cream and a bottle of vodka days after we hooked up because he either ghosted me or said he liked me but *didn't want anything serious*.

'Melody? Melody?'

'Oh, sorry!' I snapped out of my thoughts. I had no idea what Toby had just said. 'Apologies. I was miles away. I just remembered I didn't turn off my straightening irons in my bedroom,' I lied. I wasn't about to tell him I was busy fantasising about another man licking my pussy. 'Last thing I want to do is burn down the castle! Actually, I should really go and check. Sorry.'

'O-okay,' said Toby.

God, I felt awful. But the more I spoke to him, the more I knew I wasn't interested. I had no idea whether I should be upfront and tell him that. Normally I was the one that guys were rejecting.

Shit. I forgot to ask for his number so I could call when I got back to London about my jewellery. Then again, his offer to help seemed conditional on me inviting him to my room. Best not to give him the wrong idea.

As I approached the door, Nate walked towards me.

'*Bangles*.' His gaze skimmed my body again.

'*Nate*. So? What do you think of the dress?' I wanted him to compliment me.

'Like I said earlier. It's *fire*. You look good.'

Heat flooded every inch of me.

'Thanks. I like the idea of wearing a dress that's fire. It's like the word *flame*: hot, glowing and filled with passion. If I ever did my jewellery again, that's what I'd call my brand: *Flame*.'

'You should. It suits you…'

I blushed. Hearing that literally made me want to burst into flames.

'So…' It was time to put the confidence this dress had given me to good use and see if he'd reconsider the whole platonic thing. 'Do you want to, like, *hang out* later?'

Nate's eyes widened and I couldn't tell whether it was good or bad shock.

'I-I have to do something for my mum, so I can't.'

'Oh.' My stomach plummeted. Well, I couldn't argue about him doing something for his mum. It wasn't like he didn't *want* to be with me, more that he couldn't. His mum had to come first. 'No worries!' I said, like it didn't bother me. 'Anyway, I've got to go back to my room.'

'Right.' He nodded, his eyes like charcoal. Despite what he'd said about only being friends, there was definitely electricity between us. I could *feel* it. He went to say something, but then Carlos came over and, after greeting me, pulled Nate in for a hug.

'I'll leave you guys to catch up!' I made my exit.

After going to my room, I returned to the hall and chatted to Lily whilst I ate. It was so nice to eat proper food again without worrying about bursting out of my dress.

'So did you find a date for tomorrow?' Lily asked, plucking two glasses of champagne from the waiter and handing one to me. 'Cassie said you had a lot of men checking you out earlier.'

'Well, I'd hardly say *a lot*. But yeah, there might be *someone* I have in mind...' The words slipped out. I didn't know if Nate would be game, but seeing as we were both single and didn't hate each other anymore, we could just say we were sitting together. If we made it sound casual, maybe no one would bat an eyelid.

'Oooh! That's so exciting! You deserve to find someone amazing! I never knew I could be so happy. Carlos is just... *everything*. And Mum and Dad love him too. She's relieved that almost all of her kids are settled— well, apart from Nate, but we all know he's going to be an eternal bachelor. Hasn't stopped Mum from playing matchmaker, though. Speak of the devil.' She nodded across the room, where I saw her mum, Janet.

'Oh! I thought your mum was working on something with Nate this evening?' They must've finished early, which was good news. Maybe he'd have time for us to hang out after all...

'What? No! Nate's on a hot date with some leggy model right now. And this one sounds like a keeper. She graduated with a first-class degree from Cambridge, runs her own business *and* models. Brains *and* beauty! Knowing him, he won't have time to help Mum or anyone with anything tonight. You know my slut of a brother. He'll be otherwise engaged!' She laughed.

I felt like someone had reached inside my body and tugged violently on every organ.

Nate was on a date?

And no ordinary one either. She sounded like she was the total package. Too often I'd made the mistake of labelling models as bimbos, which was wrong. Of course there were loads that were intelligent. Just like in every other profession. And this woman sounded like the perfect example.

But Nate told me he was helping his mum.

He'd lied.

Maybe this was karma. After all, I'd also given Toby the brush-off earlier.

'Yeah,' I laughed weakly before downing the entire glass of champagne. 'I think I left my straightening irons on,' I said to Lily. I'd lost count of how many times I'd used that excuse tonight. 'I'd better check.'

'Oh God! Yeah! I'll see you later.'

After leaving the room, I stumbled down the long corridor. How many times was I going to let Nate reject me before I finally got the message that he didn't want me?

33

MELODY

Such a fool.

So stupid of me to think that Nate wanted us to get together. Especially when he'd made it clear that he wasn't interested in taking things further.

My bottom lip quivered and I quickly told myself to woman up.

It was only after I'd walked for another minute that I realised I'd wandered down the wrong corridor. I hadn't been down this part of the castle before.

I looked at the room on the left. It was empty. Then I heard voices coming from the small room on the right. As I looked inside, I wanted to throw up.

There standing next to a candlelit table for two was Nate.

So it *was* true. He really was on a date.

The woman was sitting down and Nate had his hand on her shoulder. I froze.

Nate looked up and saw me and his face fell.

I turned and started running down the hallway.

A few seconds later, I heard heavy footsteps in the distance behind me.

'Melody!' Nate called out.

'Leave me alone!' I shouted back. I quickly turned a corner which led to a crossroads in the hallway. I could go left or right and Nate was far enough behind me that he wouldn't know which one I'd taken.

After deciding to go right, I ducked into the nearest room. I couldn't run anymore in these heels. But he wouldn't know that. I had no idea why he'd followed me, but hopefully he'd assume that I'd gone to my room. If I hid here, he'd never find me.

I scanned the surroundings. This was the games room. It had a pool table in the middle. Apart from the large light shining above it, the rest of the room was dimly lit.

There was a bar in the corner with three stools in front of it and an area with a chessboard. It reminded me of those private members' lounges.

The sound of Nate calling my name vibrated in my ears. Shit. He was close. I quickly hobbled over to the pool table and hid behind it.

Seconds later, I heard footsteps in the room.

'Melody, come on. I know you're in here.' How the hell did he know that? He was just guessing. I was staying right here. 'I can smell your perfume. Come on. Come out. Look. What you saw—it's not what you think.'

Not what I think?

Fuck it. If he didn't want to be with me, I'd have to accept that. But I was tired of men treating me like an idiot.

I wasn't going to sit here hiding. I was going to tell him *exactly* what I thought of him.

'No?' I stood up with my hands on my hips. 'So you accidentally stumbled into a room with a candlelit dinner table and a beautiful woman? You know what? It doesn't matter. You don't have to explain. It's none of my business. And I'm used to you rejecting me. You've done it enough times.'

'What?' Nate frowned, strode over and stood in front of me. I backed away, my body hitting the pool table. 'When did I reject you?'

'Ha!' I laughed. 'Where should I start? When we matched on Tinder last year and I messaged and you didn't reply? At Cassie's thirtieth birthday party when you told me you weren't interested? Or later that night when I heard you telling your friends that only idiots dated a woman with a kid? Or tonight when you lied about doing something for your mum instead of just saying you didn't want to be with me.'

Just hearing myself say all of this out loud made me feel stupid for even thinking something could happen. And ashamed for ever wanting it to.

Nate dragged his hand over his face and squeezed his eyes shut. I could tell he felt bad. And so he bloody should.

'Look, I'm sorry. I haven't been on Tinder for ages, so I didn't even know that we'd matched. And Cassie's party, fuck, I'd forgotten about that. I… I'd had too much to drink, but that's no excuse. I'm sorry. I didn't mean to upset you. I remember the stuff you overheard and that definitely wasn't about you. Someone close had just gone out with a woman with a kid and was really cut up when it ended, which was stupid because there were so many red flags. He should've seen the signs. So that's why I said what I said. It wasn't personal.'

Yeah, I didn't specifically hear him mention my name, but seeing as I was a woman with a child, of course I took it personally.

And when I'd flirted with him at the party, although he hadn't said 'fuck off' or something mean, I liked him, so I wanted it to be mutual. The rejection, no matter how it was delivered, was always going to hurt.

'And tonight, yeah. My mum *did* say she needed my help with something. She texted in the car on the way back from that boutique. I knew she was trying to set me up with someone again, but even though I didn't want to, I went anyway.'

'Since when do you do things you don't want to?'

Such a lame excuse.

Anyone who'd spent two minutes with Nate knew he was his own man.

'Since I needed to find a distraction. Since I'm trying to do the right thing and stop myself from doing something I shouldn't.'

'What do you mean?'

'*Seriously?*' He stepped forward. 'Do you really need me to spell it out?'

'Yeah.' I swallowed hard.

'Can't you see that I want *you*?'

'No, you don't!' I scoffed.

'That's bullshit and you know it. Look at *this*.' He pointed between his legs. 'Does *this* look like I'm not interested? I've had a permanent boner ever since I saw you at the fucking airport.'

'What?' My eyes were like saucers. At first I thought I

must be dreaming, but as I looked down and saw his raging hard-on straining against his trousers, I realised I wasn't.

Holy shit.

Nate was hard. For *me*.

'That wasn't morning wood at the hotel. Well, yeah, partly, but I wanted to fuck you. I've been wanting to fuck you since I saw you. And I'm running out of willpower here.'

Nate took another step forward. Now he was so close I could feel his sweet breath on my skin and smell his hypnotic scent. He reached up and stroked my cheek.

'I hoped that by going on that date I could push you out of my mind or make you hate me. But all I could think about when I was sitting there was how much I wanted to push up that damn dress and bend you over. When you walked past, I was leaving. Telling her that she was nice, but I couldn't go through with the date. I was coming to find *you*. To ask if you wanted me to fuck you.'

My jaw dropped.

I wanted Nate to do everything he'd just said and so much more.

'You really want to?'

'Melody, you have no idea all the things I want to do to you.' Nate closed the gap, running his hand up my thigh. I wanted to pull him down on top of me. 'But I know I shouldn't.'

'Why?'

'I'm not a hearts and flowers kinda guy. This would just be sex. Pure and simple. Carnal need. No cuddles. No holding hands. Just deep, dirty fucking. You down for that?'

Given the choice, obviously I wanted a relationship, but I knew that was never going to happen. Men only wanted me for fun, so this would be no different than every other guy I'd slept with.

And I wanted this. As illogical as it was, despite what had happened in the past, I'd wanted Nate for so long, there was no way I was turning him down.

I felt Nate's hardness pressing against me and it was like it had hypnotic powers. I bit my lip. Right now I wanted to feel his cock inside of me so badly I'd agree to anything.

'Yes,' I said quietly.

'What was that?' He lifted my chin. 'I can't hear you. Tell me what you want.'

'To fuck.'

'To fuck? *Who* do you want to fuck you?'

'You.' I raised my voice a little.

'Melody.' His hand traced my inner thigh. 'We're about to cross a very dangerous line. So if I'm going to put my long, thick cock inside you, I need to know with absolute certainty that you want it. One hundred per cent. If you have even one per cent doubt, I'll leave, right now. So I'll ask you one last time: tell me what you want,' he growled.

'I want you to *fuck* me, Nate!' I panted.

'That's better.'

Nate's hot mouth crushed onto mine and my whole body felt like it'd been dropped in a volcano.

We kissed like two hungry wolves. Lips crashing, tongues thrashing, desire ripping through us like wildfire.

It was like all the hatred we'd bottled up had suddenly shattered and we needed to get all those years of sexual frustration out of our systems as quickly as possible.

The intensity of his kiss was off the scale. Every atom in my body vibrated. I groaned loudly. The fact that I hadn't had a good snog in a while was one thing, but I'd never been kissed like this before. Like, *ever.*

Nate's hands tugged at my dress. He yanked it up and grabbed my arse. I pulled him in closer, desperate to feel more of his hardness pressed against me. Then in one swift move, Nate lifted me onto the edge of the pool table.

'Open your legs,' he commanded and I instantly missed the feeling of his lips on mine.

'We—we're going to do it here? On the pool table?'

'The bedroom's too far. I can't wait. Everyone's in the dining room. No one will see. But if you don't want it…'

'I told you what I want.' I reached between his legs and stroked his hard length. 'Let's do it here, I don't care. Just bloody hurry up and put your dick in me.'

I spread my legs as instructed and leant back.

'No,' Nate growled. 'I'm not one of those one-minute men you're used to. I like to take my time. The only thing that's gonna be fast is how quickly I make you come.'

He hiked my dress further up around my waist, then started trailing his warm fingers up my inner thighs.

'But I want you *now*,' I pleaded. Normally I enjoyed foreplay, but I'd already waited years.

'Are you wet enough for me yet, Bangles? You really think you're ready for my big cock?'

'Yes!' I struggled to catch my breath. He was killing me.

'Let's see, shall we?' Nate continued trailing his hand up my inner thighs, then dipped his fingers beneath my damp knickers, pulled them to one side, then slid his fingers between my folds. I gasped. His touch was electric. 'Good. You're so fucking wet.'

'I know,' I panted. 'For God's sake, fuck me!'

'Not yet. You're not getting my dick until you come first.'

'Looks like I-I won't be getting it, then,' I said breathlessly. It was hard to speak with his hand in my knickers, but I persevered. 'I told you. Men never know how to make me come.'

'*Other* men might not know, sweetheart, but I do. Trust me. First I'll make you come with my hands. Then when I fuck you, you'll scream my name and come so hard you'll see stars. And then you'll beg me to do it all over again.'

'You're so...' I steadied my breath, trying to control the flutters between my legs. 'You really think a lot of yourself, don't you?'

'It's the truth. You'll see.'

Before I even got a chance to respond, Nate rubbed his fingers over my clit and I cried out.

Holy shit.

As he moved them back and forth, I already felt my body reacting.

If what he'd just done was anything to go by, maybe he was right.

My heart rate shot through the roof and blood pulsed through my veins. I bucked onto his hand and threw my head back.

'Open your legs wider,' Nate growled.

I spread myself on the pool table, excited to feel what he'd do next.

Nate rubbed his thumb over my clit, then plunged two fingers inside me.

'Oh God!' I gasped. It was like all the air had been sucked from my lungs. I couldn't breathe.

'You like that?' His eyes were pinned on mine.

'Y…' I opened my mouth, but no words came out.

As Nate continued working his thumb over my sensitive spot, stroking me in long, slow, delicious circles and pumping his fingers in and out of me, my body spasmed and my eyes rolled back.

Every stroke, every movement sent a pulse of electricity through me.

'I'll take that as a yes.' He smirked.

There was no way I could speak. Breathing was hard enough.

As he picked up the pace, pleasure ripped through me. Fuck. The impossible was happening.

The sensation of Nate fucking me with his fingers and stimulating my clit sent me hurtling towards the edge at lightning speed.

Not even my vibrator got me off this quickly. Even on the highest setting. But Nate wasn't a piece of hard plastic. This man's fingers had magical powers.

I felt the wave building. My body bucked against his hand. His touch made me lose complete control and I bloody loved it.

'That's right,' Nate said, sliding in another finger and rubbing my clit harder. 'Come for me, Bangles. Show me you're ready for my cock.'

'Fuuuuckkk!' I cried out, my orgasm hitting me like a high-speed train crashing into a wall at five hundred miles an hour.

Every part of me sparked and shuddered. From the tips of my toes all the way up to my head, which was light and fuzzy. My head flopped to the side of the pool table.

'Wow,' I said. I didn't care if Nate was about to gloat. He deserved all the accolades. If he could make me come like that with just his hand, what the hell was he able to do with his dick?

'Do you need time to recover, or are you ready for me to fuck you and make you come again?'

The truth was, I needed a minute. Well, several. I was still basking in the glow of that amazing orgasm. But now I'd had a taste of him, I was already craving more. I couldn't wait to feel his dick inside me.

'I'm ready.'

'Get up and turn around,' he commanded. 'I want to fuck you from behind.'

'What?' My eyebrows shot up to my forehead. 'I'm not sure I'm quite ready for anal…'

'No. I'm going to fuck your wet pussy from behind. I want to see that magnificent arse of yours.'

'*Magnificent?*' I frowned.

'Yeah. Your backside is fucking amazing. I've been fantasising about it ever since I saw you at the airport in those jeans. Damn, Melody. Are you going to let me do you or not? I'll beg if you want me to.'

My body was already trying to recover from Nate's touch. And now he'd called my arse *amazing*, every inch of my skin buzzed. I didn't think it was possible, but hearing that he loved it made me want him even more.

'Do it.' I climbed down from the pool table, turned my back to Nate, bent over, resting my chest on the table, then spread my legs wide. 'Fuck me, Nate. But do it good.'

'Sweetheart, it's the only way I know how.'

I heard Nate unzip his trousers, then the sound of a condom wrapper ripping.

This was crazy. The room door was wide open. Nate was about to fuck me on a pool table, in full view. Anyone walking by could see us. Our friends, his family or the staff. But I didn't care. All I could think about was that I was about to get the ride of my life on Nate's cock. And I couldn't bloody wait.

Before I had a chance to register any other thoughts, Nate's hand grabbed my knickers, then ripped them off in one move, leaving my arse bare.

'Fucking beautiful. You won't be needing any underwear this weekend.' His hand reached between my legs again before sliding his fingers between my folds and rubbing my clit. It was still sensitive from my orgasm, so I jerked against the table. 'You ready, Bangles? Last chance to back out before I bury myself inside you.'

'Just stop talking and do it.'

As Nate plunged into me, I cried out so loud my eardrums almost burst.

Holy shit.

There was no way that was a dick inside me. It felt like a baseball bat. *God help me.*

'Relax,' Nate whispered as he stroked between my legs. My knees buckled at the feel of his touch and once I got out of my own head and stopped thinking about how huge he was, I started to enjoy the sensations.

'You good?' he asked.

'*More* than good,' I said, my blood simmering.

'Nice. Now I'm going to fuck you properly.'

'Wh…' I didn't even get a chance to ask what he

meant by *properly*. Nate slammed into me and holy shit. If I thought what I'd felt before was good, then this was off the scale.

As Nate pounded like he was competing in the sex Olympics, the pool balls shook from the vibrations. It was a good thing the table was fixed to the floor. Otherwise it'd be halfway across the room by now.

Whoever said men couldn't multitask was wrong. Whilst he continued pumping in and out, Nate's hand did some magical stuff to my clit. He rubbed and squeezed, sending the sweetest sensations racing through every inch of me.

'Harder,' I panted. 'Fuck me harder.'

'You asked for it.' Nate ploughed into me and I cried out. 'You okay?'

I knew I'd bitten off more than I could chew, but this was what sex dreams were made of. If the world ended today, knowing that Nate had fucked me into oblivion on the pool table in a castle was my last act on earth meant I'd die happy.

'Yes. More. Please.' I could barely speak.

'Good. I like that you can take my cock.'

Nate gripped my arse, then adjusted his position. The way he angled his body hit me in exactly the right place. No other guy had come close to finding my G-spot, but sex god Nate had just scored the bullseye without even trying.

'Fuck, I-I—' I rocked against the table, dragging my nails down the green fabric. 'I can't hold on.'

'Not yet,' he growled, gripping my hips and driving into me, harder, faster.

Holding on for another minute might've been possible if he hadn't started squeezing my clit whilst he kept thrusting that delicious dick in and out of me like his life depended on it. But he continued, relentlessly making me feel sensations and pleasure that I'd never experienced before.

My legs shook and the rest of my body followed.

'I-I'm… oh, Nate. Nate… Nate! Ohhhhh!'

As the wave ripped through me, I bit down onto my hand. Nate might think no one came down this end of the castle, but he'd made me scream so loud they could hear me in the dining room and probably back in London.

'That's right.' Nate pumped harder into me, once, twice, three times before a loud grunt flew from his mouth. He gripped my arse tighter and jerked once more before collapsing onto my back.

'Fuck,' he muttered into my chest. I could feel his heart thundering against me.

'Yeah,' I added. *That certainly blew away the coochie cobwebs.*

I wasn't going to say it out loud, but that was even better than I'd imagined. That was so bloody amazing I wanted to run to the top of the castle with a megaphone and tell the world that not only had I ended my dry spell, I'd had two of the most amazing orgasms in my life, without watching bloody porn or using my vibrator. And those orgasms had been given to me by the hottest man I'd ever laid eyes on.

Nate slid off me, then passed me a couple of tissues. I was glad he was prepared.

From the corner of my eye I saw him roll off the condom and put it into a tissue before throwing it in the bin. Then he moved back towards the pool table.

'So…' I heard him zip himself up, which was a shame

as I hadn't got to see his dick yet. I'd only felt it. 'Shall I say "I told you so" now, or later?'

God, he was so cocky, but he was right. He knew what he was doing. And I'd be leaving this room more than satisfied. If I was rating his performance, he'd be getting six out of five stars. Not technically possible, I know, but he deserved it. I'd keep that praise to myself, though, because his head was already big enough.

'Later?' I used the last ounce of energy to turn around slowly and face him. Just like I'd thought, sadly he'd already put his dick away like he hadn't just fucked me senseless on the pool table.

Feeling self-conscious, I pulled down my dress and picked up the lace on the floor which used to be a decent pair of knickers but was now ripped to shreds. 'What do you mean?'

'You think we're done here, Bangles?' Nate looked at me like I'd just suggested I was going to fly to the moon. 'I didn't cross the line to just have a fuck on the pool table, sweetheart. As much as you might pretend to hate me, I know you enjoyed this little taster session just as much as I did.'

'I think that's obvious.' I rolled my eyes. He knew how hard he'd made me come. Denying it would be pointless.

'And I'm just getting started. If you're up for it, I'm going to fuck you so good this weekend, you won't be able to walk straight by the time you leave on Monday. But if you want to stop now, no pressure. It's your choice.'

'No.' I stepped forward and rubbed my hand between his legs. He was already hard again and I loved it. 'I definitely want more of this.'

'Good. Meet upstairs in half an hour for round two.'

'Your room or mine?' I didn't think it was possible for me to get any wetter than I already was, but hearing Nate wanted to go again caused another tsunami to erupt between my legs.

'I don't care. I'll find you. And, Melody…' Nate started walking towards the door. 'Get a coffee or an energy drink. We won't be getting much sleep tonight, so you're gonna need it.'

34

———

NATE

H ot. Damn.

That was even better than I'd thought.

I'd known fucking Melody would be good, but *jeez*. I wasn't expecting *that*. And what I'd said to her was true. I was only getting started. I hadn't even done anything to her yet. Not really. I'd fucked her with my hands and my dick, but there was still so much I wanted to do.

I wanted to taste her. I wanted to bury my head between her thighs. I wanted to suck on those tits. I wanted to have her on every surface of her room and mine. Have her in and outside of this damn chateau.

I felt like an animal who'd been starved for years and she'd just handed me a pass to an all-you-can-eat buffet. And I intended to devour every crumb she wanted to offer me.

Lately, I'd been bored in the bedroom. But tonight Melody had set my whole body alight. I didn't know what it was about her, whether it was that arse, her smart mouth or the fact that she challenged me, but it really got me off. And I was itching for round two.

But first, I had to take care of my responsibilities. After going to the nearest bathroom to wash my hands and check I didn't have any obvious signs of fucking on me, I headed back to the dining room.

Nico had his arm around Cassie and was leading her to the door just as I walked in.

'You okay, sis?' I frowned.

'Yeah, just…'

'She is a little tired,' Nico jumped in. 'I am going to take her up to rest.'

'You need anything?' I rested my arm on her shoulder.

'No, just sleep. Thanks, bro.'

'I will message you in the morning, Nate. About when we will meet.' Nico had mentioned earlier that the guys could have breakfast in one of the suites and get ready. He'd invited some of the staff from his salon to the wedding, and there'd be a few barbers there to groom us if we needed it.

Even though I'd had a trim a couple of days ago, I liked to look sharp, so I planned to take him up on his offer.

'Cool, thanks, man. Cass, I don't know if you and Nico are doing the whole not sleeping in the same room the night before the wedding stuff, so if he's not there and you need anything, just shout, yeah?'

'Will do.' She nodded. She did look tired. Must be all the stress from the last couple of days.

'Laters.'

Now that I'd checked on Cassie, it was time to finish taking care of business with Melody.

I headed upstairs, excited about what was waiting for me. We hadn't decided on whose room we'd meet in, but I guessed Melody would feel more comfortable in her own.

I could've played it safe and entered via the interconnecting door, but after our screwing on the pool table, I wanted to continue the thrills. After looking left, then right down the corridor, I knocked on her door.

'Room service,' I called out.

After a few seconds, I heard footsteps, then silence, before Melody cracked the door, so I could just see her head.

'Just checking it's you because I didn't order room service.'

'No?' I raised my eyebrow. 'Yesterday at breakfast you said you wanted a *long, thick sausage*, so I came to deliver it. *Personally.*'

'Well, in that case, you'd better come in.' She licked her lips and opened the door.

I swallowed hard.

Sweet Jesus.

She was wearing that red nightdress she'd had on at the hotel, and as my gaze travelled over every inch of her, I nearly lost my damn mind.

I stepped inside the room, my eyes still transfixed on her body, kicked the door shut, strode towards Melody in silence, then pushed her up against the wall.

After pressing my body against her, I grabbed both hands and pinned them above her head. She moaned and her eyes widened. I knew she couldn't wait to know what I was going to do next.

'Spread your legs,' I growled.

Melody did what I'd asked and I trailed my free hand

along her inner thigh, slowly. When I reached between her legs, I smiled.

'No knickers. *Good*. I like that you're prepared. Let's see just how ready for me you really are.' I slid my fingers between her folds and started rubbing her clit, before thrusting two fingers inside her. She whimpered.

My cock swelled as desire ripped through me. There was so much I wanted to do to this woman that I didn't even know where to start.

As I continued fucking her with my hand, she bit on her lip and her chest heaved. Her tits were practically spilling out of the top of her nightdress and they were taunting me, begging to be sucked.

I leant my head forward and, using my mouth, I tugged at the front of her flimsy nightdress.

After one sharp pull, one breast popped out. With my teeth I slid the strap of the other side down, causing the fabric to fall just beneath them.

Fuck.

She had the most incredible tits I'd ever seen in my life.

I took her nipple in my mouth and sucked on it. Hard.

'Oh, fuck, Nate. I can't take it. I'm going to come.'

'Not yet.' I pulled back. 'I want to feel you come on my cock.'

I reluctantly slid my fingers out of her and released her hands from above her head. After reaching in my pocket, I pulled out my wallet, removed a condom, then placed it on the table beside us.

Melody's eyes dropped between my legs as I tugged at my belt, unzipped my trousers, then dragged them down with my boxers before stepping out of them and kicking everything out of the way.

'See something you like?' I teased, rubbing my hand over my solid cock.

'Yeah,' she panted. 'Shall we go to the bed?'

'We'll get there—eventually, but first I'm going to fuck you against the wall. And after that, over the edge of that sofa. I want to have you on every surface and every part of this room.'

I swiped the condom off the table, ripped it open, rolled it down my length and after flicking my tongue over Melody's nipples, I dragged the nightdress down from underneath her breasts to the ground. She stepped out of it quickly and parted her legs.

After pressing my naked body against hers, I grabbed my cock and rubbed it against her wet opening.

'Oh God,' she gasped.

'God can't save you now, sweetheart,' I growled. 'Are you ready for me to fuck your brains out?'

'Yes,' she pleaded. 'Now. Please.'

I lifted her up so she was at the right height, lined my cock against her pussy, then ploughed into her.

Melody cried out, wrapping her legs around my waist.

'You're so fucking tight,' I groaned, gripping her arse to hold her up.

Need ripped through me and I powered deeper. Fucking her like my life depended on it. With every thrust, Melody's head bashed against the wall. Just as I was about to ask if she was okay and whether she wanted me to go easier on her, her pussy clenched tighter around me.

'Yes, oh God, yes,' she said breathlessly, digging her nails into my back. The sharp pain was delicious.

The sensation of having her pinned against the wall and my dick buried deep inside her was addictive. I knew some guys shied away from this position, but for me this was the perfect workout. A good test for my stamina and strength.

As I picked up the pace, powering into her harder and faster, the table beside us started to shake. The glasses on the tray with the bottle of water rattled loudly and the TV on the wall looked dangerously close to falling off, but I didn't give a damn. Nothing was going to stop me from giving Melody the orgasm she fucking deserved.

Melody wrapped her arms around my neck, then used them to pull herself up and down on me and it felt un-fuck-ing-believable.

'Don't stop. I'm so close,' she panted. Her breaths were ragged. As she writhed against my body, I felt her clench around me.

That was the only sign I needed to bring her to the finish line. I drove my cock into her over and over again.

'Fuck! Nate. Oh fuuucckkk!' she screamed, jerking against me. Now I knew she was coming, I could release.

As Melody's body stilled, my orgasm ripped through me. A low, guttural growl shot from my lips as I exploded inside her. I thrust one last time before my head dropped to her chest.

Using the last ounce of energy, I carried her to the foot of the bed, lifted her off my dick, then laid her down before collapsing beside her.

Our chests heaved in harmony, our breaths short and shallow.

'So…' I turned to face her. 'Third orgasm of the night for you. Just saying.' I smirked.

'Yeah, yeah.' She rubbed the back of her hand over her forehead to wipe away the sweat. 'You're doing well so far. But I might need a few more before I change your nickname from King of Knobs to King of Orgasms.'

'How many more are we talking?'

'Well, it's a big title, so I can't just hand it out willy-nilly. I think at least another three. No. Let's make it four. You need to give me a grand total of seven to prove that you're worthy.'

'Seven? Easy.' I smirked. 'But I've already given you three more than any other guy, so that makes me the GOAT, right?'

'Goat?' Melody frowned.

'Greatest of all time.' I ran my fingers across her breasts, squeezing her nipples.

'I'll have to think about it,' she panted as my hands travelled down her stomach, then slipped between her legs. I shamelessly ran my fingers back and forth over her clit.

'Does *this* help your thought process?' I squeezed it gently.

'Fuck.' She bucked against me and I removed my fingers. 'What? Why did you stop?'

'Because I'm waiting for your answer.'

'Yes, you big knob. You're the GOAT. Now put your fucking fingers back where they belong and give me orgasm number four.'

35

MELODY

A loud ringing sound vibrated in my eardrums. I rubbed my eyes as I tried to work out where it was coming from.

I'd screamed so much when Nate fucked me that the sound could just be my ears recovering. Like when I went clubbing during my uni days and stood too close to the speakers.

My eyes fluttered open. As I stretched my legs, a sharp shooting pain swept through me.

Sweet memories of last night, or should I say earlier this morning, flashed into my brain and a grin spread across my face.

I had no idea what time Nate left this morning. The man was insatiable. True to his word, after we'd screwed against the wall, he'd bent me over the sofa, then did some position I'd never done before on the floor before we eventually got to the bed.

It was so bloody exciting. Most men wanted to stick to missionary and come as quickly as they could without giving a toss about whether I was satisfied, but not Nate. He made sure I came every single time.

And the thing was, it didn't even seem like it was hard for him to do. Whilst the men I'd been with before couldn't find the right spot if I gave them a map and directions, Nate just knew exactly where to touch, how much pressure to apply, when to speed up and when to slow down. He played my body like a fiddle and I enjoyed every second.

Bollocks.

Thinking of the word *second* reminded me I needed to check the time. I swiped my phone off the bedside table.

Shit. Three missed calls. I should've been in Cassie's room fifteen minutes ago. I'd slept through my alarm. Actually, I'd got distracted, so forgot to set it.

My phone rang and I realised *that* was the ringing sound I'd heard earlier.

'Lily, sorry, hi! I'm running late.'

'No worries! Cassie's running a bit behind too. Just wanted to check you're okay?'

'Yeah, yeah. All fine. I'll be there in ten.'

'Okay, see you soon!'

I jumped out of bed, then instantly regretted it. Every part of me ached. My back from being fucked against the wall, my inner thighs from spending most of the night and this morning with them spread open, and let's not even start on the situation down below. My poor fanny felt like it'd been impaled by a giant cactus.

That wasn't far from the truth. Nate was hung like a bloody donkey and I fucking loved it. I didn't know how I was going to walk today, but it was worth it. Call me a sadist, but the pain I'd felt when he'd first entered me was delicious. A tingle raced through me as I fantasised about us doing it all over again.

And the weird thing was, I hadn't even felt massively self-conscious when we were shagging. Nate hadn't given me a chance. I'd been too focused on the amazing things he did with his hands and dick and the incredible sensations to worry about what I looked like.

Anyway, I needed to focus. Today was about Cassie and Nico. Not about me getting my leg over.

After jumping in the shower, I put on my underwear, wrapped the big fluffy white dressing gown around me, grabbed my stuff, then headed to Cassie's suite on the top floor.

All of the bridesmaids were getting ready together. We'd have our hair done by Nico's stylists and a pro was doing our make-up. What a treat.

I knocked on the door. As Lucy, the make-up artist, opened it, a rumble of laughter filled the air.

Cassie was sat in front of a large mirror in the living room whilst a woman was running her fingers through her hair. Bella and Lily were sitting on the plush armchairs with glasses of bubbly in their hands and I wasn't sure where Flo was.

'Mel!' Cassie said loudly.

'Hello, *Mrs*! How you doing?'

'Excited! Have you met Meena?'

'Not yet!' Meena couldn't have been much more than five feet tall. She had shiny long black hair, light brown skin and a beautiful smile. 'Lovely to meet you!'

'She's one of Nico's top hairdressers at his flagship salon in Paris.'

'Nice to meet you too!' Meena smiled. 'I love the colour of your hair.'

'Oh, thanks!' I said, resisting the temptation to tell her it had happened by accident and wasn't meant to be so bright.

'Did you put make-up on already?' Lily handed me a glass of what looked like Buck's Fizz.

'No.' I frowned. 'Why?'

'Because you're glowing. Your cheeks are all rosy.'

'No…' I said coyly. 'That's not what's put the colour back in them.'

'What, then?' Lily tilted her head. 'Where were you anyway? You disappeared last night and I know you messaged in the group chat to check Cassie was okay and to say you wouldn't be back down, but you didn't say why.'

'Did you get lucky?' Cassie shouted.

'Maybe…' I tried to hold it in, but a smile erupted across my face.

'Oh my God!' Cassie, Bella and Lily screamed in unison. Flo entered the room, her eyes wide.

'What's going on?'

'Mel hooked up with someone last night!'

Flo came over and pulled up a chair. She'd been married for years and although I didn't know her that well, she was more conservative than Cassie and Lily, so I was surprised she was even interested in my holiday hook-up.

'Was it with the guy at the bar? Nico's friend?' Cassie said.

'Nope…'

'Who, then?' Her eyes widened.

'Someone else…'

'Spill!'

'No! It doesn't matter.' I waved my hand dismissively. 'Today's about *you* and your big day, not about my sexual antics. We can talk about it later.'

I really shouldn't have even mentioned it at all, but I was bursting to say something to someone. Typical that when I'd had the best sex of my life, I couldn't even tell my besties.

'Well, at least tell us if he rocked your world!' Lily laughed.

After pausing for several seconds to consider whether or not I should reply, I decided no harm could come from it. I was never going to tell them who I'd screwed, so it didn't matter.

'Oh yes, he did… *multiple times.*'

I'd said to earn the title of King of Orgasms, Nate needed to get me off seven times, and we were already close. Five big explosions in less than twenty-four hours was definitely a world record for me.

'*You go, girl!*' Lily said in a terrible American accent. 'I'm so happy for you! Are you going to sit together at the wedding?'

'Yes!' Bella jumped in. 'I need to know ASAP if you need another space at the table for your date.'

'Um, er, I don't know. We didn't get round to talking about that…' I said, thinking that was a good point. I wondered if he wanted to be my wedding date. Probably not. It would get everyone talking.

'They were too busy fucking!' Cassie laughed.

'Something like that. So…' I quickly changed the subject before I revealed too much. 'What's the plan for this morning? Are we getting ready in a certain order?'

'Don't think we didn't notice how you changed the subject!' Cassie said. 'I'll let you off for now, but I want details later!'

Bella called me over and pulled out an iPad. She had a spreadsheet with timings and a whole itinerary. She was always so organised.

After we'd had breakfast together, two more hairdressers and make-up artists arrived and worked their magic whilst we sipped on Buck's Fizz and chatted about the wedding, life and men.

They'd tried to probe me again about my hook-up, but despite feeling light-headed from the alcohol, I managed to keep my mouth shut. In a way I think that only added to the mystery and made them want to know even more, but I was determined to keep my lips sealed.

I definitely didn't do that last night.

I chuckled to myself as a flashback of Nate's mouth on mine and his giant cock between my lips down below came into my mind. I squeezed my thighs together.

For probably the hundredth time this morning, I wondered what Nate was doing right now. Whether he was dressed already. God. I could only imagine how gorgeous he was going to look in his tux or suit or whatever he was wearing. I hoped I had an opportunity to remove his clothes ASAP.

Was he thinking about me as much as I was thinking about him? Probably not. I had to be careful. As amazing as last night was, I couldn't start catching feelings.

Nate had been very clear. It was just fucking. Like every other man I shagged, he wasn't boyfriend material and wasn't looking for anything long-term. *Story of my life.*

In twenty-four hours we'd be getting ready to leave this dreamy chateau and return to normal life in London. So I had to remember to just enjoy whatever moments we had after the wedding today and possibly tomorrow morning. I couldn't get attached.

I pulled out the box I'd brought up to the room.

'So I have the jewellery. You don't have to wear the headpiece. No pressure.'

After opening the box, I laid out everything I'd made. There was Cassie's headpiece and different earrings, necklaces and bracelets for the bridesmaids to choose from. Some had love heart pendants and charms; others had sapphire-esque stones to match our dresses.

'Oh my God! This is amazing!' Cassie beamed, holding up the headpiece and admiring it. 'It's even better than the photo you sent. I'm *definitely* wearing this! And I'll tell everyone who'll listen who made it.'

'Too right!' Bella chimed in. 'You really should think about selling your stuff again.'

'Agreed!' Cassie and Lily said in unison.

'Maybe one day…'

As I watched them all sliding on jewellery that I'd made with my own hands, my heart fluttered. Especially when I saw the grins on their faces as they gushed about how good the pieces looked on them. It made all the hard work, late nights and stress to get everything finished worthwhile.

Cassie was almost ready. She looked stunning. Lucy had kept her make-up natural, so she looked like herself but just an enhanced version, and Meena had done some amazing hair magic with Cassie's beautiful curls to make them super shiny and defined before placing the headpiece I'd made at the crown.

But despite Cassie's make-up being sensational, she didn't look right. She seemed off-colour somehow. She'd been quiet for the past ten minutes. Cassie reached for her glass of water and took a large glug.

Whilst we'd been hitting the Buck's Fizz and Prosecco, she'd been drinking water all morning because she wanted to keep a clear head.

Cassie clutched her chest, squeezing the top of her fluffy white dressing gown.

'You okay, Cass?' Bella's face creased with concern. Looked like I wasn't the only one who'd noticed she didn't seem right.

'Sorry!' Cassie jumped up and raced into the bedroom, where I guessed there was an en suite. Seconds later we heard the sound of her puking.

We all rushed in after her and found Cassie leant over the toilet bowl. I held Cassie's hair out of the way.

'That's it,' Bella said gently, rubbing her back. 'Get it all out. You'll feel better once you do.'

Cassie retched again and again. Lily left the room, then returned with a glass of water.

Once Cassie had finished, we helped her up.

'Here.' I passed her a tissue and she quickly wiped her mouth.

'I'm so sorry.' She hung her head, then dragged herself to the sink to wash out her mouth. Cassie glared at herself in the mirror. 'Oh God! I've ruined my make-up. I look like death warmed up!'

'Don't worry about your make-up.' Lily rubbed Cassie's shoulder. 'Let's just get you to the bed. I'll bring the bin just in case you need to throw up again.'

Lily handed Cassie the water as Flo led her to the bedroom and closed the door to give her privacy from the hairdressers and make-up artists.

Cassie sat down on the edge of the bed in silence and we all gathered around her. For some reason, she wasn't making eye contact with anyone.

'So,' Bella said gently. 'Is there anything you'd like to share with us?'

Cassie's head jerked up quickly, her eyes wide.

In that moment, the penny dropped. Now it all made sense…

'How did you know?' Cassie looked at Bella.

'Just a feeling…'

'Know what?' Lily frowned.

'I… I'm pregnant!' Cassie's face broke into a smile.

'Oh my God!' I shouted. Even though I'd realised a minute ago, hearing it confirmed was so exciting.

Lily and Bella threw their arms around Cassie, screaming with delight.

'Congrats!' Flo said quietly. 'I'm just going to the loo.'

'How far along are you?' I said, joining the group hug.

'Around three months. We were hoping to wait a bit longer before saying anything, but you ladies just know me too well…'

'Well, all the not drinking alcohol and feeling sick multiple times was a bit of a giveaway,' said Bella. 'I know how excited you've been about the wedding, but even with the weather challenges and normal wedding stress, it wouldn't be that making you this ill.'

'God, I remember how sick I got when I was expecting

Andrea. It was a nightmare. I'm glad you have Nico around to help. Speaking of which, how did he take the news? I bet he's chuffed!'

'He's over the moon! Probably even more excited than me and that's saying something because I'm *so* happy. It's crazy to think that a couple of years ago I was single and wondering if I'd ever find someone and now I'm living in Paris, about to get married to the man of my dreams and in the New Year, all being well, two will become three and we'll be a little family!'

'Sis, I'm so happy for you both!' Lily gave Cassie another squeeze. 'You deserve all of this and more. I can't believe I'm going to be an aunty! Oh my God, does Mum know?'

'Not yet…'

'She's going to be so excited!'

'That's the understatement of the century!' Cassie laughed.

'At least that takes the heat off me and Carlos for a while. Every time Mum sees him she drops hints about kids. And Nate will be relieved—she's trying to get him to settle down too.'

Hearing Nate's name instantly made my heart flutter. Then it twisted as I remembered the context of the conversation. It was a reminder that Nate was just on loan. For one more night only.

'Ha!' Cassie replied. 'Good luck with that! Nate will still be having one-night stands in his eighties.'

'Yeah! The eternal playboy,' Lily added.

My stomach was currently several thousand metres beneath the earth. I got up and took a gulp of my Buck's Fizz.

Beads of sweat pooled below my hairline. I didn't know what to do to keep myself calm and also not give anything away. If I stayed quiet, they might suspect something, but I also didn't trust myself not to say something incriminating if I opened my gob. Luckily Bella piped up before I got the chance to decide.

'You never know,' said Bella. 'I used to think Mike was a player and would want to live the single life forever, but I was wrong. He's an amazing husband and father. And didn't you think Carlos was a Casanova too, Lil? Sometimes when guys meet *the one*, everything can change.'

Yes, Bella!

My stomach resurfaced above ground. I liked the sound of what she'd said. As soon as that thought entered my head, I chastised myself. What did Nate changing have to do with me? We were just fucking. I had to get a grip.

'But this is *Nate* we're talking about!' Cassie added. 'The man changes women more often than his underwear and he showers at least once a day, so…'

'Your mum has certainly been lining up loads of ladies for him since he arrived,' I jumped in. Fingers crossed that was a neutral comment and wouldn't land me in hot water.

'Yeah! I almost felt sorry for him when he sat with me and Carlos at dinner the other night. He looked so bored with that woman. He made a run for it as soon as he could.'

As much as I shouldn't, I loved hearing that. Now that I thought about it, whenever we spent time together, it was never boring. Even if we were at each other's throats or bantering, it was exciting and fun. Although we clashed sometimes, I was confident he'd at least agree with me on that.

'Like I said, people can change,' Bella said. 'Nate might surprise you one day.'

'True,' Cassie said. 'Has anyone seen Flo?'

'She said she was going to the bathroom,' I said.

'Shit!' Cassie said. 'I didn't think.'

'I'll go…' Lily jumped up. 'Just focus on getting ready. I'll take care of Flo.'

Oh yeah. I didn't know all the details, but from what I'd heard, Flo and her husband had been trying to have a baby for a while, so hearing Cassie's news must be bittersweet. My first instinct was to go and see if she was okay, but we weren't that close and I knew Lily had it under control.

'You feeling better?' I rubbed Cassie's back.

'Much.'

'Come on, then.' I stood up and Bella and I linked arms with Cassie, leading her into the living room. 'Let's finish getting you ready. You and your beautiful bump have got a wedding to get to!'

36

NATE

I stretched my arms up to the ceiling and yawned.

'Late night?' Carlos handed me a cup of coffee, then sat beside me on the sofa.

'Yeah.' I took a sip, then rested the cup on the antique gold coffee table in front of us.

We were in Nico's suite. He called it a *suite* but it was more like a damn mansion. Me and Carlos were in the living room, which was the size of half of my house. Nico was getting his hair cut in the bedroom and some of his other mates were still in the dining room finishing breakfast.

I yawned again, squeezing my eyes shut. I was so fucking tired. But it was worth it.

A mischievous smile spread across my face as flashbacks of Melody pinned against the wall, with her arse in the air as I fucked her on the sofa, then on the floor and on the bed, flooded my thoughts.

My cock strained against my boxers. Jesus. Just

thinking about her made me hard. She was really into it and that was so refreshing.

I loved how Melody just let herself go. She wasn't worried about making sure her hair looked good or that she was making too much noise—she was just free.

It wasn't just the way she had no inhibitions. Melody was also fun. The first time we'd tried the wheelbarrow position, where she got on her hands and wrapped her legs around my thighs whilst I held her up, she fell over. And the second time her hands gave way, but she just laughed. We both did. At one point we creased up so much my stomach felt like it was gonna split.

And that body. *Damn*. It was so soft, so sexy, so welcoming. My dick fit her pussy like it was made for her. Who knew that screwing someone I thought I hated would feel so good? I couldn't wait to bury myself in her all over again.

'What are you thinking about?' Carlos said, pouring cold water over my thoughts.

'Nothing.'

'You are smiling.' Carlos's eyes narrowed.

'So what? Smiling is a crime now?'

'No, but... I haven't seen you smile like *that* for a while.'

'You make it sound like I'm a miserable bastard!'

'Your words, not mine!' Carlos laughed. 'So tell me. Did something happen last night? Were you with a woman?'

'What? Why do you wanna know?'

'Just curious...' He held his hands up in surrender. 'You left dinner early last night, but you are tired this morning and I do not think it was because you stayed up doing your crossword puzzles…'

Carlos gave me his cheeky smirk. I hated that he knew me so well.

'Yeah. I hooked up last night. No big deal.' I shrugged.

It was true. Melody was cool. She was fucking amazing in bed, but that was all it was. It was all it ever could be. Like I told her, it was just a sex thing. Carnal. Nothing more. To get the sexual tension out of our systems.

My mind flitted back to our journey in the taxi where the driver had said he felt the sexual tension. He'd realised it before we did.

But yeah, it was just a temporary thing. I'd hoped that fucking Melody on the pool table would sate my appetite for her. I usually only screwed a woman a few times, then moved on. Partly because I'd never really enjoyed it enough with one person to want to repeat more than that, but also because doing too many repeats gave them the wrong idea.

The last time I'd gone back to the same woman four times (not because I liked her that much—I just hadn't had time to find someone else), she'd started talking shit about meeting her parents, then asking how many kids I wanted and when.

I'd bolted out of her flat so fast after that. The last thing I needed was to get caught up in a relationship or start thinking about all that forever bullshit. Been there, done that, got the scars to prove it.

An ache burned in my chest as I thought about the woman who'd ruined me. Who'd taken my heart, chewed it up and spat it out. I'd never let that happen again.

'If you say so.' Carlos raised his eyebrow.

'What?' I'd zoned out. I couldn't remember what we'd been talking about. Oh yeah. Melody. 'Nah, Carlitos—I'm telling you. It's just some fun. You know me. Just because you're all loved up doesn't mean I'm getting handcuffed too. Bachelor until the day I die!'

'That is sad.' Carlos shook his head. 'Being in love with the right woman is amazing. You will see one day.'

'*Hombre*, please.' I shook my head. 'Never gonna happen.'

'Do not let what happened before affect your future, you—'

'You ready, guys?'

Karim, one of the barbers, stepped into the room, cutting Carlos off mid-sentence. I was relieved. If I had to hear his *love is wonderful* speech one more time I was gonna gag.

I loved Carlos like a brother, but since he'd got with my sister, he'd become unbearable. So gushy and sappy.

Don't get me wrong. I was glad he was happy and, most importantly, that he was making my sister happy, but just because he'd found his *bliss* didn't mean he had to preach to me. I was happy being single. I didn't want what he had. I was fine just the way I was.

'Yep!' I stood up. Getting my haircut meant escaping this conversation.

'We will talk later.' Carlos stood up. *Great.* The man was like a dog with a bone. 'You want another coffee?'

'Yeah. And another croissant if you're offering.' I winked. Carlos nodded, then headed to the dining room.

I wasn't just tired, I was fucking starving. Melody had given me a full-body workout last night and this morning.

And even though I'd already had a big breakfast, it'd take a lot to replenish all the calories we'd burned.

After I'd explained how I'd like my hair trimmed to Karim, I pulled my phone out of my pocket. A load of messages had come through last night. Some from clients, others from more women asking if I was *around*, which was code for whether I was down to fuck, but I skipped past the preview panes, not bothering to open the messages to read them properly, and landed on Melody's name.

I zoomed in on the profile picture. Melody was wearing a tight green dress, her arms laden with colourful bangles, her hair piled high on top of her head with loose tendrils falling around her face. Her smile was wide and her lips were painted with that fire-engine-red lipstick that I loved. My heart did some jumpy thing and I quickly clicked off the picture.

What was I even doing looking at her photo? I'd just seen her a few hours ago. After we'd finished fucking on the bed, I'd left Melody sleeping, her hair spread across the white pillows, her cheeks flushed. She looked so peaceful lying there exhausted. I'd covered her up, then crept back to my room.

When I woke up at six thirty to go for a run around the grounds, I was tempted to go and see her, but I knew she needed her rest. Even when I got back to my room an hour later, I still held back from knocking. Not everyone was a morning person like me, so I had to respect that.

Now that I thought about it, Melody was pretty worn out. What if she'd slept in? I didn't want Cassie to worry if she didn't turn up on time. I'd better message Melody. Not because I wanted to see her. Just to check she was with Cassie and everything was okay.

Me
Where you at?

I stared at my phone, waiting for her reply. What was wrong with me? I never did that. If she replied, she replied. No big deal.

If I wanted to know how everything was going with Cassie, I just needed to message Lily. Simple.

Me
How's it going there, sis?

Carlos came back in the room. I shoved my phone back in my pocket and took the coffee from him.

'Good for you?' Karim held the mirror behind my head.

'Nice, man.' I turned my head to the left, then the right, to admire his work. '*Merci.*'

'You want me to do your beard?'

I felt my phone vibrate in my pocket. Must be Melody. I wondered what she'd said. If Karim started shaping my beard, I wouldn't be able to read the screen to check.

'Maybe. But do Carlos first. I'll just be over here.' I walked over to the armchair a few metres away, then quickly pulled out my phone.

Oh. It wasn't Melody.

Lily
All good here! In fact, more than good!

Lily
Mum's just arrived and it's all getting *very* emotional. But in the best way! How's Nico doing?

.   .   .

Even though Melody hadn't replied, I was happy that they were all okay.

'Let me check.' I headed to the bedroom, then knocked the door.

'*Entrez!*' Nico called.

I opened the door and saw Nico looking in the mirror as his tailor brushed down his suit.

'Looking sharp!' I said. 'That suit's the business! How you feeling?'

'Like the happiest man in the world!' The size of his smile said it all.

'Well, you're definitely one of the luckiest. My sister is amazing.'

'Is this where you give me the big brother warning speech?' Nico raised his eyebrow. 'Don't worry. I know how lucky I am. Cassie means everything to me. I will take good care of her.'

'I know. You're a good guy. I'm happy for you both.'

'*Merci.* That means a lot. I know how important you are to Cassie. And we both hope that one day you will find the same happiness with someone special.'

Just when I'd thought we were having a nice brother-to-brother moment, he had to spring that whole love shit on me again.

'And on that note, I'll leave you to it. Shout if you need anything, yeah?'

'Will do.'

I closed the door and exhaled. I needed to get some air. All this talk of love was fucking suffocating.

My phone chimed again, reminding me I needed to

reply to Lily to let her know that everything was cool with Nico.

As I looked at my mobile and saw who'd messaged, my whole body lit up.

It was Melody.

Yes.

37

MELODY

The sound of Janet shrieking with joy when Cassie told her she had a bun in the oven nearly burst my eardrums.

She'd squeezed Cassie so tight, I was afraid the poor girl was going to break.

'It's about time!' Janet shouted before hugging her again. 'I'm going to be a nana!'

I'd never seen her so happy. Such a different reaction to when I'd eventually told my parents I was expecting. My mum had shook her head with disappointment, and when I'd seen my dad, he'd said, 'You stupid bloody cow,' then tutted and changed the TV channel.

Andrea had only seen them a handful of times in her life and they'd barely given her the time of day. That was one of the reasons I cut ties with them years ago. Blood or not, there was no point staying in contact with people who didn't give a toss about us.

Even though Cassie's parents could be hard on her

sometimes, at least they loved her. She was lucky that her baby would be surrounded by people who cared.

With all the happy commotion, I hadn't noticed that a message had come through from Nate. My heart fluttered. I quickly looked over my shoulder.

Everyone was so caught up in the emotions of the good news they wouldn't have time to see what I was up to. I quickly opened the message.

Nate
Where you at?

Oooh. Sounded like he wanted to see me for another round. I typed out my reply.

Me
Where do you want me to be?

With each second that passed, my pulse raced faster. Talking to Nate always gave me such a rush. I didn't know if it was because we were doing something that was kind of forbidden or because he was so bloody hot. Most likely a combination of the two.

The *typing*... flashed on the screen and blood pumped through my veins. I couldn't wait to see what he was going to say.

Nate
I want you over my knee, so I can spank that gorgeous arse of yours...

· · ·

My cheeks heated and a flurry of fanny flutters erupted between my legs. I'd love him to do that and other things.

Me

And what would you do next?

Nate

Give you your sixth orgasm.

Nate

And then the seventh and the eighth …

A huge grin spread across my face and my whole body tingled. I didn't doubt that for a second. If I could, I'd go to him right now and spread my legs for him. But I couldn't. This was Cassie's day and as much as I wanted Nate to fuck me, I had to put her first.

Me

I like the sound of that…

Me

As soon as the ceremony is over, come and find me…

Nate

Yes, ma'am!

Nate

Make sure you're ready for me.

Me

Oh I will be.…

I slipped my phone back in my bag and joined the rest of the girls. Lily and Flo were back in the room now.

'Okay, ladies, I hate to break up the celebrations, but we're running behind schedule. We need to start getting dressed. Especially the bride!' Bella smiled at Cassie.

Taking our cue, we dispersed and headed to where our bridesmaids' dresses were neatly hung up on a rail.

These weren't your traditional poufy bridesmaid dresses. They were pretty sapphire blue designer gowns that probably cost more than my monthly salary: *each*.

It was the moment of truth. Time to see if the altered dress would fit.

I plucked it off the rail, slipped behind one of the changing screens dotted around the room, took off my dressing gown and stepped into the dress. I let out a victorious shriek of joy when the zip slid past my bum and up behind my back.

It fitted!

Thank God for that.

All that worrying for nothing. I glanced at the mirror and blew out a breath. What a relief. And I actually looked half decent.

Lily was right. I was kind of glowing. And it wasn't just the ace make-up Lucy had put on me. My eyes sparkled too. I felt something that I hadn't in a long time: happiness. Pure unadulterated joy.

Here I was, in France, surrounded by my closest friends. And then there was Nate. Temporary fuck buddy or not, I'd had so much fun with him last night. The weekend wasn't even over yet, but I already knew I'd remember this experience for a lifetime.

Once everyone was dressed, we all stood by the bedroom door, waiting for Cassie to appear. As soon as she stepped out, a collective gasp filled the air.

I felt my lip tremble and my eyes began to water.

'Tissues!' I shouted. 'Where are the blimming tissues?

Cassie, love, you look so bloody beautiful I'm going to cry.'

And I wasn't the only one. Bella already had a tissue in her hand and was dabbing underneath her eyes so she didn't ruin her make-up, Lily had her hand covering her mouth in shock and Janet was a goner. Tears were rolling down her face.

'My baby.' She stepped in front of Cassie and held her hands. 'You look gorgeous.'

'You really do, sis.' Lily smiled.

Cassie looked like a Disney princess. Rose and floral embroidery, crystals and sequins adored the bodice and illusion sleeves of her elegant white ball gown. At the back there was a lace-up corset with crystal buttons which complemented the sparkle tulle perfectly.

Once she'd composed herself, Bella stepped away and dialled the number of Maurice, who was one of Nico's best men.

'Ladies, it's time to go. I have confirmation that Nico is in position and everyone's seated. All they need now is the bride!'

'I'll leave you ladies to it!' Janet said. 'Better go and take my seat and let your father know you're ready for him to walk you down the aisle.'

'Okay. And, Mum,' Cassie called after Janet. 'Don't forget, *mum's the word*. Don't go blabbing to Dad or Nate or anyone yet about you know what…' Cassie lowered her voice. 'I want to tell them myself. Okay?'

'Okay, dear.'

As we stepped outside of the castle and into the grounds, my mouth fell to the floor. Wow. They'd done an amazing job.

Lavender lined the walkway leading down to the immaculately manicured garden where the wedding was taking place.

Nico stood at the arch, which was decorated with lush green foliage along with beautiful big blush-pink and white roses. He was dressed in an ivory suit with a sapphire-blue bow tie.

Next to him, Paul, Bella's seven-year-old son, stood proudly dressed in a mini version of Nico's suit. Cassie and Nico had wanted to get Paul involved in the ceremony, so had appointed him chief ring bearer. And judging by the huge smile on his face, he was very happy with his role.

The sound of the pianist that had performed on the night that I'd arrived playing 'Endless Love' filled the air.

The guests were sat on chairs adorned with olive branches. Everyone span around to look at Cassie, their mouths ajar as they took in her beauty.

We walked slowly behind her. I spotted Nate in the second row from the front and my stomach flipped. He looked so delicious, dressed in a rich lavender suit.

Nate's gaze met mine and he smiled before licking his lips. A dangerous action, both from the point of view of the effect it had between my legs and because anyone who saw him would ask questions. But right now, nobody was interested in looking at anyone except Cassie and that was exactly how it should be.

After Cassie reached Nico, who was wiping his eyes, I sat with the rest of the bridesmaids.

The ceremony was lovely. Lots of tears and laughter and their vows were beautiful. Before we knew it, everyone was standing and cheering for the happy couple: Mr and Mrs Chevalier.

We all followed them into the beautiful lavender fields as they posed for photos. The photographer took a few group shots with us, the bridesmaids lined up with Cassie and Nico, and after that we were led to another area where there were refreshments for us to enjoy whilst Cassie and Nico continued with their photo shoot outside.

'Our table's over here,' Bella announced. My mouth dropped open again as I took in the rows of rectangular tables in front of us. They were all decorated beautifully with white tablecloths, pretty flowers and fancy cutlery and crockery. I'd hate to think how much this wedding cost.

As we reached the table, I scanned the name cards to see where I was sitting. If I could sit next to or opposite Nate, that'd be perfect.

Once Lily and Carlos sat down, Nate approached the table and my heart flipped again. I had no idea how, but he looked even hotter close up than he had when I'd seen him several feet away during the ceremony.

He came around to where I was standing, keeping his eyes on the table.

'Am I here?' Nate said to no one in particular. He brushed against me and even though his warm, hard body only connected with mine for a few seconds, it was like someone had struck a match against my skin. *Fuck.*

Nate leant forward and picked up the wedding place card beside me. I swallowed hard as his gorgeous scent flooded my nostrils. If I hadn't had the wedding to go to this morning, I would've held off from showering for a few more hours just so I could keep his scent on my skin.

'I-I'm not sure,' I stuttered.

'No. Maybe I'm on this side.' Nate brushed past me

again. I swear he was trying to give me another orgasm. Or a heart attack.

'You are here.' Carlos looked at Nate, then at me, before returning his gaze to Nate. 'Next to me.'

'Okay, cool.' Nate walked around to the other side and pulled out the chair in between Carlos and Mike, Bella's husband.

When Nate sat down, his eyes met mine and my mouth went dry. God, had it only been a few hours since we'd been together? It felt like days. I wondered if we could slip away quickly now.

'B, do you have the itinerary handy?' Bella was like the unofficial wedding planner and had every detail ingrained in her brain.

'It's all up here.' She tapped the side of her head and smiled. 'What do you want to know?'

'Like, is the lunch at a set time, or do we have time to, you know, mingle for a bit now?'

From the corner of my eye, I saw Nate smirk. He knew exactly what I meant by *mingle*.

'Hmmm, not really. Nico and Cassie will finish their photo shoot in about fifteen minutes, so it's best that everyone is seated when they arrive.'

'Makes sense,' I replied. That was that, then. It'd take at least fifteen minutes to walk back to the castle, add another five to get up to our rooms—that meant it was a forty-minute round trip. There was no way I was risking missing their return and the speeches. And even after we'd had lunch, Nate and I couldn't disappear for almost three-quarters of an hour.

In fact, what was I saying? It would be more like an hour and a half because we'd need time to do the deed, and like Nate had said that first night, he liked to take his time. Nope. I had to face facts. There'd be no nookie this afternoon. I'd just have to cross my legs and wait until we were back in our rooms tonight.

I felt my phone vibrate in my bag. As I pulled it out, I stifled a smile.

Nate

I like your thinking…

It was so hard to stop myself from grinning as I typed out my reply.

Me

I don't know what you mean…

I added a winky face.

'Back in a minute,' Nate said to Carlos as he got up from the table and disappeared into a crowd that had gathered a few metres away.

Me

Why'd you leave?

Nate

You had your phone out at the table and so did I.

Nate

If I stayed, it'd be pretty obvious that we were messaging each other.

Me

Good thinking!

Nate

Mingling is going to be tricky this afternoon. But I'll think of something.

Me

What are you, a miracle worker?

Nate

Five orgasms and yet still you doubt me. I'm hurt.

I threw my head back and cackled. As Bella raised her eyebrow, I reminded myself that I needed to act cool before I gave the game away.

Me

True. You are very talented. I'll wait to hear about your miracle mingling plans later…

Nate

Good. It'll be worth waiting for.

Nate

Trust me.

Nate

Now put your damn phone away and stop texting so it doesn't look sus when I come back to the table.

Melody

If you insist!

I slid my phone back in my bag and crossed my legs. I kind of liked when Nate was bossy and I needed to control the situation in my knickers.

When I looked up, Sophia, one of Bella's best friends, was approaching the table. Bella jumped up and they hugged each other tight.

'Mel!' Sophia turned to me. 'Long time no see!' She rushed around the table.

'It's been years!' I gave her a squeeze.

Sophia used to live in London but had moved to Italy to live with her Italian chef boyfriend a few years ago. 'Where's Lorenzo and your beautiful son, Leo? He must be so big now!'

'Lorenzo's actually one of the chefs today,' she said, returning to the other side of the table to sit down.

'No way! I didn't know that.'

'When Cassie and Nico were in Italy, they came to Lorenzo's restaurant and fell in love with his limoncello tiramisu and asked if he'd make it as one of the desserts today.'

'Amazing! I can't wait to taste it!'

'And you're right, Leo's grown a lot! He's at the children's table over there.' She pointed. A cast of giant costumed cartoon characters were entertaining several kids. Cassie and Nico had thought of everything.

'Paul's so happy to see Leo and have a playmate here,' said Bella. 'They're happy playing together and me and Mike get to have a break too!'

'Perfect!' I said.

'By the way,' said Sophia, 'the pieces you made are amazing, Mel. Cassie told me you made jewellery, but I had no idea it was so beautiful. Where do you sell it?'

'She doesn't anymore!' Bella jumped in. 'We keep saying she should, but will she listen? Cassie even offered to ask some of Nico's contacts, but Mel wasn't having it!'

'Oh, that's a shame. Why did you stop?'

I didn't want to tell her that trying before hadn't worked how I'd hoped and had made me think I wasn't good enough. After all, if I couldn't get something right for a tiny market stall, how could I produce bigger quantities and still maintain the quality and customer service? It was too risky.

'It just wasn't the right time. Andrea was going through some stuff and things were stressful at work and so…'

'And now?' Bella raised her eyebrow. 'What's stopping you *now*?'

'Well…' I paused, scanning my brain for reasons. I was sure there were plenty. I just couldn't think of them at the moment. 'Nothing, I suppose.'

'Exactly!' Bella added.

'I was thinking, if Cassie's okay with it, I could ask the photographer to take some extra photos and close-ups of everyone who's wearing your jewellery here today. Then you could add them to your website, if you decided to start selling them again.'

My eyes widened. Sophia used to run a fancy beauty PR agency, so she knew all about photo shoots and marketing. But the brands she represented were all huge names. My jewellery wasn't on the same level. It was a good idea, though, and it was kind of her to think of me.

'Y-yeah. That would be amazing, thanks!'

'Great!' Sophia smiled. 'I'll speak to Cassie when it's a bit calmer, then I can give the photographer some direction on what would look good. And when you're ready, I know some web designers I can put you in touch with if you like? I really think your jewellery could be a huge hit.'

'Th-thanks…' I swallowed hard. Cassie, Bella, Lily and now Sophia were being so supportive. They all really wanted to help. They all believed in me. Even Nate had said encouraging things. My heart swelled. Maybe I'd think about starting up again. Possibly in the new year. Andrea would be properly settled in college by then.

I felt the air change and instantly knew that Nate had returned. I didn't know anyone else whose presence was so powerful that it affected the atmosphere around them. Tingles vibrated around my body.

'Hey, Sophia.' Nate gave her a hug.

'Hey.' She smiled. 'No date for the wedding? I thought you'd be inundated!'

'What can I say?' He shrugged his shoulders, then his gaze ran over me briefly.

'Don't tell me: too many women to choose from, so it wouldn't be fair to pick just one?' Lily added, shaking her head and grinning.

'Your words, not mine,' Nate replied.

'One day you'll find *the one*,' Sophia said. 'Maybe you just need a helping hand. A matchmaker.'

'No, *please*.' He grimaced. 'I'm good.'

'Janet has been playing matchmaker all weekend. I think he's traumatised,' Mike laughed.

'Sometimes we all need a helping hand to find the right person. And they're often right in front of us. You know *exactly* what I mean, don't you, Mel?' Sophia added and I nearly choked on my glass of rosé.

'What?' My eyes widened. Did she know something? I hadn't seen Sophia at either of the dinners, but had she seen me and Nate together?

'Remember all those years ago when Bella was in denial about liking Mike and she didn't want to go to their ten-year uni reunion and we had to give her a helping hand?'

Phew. We were in the clear.

'Yeah!' I said quickly.

'I think the word you meant to use was *blackmail*, not *helping hand*!' Bella laughed.

'What did they do?' Carlos asked.

'Basically Mel hounded me every day about going and then when she was at the reunion, she called and put Mike on the phone, knowing I wouldn't be able to say no to him. And then said if I didn't get my bum down to the reunion, she'd bring Mike to my flat.'

'It was so funny when she answered the phone!' Mike chuckled. 'What was it you said, Bells? Something like "I am *not* going to the stupid reunion! I don't care if Mike is there. I don't care if Brad Pitt and George Clooney are cavorting on the tables right now doing a striptease. I. Am. Not. Coming!"'

'That is funny!' Carlos said. 'But you are glad now that you did!'

'Exactly!' I laughed. 'You're welcome, Bella-boo!'

'*Okay, okay.*' Bella smirked. 'I owe you and Sophia a lot. You know how grateful I am that you forced me to go. This one's a keeper.' Bella kissed Mike on the lips. 'That reunion brought me and my soulmate together. I wonder who this wedding will bring together?' Bella looked directly at me and smiled.

'Yeah,' I said coyly. 'Who knows…?'

38

NATE

It was almost 8 p.m., which meant it'd been more than fourteen hours since I'd touched Melody's skin and that was fourteen hours too long. But today was Cassie's big day, so her happiness took priority.

The ceremony was nice, as weddings go. Full of love and all that mushy stuff. The food was on point, but the speeches went on for way too long and every time someone got up to say something, it was just another ten minutes that I was being kept away from Melody.

At least we were on the same table. I was still able to hear the loud rumble of her laughter and see how her face lit up when she smiled.

We'd made eye contact a few times, but that was it. She was too far away for our hands to accidentally touch. And we couldn't even play damn footsie under the table because she wasn't opposite me. It was driving me crazy.

When she'd got up to go to the toilet, I thought I had my chance, but then Lily, Bella and Sophia all got up with her. What was it with women? Why did they always want to go to the toilet together? It was a mystery I still hadn't solved.

The soul band that had been playing old Motown classics for the past hour finished their set and Carlos, who was DJing tonight, played the first song. Lily wasted no time dragging Melody and Bella up to the dance floor.

As I watched them move to the Calvin Harris track, a smile crept onto my lips. It was still hard to get my head around the fact that Lily was dancing. I loved my sister, but for years she'd had no rhythm. I didn't know what Carlos had done to help her learn, but the transformation was amazing. It was good to see her so happy.

And then there was Melody. As I watched her waving her hands in the air, whooping and shaking her hips, my chest grew warm. Everything about her was so… different.

The women I dated were much more reserved. They didn't like to let loose in case they sweated and ruined their make-up. Not that they could even dance in the heels they wore. They came to the club to look good, not to actually move to the beat.

But not Melody. She was dancing like nobody was watching. Like she was in her bedroom rocking out to her favourite tune and didn't give a fuck how she looked. She was enjoying herself and that was all there was to it. And that confidence was sexy as hell.

'You want to go and join them?' Mike asked.

'What?' I span around, reluctantly dragging my gaze away from Melody.

'You gonna dance?' Mike shouted.

'Nah, I'm good. You go.'

As much as I wanted to, that'd be too suspect. If my

dick was twitching just from watching the way Melody moved from several metres away, there was no way I could keep my hands to myself if she was in front of me. Earlier, I'd promised I'd find a solution, and I would, dammit.

Mike nodded, then went to join them. I was about to scout possible locations when I spotted Cassie heading towards me, holding Dad's hand.

'Hey, sis!' I got up and gave her a hug. 'Congrats again! You having a good time?'

'The best! Come on.' She took my hand and led us away from the reception area. 'So there's something I want to tell you.' Cassie stopped in front of a tall cypress tree. 'Dad… you're going to be a grandpa. Nate, you're gonna be an uncle. I'm pregnant!'

'No way!' I shouted. 'Sis! That's the best news! Come here.' I pulled her in for a hug.

'Move over, son! My daughter's just told me I'm getting a grandson or granddaughter. I need a hug too.'

We all stood there for minutes, just hugging and laughing. It was a beautiful moment. Even though I wasn't into the whole romance and happy families thing anymore, I could appreciate how special this was.

Wow. I was gonna be a proper uncle. Some of my friends had already had kids, so I was used to being Uncle Nate, but I knew that when one of my sisters had a child, it'd be different. *Extra special*. I was so damn happy I thought my heart might burst.

'I'm glad you're pleased. Our baby is going to need you. I want him or her to have good strong male role models around them.'

'I don't know about the role model thing, but know

that I'll be there to give you and my niece or nephew whatever they need.'

'You're an awesome role model! I know we tease you and you can be an overprotective arse sometimes, but I know me, Flo and Lily wouldn't change our brother for the world. You're amazing!'

'Thanks, sis.'

My heart started doing that weird fluttery stuff again. Hearing Cassie say that meant a lot. I knew I could be a bit much sometimes, but I was trying to relax more. My sisters were doing great on their own. If they needed my help in the future, they'd ask for it.

'You know we'll all do right by you, love.' Dad kissed Cassie on the cheek. 'So chuffed that you found Nico. He's a top bloke.'

'Yep! My hubby is a diamond! *Husband!*' Cassie repeated. 'Still can't get my head around the fact that I'm *married*! Anyway, we'd better go. Fireworks display is starting in ten minutes, so I need to find Nico.'

'Fireworks display?' I frowned.

'Did you even read the itinerary, bro?'

'There's a lot to remember…' I said diplomatically, knowing I'd only skimmed it.

'It's in the field behind the reception area in ten minutes. I think it'll last for about half an hour. I can't remember either. I'm too happy!'

'That's good, sis!'

Happiness was all I'd ever wanted for my sisters.

As we arrived back at the dance floor, the idea hit me. Cassie had said the fireworks display would last half an hour.

I could do a *lot* in half an hour. I took my phone out of my pocket and messaged Melody.

I'd told her that I'd find a way for us to meet up and let me rock her world again. Now it was time to make good on my promise.

39

———

MELODY

'I haven't danced so much in ages!'

I wiped the serviette over my forehead. As soon as we'd all taken photos of my jewellery with the photographer that Sophia had kindly briefed, we hit the dance floor. My make-up was probably fucked and I was sweating like I'd just run a marathon in a puffa jacket, but I didn't care.

It was amazing to just let my hair down and feel free without worrying about my shitty life back in London. Yeah, I still wasn't sure how I was going to handle the whole Andrea on the pill and her boyfriend situation, but for once I was pushing all of my adult responsibilities out of my head and was just enjoying myself. Like I used to at uni.

'A year ago I might've said the same!' said Lily. 'But Carlos and I go dancing most weekends.'

'I'm glad you've found your dancing mojo. And a great man.'

'You'll find your special someone soon.'

Lily mentioning that made me scan the area again.

Nate had disappeared about fifteen minutes ago and I wondered where he'd gone. A few days ago, giving him a second thought made my blood pressure rise, but now, if I didn't see or hear from him, things didn't seem right.

My heart jumped as I spotted Nate waving off Cassie and their dad and returning to the table.

Bella and Mike were at the bar and there was no one else at the table right now. This would be a good chance for me and Nate to talk.

'Here's hoping.' I rested my hand on Lily's shoulder. 'I'm knackered. I'm gonna sit down for five minutes and rest my feet.'

'Okay. I'll catch up with you later!' Lily continued dancing as I tried to stop myself from skipping back to my seat.

'Fancy meeting you here.' I sat down. Nate was still standing and his eyes met mine.

'I was just about to message you. There's a fireworks display starting in five minutes. Keep your phone with you. I'll text you where to meet.'

And with that, he walked away.

I almost whimpered. He'd barely spoken to me for thirty seconds and yet my body was crying out for him.

Five minutes wasn't even long enough for me to go to the bathroom and freshen up. I grabbed a napkin and blotted my forehead, neck and back. My heart thudded, excited about the fact that my lips were about to be reunited with Nate's.

Carlos announced on the mic that the fireworks display was about to start and the crowd started to head over to watch them.

'You coming?' Lily returned to the table.

'Maybe later. Just need to chill for a bit.'

That wasn't a lie. Netflix and *chill* was a well-known phrase. I was just planning to do the *chilling* part.

'Okay. See you there!'

Once she'd left, I checked my phone and sure enough there was a message from Nate.

I followed his directions, the music and sound of chatter fading behind me with every step.

Even though it was dark, the whole grounds sparkled under the pretty fairylights that lined the pathways and decorated the trees.

'I was starting to think you weren't coming,' a deep voice boomed from behind me.

Nate. I'd recognise his honey tones anywhere.

As I span around, he wrapped his strong, warm arms around me. I gasped as he released one hand, cupped my face, then pushed his lips firmly on mine.

God. The man kissed me like he'd had his head underwater for ages and I was oxygen.

My lips parted and as our tongues crashed against each other, my hands roamed all over his hot hard body. I groaned loudly.

Nate pushed me against a tree.

'Fuck, Melody,' he growled. 'You've been driving me crazy all day. You look so fuckable in that dress. The way it clings to that gorgeous arse. Then the way you were shaking it on the dance floor. I wanted to throw you down and put my cock inside you.'

'Do it, now.'

'No. First I need to taste you.' Nate dropped to his knees. 'Pull up your dress.'

'Wait, you want to…?' I frowned as I did what he asked.

'Why are you wearing these?' Nate tugged at my knickers. 'I told you. You wouldn't need underwear this weekend. They're pretty, but they've got to go.' He ripped them off and I gasped. 'That's better. Now spread your legs and let me fuck you with my mouth.'

'What? Wait!' I wanted Nate's mouth on me more than I wanted to breathe right now, but I wasn't clean enough. When he said he wanted to *taste* me, I thought he was going to suck my boobs like every other man.

'I'm all hot and sweaty. Don't you want me to shower first?'

On the handful of occasions I'd managed to persuade a guy to go down on me, they'd always insisted I scrub my fanny within an inch of its life minutes beforehand so I was 'clean' first.

Nate looked up at me like I'd just suggested we have sex in the middle of the dance floor in front of all the guests. I didn't know why he thought I was so crazy.

'Sweetheart,' Nate said, lifting his head, 'if I wanted to taste soap, I'd drink a bottle of shower gel. I told you I want to taste *you*. Which means it's your pussy I want to eat. So just spread your fucking legs and let me take care of business.'

My jaw dropped and before I had the chance to respond, he'd buried his head between my legs and licked like I was the most delicious thing he'd ever tasted.

Holy. Fucking. Shit.

With long, slow strokes he licked me from my clit to my opening and back again. Once, twice… fuck. What was the number that came after *twice* again? My mind went blank. All I could focus on was the incredible sensations taking over my body.

He was right about his beard being soft. The gentle friction of his facial hair between my thighs was delicious. I'd be happy for him to keep his head here all day.

Next, Nate put his warm, wet mouth on my clit and pulled on it gently. A loud cry of satisfaction shot from my lips.

My God. I'd known the man would be gifted with his tongue, but this was on a whole different level.

Thank goodness the fireworks had just started. Otherwise everyone would think there was a wild animal on the loose.

'Oh my God, yes,' I panted, grabbing the short curls on top of his head and pushing his face deeper. 'Right there.'

He growled before pushing two fingers into me, then grazing my clit with his teeth.

'Fuck!' I cried out again.

Nate took that as a signal to dial up the intensity, but I wasn't sure if I was strong enough to handle so many incredible sensations at once.

As he continued finger-fucking me, lapping, sucking and teasing my clit, every inch of me sparked.

I squeezed my eyes open to check that I wasn't dreaming. Nope. This wasn't just a fantasy. It was a fantasy that had become reality.

Nate, who in my eyes was the hottest guy in this wedding party, had his beautiful face buried between my legs. Eating out my pussy like it was his first meal in days.

And we weren't even doing it on a bed. We were in the grounds of a French castle. Outside. Where he had me up against a tree, my legs spread wide, whilst he fucked me with his tongue and fingers under the moon-light. There were hundreds of people probably just a stone's throw away, but they had no idea what we were up to.

Bloody hell. Even when I'd pictured this in my wildest dreams, it wasn't as hot as this.

Nate flexed his fingers inside me, then licked me harder and faster. The wave was building within me. I bucked against him and my legs started to shudder.

'Oh, Nate! I'm fucking coming!'

He thrust another finger in my entrance, pumping all three of them in and out of me whilst he moaned against my pussy like he was getting off on this just as much as I was.

As my orgasm ripped through me, the loud fireworks in the background exploded in unison.

'Fuuuuuckk! Nate!' I screamed. Knowing that the explosions would cover up my cries of ecstasy, I was able to let go completely. And it felt fucking fantastic.

The intense sensations rocketed through my body. From my scalp to a powerful roar of blood in my eardrums, my nipples, between my legs, all the way down to the tips of my toes. I didn't even know it was possible to feel so many earth-shattering sensations at once.

My legs couldn't take it. I slid down to the ground and looked at Nate through hooded eyes. He was still on his knees, his lips and beard soaked with my arousal.

I almost felt a twinge of embarrassment about the fact that I'd been so wet for him and that his face was now covered with my juices, but then he licked his lips.

'You taste fucking amazing, Bangles,' he panted.

Oh my God. I was already struggling to recover from

the orgasm and then he'd made my insides go even more crazy by saying those words.

Getting a man to go down on me always seemed like a big enough challenge, so the fact that Nate had done it voluntarily was one thing. But the fact that he'd loved it so much that he was licking his lips like they were covered with honey was just… mind-blowing.

'Th-thanks?' I said, unsure whether I was making a statement of gratitude or asking a question.

'The pleasure was mine.'

'Now it's my turn to return the favour,' I said. After how much he'd rocked my world, I couldn't wait to wrap my lips around his dick.

'I'd love that, but we don't have much time, so I need to fuck you before my cock punctures a hole in these trousers. You cool with that?'

'Do you even have to ask?'

'Actually, yeah.' He started unbuckling his belt. 'When it comes to fucking, I never assume. You have to want it too.'

'Well, let me make it absolutely clear: I want your cock in me, right now.'

'Good.' He ripped open the condom packet I hadn't even seen him take out.

'Let me do the honours,' I said as Nate stood up. I unzipped his trousers, then pulled them down with his boxers in one swift movement. His ginormous cock sprang free and almost took my eye out. The man should have a licence for carrying a weapon that big.

I snatched the condom from his hand and rolled it down his length.

'Lay down and open your legs.'

It didn't even take me a second to comply with Nate's demands. As my back hit the ground, the scent of the rows of lavender a few metres away flooded my nostrils. Getting fucked next to a lavender field was definitely a sweet memory I'd never forget.

Nate thrust into me at full force and the noise that flew from my mouth didn't even sound human. It was like a strangled cry from a feral beast. Jesus. I didn't know how it was possible, but he seemed even bigger than he was this morning.

'Normally I like to take my time,' Nate panted as he slammed into me. 'But the fireworks are going to finish in a few minutes, so this has to be hard and fast. Okay?'

'Fuck, yes.'

'I mean it. I'm not gonna hold back, so you might want to cover your mouth.'

I was just about to scoff at his suggestion when he lifted my legs up off the ground, pulled them onto his shoulders and pounded into me.

'Jesus, Christ!' I called out.

I lifted my hips and ground them into him before wrapping my legs around his neck.

'I'm coming,' I said as I felt my body begin to shudder.

'Not yet!' he growled. 'I know I said quick, but not *that* fast.'

'I can't help it!' I whimpered. 'It feels—it feels too good!'

Nate pulled out and my body instantly mourned the loss of the sensation.

'What are you doing!' I protested.

'Turn over,' he commanded. 'Get on your hands and knees.'

After I did what he asked, Nate got behind me and I felt the tip of his cock nudging my entrance.

He slapped my bare arse, once, then twice.

'I fucking love your backside,' he said before thrusting inside my pussy.

I didn't even have time to fully register the shock at him saying he loved my backside again because all I could think about was how good everything he was doing felt.

As he pumped in and out of me, with one hand gripped firmly around my waist, he started rubbing my clit with the other and I felt the wave building again.

His thrusts came faster and harder and I tried to stifle my cries, but I couldn't. Especially when he started squeezing my sensitive clit. Blood flooded furiously through my veins.

'I can't...'

'*Now* you can come,' he growled, fucking me like the future of mankind depended on him taking me over the edge. 'Fuck, Mel. Melody!' Nate grunted as I trembled around him.

My orgasm detonated inside of me. I saw stars and the whole universe as the sensations ripped through my core. I wanted to collapse and soak up every sweet tingle and ripple, but I knew Nate was close, so I let him finish.

Seconds later, he gave one long thrust before a loud, guttural groan shot from his mouth and he collapsed on my back.

We stayed there for what might've been seconds or minutes, I was too tired to tell, our chests heaving. Nate's heartbeat pounded on my back, eventually slowing before we both fell onto our sides.

He slid his arm underneath me and wrapped it around

my waist as we lay on the grass, now just inches away from the lavender rows, catching our breaths.

The fireworks had stopped and there was an announcement on the mic, but I only caught every tenth word. My brain and body were still struggling to recover from two more fan-fucking-tastic orgasms.

This man had completely ruined me. How the hell was I going to go back to normal life after experiencing this? How could I continue mindless swiping on apps? How could I go back to disappointing one-night stands or short-term dalliances, knowing that nothing could ever compare to *this*?

And I knew it was supposed to just be fucking, but when our bodies were pressed against each other it felt like two pieces of a jigsaw puzzle slotting together perfectly. Our movements were so in sync. Nate knew what to do and when. Where to touch and how light or firm I wanted it. Somehow it was like we'd been having sex for years not days.

'So that was…'

'Yeah.' Nate paused. 'Amazing. I gotta hand it to you, Mel, you're a fucking sex goddess. My cock can't get enough of you.'

My stomach flipped like it had a whole aquarium of excited fishes swimming around in it.

It wasn't just that he'd called me a sex goddess— which, I mean, *hello?* Mind. Blown. He'd also called me *Mel*. And it wasn't the first time. He'd screamed my name when we were having sex. My memory might be crap, but I could've sworn that on the journey here, he'd told me that he never called women by their name when he was fucking them. Hadn't he? I wondered if that meant anything.

No. Stop getting carried away. By this time tomorrow I'd be in London and back to settling for watching my ethical porn. Wondering whether these last few days really had happened.

At some point I should get a picture of us together. Not one of *those* pictures. Although, I wasn't gonna lie. If Nate wanted to send me a dick pic, this was the one time I'd happily accept. The way he'd repeatedly made me come, I'd gladly print the bloody photo, pin it inside my duvet and worship it every night. The man and his talented appendage were more than worthy.

'Thank you.' I beamed. 'I won't tell you how much you rocked my world, because it's obvious from the way you make me scream your name.'

'Well…' Nate sat up and pulled off the condom. 'You know I'm one for clarity and communication in the bedroom, or by a lavender field, so it's important for you to tell me.' He smirked, wrapping the condom in a tissue.

'Nate, *you* are a sex god and you bloody well know it! This castle might be huge, but if I say any more, your head will expand so much there'll be no room for the guests.'

He broke into a fit of laughter and the sound made my whole body light up all over again.

'As long as you're satisfied, that's the important thing. Come on.' He stood up, dragging his boxers and trousers up his solid thighs. My insatiable fanny groaned with disappointment. 'We better get back before someone notices we're gone.'

He had a point. The display must've finished fifteen minutes ago.

I pulled my dress down and picked up the ripped fabric that used to be a pair of knickers from the ground.

'That's *two* pairs of knickers you've ruined!' I laughed, holding it in the air.

'Maybe now you'll listen when I tell you not to wear any.' Nate smirked as he buckled up his belt and started heading back to the reception.

'Whatever.' I rolled my eyes, secretly loving the idea. 'I think I should go back first. I'm going to need to go to the loo and try and make myself look like I haven't just been fucked senseless in the middle of a field.'

'Good luck with that.' Nate grinned. 'And, Mel…'

'Yeah?' My heart fluttered again at the sound of my name.

'Don't bother spending too much time putting on make-up or fixing your clothes. I'm not done with you yet. It won't be long before I'm smudging that lipstick and pushing up that pretty little dress so I can fuck you all over again.'

40

———

NATE

That woman must have cocaine inside her pussy.

Either that or she'd put some kind of voodoo spell on my dick, because I couldn't get enough of her.

I'd pretty much always lived a clean life. No drugs, no cigarettes and alcohol in moderate levels. Well, except when I was celebrating. I was only human, so I got drunk just like everyone else.

But my job was all about encouraging a balanced lifestyle. Everything in moderation. Exercise, food, even sex. Despite what people thought, I didn't swing from the chandeliers seven days a week. I went through phases where I had it a lot and others where I'd just let my hands do what was necessary. But one thing was already crystal clear. When it came to Melody, my cock didn't give a shit about balance. It wanted to binge. It wanted to fuck her. Again. And again. And again. It wanted to devour her. Overdose on her. And I didn't know how to control it.

I craved her. More than anything. Even chocolate. And I fucking loved chocolate. It was my weakness. But even if

I was having a bad day, normally after I had a bar or sometimes two, it was enough. Any more than that and I'd be sick. But with Melody it was different. Somehow with her, I hadn't reached my limit.

Not even close.

I didn't get it. We'd fucked multiple times last night and this morning. And again just now in the fields. That was probably at least double if not *triple* the amount of sex I normally had with the same woman. By that point I'd be counting down the minutes before I could say a polite goodbye and get the hell out of there.

But now, the opposite was true. As I walked back towards the reception I anxiously scanned the grounds, looking for another location where we could slip away to be together.

For some crazy reason I was counting down the seconds until I could feel her soft skin pressed against mine. I craved her sweet coconut and sherbet scent. I couldn't wait to feel my mouth on hers one more time.

I needed help.

After ducking into the gents quickly to reluctantly wash my mouth, remove the rest of her juices that were still on my chin, and check I didn't have any stains on my trousers, I headed out to the dance floor.

Carlos had taken a break from DJing and was dancing with Lily. When he spotted me, he whispered something in her ear, then excused himself and came over to me.

'There you are! Did you have a good time?' He raised his eyebrow.

'No idea what you're talking about, man.'

'Sure. So if I think that you disappeared to be with a woman, I would be wrong, *sí*?'

I paused. I didn't know what to say. Part of me wanted to deny it, but Carlos and I rarely kept secrets from each other. Everything always came out eventually.

'You might be right.'

'I know I am, and I am happy for you. It is good to see you have found someone special.'

'What?' I frowned. 'It's not like that. We're just fucking. It's not the hearts and flowers soppy stuff like you and Lily.'

'*Si tú lo dices*,' Carlos scoffed.

'Wait, that means, *if you say so*, right?'

'Correct.' He smirked.

'Like you said, you know me. I'm a fuck 'em and leave 'em guy. Always have been, always will be.'

'We both know that is not true. You think that you are being honest by telling women you are a wild wolf who cannot be tamed and not to expect anything from you. You pretend not to care—like you do not need love, but you are lying to yourself. You are a sheep in wolf's clothing. It is not just them you do not want to hurt. It is your own heart you are scared of breaking.'

'You're chatting shit!' I rolled my eyes.

'I keep telling you: do not let what happened with one woman in the past ruin something good with another woman in your future. I almost made the same mistake, and if I had, I would not have the happiness I have found with your sister now.'

A sharp pain ripped through my chest. He knew I hated talking or thinking about what had happened before. And anyway what he said was bull. It had no relevance to what I was doing with Mel right now.

'Carlitos.' I rested my hand on his shoulder. 'For the

last time, it's not the same. This is just some fun for the wedding.'

'Who is it?' he asked.

'Doesn't matter.'

'Is it Melody?'

My eyes bulged from my head. At first I thought I'd given the game away, but then I realised that as far as everyone was concerned, I hated her guts, so my reaction could just be because of shock. Pure and simple.

'What? Everyone knows we hate each other,' I said, being careful not to lie.

'But hate can also lead to intense passion. I have seen the way that you look at her. The way she looks at you. And it is not hate that I see. It is lust. And perhaps more.'

'*Come on!*' I laughed. 'Now you're talking crazy.'

Obviously he was bang on with the fact that it was lust. But the whole *something more* bullshit was totally off base.

'*Si tú lo dices…*' He raised his eyebrow again.

'I'm going to get a drink. Laters.' I slapped him on the back.

Carlos knew me well. He was my best friend and sometimes he called me out on things that I didn't like hearing, but I didn't mind because usually he was right. But not this time.

I didn't have *feelings*. I wasn't some *sheep* worried about getting hurt. That was pure foolishness.

Like I'd said, me and Melody had a sexual connection. That was all.

I spotted her over by the bar and my dick instantly jerked. *See?* Carnal. That was what we shared. A love of fucking.

This wasn't some romantic, sweet, lovey-dovey holiday romance. This was two people enjoying each other.

I was lust-sick and Melody was my medicine. Simple.

Speaking of which, it was time to get my next dose.

41

MELODY

I didn't often credit myself with good ideas, but deciding not to join the queue for the toilets closest to the wedding reception area but head back to the ones closer to the castle instead was definitely a good decision.

After taking a quick glance at myself in my mirror compact, I knew I wasn't fit for being seen in public without a proper clean-up, and one look in the mirrors of the brightly lit loos confirmed it.

If you looked up 'just fucked' in the dictionary, there'd be a photo of me. The remains of my red lipstick were smudged across my chin and even on my neck where Nate had kissed me. Either that or it was a love bite. My cheeks were flushed pink, my hair was a complete bedhead and my dress had grass stains all over it.

Well, the part that I'd had hitched up around my waist whilst Nate fucked me was less soiled, but it was crumpled like it'd just had a couple of spins in a tumble-dryer.

And as for the carnage between my legs… let's just say I needed to have a good wipe down there.

It was hard to know where to start. If I had another outfit, I would've hotfooted it upstairs and changed. But the only thing that could fit me was the dress I'd worn to the rehearsal dinner, my jeans and a casual dress. No. I'd have to find a way to straighten myself up.

Just as I was wondering how many paper towels it would take to clean my dress, the toilet door opened.

'Meena… hi!' I leant on the sink, trying to look casual.

'*Salut*, Melody. Are you okay?'

'Y-yeah, fine. Just trying to, um get these stains off my dress.'

'Come.' She stepped forward. 'I have something that will help.'

Meena reached into her handbag and pulled out a pack of wet wipes.

'Amazing!' I took them from her and started pulling a few out of the pack.

'I have five minutes before I must return to fix Cassie's hair for some more photos, so I can help you until then.'

'Thanks, but I can manage. You've already helped by giving me these!'

I insisted she go to the loo whilst I started scrubbing. Once she'd finished, Meena offered to help again and was about to fix my hair when her phone rang.

'It's okay! Go!' I said. 'I don't want to make you late. You've been a diamond. Thanks so much again.'

'My pleasure.'

Meena was so kind. And she hadn't even asked how I'd ended up in such a state, which was a relief.

Ten minutes later, I headed back to the dance floor. No one would be any the wiser about the fact that I'd been rolling around in the fields with Nate half an hour ago.

My whole body tingled as I thought about what we'd just done. I'd massively downplayed my feelings when I'd said Nate had rocked my world. The man had rocked my bloody universe.

And when he'd said he wasn't done with me yet, my whole body had erupted with need. The sooner the better as far as I was concerned.

First stop. Bar. After that intense cardio workout, I was parched.

'The wanderer returns!' Cassie slid up beside me, her arm linked in Bella's.

'Hey, Cass! Hi, B!' I said in my best *I have absolutely nothing to hide* voice.

'What happened to your dress?' Bella started brushing it down.

'And you've got lavender in your hair.' Cassie reached to the back of my head and pulled out a sprig I must've missed.

'Oh… th-thanks,' I stuttered. There I was thinking I'd done a good job at tidying myself up. My eagle-eyed besties never missed a trick. 'I fell over in one of the fields…' I added, hoping they'd move on.

'Are you okay?' they said in unison, their faces creased with concern.

'Yeah, I'm good.'

'Thank God for that! Seeing you like this reminds me of when Nico I got busy in a park and I ended up with grass stains all over my clothes and a twig stuck in my hair!' Cassie threw her head back laughing, whilst the tension in my chest deflated a little.

'Ha! You and Nico and your al fresco fucking!' I cackled, hoping that deflection would help. 'No wonder you've got a bun in the oven. You two are at it like rabbits!'

'Yeah… anyway, ladies, I'll catch you later on the dance floor. I need to go and find out what's happening with the live feed thingy. Nothing's showing up on the screens.'

'Definitely!' I breathed a sigh of relief. I was in the clear. No idea what live thing Cassie was talking about. There were two screens either side of the stage which had shown the band earlier, but what they'd be screening now was anyone's guess.

After ordering a vodka and Coke and a glass of Chardonnay, Bella and I stood at the side of the bar.

'So, did you enjoy the fireworks?' Bella cocked her head to one side.

'Um, yeah! They were… *explosive*!'

The only fireworks I'd experienced this evening were the ones that had gone off when Nate had made me come.

'It's funny, because I looked but I couldn't see you. And Nate was missing too…'

My eyes widened and my jaw dropped open.

'Nate?' I repeated as my brain scrambled to find something that wasn't incriminating to say. 'What's *he* got to do with anything?'

'You tell me…' Bella raised her eyebrow. 'Speak of the devil.'

I looked up and saw Nate heading towards us. The hairs on my arms stood up and I swear the lips on my horny vagina parted.

'Ladies.' He smiled before walking over to the barman.

Bella's eyes burned into me.

'I'm going to check on Paul, but I look forward to

catching up later.' Bella smirked. 'I'm sure you'll have *lots* to tell me.' Her gaze flipped over to Nate.

She knew something. But how? I wouldn't be surprised if Bella had linked the fact that I'd disappeared with the grass stains on my dress and guessed what I'd been up to. *Oh well.*

If we got a chance to talk later, I'd tell her. She was my bestie after all and Bella was always calm about things. It would be much easier telling her than confessing to Cassie and Lily that I'd been shagging their brother.

They'd always known that I fancied him. Most women did. But they'd warned me off Nate so many times. Not because they'd be bothered about whether we dated, but more because they were trying to look out for me. To protect me from getting my heart broken. But it was fine. I'd gone into this knowing that it was just temporary. Things with men always were.

As much as he said he liked my arse, being a personal trainer, he'd be embarrassed to be seen in public with someone like me. Especially as I was older than him. A younger woman with a toned, slim body would be more *on brand.*

Once Nate was back in London, he'd forget about me and move on to his next pin-up girl and that'd be that.

Thinking about it, I should just fess up to Lily and Cassie too. It'd be better that they heard it from me, rather than Nate.

Yeah. If we had time to catch up later, I'd tell them.

I took another sip of my drink. As I looked over at the bar, Nate caught my eye. My heart fluttered. He was so bloody hot. I still couldn't believe that beautiful face of his had been between my legs just an hour ago. I wondered when we'd start the next round.

Just as I went to check my phone, I saw Sophia walking towards me with a handsome man. Must be her fella.

'Hey, Mel! Have you met Lorenzo?'

'I haven't, no, but I've heard a lot about you. Nice to meet you!' I held my hand out.

'Pleasure to meet you too,' he said in his thick Italian accent before ignoring my hand and leaning forward to kiss my cheeks.

'Italians prefer cheek kisses to handshakes!' Sophia laughed.

'Course! I forgot!' I said.

'I hope it is good things you have heard?' Lorenzo's face broke into a smile.

'Well, there was one very interesting story…' I raised my eyebrow and Lorenzo's eyes widened. 'Only joking! All good things. In fact, I heard that you were responsible for the delicious limoncello tiramisu?'

'That is true. I am glad you enjoyed.'

'You should come to Italy and see us sometime. Lorenzo will cook up a feast! Anyway, we're going to check out more of the things in the fun area quickly before we take Leo to bed.'

'The *fun area*?' I frowned.

'Yeah. They've got all different things there. We just came back from the interactive photo booth.' Sophia handed me a printout of photos of her and Lorenzo wearing bright-coloured wigs and fake moustaches.

'That's hilarious!'

'You should go! It's quietened down now. When they

first announced it at the fireworks display, there was a big queue, but when we left, there was only one couple waiting. They've got some great fancy dress stuff there.'

'I'll check it out!'

'See you later.'

'*Ciao.*' Lorenzo waved.

I'd said earlier that I'd like a picture of me and Nate together to remember our time here, and getting one from the photo booth sounded more fun than just a simple phone selfie.

Nate was still leaning against the bar, so I walked over casually and stood in front of him.

'There's a photo booth over there by the olive groves. Could be fun. And who knows what we could do behind that curtain? Meet there in ten.'

Without waiting for his reply, I walked off. My heart thudded, wondering if he'd turn up or shun it because he didn't want any photographic evidence of our time together. At least I didn't need to wait long to find out.

I headed straight there. Sophia and Lorenzo hadn't returned here after all, and there was a couple in their fifties going in the booth when I arrived.

The man had a plastic snake wrapped around his shoulders and the woman was wearing oversized pink sunglasses. They looked hilarious. This was going to be brilliant.

The light in the booth flashed multiple times and the sound of the couple's laughter was infectious. Whilst I was waiting, I looked through the dress-up box nearby to see what we could wear.

I pulled out a huge fake gold medallion. That would look good on Nate. *Any excuse to get him to undo his shirt.*

I didn't mind wearing it either. I could slide it between my breasts and insist that he retrieve it. The feather boa also looked cool, so I took that along with a few other things.

Just as the couple pulled the curtain back and stepped outside, I saw Nate walking towards me. Perfect timing.

I headed to the booth and heard the woman talking in French. That was good. It meant they were from Nico's side rather than Nate's, so they wouldn't know who we were.

'You came!' I smiled, resisting the temptation to throw my arms open and hug him. Fuck buddies didn't hug. I needed to remember that.

'Why? Didn't you think I would?'

'I thought you'd be worried in case someone saw us together.'

'It's inevitable. Carlos guessed and he doesn't keep anything from Lily, so…'

'I think Bella's guessed too.'

'I don't give a fuck.' Nate shrugged his shoulders. 'It's our business. It doesn't matter what they think.'

'Exactly!' I pulled back the curtain and stepped inside. Even if anyone saw us in here, it'd be fine. Taking photos with someone wasn't a crime. If anything, people should be happy we'd called a truce. 'Here.' I handed Nate some of the items.

Part of me thought he'd refuse to dress up because he was too cool for school, but he took them enthusiastically. Once we'd put everything on, we looked at each other and burst out laughing.

'How is it that you're wearing a ridiculous moustache and a feather boa and you still look hot?' I folded my arms in mock protest.

'What can I say?' Nate smirked. 'It's a gift.'

'Your giant ego strikes again!' I cackled.

'I'm not the only one who looks hot. That medallion suits you, and those devil horns—*damn, girl*.' Nate licked his lips. 'Let's take some pictures to remember.'

After pressing the button for the photo countdown, he leant forward and pressed his lips on mine.

My body instantly sparked. I could kiss this man all day. The softness of his lips. The sweetness of the rum he'd been drinking still on his lips, mixed with his gorgeous scent, was intoxicating. I ran my hand over his chest before fumbling with the buttons and underdoing them whilst Nate slid his tongue in my mouth.

He must have pressed the button again because there was another snap. Goosebumps erupted across my skin as Nate's lips moved from my mouth to my earlobe, then down my neck.

'Oh God,' I groaned as his tongue trailed my collarbone, then down to my breasts. He reached behind my dress to undo the zip, causing the front of the dress to loosen enough for the tops of my boobs to show.

'I can't find the medallion,' Nate said softly. 'I think it's got lost down here…' His lips moved between my breasts, and the light from the camera flashed again. I couldn't wait to see how these pictures turned out.

'Yeah, I think it's buried in there, *somewhere*.'

His hand trailed up my thigh and my legs parted in anticipation. As he slipped his fingers inside me, I groaned and tightened around them.

'See? This is what happens when you don't wear underwear. Less restrictions. More fun. Speaking of underwear, maybe I should remove your bra to have a closer look for that missing medallion.'

'Do it,' I panted.

Still keeping one hand between my legs, Nate reached behind me and used the other to unclip my bra. Wow. Most men struggled to undo it with two hands. Clearly being a ladies' man had its benefits.

The front of my dress loosened more and he dragged it lower with his teeth until my breasts were exposed and he nuzzled his face in my chest.

'Oh God,' I groaned. 'Don't you want to take a photo?' I said breathlessly.

Nate lifted his head up, his eyes wide with shock. He removed his fingers from inside of me and I instantly missed them.

'With your tits showing? You sure? I wasn't doing this to get a photo. I'm just happy to have the chance to enjoy you behind this curtain.'

'I don't mind. It'll be a memento. It's not like I've got my flaps out or anything,' I cackled.

'The memento of you will always be here.' Nate tapped the side of his head. 'I'll leave it up to you. Don't feel like you have to. I want you to feel comfortable. We have one more shot left, you press the button whenever you want. Now if you'll excuse me, I'm gonna get back to enjoying these…'

He leant forward and buried his head between my boobs, then groaned. As I looked down, the sight was beautiful. Artistic. He might not want or need a memento, but I did.

I pushed the button and a few seconds later the light from the camera flashed. *Beautiful.*

Nate squeezed my boobs together and started sucking on my nipples slowly. Jesus. This man.

'You don't know how much I want to fuck you right now.' Nate's warm breath tickled my skin.

'What's stopping you?' I said. 'The curtain almost goes to the floor. We could try.' I'd developed a taste for the risky outdoor sex and I was sure that no matter how much Nate wanted me, I wanted him even more.

'I'm all for taking risks, but only calculated ones. The way I want to have you will be too much for this flimsy cubicle.'

'Come on.' I reached for his belt buckle. 'Don't be such a wuss!'

Just as I slid my hand inside his trousers, I heard someone call my name.

'Mel!' Sounded like Bella. 'Get out of there! Quickly!'

What the hell?

Nate and I both jumped. He did up his trousers and I just managed to pull up the front of my dress before the curtain was yanked back.

Bella and Mike were standing there, their eyes wider than two giant dinner plates.

'Get out!' she repeated.

'Yeah, yeah, we know you guessed that we've hooked up.' I rolled my eyes. 'So what? We're both consenting adults, so sue us!'

'It's not just *us* that know now, Mel. The whole wedding party does.'

'Huh?' I frowned. 'How?'

'Come out and we'll explain.' Mike ushered us out of the booth. Nate and I stepped out and he zipped my dress up at the back.

'You really weren't at the fireworks display, were you?' Bella said softly. 'That's when they announced that there'd be a live feed from the photo booth onto the big screens so that everyone would get to see the funny poses people did.'

'But I saw the screens when I was at the bar and there was no live feed… wait.' My stomach dropped as the realisation hit me. 'Was that the thing Cassie said she had to go and fix when she left us at the bar?'

'Yep.' Bella nodded.

'No way!' Nate gasped. 'Mike, is this true?'

'Yeah.' He nodded.

'So, they just saw when I was…'

'Yep, sorry, mate.'

That meant that Nate's entire family and the whole wedding party had seen us kissing and Nate burying his head between my boobs.

Fuck.

42

MELODY

The word *embarrassed* didn't even begin to cover how I was feeling. Right now I wanted to climb under a rock and hide there for a month.

It was hard to remember how revealing the photos were. I was too busy enjoying Nate's hot mouth roaming all over me to think about how much my boobs were hanging out.

Nate handed me the photos. *Of course.* All I had to do was look at the printout to see what everyone else in the wedding party had already got an eyeful of.

There were some of us kissing and the one with his head between my breasts… yeah. That one was pretty revealing.

Thanks to Nate's broad shoulders blocking some of the view, there was no nipple on show, though. That was something.

'So sorry,' Bella said. 'Mike spotted the photos on the screen at the same time as me and we got here as soon as we could. Most people are probably drunk and didn't even notice.'

'You're sweet, Bells, but I'm sure a lot of them did. I was gonna tell you, Cass and Lily later about, *y'know*'—I gestured between me and Nate—'but… now Nate's entire family has seen my tits, the cat's out the bag.'

'The only thing that I'm pissed about,' Nate jumped in, 'is that you were exposed. I hate that it's made you uncomfortable. But I don't care that people know that we were together. It's none of their damn business. Come on.' He took my hand and led me towards the reception area.

'Wait! Where are you going?'

'Carlos is playing my tune. We're gonna dance.'

My brain whirred as I tried to process what he'd just said, but it was difficult because I loved the sensation of Nate holding my hand. The heat from his big palm was so comforting.

Seconds later we were heading to the dance floor. Our photos were still rotating on the screen. Shit.

Lily rushed over.

'Cassie and Miriam have gone to get the tech guy to stop the live feed. It should be off any second… there.' She nodded towards the now-blank screen. 'So… you two. I never would've guessed…'

'Yeah,' was the only response I could muster.

I felt the heat of a hundred eyes on me at once. I tried not to look, but it was hard to avoid the open mouths around us.

'I cannot believe he chose *her* instead of *me*!' One of the models that Nate had been talking to on the first night breezed past us.

My chest tightened and my stomach twisted. Nate squeezed my hand.

'Don't listen to that bitch. Come on. I told you, this is my tune. I need someone to dance with.'

The horrible feeling in my stomach was suddenly replaced by a basket of butterflies. Nate knew everyone was looking, he'd heard that girl's catty comment and yet he hadn't run or dropped my hand. He'd gripped it tighter to reassure me. To make me feel better. And now he wanted to dance with me. In front of everyone.

As we reached the centre of the dance floor, Nate lifted up my arm and spun me around, then pulled me close as he gyrated his hips to the reggae beat.

God. We were really doing this. Showing the world we were having a good time and didn't care what they thought.

Fuck it.

I turned around and pushed my bum back into him and started dancing close. I'd never cared what anyone thought of me when I was dancing before, so I wasn't about to start now.

'That's it, Bangles. Show them what you've got!' Nate smiled.

Shortly afterwards, the track changed and Lily, Bella and Mike came and joined us on the dance floor, then Cassie headed over with Nico.

'You dark horse!' she shouted in my ear as she moved to the soulful beat. 'I didn't even notice you'd hooked up with this one! We'll speak tomorrow at breakfast, young lady.' Cassie smirked.

Out of Lily and Cassie, Cassie had been the most vocal about warning me off Nate. Even though it was clear I hadn't liked him as a person back then, I had admitted on a few occasions that I still thought he was fit. And she'd told me repeatedly that getting involved wasn't a good idea, so I suspected another warning would be coming my way.

'Won't you be on your honeymoon?' I shouted back. It was the only way to hear each other over the music.

'Nope, not until tomorrow night, so we'll have *plenty* of time to speak.' Cassie raised her eyebrow.

'Okay,' I said, knowing she only had my best interests at heart.

After that, neither Nate or I gave anyone else a second thought. Carlos played banger after banger, so once that song had finished, we danced to another tune and another.

Although Cassie, Nico, Lily, Bella, Mike, Sophia and Lorenzo were all on the dance floor with us, with the exception of a few songs, I spent most of the night dancing and laughing and dancing again with Nate until sweat dripped down our faces and backs.

When a slow soul song played, all my besties paired up with their partners. Even Carlos came down from the DJ box to slow dance with Lily.

Nate looked into my eyes. I froze a little, not sure what to do next. A slow dance was something intimate. Something between couples. Rocking out on the dance floor to the soul, dance, pop and reggae Carlos had played all night didn't have to involve close body contact. But this was different.

I didn't know if putting our arms around each other and pressing our bodies together in public was really hook-up territory.

Plus, I was sweating so much that my dress was stuck

to my skin. There was no way he'd want to touch me when I was like this.

'I'm going to get a drink. I'm parched!' I said quickly, to avoid the awkwardness of Nate's rejection, which I knew was coming any minute now…

'Wait.' He grabbed my arm. 'Don't you want to dance?'

'You want to dance, like *slow dance*, with me?' My eyes widened.

'I know the music is loud, Bangles, but I'm pretty sure you heard exactly what I asked.'

'Oh, it's just, I'm all sweaty and…'

'Mel.' He pulled me into him. 'Considering a few hours ago my tongue was licking out your pussy, I think we're past the point of worrying about bodily fluids, don't you?'

I swallowed hard and my pulse raced at the memory. The man had a point. It was just that after decades of men rejecting me and making me feel like I wasn't good enough, it was going to take more than a few days of Nate's acceptance and enthusiasm to erase that.

'Okay.' I stepped forward and Nate wrapped his arms around my waist.

'Come closer,' he mouthed, holding my gaze. I pressed my body against his and felt his heartbeat. The warmth of his body radiated, lighting me up from the inside.

He moved his hand up to the back of my head and pushed it forward gently until it was resting on his chest.

Oh my goodness.

I inhaled deeply, drinking in his hypnotic scent. Nate was sweating too, but whereas other men's perspiration reeked of mouldy socks and onions, Nate's pores seemed to be capable only of leaking *eau de manly deliciousness*. He smelt so bloody good. If I could, I'd rip off his shirt right now and lick his chest. That was how lush he was. I could literally keep my head here all night.

As we swayed to the beat, I wondered if we really had to say goodbye forever tomorrow or if Nate would be up for meeting again.

He didn't do relationships. That was clear, but maybe we could continue this arrangement back in London. Short-term hook-ups were all I'd ever had back home, so if I was going to settle for that, I'd much rather do it with Nate than some random stranger from a dating app. Maybe we could talk about that tomorrow.

Nate moved his hand down to the small of my back and pulled me in tighter. I'd been so entranced by his heartbeat and scent that I hadn't even noticed his hard on pressing against me. The friction as we ground against each other was amazing.

'Do you want to get out of here?' I asked.

'Not yet.' He rested his head on top of mine. 'Let's keep dancing.'

That was a surprise. I would've put money on him grabbing the first opportunity to go back to our room and fuck.

Most guests had left hours ago. It'd been a long day. Even Cassie and Nico looked like they were getting ready to call it a night. But yet, Nate wanted to stay here. With me.

I wrapped my arms around his back, nuzzled my head deeper into his chest, then closed my eyes. This was heaven.

After dancing for three more songs, my limbs grew heavier and a yawn escaped my lips.

'Tired?' Nate spoke into the top of my head.

'A bit.'

'Let's go.'

I opened my eyes and was surprised to see that there was only Lily and Carlos on the dance floor, right in front of the DJ box, probably so he could still keep on top of playing the music, and two other couples. Bella and Sophia, who were with Mike and Lorenzo the last time I'd looked, had gone.

Nate took my hand and led me away from the reception. It was like being in a princess in a fairy tale, walking towards the huge castle with the pathways illuminated with pretty lights.

'Slower,' I slurred. 'I can't keep up. I'm too tired.'

Without saying a word, Nate scooped me up in his arms.

'What are you doing!' I screamed.

'Looks like Captain Obvious is back!'

'For the last time, I knew why you were at the airport, I was just surprised!'

'And now? Isn't it obvious that I'm carrying you because you're tired?' Nate laughed.

'I just meant that you shouldn't be carrying me! You'll break your bloody back!'

'Shhh!' He pressed his finger against my lips. 'You'll wake everyone up. Now unless you have the energy to walk back to your room, just put your head on my chest and keep quiet.'

My stomach fluttered again and because I was too tired to overthink it, I wrapped my arms around his neck and just enjoyed the sensation of his heartbeat. No man had ever carried me before and there was something so comforting about it.

I closed my eyes and relaxed.

I'd had the most amazing day with an amazing man. Having sex under the stars, dancing until our feet hurt, and now he was carrying me back to my room in a fancy castle. It felt like a dream. And if it was, I never wanted to wake up.

I gently kicked the interconnecting door, stepped through it, switched on the lamp, laid Melody on the bedcovers, slid off her heels, then sat at the edge of the mattress.

She was out like a light. Even when I'd had to root around my wallet with one hand to pull out my room key card, she hadn't stirred. I wasn't surprised. I was knackered too.

It was almost two a.m., which meant I'd been awake for nineteen hours. Longer if you took into account the fact that we'd been up fucking most of the night before. I'd only got a few hours' sleep before my run. After that was the ceremony, more fucking, then the dancing. Damn. I'd need to sleep for a whole day to feel human again.

A strand of hair fell onto Melody's cheek and I brushed it away with my thumb. She looked so peaceful. A funny sensation vibrated in my chest. I'd felt the same thing when we danced. I didn't really know how to describe it. It was kind of like a feeling of calmness.

No one was more surprised than me when Melody had suggested we go back to her room to bang and my damn mouth had said no. Yeah, I loved dancing, but we were *slow* dancing.

I *never* slow danced. Okay, *never* was too much to say. I *used* to slow dance. With my ex. Years ago. But I hadn't since then. It was too intimate. If I was going to press my dick up against a woman, I preferred to do that with her naked. So why I'd wanted to keep vertical rather than horizontal dancing with Melody was a mystery I was too tired to solve right now.

Maybe it was because I wanted to make her feel better. To protect her. *Yeah. That makes sense.*

I'd felt her shaking when we'd stepped back out onto the dance floor after the photo booth shit hit the fan. I knew she was embarrassed. Especially when that bitch made that comment about me choosing Mel. *Damn right.* Melody was worth a thousand of her. She was kind, funny, smart and naturally beautiful. I ran my thumb over her cheek again and gazed at her for a few seconds before pulling my hand back.

If Melody opened her eyes and saw me staring she'd think I was a creep. I needed to get back to my own room. I went to get off the bed, but as I moved, Melody reached out and grabbed my arm.

'Where are you going?' she said softly, her eyes still squeezed shut. 'Stay with me tonight. *Please.*'

Hearing her say *please* set off something in my chest. I supposed I could stay. Just for a few hours. Then I'd go back to my room. It'd be cool.

'Okay.'

After switching off the lamp, I removed my shoes and

climbed on the bed behind her. Neither of us had the energy to take our clothes off. Seconds after I closed my eyes, sleep took me.

The vibration on my watch woke me up. I looked to my right and then left, which was when I realised I was in bed with Melody. But not in the normal way that I slept with a woman. She was still wearing her dress, and although I must've taken off my shirt in the middle of the night, we weren't naked. And I had my arms wrapped around her.

Wait, what?

I was fucking *snuggling*.

What the hell?

My brain warned me to move my arms, but my body told logic to shut the fuck up. It didn't mean anything. It was comfortable, that was all.

My hands were resting between Melody's stomach and her breasts and it was... *nice*. I nuzzled my face deeper into the back of her neck and inhaled her sweet scent. Fuck. I could stay here all morning.

Melody stirred. She moved her hands on top of mine, then our fingers entwined. I knew I should let go, but it was like my palms were magnets and she was metal. The pull was too strong. I took the hint and stayed exactly where I was.

Anyway, we'd held hands a few times yesterday. And that was in front of people. No biggie.

'Morning,' she croaked.

'Hey,' I whispered into her neck. 'How'd you sleep?'

'Okay, I think. I don't remember. I could still sleep for

another week.' A soft laugh made her body vibrate against mine. She felt so damn good.

'Same.'

'Judging by that big baguette I can feel poking me, it's not *sleep* that you want.'

I hadn't even realised I was hard. Then again, these days it was easier to say when I *wasn't* hard around her.

'Sorry.'

'No apology needed. *I'm* sorry I passed out. I'd wanted to, *y'know*… seeing as it was our last night. But we still have time. When's your flight?'

'Three.'

'Oh. You're on the earlier one. I think mine is about six. It was cheaper.'

'I thought Nico was covering your flight?'

'Yeah, he is. Because the wedding was postponed, he insisted. But even so, I didn't want to take the piss.'

'That's thoughtful.'

It was true. I didn't know many people who would be concerned about a billionaire's expenses. But that was Melody all over. She was always thinking about other people. Everyone except herself.

'Money doesn't grow on trees. Even when you're loaded like Nico. Not that I'd know, but if you look after the pennies, the pounds look after themselves. Anyway, I need the loo and a shower before you *ravish* me.' She uncurled herself from my arms. It felt like the room temperature had dropped twenty degrees. 'Fancy meeting back here in twenty minutes so you can fuck my brains out?' She chuckled.

'Yes, ma'am!' I saluted as I watched her walk to the bathroom.

What'd happened over the last few days ran through my head. Everything had been so unexpected.

When I'd left home on Thursday morning, I'd thought I was just getting a plane to France to see my sister get married. I'd have been lying if I'd said I didn't think that I'd hook up with someone, but I wasn't expecting *this*. That on the morning I was heading home, I'd be snuggling with the woman I'd spent years hating.

And this was supposed to be a fling. So why was I lying here wondering if I'd be able to keep seeing her back home?

The toilet flushed, then I heard water running from the sink and, after that, in the shower. I sniffed my pits. I needed to shower too. But I didn't want to be away from her. Even though my room was just next door, somehow it seemed too far.

After jumping off the bed, I knocked on the bathroom door.

'Come in!' Melody shouted.

I swallowed hard as I took in the sight of her. Water running down the soft curves of her skin, soap dripping from every inch of her.

My gaze travelled from her pretty eyes, down along those delicious breasts, along her thighs and between her legs.

So fucking beautiful.

As she ran her hands over her nipples, a bolt of desire hit me.

I reached for my flies and unzipped my trousers.

'Mind if I join you?' I asked, my gaze still fixated on her gorgeous body.

'Be my guest.'

That was all I needed to hear. I made fast work of rolling down my boxers. My cock sprang free. It'd been several hours since it was buried inside her and it was desperate to return.

I stepped inside and pinned Melody against the shower wall.

'Do you mind if we—'

'Yes,' Melody jumped in. 'I mean, no, I don't mind and, yes, please fuck me.'

I pressed my body against hers before bending down to line my cock up with her entrance, then thrusting inside her.

'Whoa!' Melody cried out and slipped. I quickly caught her arm and pulled her upright.

'Sorry, I just… I needed to be inside you.'

'It's okay. I told you. I want it too.'

'You feel so fucking good.'

As I slid in and out of her, I noticed the sensation was different. That was when I realised. Fuck. I wasn't wearing a condom. I *never* went bareback. Never. I didn't want some woman calling to tell me I was about to be a father. I paused.

'Why'd you stop?'

'Condom. I forgot.'

'Oh shit, yeah. I know I'm clean, but you like the ladies, so…'

'I never fuck anyone without one. And I get tested regularly.'

'I'm okay to carry on if you are?'

Like I'd said earlier, the pull between us was too strong. I knew I should stop, but I also wasn't sure if I had another condom in my wallet, so I'd have to go to my room, into my suitcase… fuck it. I'd pull out before I came.

I continued pumping in and out of her, but slower this time. I lifted up her leg and she wrapped it around my waist. But the longer I was inside her, the more I wanted. I wanted to be deeper.

After gripping underneath her arse, I lifted her up.

'Put both legs around me.'

She did as I asked, but after I thrust into her a few times, I slipped. Melody dropped her legs back on the ground.

'I've always wanted to be fucked in the shower, but it's not as easy as it looks in the films, is it?'

'It can be, but this base is extra slippery. Let's do something else instead.' I pulled out of her. 'Turn around and stand here.'

As Melody pushed her back against me, I reached for the shower gel and pumped it in my hands before rubbing them together. Next I moved my palms slowly over her shoulders, then down over her breasts. Her arse bucked against me.

My hands travelled along her belly, then down across the tops of her thighs. I carried on soaping her up and massaging her from her shoulders to her toes. Seeing her body vibrate under my touch was almost as good as being inside her.

I span her around to face me, then dropped to my knees, drinking in the sight of her lower body and running shower gel over her hips.

'Told you,' I whispered, trailing my fingers between her smooth inner thighs.

'What?' she panted.

'No rash after I ate your pussy last night. Did you like having my soft beard between your legs?'

'Yes.' She gasped for breath. 'God, yes. You licked me so good.'

I skimmed the sides of her pussy, deliberately avoiding touching her clit or slipping my fingers inside her. I wanted to show her there were so many ways I could take her to the edge.

'Oh, Nate!' she cried out. 'It's too much.'

'It's never too much. Let go, Mel. Come for me.'

As I moved my fingers closer to her entrance, she bucked again. I relented and finally slid my fingers inside her, using another to rub against her clit. I'd barely built up a rhythm before she tightened and exploded around me, crying out my name.

And it was the sweetest sound I'd ever heard.

44

MELODY

As my body erupted into yet another orgasm, I fell forward. Luckily Nate gripped me, holding up my lifeless frame.

Jesus. The man had barely touched me down there for a few minutes and I'd exploded. There was something about the way he'd lathered me up before with shower gel that was so erotic.

At first when we'd abandoned the shower sex I was a bit disappointed. But the way he'd touched me was more intimate. The connection felt deeper. And I was all for it.

'That's right,' Nate whispered in my ear as the sensations continued to flood every inch of me. 'That's what I like. I love hearing you scream my name. I know you're tired, but do you have the energy for one more orgasm?' I nodded, still catching my breath. 'Good. Come out here.'

He led me out of the shower, our bodies still dripping with water. After we towelled ourselves down quickly, he took my hand again and stopped in front of the sink and bathroom mirror.

'Stand here,' he commanded.

'No, thanks. Can't we do it somewhere else? I'd rather not look at myself.'

'Why?'

'I don't want to look at all the things that are wrong with me. All my lumps, bumps and cellulite.'

When Nate was inside me, I was too lost in the moment to feel self-conscious. But standing in front of the mirror, looking at myself, was different. I felt more exposed.

'What?' Nate's face crumpled. 'Have you not listened to anything I've told you these past few days? Melody, you are fucking beautiful.'

I swallowed hard. My heart fluttered, then I froze again. My guard immediately flew up and told me he was just saying that to get in my knickers. But that couldn't be right. I was already naked. He'd already fucked me multiple times.

'Look at these shoulders.' Nate ran his hands over me. Reluctantly, I looked at myself in the mirror. 'Do you know how many women would kill to have shoulders like yours? And don't even get me started on these...' He trailed his hands down over my breasts. 'Women spend thousands to get tits like this, but even then, no money could buy breasts this good. And this fine arse.' He stood back, dropped to his knees and cupped my butt cheeks like he was worshipping them. 'Your backside is so perfect it's hard to even believe it's real.'

My stomach dropped several floors before an army of butterflies lifted it up again and danced inside my belly like they were high on crack. No man had ever said anything that nice to me before. And definitely not someone as desirable as the one stood behind me.

'Nate, I… I don't know what to… thank you.'

'Shhh.' He stood up. 'Bend over. I'm going to put my cock inside you and I want you to look in the mirror and see what I see. I want you to see how beautiful you are. And then I need you to look at my face, properly, as I slide in and out of your sweet pussy and ask yourself if you really think I have even the smallest concern about your body or if I fucking love it.'

I went to talk, but no words came out. I couldn't believe he'd really just said that.

My head was fuzzy, clouded by the aftermath of my orgasm, but also trying to process Nate's words.

Once I'd bent over, Nate slid into me and I threw my head back, revelling in the delicious sensation of feeling him inside me completely bare, nothing between us.

I knew I was being reckless. Normally I was so terrified of falling pregnant that if I could've asked a man to wear three condoms, I would've. But this felt different.

Nate sank in and out of me. Whilst one hand gripped my waist, he slipped the other between my legs.

'Oh God,' I groaned, squeezing my eyes shut.

'Open your eyes and look in the mirror,' he growled.

I did what he asked and watched as Nate buried himself deeper.

My face was flushed, my wet hair was all over the place, and my boobs jiggled with every long, slow, hard thrust.

Nate had said my breasts were beautiful. As I looked at my reflection, I supposed they didn't look half bad. Full, round, sexy even.

And it was kind of hot seeing him thrusting inside my pussy from behind. He moved his hand from my waist, slapped my arse, then squeezed it. He seemed quite obsessed with my bum this weekend and I liked that.

Actually, Nate looked pretty mesmerised with my whole body. If anyone else saw his expression, they'd think that he was fucking a supermodel. But yet, he was shagging me and loving every second.

He wasn't lying. Nate thought I was hot. Now *I* was the one who needed to believe it.

I pushed myself back onto him, moved my hips, gyrating on his dick.

'Fuck yeah,' he groaned as he picked up the pace, pumping faster. I rotated my body to the side a little so we could both get a better view of him thrusting inside me.

'How about *that* for a view? Now you can see my arse in the mirror,' I panted.

'I fucking love it.' Nate grabbed one of my boobs, which was jiggling so much I was in danger of getting whiplash. Or should I say *tit*-lash. 'I know I said before that I wasn't a one-minute man, but watching you in the mirror and seeing my cock slide in and out of you is so damn hot.'

'Do it. Come. I'm almost there too.'

He'd already lasted several minutes, which was a lot longer than most of the shags I'd had. But something told me that even if Nate was inside me for hours, it'd never be long enough.

Nate gripped my waist tighter and pumped into me, squeezing my clit.

'Mel, fuck, Mel, oh fuck!' he cried out.

His hand was working some serious wizardry between

my legs. The fuse inside of me was already lit and now it was seconds away from detonation.

As Nate collapsed on my back, the wave hit me. I continued rubbing myself against his hand as I hurtled over the edge.

His chest rose and fell against my back and I twisted my body to the front, then rested my head on the cold marble sink.

After a few minutes, we stumbled back into the bedroom and flopped onto the bed.

I closed my eyes and gripped the sheets. I felt so light. Like if I didn't hold on to something, I'd float into the air.

I couldn't calculate how many times we'd shagged since that first night, but one thing was for certain. Just like every other time, sex with Nate was mind-blowing.

Yet this morning, something was different. Not just because we hadn't used protection. The actions, the connection, the emotions weren't the same.

When we'd first screwed, it was wild and feral. All those years of pent-up anger and tension were finally released. We were just two horny people fucking.

But today, it was more tender. More gentle somehow. The way he'd looked at me. How he'd soaped me up in the shower. The things he'd said in front of the mirror. The way he'd touched me like I was the most beautiful woman he'd ever seen.

It didn't feel like sex. It didn't feel like fucking. It felt like making love. I wondered if he felt the same. Because if he did, then we'd both need to admit that this was more than just a fling.

And most importantly, have a conversation about the future and decide what should happen next…

45

———

NATE

It was only a few minutes after we'd been lying on the bed that I realised I'd come inside Melody. I'd meant to pull out.

Fuck.

My head was all over the place. Whenever I was near her, I couldn't think straight.

Everyone knew I'd been with a lot of women, but this was different. I couldn't get enough of her. It was like my cock wanted to take up a permanent residency inside her.

But that was the thing. It wasn't just about the sex. I'd lay with her all day, even if she didn't let me put a finger on or in her. I couldn't believe there was only an hour left before I had to leave. This sucked.

'I should get ready.' I propped myself up on one elbow.

'Yeah. So…' Melody paused. 'I suppose this is good-bye, then.'

'I guess it is.' A long silence stretched between us. Maybe it was only a minute. But it felt like twenty. I should say something. *Anything.* Let her know what she meant to me. 'Thanks for, y'know…'

Tell her how you feel.

'No, I don't.' She smirked, and I resisted the temptation to kiss her.

'For a great weekend. I-I enjoyed being with you.'

'You mean your *knob* did,' Melody cackled.

'Yeah, it did. But it wasn't just…'

I wanted to tell her that it wasn't just about us banging. That I really had an amazing time with *her*. I enjoyed talking to her, dancing with her, playing cards, just hanging out. But somehow the words wouldn't come out.

'Well, thank *you*, for all the orgasms. I think I had nine! You blew your target of seven out the water, so I'll contact Guinness World Records to formally request that you're included in the next edition as the official King of Orgasms.'

'Nice. Thanks! Is there a presentation ceremony? You know, like with the Oscars? Do I need to prepare my speech?'

'Possibly. It's not a title that's given out lightly.'

We both burst into a fit of giggles. Melody threw her head back laughing and as the sound of her loud cackle filled the air, I wondered how I'd ever found it loud and annoying. It was infectious.

I had to admit, I was kind of gutted that I wasn't going to hear that any time soon. The next time would probably be when my niece or nephew was born, if Cassie and Nico threw a party or something. Other than family gatherings, me and Mel didn't really have any other reason to see each other, which was a damn shame.

'I'm gonna get going.'

I jumped off the bed. There was no point in prolonging the inevitable. Just like ripping off a plaster, the quicker I left, the less painful it'd be. Not that I was in pain or anything. I just meant, it would be easier. For Melody. In case she'd started catching feelings. *I'd* be fine.

'Okay.' Melody fidgeted with her fingers, then leant over to the bedside table and started sliding bangles onto her arms.

She looked so wounded somehow and something inside my chest cracked.

'We could have breakfast together if you want?'

Her head shot up and her eyes brightened.

'Ye—oh, actually, no. I can't. I'm meeting the girls.'

'Oh yeah. Something tells me that it won't just be the bacon that's getting grilled this morning.'

'Tell me about it!' Melody smiled. Damn, I loved the way her smile reached the corners of her beautiful eyes and made them sparkle. 'Don't worry. I won't reveal your deepest, darkest secrets to your sisters.'

I swallowed hard. When it came to women, there were things I didn't want my sisters to know about, but being with Melody wasn't one of them.

'Good to know.'

The alarm on my watch sounded, reminding me I had to leave. Now I wished I'd booked a later flight. If I had, maybe after breakfast I could've played another round of cards with Mel. Or gone for a walk or something.

What the hell?

Why was I thinking about going on romantic walks? I needed to eat something. My brain was getting all fuzzy.

I went over to Mel. She froze and looked up at me with those fucking adorable eyes. I wanted to push my mouth onto hers and kiss her until the sun went down, but instead I just pecked her on the cheek.

'See you around.'

Damn, that was so lame.

'Bye.' Her voice cracked.

Everything inside me said to turn and look back, but I kept on walking towards the door, then went into my room.

I took out my phone, launched Spotify and played my favourite playlist on full volume.

After that crap goodbye, I needed something to drown out my thoughts and the constant pounding of my heart.

46

____

MELODY

The music from Nate's room switched off and seconds later I heard his room door slam.

So that was that, then. He was gone.

I sat up in the bed and pulled my knees up to my chest.

Why was it suddenly so cold in here? I dragged the covers around my body. I knew I should get ready for breakfast, but for some reason, I didn't feel like eating. Not even the prospect of toast and fresh croissants was enough to make me want to get my arse out of bed.

My phone lit up with a text, and a flash of excitement ripped through me. Maybe it was Nate saying to come and meet him so we could say a proper goodbye. Not just that limp cheek kiss he'd given me.

I understood that we were just casual for this weekend, but I'd thought we'd at least have a passionate goodbye snog. We were in bloody France. Cheek kisses were normal. For all I knew, it was something French people did to their doctor or even a stranger they bumped into on the street. Surely our last few days together meant more than that?

When I picked up the phone, the message wasn't from Nate.

Cassie

You coming up? Flo's already left but Bella, Lily and Sophia are on their way here.

Crap. I needed to get my arse in gear. I dragged myself out of the bed, threw on my pink jeans and a T-shirt, then headed up to Cassie's suite.

'Here she is!' Lily said as I stepped inside. 'The dark horse.'

'The *undercover lover*!' Cassie shouted.

'*Here we go…*' I rolled my eyes. 'Not even a hello before you start grilling me like a pack of bacon,' I said, remembering Nate's words.

'Sit!' Cassie patted the space on the sofa beside her. Bella, Sophia and Lily were curled up in the big armchairs opposite.

'Can I at least get a coffee first? I'm knackered.'

'We can all guess why *that* is… actually, no, that's gross!' Cassie's hand flew to her mouth. 'I really don't want to think about what you've been up to with my brother.'

'So come on, then!' Lily's eyes widened. 'Tell us what happened. I thought you hated Nate's guts! What changed?'

'First, I need *coffee*!' I huffed.

'I'll get it!' Bella offered.

'Looks like they're not letting you off the hook.' Sophia smiled.

I slumped down on the sofa, admitting defeat. They weren't going to rest until I'd spilt the beans, so it was better to just get it over and done with.

'I *did* hate his guts. But then, I dunno. He did some nice things like coming with me to get my passport and, well… we had to spend a lot of time together, y'know, travelling, and then all the hotel rooms were booked, so we had to share a bed and…'

'What!' Cassie screamed! 'There was only one bed? *Classic!*'

'So was that when things, *y'know*, happened?' Sophia asked.

'La-la-laaaaa!' Lily sang loudly. 'Please do not reveal any details!'

'No!' I shouted. 'And, no, I won't. Nothing happened until we were here. On the second night. And, y'know, a *lot* since then.'

'Oh my God. You and my brother were knocking the boots at my rehearsal dinner. I can't work out whether that's romantic or not!' Cassie's face contorted, interchanging between frowns and smiles.

'*That's* why you're glowing!' Lily took a sip of her Buck's Fizz. 'Is that why you were late coming to get ready yesterday morning?'

'Kinda…' I winced.

'I just can't get my head around it. *You and Nate!*' Cassie shook her head. 'You've spent years giving each other dirty looks. I never left you two in the same room alone for more than two minutes in case World War III broke out, so the fact that you've been spending time together and getting down and dirty is… wow. Mind blown!'

'I know, right?' Lily added. 'When those pictures flashed up on the screen last night, I thought someone had spiked my drink and I was hallucinating.'

'Same here!' Cassie shouted. 'When we were thinking about live-streaming on the big screen, it didn't even cross my mind that there was a chance two horny guests would've seen the photo booth as the perfect place to bang.'

'We weren't *banging*!' I protested, before remembering that I'd wanted to and it was Nate who'd warned against it. Thank God he had.

'I don't want to know details!' Cassie reminded me. 'Whatever you were doing in there, you certainly earned yourself a fan. Doris thought you were a legend!'

'I knew I liked that woman!' I smiled. 'I didn't feel like a legend when Nate dragged me back to the reception and everyone was staring.'

Thinking about that again made my stomach jolt. The words of that model rang loudly in my ears. Telling me that I wasn't pretty enough to be with someone like him.

'You had nothing to be ashamed of,' Cassie said. 'I liked that you just ignored it and headed to the dance floor. It was so strange seeing you guys dancing together. You seemed like you were having a great time, though.'

Lily lifted the jug of Buck's Fizz and filled four glasses with it, then poured Cassie some orange juice. I wasn't sure if I'd have mine. I was still recovering from last night, so coffee was better.

'We were. We did,' I replied.

'So what happens now?' said Bella, the voice of reason.

'Nothing, I suppose. It was just something temporary.'

'That sounds like Nate.' Lily nodded.

'I don't know…' Sophia added. 'I saw the way he looked at you. From where I was standing, it seemed like he was really into you.'

'You don't know Nate as well as we do,' said Cassie. 'He's not a relationship guy.'

'True. But then again, neither was Carlos,' Lily said.

'At least Carlos had *had* a long-term relationship. Even though he's pushing forty, I've never known Nate to date anyone for more than a few months. If that.'

'What do *you* want to happen, though?' Bella asked.

'We agreed that it would just be a hook-up,' I said, my stomach twisting. Having this conversation was uncomfortable.

'That wasn't what I asked.'

'It doesn't matter what I want. It's reality. Once we're in London, everything will just go back to normal. Nate will carry on screwing around and I'll go back to, well, dating apps, I suppose.'

'Oh, Mel.' Cassie squeezed my hand. 'I'm sorry. I think you're right to manage your expectations just in case. I don't want you to get hurt.'

'I won't! I'm fine!' I waved my hands dismissively. 'I knew it wasn't going to last beyond today and I'm okay with that.'

If I said it enough times, maybe I'd start to believe it.

'Hmmm,' said Bella, clearly not convinced. 'I know you're putting on a brave front. But I can tell you'd like more to happen.'

Dammit. That was the thing about having besties. Cassie and Bella could read me like a book.

'Yeah, okay!' I huffed. 'I'd like more, but it's never gonna happen.'

Even if Nate was interested in meeting again, there was no way he'd actually settle down with me. I was five years older than him. Not a big deal if we were both in our twenties or thirties. But a guy like him would want a house full of kids at some point and the reality was, that was something I couldn't give him.

Anyway, it was a non-issue. Like I said, it was just a hook-up, so I didn't even know why I was thinking about children. FFS.

'Never say never!' said Sophia. 'If you think about all of our relationships, I'm sure there was a point that we all said the same thing. After what I went through in the early days with Lorenzo, I never thought we'd get together. Bella, I'm sure you felt that way about Mike too.'

'One hundred per cent.' Bella nodded.

'Same here with Carlos,' Lily agreed.

'It was all smooth sailing with me and Nico... *not*!' Cassie laughed. 'We had so many obstacles. There was no way I thought France's most eligible *billionaire* who had women throwing themselves at him left, right and centre would be interested in a PA from South London. But here I am, newly married with a baby on the way. So, yeah. Don't give up hope completely. Maybe you can be *cautiously optimistic*.'

'That sounds like a good plan,' Bella said. 'Ultimately, time will tell. When you're both back at home, living your normal lives, you'll know whether it was more than just something casual. If weeks pass and you both still can't stop thinking about each other and you feel emptier without him, there's a chance you could try making a go of things.'

I resisted the temptation to say that I was already feeling like that. It was too soon. He'd only left my room less than an hour ago.

But maybe there really was a chance? Nate did look at me like I was special. I felt that connection. It was real. Different than anything else I'd experienced before. Surely that counted for something?

'Yeah, we'll see. Anyway, do you have any pain au chocolat here?'

'Sorry! I took the last one,' Lily said.

'No worries! I'll get another one from the dining room.'

'You sure?' Cassie asked. 'I can ask room service to bring it up.'

'Nah, I can get it myself. I'm not all *la-di-da* like you yet!' I laughed.

And hopefully, Nate might still be down there. I just wanted to see him one last time.

If I did, I'd tell him I wanted more. Or give him a proper goodbye kiss so he'd know I was interested. I'd do something. *Anything.* This was the modern age. I didn't need to rely on the man to make a move.

Yes. Speaking to my girls had hyped me up. I was going for what I wanted. I'd seize the day. Or in this case, the man.

'Anyone want anything whilst I'm down there?'

When I got to the dining room, I was disappointed not to see Nate. He must've already left. After our nightmare journey here, I couldn't blame him for wanting to get to the airport extra early.

I held the plate with the pastries in one hand, but when I reached into my pocket to check my phone to see if he'd messaged, I realised I'd left it in my room.

As I climbed the staircase to get it, I heard voices above me.

I'd recognise that deep, honey-coated tone anywhere. It was Nate. *Excellent.* He was talking to a woman. I paused.

She had a St Lucian accent, so I assumed it was his mum or one of his relatives who'd flown over for the wedding. Phew. Nothing to worry about.

'…at least now I know why you weren't interested in the women I arranged for you.'

'Mum…'

'And isn't she Bella's age? She'll be too old to have children.'

My stomach twisted. They were talking about me. Nate's mum was assessing my ability to provide her with grandkids. Shit.

Janet was right. Like I'd said to myself earlier, I probably *was* too old.

Of course there were women who had kids in their mid forties. But the truth was, I didn't want another child. That was why I avoided dating younger men. They'd want their own family. Something I couldn't give them.

'I'm not interested in having children with her. It was never about marriage and babies…'

Now my knotted stomach plummeted through the floor. Even though I knew that was true, hearing Nate rule it out so strongly completely ripped any fantasies of a future together right out of my crazy mind.

'I didn't think Melody was your type,' Janet jumped in.

'She's not b——'

Oh God.

I raced down the stairs. I couldn't listen to any more. Hearing Nate's reply would destroy me. I already knew all of the reasons he wouldn't be interested. I didn't need to hear him spell them out one by one to his mum.

At least now I knew where I stood. I'd heard it straight from the horse's mouth. I wasn't relationship material.

This wasn't like the romantic films or books where the woman transformed the hero and convinced him to change his ways.

I was just a bit of fun. I was only good for sex. Like always.

Nate might be great in bed, but he was just like every other man I'd been with.

He didn't want anything long-term. He'd told me that himself.

And I was stupid to ever think otherwise.

47

———

NATE

Talking to a brick wall would've been more productive than trying to have a conversation with Mum. She wasn't listening to a damn word I said.

After breakfast, I'd wanted to get my case, then text Melody to say a proper goodbye. The kiss I'd given her before was lame. I could do better. I *wanted* to do better than that.

There was so much more I needed to say to her. I didn't know how, but I was gonna try.

But I didn't get the chance. When I got to my room, Mum was already there, knocking on my door.

'You avoided me last night,' Mum said as she saw me approaching.

'I was dancing,' I snapped. I could already tell I wasn't going to like this conversation. 'It was a party. That's what people do.'

'Don't get smart with me, son. I know you're a grown man and you like to fool around with women, but did you have to expose yourself so publicly at your sister's wedding?'

'*Expose myself?*' I ground my jaw. 'You make it sound like I got on the stage and pulled out my dick!'

'Language!' Mum warned.

'Mum. Drop it. I don't want to get into this with you now. Or ever. What I do is my own damn business.'

'Not when it affects the family. Everyone saw those filthy pictures on the screen last night.'

'And? So what?' I ground my jaw. Cassie and Nico were fine about what happened when I'd spoken to them briefly last night. It was their wedding, so as long as I hadn't upset them, I wasn't bothered about other people's opinions. 'I'm trying to be respectful, Mum, but you're pushing my buttons.'

She was the only one I'd tolerate this nonsense with. If it was anyone else, I'd tell them to fuck off. But she'd given birth to me. Raised me. Biting my tongue had to be done sometimes.

'At least now I know why you weren't interested in the women I arranged for you.'

'Mum…' I warned. But she didn't listen.

'And isn't she Bella's age? She'll be too old to have children.'

I didn't give a fuck whether Melody could or couldn't have children. I doubted I wanted them now anyway.

Don't get me wrong. I loved kids. But all those late nights, feeding and changing nappies and all the millions of other responsibilities that came with raising a child looked like too much hard work.

Between my sisters and my mates, I'd have plenty of kids around me. Being a cool uncle sounded like it was more my thing. Hang out with the nieces, nephews and godchildren for a few fun hours, then hand them back to their parents afterwards.

'I'm not interested in having children with her. It was never about marriage and babies…'

'Good,' Mum jumped in before I even had a chance to finish my sentence.

For fuck's sake.

What I'd said was true, though. When I'd first hooked up with Melody, the whole commitment thing was one hundred per cent *not* on the cards. I had no interest in marriage or kids with her or anyone. But now, as much as I hated to admit it, I'd been thinking about whether I *could* do the relationship thing.

Every time those thoughts came into my head, I pushed them away, because of what had happened the last time I'd committed to someone. But maybe Carlos was right. Maybe I was finally ready to try again.

That was why I wanted to see Melody before I left. I looked at my watch. Shit. I should've left ten minutes ago.

'I didn't think Melody was your type.' Mum put her hands on her hips.

'She's not, but like I tell my clients, you can't keep doing the same thing and expect a different result. Sometimes it's good to change. Melody's great. A million times better than the women I've been with before. Dating *my type* isn't working for me anymore. I'm just not feeling it.'

'Well, you should've said! Then I would've—'

'No!' I shouted. 'Enough! Mum, I've spent the whole damn weekend asking you to butt out of this. I know you're doing it because you want a house full of grandkids, but I've told you before, count me out of that. I'm finding my own way. Making my own choices. Not every man or woman wants to procreate. Things are different these days, so just leave it, yeah? Look, I've gotta get to the airport. I'll see you in London, okay?'

Mum was rooted to the spot, her jaw open. I didn't have time to wait for her reply. I had a special lady to see and a flight to catch.

After kissing Mum on the cheek, I went into my room and did one final check before putting my charger in my suitcase and zipping it up.

I walked to the interconnecting door and knocked. I knew Melody was having breakfast with the girls, but there was still a chance she might've come back to her room by now.

Fuck. If she was there, she would've heard that conversation with my mum.

Then again, even if she did, it wouldn't be a big deal. She would've heard me bigging her up and telling my mum to butt out of my business, so it'd be cool.

I waited a few more seconds, then pushed the door open. The room was empty. She must still be with Cassie and the crew.

Once I'd wheeled my case out of my room and was in the hallway, I pulled out my phone to text Melody.

Me

Where you at?

Me

Wanna meet quickly before I catch my flight?

I thought about going up to Cassie's suite but then saw sense. There was no way I'd make my flight if I stepped foot in that room.

When I'd gone to say bye to Cassie earlier, not long after I'd left Melody, she was on a call, so just gave me a quick hug and said we'd speak later. I'd escaped the grilling then and last night during my chat with her and Nico, but I wasn't going to chance it again. Especially not when there was a pack of women there. They'd throw a million questions at me and I couldn't miss this flight.

Melody always had her phone glued to her hip, so by the time I'd checked out at reception, I could see her quickly to talk.

After handing over my key and saying bye to Nico and Carlos, I checked my phone again.

No reply. Strange.

My phone buzzed. I'd had two messages from the driver saying we had to leave now to get to the airport in time.

Fuck.

I dialled Melody's number. The phone rang out. So I tried one more time. Same.

The driver called again. Shit. I had to go.

I'd called and texted. She must be busy catching up with her girls, so I wasn't going to hound her down. It would've been good to talk today, but looked like it would have to wait.

This may have started as a holiday thing, but at least we lived in the same city, so it wasn't like it would be hard to see each other again.

The ball was in Melody's court now. If she wanted to continue things, she'd message back.

And I guessed if she didn't, then that was it.

I'd just have to wait and see what happened.

48

MELODY

As I walked to Gatwick train station, memories of when I was here with Nate flooded my brain.

It was nuts how much could change in a few short days. If someone had told me back then that I'd end up having non-stop nookie with him during that trip, I would've laughed and told them they needed their head tested. But yet, it'd happened. I had the photos to prove it.

I pulled the photo booth pics out of my purse and scolded myself.

So stupid.

Bella always said: *If someone tells you something, believe them.*

Nate had said from the start that he didn't want anything serious, so why was I so upset when I heard him telling his mum that we were just a bit of fun? He'd been honest from the beginning, which was more than I could say for most of the men I'd been with.

After taking the pastries to Cassie's suite, I'd pretended I was okay, listening to stories from Lily,

Cassie, Bella and Sophia about their amazing partners. I was happy for them, but it just reminded me that I'd never have that, which was hard. So I'd said I needed to pack and went to my room.

When I got there, I saw that Nate had messaged and called a couple of times. I couldn't lie. My heart jumped with excitement when I saw his texts. It meant he hadn't forgotten about me. But when I opened it, my heart sank again.

He hadn't messaged to say he'd changed his mind and wanted to give things a go back in London. He'd just asked where I was and if I wanted to meet. So basically, he wanted a quick shag before he left. That was all.

And if I hadn't overheard his conversation with his mum and forgotten my bloody phone, I probably would've run to him, opened my legs and let him fuck me like I always let men do. And I would've enjoyed it. At the time. But afterwards, I would've felt worthless. Just like I felt now.

I was tired. Tired of just accepting scraps that men wanted to throw at me. Tired of settling. Tired of just being the woman that men wanted to shag, but nothing more. Tired of feeling like I wasn't good enough to have a proper relationship like all my friends had.

I wanted more. Was that really too much to ask? Was I really that unlovable?

When would my time come? I'd hoped that I'd meet someone in my thirties. Now I was in my forties and still no Prince Charming. In six years, I'd be fifty. *Blimey.* Yeah, at least by then Andrea would be at uni or, knowing her, living with friends or a boyfriend, so I'd have more time to go out and enjoy myself. I wanted to keep having fun, but I didn't want to only be known as someone who was just there for a good time.

So as much as I liked Nate, and I *really* liked him, I wasn't going to reply. I wasn't going to become his booty call. I couldn't be the woman he thought was only good for a quick bang. Because we'd only spent a few days together and I'd already fallen for him. Hard.

If I spent any more time with him, I wouldn't recover. I might've thought I was okay with just sex before, but I wasn't now. And that was all he wanted from me. He'd said so himself. I'd heard it with my own ears.

Forgetting about him wouldn't be easy, but it had to be done. I didn't want to do anything as drastic as blocking him. He hadn't done anything wrong. But I knew I couldn't stand to see his profile photo or message every time I logged into WhatsApp, so I archived him. Just like I planned to do with the memories of the time we'd spent together.

What happened in France stayed in France.

Nate and I were in the past. And that was where all thoughts of him would be locked away, forever.

The sound of Andrea dumping her bag on the living room floor woke me up. I must've dozed off on the sofa. I didn't want to go to bed until I knew she'd got home safely, and all those late nights had caught up with me.

'Hi.' I squinted before turning on the lamp.

'Hey,' Andrea replied, her voice low and moody.

'How was your trip?'

'Alright.'

'Is that it? Just *alright*?'

'Yeah.'

Sometimes talking to Andrea was like getting blood out of a stone.

'Come here.' I stood up, my arms open wide. Andrea frowned before stepping into them cautiously, her hands still at her sides. I pulled her in for a hug. 'I missed you.' I kissed her head and I felt her body loosen a little. 'Even though we argue sometimes, it doesn't change the fact that I love you more than anything in the world.'

'Really?' She looked up at me.

'Yes, *really*! More than bread and all the pizza in the universe.'

'Now I *know* you're lying!' She laughed.

'It's true! You're the best thing that ever happened to me. And I need you to know that.' I squeezed her tighter and thankfully she didn't resist.

It was true. Having Andrea when I did might not have been what I'd planned, but I wouldn't be without her.

'Even though you didn't get to follow your dreams because you had to look after me?'

'Despite what you think, I'm still young… ish! I still have time to follow my dreams. I'm just doing things in a different order.'

'What do you mean?' She frowned.

'Well, some women have a career, then decide to have kids. Others have children and focus on raising them full-time. Others choose not to have any at all. There's no right or wrong way. Everyone has to do what's right for them and sometimes things don't turn out exactly how we think they will. Yeah, I had you earlier than planned, but now you're all grown up and strong and independent, there's no reason why I can't start following my dreams. And I'm going to. I'm blessed to have a daughter like you. And I want to show you that anything is possible. I'm so proud of you, darling.'

Andrea threw her arms around my waist and gave me a big squeeze, and my heart melted. Every time I thought she'd let go, she hugged me tighter and I did the same. If we kept going on like this, I might squeeze all of the air from her lungs.

'I'm sorry, Mum,' Andrea whispered.

'What for?' I stroked her hair. She pulled away gently. 'Come on.' I sat on the sofa and patted the space beside me. 'Sit. Talk to me. You can tell me anything and I promise I won't get upset.'

She looked as if she was debating whether or not to open up. I didn't say a word. I just sat and waited, hoping that she'd feel comfortable enough to get whatever it was off her chest.

Andrea opened her mouth, then closed it again. I wanted her to confide in me so badly, but I couldn't push her. I had to be patient.

'I… I'm sorry I didn't tell you, about, *y'know*. Taking the pill.' She looked at me, waiting for me to speak, but I kept my mouth shut. I knew she had more to say. 'It's just, I knew you'd freak out, if I told you I had a boyfriend and… I really liked him. But he was older. Not like, massively, just, y'know, eighteen. I knew he'd had sex with his other girlfriends and he told me he wanted us to and I wanted to be careful, y'know?'

'Yeah.' I nodded, trying to keep my blood pressure under control. I didn't like the sound of this boy already.

The fact that Andrea had said that he told her that he wanted them to do it didn't sit well with me.

'I know you think I don't realise, Mum, but I see how hard you work. I know it hasn't been easy trying to bring me up on your own, and no offence, I want to do things with my life. Like, travel and stuff, and I'm not ready to have a baby, so I thought, if I was gonna do it with him, I needed to be careful.'

My little baby girl. I'd really underestimated her. That was wrong. I should've known she wouldn't have taken something like this lightly.

'I'm sorry too.' I squeezed her hand. 'I shouldn't have shouted at you. You were sensible to take precautions. It was just that—I was shocked. I didn't know you were having sex and even though you're sixteen and becoming a woman, to me, you'll always be my baby.'

As those words fell from my mouth, my thoughts went to Nate again. I remembered that Janet had said the same thing about him when we'd arrived at the castle.

Nate had also said that I should be glad Andrea had taken precautions, and he was right.

'I know, Mum.' The corner of her mouth twitched. 'And I know you probably spent the whole weekend worrying that you were gonna come back to London and be a granny, but you don't need to. I didn't do anything with him. I told him I wasn't ready.'

It felt like a ten-tonne weight had been lifted from my shoulders. I wanted to race down the street screaming, *My daughter didn't have sex!* But instead, I just blew out a breath. Like Nate had said, it was inevitable. It hadn't happened this weekend, but it was only a matter of time. I just had to hope that when it did, Andrea was still mature enough to take precautions.

Pff. That was rich coming from me. I was a grown woman and knew full well what could happen when you did the naked dance without a raincoat. Yet I'd jumped on Nate's cock without protection. And if that wasn't dumb enough, I'd let him come inside me. What a bloody idiot.

In the cold light of day it was hard to justify my actions. At the time, I was so caught up in the moment and believed we had deep feelings for each other. That I was special to him. Which was exactly what had happened with Rodney. After all these years, I still hadn't learned my lesson.

What right did I have to lecture Andrea on taking precautions if I hadn't even practised what I preached? I hoped to God that I wouldn't have a permanent souvenir of our night together. My period was due in a couple of weeks and I was already shitting myself. It felt like I had to wait an eternity to find out.

'I'm glad you didn't jump into it, love, if you didn't feel ready. You should never feel pressured.'

'I know. I remembered you telling me that. He wasn't happy, though, so he broke up with me. When you called that morning, he'd just left. So I was upset. That's why I put the phone down.'

When Rodney had said the boy had left, I hadn't believed him. But I was relieved that for once he'd told the truth.

'Oh, love.' I pulled her into me and she rested her head on my shoulder. 'He didn't deserve you. You'll know when the time is right and when it is, if you need anything

—condoms, advice or just someone to talk to—I'm here. And I promise to try and not make it weird.'

'Thanks, Mum. And how about you? Did you enjoy the wedding? Did you meet anyone *special*?' She sat up and smiled.

'I had a good time, thanks. And, well, I did meet someone, but it wasn't meant to be.'

My heart sank. I knew she'd like having a decent father figure in her life. I saw how excited she was whenever her poor excuse for a dad showed an interest in her. But I also saw how disappointed she got when he let her down. Which was often.

Even though it was awkward for a child to think of their parents meeting someone new, I also knew Andrea would like me to find someone. She wanted me to be happy. Hopefully I'd find that companionship one day. Until, then, I'd focus on creating my own happiness.

'Sorry to hear that. But it'll happen soon. I can feel it in my waters.'

'*In your waters?*' I laughed.

'That's what Aunty Bella says all the time.'

'Yeah, she does!'

It was good that Andrea felt optimistic, so I didn't burst her bubble by telling her that I'd been *feeling things in my waters* for years about finding a decent man and nothing had ever happened.

I didn't want to tell her that finding *the one* only happened to the lucky few. But one thing I *did* want to do was show her that even if you didn't meet a Prince Charming, it didn't mean you'd be unhappy. So I decided that tomorrow I was going to get back to pursuing my dreams.

I was going to start making my jewellery again. For me. And for Andrea.

Instead of holding me back, my daughter had inspired me to succeed. To set an example. She'd made me proud of her and now I wanted her to be proud of me.

I was starting afresh. No more chasing men who didn't deserve me. No more staying in a shitty job I didn't enjoy and doing nothing about it. No more dieting and trying to look how I thought people or men wanted me to.

It was time to be me. It'd taken a long time to get to this point, but I was finally ready to start being my true, authentic self.

49

———

NATE

'Hold for ten more seconds. That's right. Keep that leg straight,' I said, towering over my client as she lay on the mat, doing a hamstring stretch.

I rubbed my eyes. Thank fuck we were almost done. I was knackered.

Luckily, Maddie was one of my regulars, so she knew not to take it personally when I started yawning during our session.

I hadn't slept properly again last night. Not even doing my crosswords helped, which was bad. It'd been the third night in a row that I'd tossed and turned. I was off my game.

Normally when I was tired on the job it was because a client had requested me at short notice and I was jet-lagged from flying to see them.

And it wasn't because I'd been out partying. I didn't do that if I had work the next day. Right now, raving was the last thing I wanted.

The truth was, I knew exactly why I wasn't sleeping. It

was because of Melody. I hadn't felt right since I'd left that damn chateau without speaking to her.

As soon as I'd got in the car, I noticed it. The journey to the airport was so fucking boring. No laughter, no banter, no fun.

I'd thought back to our first journey to the chateau and how much I'd enjoyed it. My cheeks and stomach hurt from the jokes me and Mel had caught. Even though I was pissed she'd beaten me so many times at cards, I secretly liked it. She challenged me. Made me want to be better. And, yeah, there were the sexy times too. My dick had been so hard around her. But these days it'd gone into mourning. It was limper than a rotten lettuce leaf.

I thought I'd feel better once I was home, back in familiar surroundings, but if anything it was worse. When I'd gone to bed that night, it felt bigger than I'd remembered. Emptier. And the smell wasn't right.

The sheets were clean. But as my head hit the pillow, it was washing powder that I smelt, not coconut and sherbet like Melody's scent.

Even though the temperature was warm, the bed felt cold. I couldn't believe I was thinking it, but I missed cuddling. I missed the heat from Melody's body. The feel of her soft skin next to mine.

I didn't know what the fuck was wrong with me.

We'd only slept in the same bed for a few nights. So how was it possible to get some kind of separation anxiety that quickly? It made no damn sense.

'That's it. You're done. Good work today.'

'Thanks. So, we're going to Lisbon this weekend. You free to come?'

'This weekend?' I repeated, buying myself some time.

I knew I wasn't working because a client had already asked me yesterday if I could train them and I'd checked before turning them down. 'Sorry, I can't. When are you back in London?'

'Not for another week.'

The reason I'd turned down the job was because I was hoping that if Melody got back to me this week, we could meet up this weekend. And if I was travelling, there'd be no way I could see her.

This was crazy.

Before I'd left for France, I'd said I wanted to get back to doing more travelling for work. And I'd always promised myself I'd never let pussy come before my career again.

But I knew Melody wasn't just *pussy*. I didn't care if we fucked or not. I just wanted to be near her. Fuck. I didn't like where my head was at. Or where this was going. I needed to sort my shit out.

'If anything changes, I can let you know, okay?'

'Okay. I'm going in the shower. You should go home and get some sleep. You don't seem right today.'

No shit.

'Yeah, thanks. I'm gonna head off. Say hi to Darnell and the kids.'

'Will do. Take care of yourself, Nate.' Maddie patted my shoulder before leaving her home gym and disappearing down the grand hallway.

She was right. Sleep was what I needed. I didn't have any more clients for today, so I'd just go home and rest.

Hopefully by tomorrow, everything would feel better.

Pushing my hand out of the bedsheet, I reached to the bedside table and picked up my phone. I scanned the messages that had come in overnight. Two from Carlos and several from different women who were still texting despite the fact I'd politely told them I wasn't interested. But there was still nothing from Melody.

I'd caved last night and sent her another text. Just a 'Hey, what's up?'. I was trying to keep it light, but it ended up sounding lame. Maybe that was why she hadn't replied.

Fuck. I couldn't remember the last time I'd obsessed about checking my phone or waited for a woman to reply. Normally *they* were the ones hounding *me*. This sucked.

What did I expect, though? I was the one who'd said it was temporary, so I couldn't be mad that Melody was just doing what we'd both agreed.

It was *me* who was stupid enough to catch feelings.

Yeah. That's right. I liked her. A *lot*.

The bed still felt empty. Just like it had yesterday and the day before that. Like every fucking day since I'd left France. Somehow I needed to forget about her, just like she'd forgotten about me.

I opened Carlos's message and my mood lifted. He was back in London and wanted to know if I fancied meeting. The sooner the better.

Me

Hell, yeah. You free for breakfast?

'So, how are things with Melody?' Carlos pulled up a chair at my breakfast bar. I wasn't expecting him to be awake and free to come over, but I was glad he was.

'There are no *things* with Melody.' I shrugged my shoulders. Meeting Carlos was supposed to be a distraction from thinking about her.

I couldn't blame him, though. We hadn't really spoken about what had happened on the wedding night, so it had to come up sooner or later. I would've just preferred if it was later. Like in the year 3000.

'What do you mean?' Carlos frowned.

'It was casual. We were just fucking whilst we were at the wedding.'

Carlos laughed.

'*Si tú lo dices.*'

'What? It's true!' I raised my voice, convincing no one.

'You remember that I was the DJ at the wedding, *sí*?'

'What kind of dumb question is that? Of course I know you were DJing there!'

'*Hombre*, I had to check because it seems like you have forgotten that I was standing on the stage for most of the night. I had the perfect view of the dance floor and everyone who was on it. Including you and Melody. And the two of you did not look like people who were *just fucking*. It is true that there was a lot of sexual chemistry. But there were enough lights shining for me to see the way that you looked at her when you danced together and when she danced by herself. And how sad you were when she left your side even for a few minutes. *Amigo*, that was more than just sex.'

'Shut up!'

'Why? You do not want to hear the truth?'

'I can't go there again, man. You saw what happened last time.'

'Melody is not Gigi. Just because she hurt you, it does

not mean Melody will. She is into you. Like, *really* into you. I saw the way she looked at you too. And Lily told me.'

'Melody spoke to Lily about us?' I sat up straighter. I'd wanted to ask my sisters if they'd heard from her, but it was too awkward. Exactly why I always thought it wasn't a good idea to get involved with people we all knew. 'What did she say?'

'So you admit there is an *us*.' Carlos smirked.

He'd been right all along about me having feelings for Melody and being worried about getting hurt and he knew it.

After the stick I'd given him about dating Lily when I'd first found out, something told me he liked the fact that the tables were turned and now I was the one squirming.

'Just answer the damn question.'

'*Sí*. Melody spoke to Lily about you. I told you. She likes you. They all spoke about what had happened that morning during breakfast.'

'And after that? What has she said about me since then?'

Jesus. I hadn't had to worry about whether a woman was into me or not for years. They came and went and that suited me just fine. But now I was hanging onto Carlos's every word. Hoping and praying that he'd throw me a little crumb. Give me a sign that Melody was still interested.

So fucking pathetic.

'I have no idea. We only returned from Madrid yesterday, so I do not think that Lily and Melody have spoken much since then. If you want to know what Melody thinks, you should ask her.'

'Don't you think I've tried? I messaged and called

when I was leaving. And again last night, and she hasn't replied. We agreed at the beginning that it was just casual, so looks like that's it.'

'You say that you have tried. Try harder.'

'I don't know, man. What more can I do?' I huffed.

'Think about something she likes. Something that is important to her. You say that in the beginning it was just about sex. So do something that will show her that you are interested in more than that. With Lily, I knew she liked her cheesy pop music, so I thought of something related to that. What could you do that Melody would love?'

This was tough. If I ever wanted to woo a woman, usually turning on the charm or pleasing her in the sack was enough. If I really wanted to push the boat out, then flowers or taking them somewhere expensive to eat would have them swooning in seconds. But although Melody would probably love that shit too, I wasn't sure that just doing that would be enough. I needed to bring my A game. Prove to her that I was serious.

My brain whirred as I tried to think of ideas. Then it hit me.

Yeah. That could work.

'I've got it. I know what to do. But I'm gonna need help.'

'Whatever you need. I will never forget what you did to bring me and Lily together. And I want to see you happy like us. I am proud of you.' He patted my back. 'You are finally settling down.'

Shit. I really was doing this.

I was going to tell Melody how I felt.

And I was man enough to admit that I was fucking terrified.

50

———

MELODY

'Right, I'm off.' I switched off my mouse and checked the computer was turned off before getting up from my desk. 'Have a good weekend.'

It'd been another monotonous week at work, but for once, it didn't bother me too much. Not just because I had two whole days away from this place. It was because I had my eye on bigger things.

For the past week I'd been working hard on my jewellery. The day after my chat with Andrea, I'd gone online and ordered a load of supplies. And even though next-day delivery cost more, I went for it. After all, it was an investment in my future, and after procrastinating for so long, I didn't want to wait to get started.

When it'd arrived, I'd stayed up late into the night working on a gold necklace with a matching gold pendant in the shape of a pizza slice dangling from it. I'd decided I wanted to make cool jewellery that reflected people's personalities, and loads of people loved food. I knew I did. So since then, I'd be working on different designs.

There was also the cupcake collection and chocoholic collection.

It'd take a while to get everything done right, especially as I'd had to work at a friend's workshop to create the pendants because I didn't have all the equipment at home, but the important thing was that I'd started.

As well as Andrea's conversation inspiring me, seeing the photos from the wedding that Cassie had sent over a few days after I got back to London also encouraged me.

The photos that Sophia had asked the photographer to take of my designs were beautiful. I'd never looked at my stuff objectively before, but now, with my newfound motivation and positive outlook, I was able to see that I *did* have talent. And I was going to make a go of this. Properly this time.

After getting the bus home, I put down my handbag, washed my hands, headed to my jewellery bench and pulled out some beads, beading wire, crimp beads, a clasp, pliers and scissors.

Lily had asked me to make a necklace for Carlos's aunt, so tonight I'd be focusing on that. I'd already measured the length, so was able to get stuck in faster. I used the pliers to attach the clasp to one end of the wire, then threaded a crimp bead onto it, followed by a jump ring that I'd attach to the clasp. Next I used pliers to crimp the bead in place, securing the clasp and jump ring together.

'Hi, Mum!' Andrea poked her head into the living room. 'How was work?'

'Crap as usual, but y'know.'

'You won't have to be there for much longer! Soon your jewellery's gonna take off. I can feel it in my waters.'

'You really love that phrase, don't you?' I laughed as I began stringing the beads onto the wire.

'Yeah, it's funny.'

'Maybe I'll make a necklace with that on it.' That actually wasn't a bad idea. I could do slogan necklaces, like 'Boss Girl' or 'Badass'. I was sure lots of people would want to wear those.

Saying the word *badass* made me think of Nate. Again. It was probably easier to say when I *wasn't* thinking about him than when I was, because it was constant.

When I went to bed, I missed having his big strong arms wrapped around me. I missed his scent. I missed his laugh. I missed his smile. I missed the way he looked at me. Like he was in awe. Like I really was *badass*.

I missed the way he encouraged me. Even when we hadn't completely stopped hating each other, he'd encouraged me to pursue my jewellery making. I wondered what he'd say if he knew what I'd been working on. Actually, I didn't need to wonder. He'd be happy and say he knew I could do it.

My heart fluttered. Nate was a good guy. He'd make some lucky woman very happy one day. It was just a shame that it wouldn't be me.

I almost messaged him the other day. I missed talking with him. And, yeah, I missed the sex, but I was going to go without that for a while. If I was serious about making a go of my business, I needed a clear head.

Nate had ruined sex for me. I couldn't even think about going back to using my vibrator after being with him.

And I had zero interest in watching porn. That had nothing on the kind of things Nate and I had got up to that weekend. Watching other people at it wasn't going to cut the mustard anymore. It was like spending a weekend dining at a fancy Michelin-starred restaurant and then going back to eating beans on toast. There was no comparison. And coming from someone who loves toast with *everything*, that was saying a lot.

Speaking of toast, I wasn't starving myself anymore. I'd been eating healthily. Enjoying what I liked, but in moderation. I'd also been getting off the bus a few stops earlier and walking the rest of the way home. I'd kept up my legs, bums and tums class. I reckoned it'd been working, but I wasn't being kind enough to myself to see it. As we got older, our bodies changed and that was okay. Being fit and healthy was the important thing. And even though it was early days, I was feeling better than ever.

Despite feeling better inside and out, I still had no intention of getting back on the dating apps. Again, I knew no one could compare to Nate. Even putting aside his looks and his shagging prowess, I'd never been with a man who'd made me laugh as much as he had during those few days. Who'd encouraged me, who'd made me feel like I had something to offer the world. That I was enough.

Yeah, I wasn't enough for Nate to want a relationship with, but for once, I knew that was on him, not on me. He clearly had his own shit going on. Reasons why he didn't want to commit that had sod all to do with me. And that was fine. I was slowly learning that everything bad that men did wasn't always because of something I didn't have. Nate was just an eternal playboy. Not all men could be changed.

One day, I'd find a partner. I had to believe that. But for now, I was happy trying to be a good mother and role model for Andrea, focusing on my future and building my career.

'Yes!' Andrea shouted. 'Could you really make that?'

'I think so! I'd have to probably have to use Vi's workshop again because I don't have the right equipment here, but I'm sure there's a way.'

'That would be so cool!' Andrea looked like all of her Christmases had come at once. 'Do you want me to help you again?'

'Have you tidied your room yet?' I raised my eyebrow.

'Yes, Mum.' She rolled her eyes.

'Well, in that case, I'd love that!' I beamed.

That was another thing that'd been great about these past couple of weeks. Instead of being glued to her phone screen or the TV or locked in her bedroom, Andrea had been spending more time with me and offering to help with my jewellery. Just simple things, like last night she'd helped me to measure the length of the necklace to make sure it fit comfortably. Or sometimes she'd hand me the pliers or get the bits and bobs I needed from my little ziplock bags. It'd been so lovely.

Sounds crazy now, but I was glad that I'd found that pill packet in her bedroom. Since we'd had that talk, it'd brought us closer together. Now I really felt that if she got another boyfriend or was thinking about having sex, she'd talk to me about it. That was a breakthrough in my book.

So yeah, even though the romantic side of my life hadn't turned out how I'd hoped, my relationship with Andrea and my career were blossoming.

Which reminded me. Tomorrow I definitely needed to contact Cassie about getting Sophia's number so that I could sort out a website. She'd said she knew someone who could help and I didn't know the first thing about building an online shop, so I needed all the support I could get.

Then once I'd finished my collections, I'd make a list of some shops to contact. See if they were interested in stocking my designs. I'd try putting some stuff on Etsy again and those kinds of sites too. If I was going to make a go of this, I really needed to be in as many places as possible.

My phone chimed. It was still in my bag. I'd been so excited to get back to working on my designs that I hadn't even bothered to take it out of my bag. Or get a drink and something to eat.

'Want me to get that for you?' Andrea said.

'Can do.' I shrugged my shoulders. I wasn't fussed. I'd unarchived Nate last week, so I knew he'd messaged a few times, but I hadn't replied, so I doubted he'd message again. My stomach twisted.

I needed to contact him, though. To sort out the money for the taxis and my Eurostar ticket. And—oh shit! That reminded me, I hadn't thanked Nico for the dress. I'd do that right now before I forgot again.

So yeah, back to Nate. I needed to arrange some sort of payment plan. Money was tighter than ever after I'd maxed out my credit card paying for the jewellery materials, but I'd promised to pay him back so I would. Even if it was only ten pounds a week, I'd make sure I gave him every last penny.

'It's from an international number.' Andrea looked at the screen.

'What, there's no name?'

'No. Just a number. They said it was nice to meet you

at the wedding, but I can't see the rest of the message unless I go into your WhatsApp.'

'I'll take that, thank you!' I grabbed the phone from her hand. I had no idea who it could be because I'd met loads of people at Cassie's wedding.

I know I said earlier that Andrea and I had grown closer, but not close enough that I wanted her reading my messages.

'Ooh, is this that person you said you met but it didn't work out?'

'No!' I said immediately. Nate's name was saved with his number, so even if he was abroad, his name would show up. It definitely wasn't him.

I was desperate to see who it was from, but first, I needed to message Nico.

Me

Bonjour! Hope you're enjoying your honeymoon!

Me

I forgot to say thank you so much for the dress you paid for—for the rehearsal dinner. Nate told me.

That was really kind of you.

Thanks again for everything and tell Cassie I'll message her later x

There. I'd wanted to thank him a million times but it kept slipping my mind.

I clicked on Nate's message and went to reply. I didn't know what to say. I knew what I *wanted* to say. That I missed him. That I wanted to see him. To hold him. To inhale his gorgeous scent.

To tell him how I felt.

Me

Hey, how are you? I miss you. Want to meet?

I paused, my finger hovering over the send button.

Press it. Go on. Do it.

I clicked the delete button and erased the message.

Maybe I should write something about owing him the money first.

No.

Ever since I'd got back, I'd wanted to ask my friends about what to do, but Cassie was still on her honeymoon and still suffering from morning sickness, Lily and Carlos had been travelling a lot, and I knew what Bella would say: he told you what he wanted from the beginning, so believe him.

I'd bent my friends' ears too many times about doomed hook-ups that I hoped would become relationships. And they'd already warned me about Nate, so I had to work this out for myself.

Then again, Bella had also said that if I was still thinking about Nate a lot, then we might have a chance. Every day I missed him so much my chest hurt. But it had to be mutual, so…

Oh God. My brain was like a bowl of spaghetti: tangled and messy. I needed to think. I didn't want to mess things up by saying the wrong thing.

In the meantime, I'd open this mystery message…

+ 33 1 21 34 76 12

Hello, Melody,

It was very nice to meet you at Nico's wedding.

Cassie gave me some of your jewellery and I have

spoken to the buying team at our store and they are interested in seeing more samples of your designs.

I am currently in London. Would it be possible to meet later tonight to get something to take back to Paris?

Toby

What? Cassie gave him samples? When?

OMG. OMG. OMG.

His store is interested in my designs.

Wow. This could be major!

My brain whirred, a million questions racing through it.

'So?' Andrea asked.

'What is it?'

'It's from a guy I met at the wedding!'

'I knew it!' She smiled. 'It's the man you were talking about.'

'No! It's not like that, it's…' I paused.

It wasn't like that, was it? He'd wanted more from me at the wedding and I'd declined. And now he wanted to meet *later* tonight. It was already fast approaching eight in the evening, so how late exactly was he talking?

How did I know he wasn't trying to take advantage and use me for a quick shag whilst he was in London? It wouldn't be the first time a bloke had tried to take advantage of me.

But, what if it was genuine? I'd kick myself if I didn't at least try and find out. This could be a big deal for me. I couldn't afford to turn it down.

Me

Hi, Toby, nice to hear from you. I'd love to give you

some samples. I'm afraid I'm busy tonight, though. When are you going back to Paris? Maybe we could meet tomorrow morning instead?

Let me know.

There. Done.

If he wanted to meet later, I doubted he could be going back to Paris tonight, so he must still be around tomorrow morning.

I'd wait to hear what he said. If he insisted on meeting this evening, I'd do it, but I'd keep Andrea with me. I didn't want to give him the wrong idea.

Typing... appeared on the screen and a flutter of excitement raced through me.

+ 33 1 21 34 76 12

Thank you for your reply.

Tomorrow morning is fine. I am flying from Gatwick. I remember that you said you lived in South London. Is that near the airport? Perhaps I can come early. On my way to the airport. Around eight in the morning. Is this okay?

Toby

Oh. I hadn't thought he'd want to come to my flat. It wasn't fit for visitors.

Fuck it. This was me. This was where I lived. It was never going to compare to a millionaire's mansion like he probably had, but it was home.

Normally I'd suggest we meet somewhere away from home first, but now that I thought about it, he knew Nico. So if he put one foot out of line, I'd call Cassie. Nico was influential, so it wouldn't make sense for Toby to risk getting up to any funny business. It was fine.

I sent Toby my address and then exhaled.

Things really felt like they were finally coming together. I'd tried doing my jewellery business so many times. But now, it felt different.

I had a feeling that tomorrow was going to be the start of something.

I was on the cusp of my life changing forever.

And I couldn't bloody wait.

51

NATE

Today was the day.

I was ready.

I'd spent the whole week preparing. Now it was time to put everything into action.

For whatever reason, Melody hadn't replied to my messages. But like Carlos had said, I couldn't give up that easily. What was that saying? *If the mountain won't come to Muhammad, Muhammad must go to the mountain.*

There were several parts of my plan. Most of them I'd put in place tonight, if Melody accepted my invitation.

I wanted to take her out on a date. Do things properly. Start from the beginning. Not fucking. *Courting.* Taking her out, wooing her. The sex stuff could come whenever she was ready. I didn't give a shit about that. I just needed to be with her.

It had been almost two weeks since I'd seen Melody and my chest ached constantly. As corny as it sounded, I felt like my fucking heart had been cut out.

The only way to fix the empty hole in my chest where

my heart used to be was to go and see her. I'd look her in the eye and ask once and for all if she wanted more. If she wanted to make a go of things.

After another sleepless night, I had two choices. Lie here in bed tossing and turning and thinking about her, or get my arse up and go to her.

I looked at the clock. It was just after seven. If I was quick, I could get there by eightish. I'd bring her breakfast. Yeah. She'd like that. Croissants and some French bread. The stuff that I knew she'd enjoy.

Once I'd showered, I got dressed and went to the bakery before ordering a cab. I still remembered the name of her road. I didn't know the number, but I'd know the building her flat was part of when I saw it. Once I was there I'd call her.

'Excuse me, mate,' I called out to the driver. 'Any chance you can put the air con on?'

I was burning up. I pulled out a tissue and wiped my forehead. It wasn't even that hot. I was sweating because I was nervous.

This was fucking insane.

The last time I was nervous about talking to a girl was probably when I was a teenager. Since then, I'd loved the challenge of approaching women. Chatting them up. Getting their number. It was like sport to me. But this was different.

This time there was a real chance of failure. Of rejection. Melody could say she wanted nothing more to do with me. And I couldn't blame her.

I'd asked Carlos again a few days ago if Lily had mentioned Melody speaking about me, but he said there was no news. Melody had been busy, so hadn't had time to chat. Busy doing what, I wondered.

'Whereabouts is it?' the driver called out.

'I'll let you know.'

I scanned the road from left to right. Pretty sure it was a bright-coloured door. That was so Melody. Living in a place with bold decor. I didn't think I'd ever seen that woman wear black or grey. Everything about her was so vibrant. I couldn't wait to see her.

Shit. Maybe I should call first. She might not want Andrea seeing me. I had to remember it wasn't just her. They were a package deal.

I'd met Andrea briefly before, though, and she seemed cool. If being part of Andrea's life was what I needed to do to be with Melody, I was ready.

There it is.

I recognised the orange door.

But, wait.

There was a big fancy car parked outside. Couldn't tell whether it was a Rolls-Royce or a Bentley, but it obviously belonged to someone rich.

It was strange for a car like that to be in a neighbourhood like this. That car probably cost more than some of these flats.

An ache filled my chest.

But just because it was outside Melody's flat, that didn't mean that the person who owned it was in her building. They could be next door.

'Pull over here, please.' I slid the box of pastries back on the seat and moved closer towards the window.

The driver pulled over opposite Melody's building and just as he did, the door opened.

A tall dark-haired guy stepped out, tucking his shirt into the back of his trousers, and then Melody joined him on the doorstep.

WTF.

Wait. I recognised him. That was the French dude from the wedding. The one she'd sat with at dinner that first night. The one that wouldn't stop fucking looking at her.

What the hell was he doing leaving her flat at eight on a Saturday morning, not properly dressed?

I wasn't an idiot. It was obvious. They were fucking.

Just in case I didn't already get the memo, Melody leant forward and threw her arms around him.

Everything started spinning around me, like I was trapped in a cyclone.

Everything ached. My head, my chest and my gut.

It'd happened again.

This was just like last time.

Melody had chosen a more powerful, richer man instead of me.

I'd come here to find out if she wanted more. And now I knew she didn't.

I might have caught feelings, but it really was just a fling for her.

Melody didn't want to pursue anything with me because she'd already chosen the French guy. That was why she'd been *busy*.

Message received loud and clear.

52

MELODY

Yes! I stepped out of my front door to say bye to Toby. I was so happy I could dance.

Things had gone better than I'd hoped. I hadn't bothered dragging Andrea out of bed. I knew how much teenagers needed their sleep and I was confident it would be fine with Toby—and I was right. He hadn't tried it on. In fact, as soon as he'd arrived about twenty minutes ago, he'd said he couldn't stay long because he needed to get to the airport.

I already had some of my best designs laid out on the coffee table in the living room, so I was able to show him everything straight away.

As well as complimenting the colourful decor in my flat, which took me by surprise, he was enthusiastic about my pieces.

'These look very good,' he'd said, making a beeline for the love hearts collection. 'I will only take a few things. Cassie has also sent me some photographs of the jewellery taken at the wedding. And she told me you made the headpiece that she wore. This should be enough.'

'I'd be happy to send your buying team whatever they'd like to see.'

'*Merci*. That will be helpful. I really must go now. But first, can I use your bathroom? It was a long drive here from Mayfair.'

'Course!' I'd said. 'It's just at the end of the hallway.'

Toby had gone to the loo, but as he walked to the front door and opened it to leave, I'd told him that he hadn't tucked his shirt back in his trousers properly.

He turned to face me, his cheeks flushed with embarrassment, and quickly tucked it in.

'I was rushing!' he laughed. I didn't bother to check whether he'd forgotten to do his flies up. That'd be inappropriate. He'd know soon enough, though, if he felt a draught between his legs.

'It happens to us all!' I smiled, remembering a drunken night at uni when I'd tucked my skirt into my knickers. Thank God Bella had noticed before the rest of the pub did.

'I will be in touch, when I have news. It may take a few weeks.'

'Okay. And thank you!' I threw my arms around him. It was probably too much, but I was happy. Although nothing was guaranteed, there was a chance of having my products stocked in an actual department store. In Paris! That would be a dream.

'I have not done anything yet, but I hope that I can help. Your designs are exactly the kind of thing the buyers would like as part of the emerging designers pop-up in our store. Enjoy the rest of your weekend.'

'You too!' I waved him off as he climbed into the flashy car that was parked in front of the building, then drove off.

I was just about to head inside when I spotted a silver Prius pull up opposite. I thought I'd spotted a similar one a few minutes ago. When I looked closer, I saw there was a guy at the back looking out of the window.

Wait.

Was that…?

It couldn't be, could it?

The car pulled into the space that Toby had just left and my mouth dropped when the passenger stepped out.

My eyes weren't deceiving me.

Stood in front of my building was *him*.

Nate was here.

OMG.

53

———

NATE

Nah.

I wasn't going out like that.

I wasn't gonna let history repeat itself.

I'd got as far as the end of Melody's road before I'd asked the driver to turn back.

I wasn't some pussy who was gonna go home and feel sorry for himself and sit there for hours drinking, wondering what had gone wrong. I had to man up and confront the situation head on. I'd speak to Melody. I wanted her to look me in the eyes and tell me she hadn't been suffering like I had these past couple of weeks.

The only way I'd believe it was if I heard her say it.

I didn't give a fuck if that French guy was still there. There was no way I was giving up so easily. I'd come to fight for Melody and tell her how I felt and I wasn't leaving until I'd done that.

The flash car had gone. *Good.* That'd make things less awkward: for *him.*

As soon as the cabbie pulled into the empty space, I jumped out.

Melody was still at the door and she looked so fucking beautiful.

Her hair was tossed up in a bun and she was wearing that beautiful fire-engine-red lipstick that I loved so much.

I liked the dress she was wearing too. It clung to her curves and it took everything I had not to run over and pull her into me.

Melody's eyes almost flew from their sockets when she spotted me.

'N-Nate?' she said before laughing. 'Okay, before you say it, I know it's you. I'm just shocked. Thought I'd say that before you accused me of stating the obvious again!' she cackled, and it was like a brand-new heart started growing in my chest.

Damn, I'd missed that laugh. I'd missed everything about her.

I stepped forward in a daze.

'I brought you breakfast. I was hoping we could talk.'

'I'd like that,' she said quickly and my chest almost exploded with happiness. She wanted to talk. That was a relief. 'There's a little park across the road. We can sit there. Andrea's upstairs and even though she's still sleeping, I wouldn't put it past her to wake up and eavesdrop.'

'Cool.' I nodded.

'I'll just get my jacket and put on some shoes.'

I glanced down and looked at her slippers. They were giant fluffy yellow ones. *So Melody.* I fucking loved them.

We walked across to the park in silence. I looked at her and went to speak but then clammed up. It was crazy. Since I'd left France I'd wanted to talk to her. I'd dreamt about it, replayed this scene a million times in my head, but now I was here I didn't know what to say.

Actually, scrap that. I knew what I wanted to say but didn't know *how* to without fucking up. This was important. The words had to come out right.

From the corner of my eye I saw Melody look at me and then look away. I had so many questions.

I was desperate to know what she was thinking and if she felt the same. And I wanted to know what that damn rich guy was doing leaving her house this morning. But I had to be patient. I'd find out soon enough.

'Let's sit over here.' She pointed to a bench. I followed her lead.

There was a playground in the centre of the grass and a mother was pushing her kid on the swings.

We sat down and I rested the pastries on my lap.

'So, what did you bring?' She signalled to the box.

'Er, croissants and some pastries.' I opened it up to show her.

'Oh my God! This looks amazing! Thanks. I'm bloody starving!'

'And I got a baguette. I know how much you like bread. But I guess you can't eat that here. I didn't bring any butter or jam.'

'I'll eat bread any way it comes! With or without butter, I don't care. Give it here.' She held her hand out and I put the baguette in her palm.

Melody wasted no time biting into the end of the baguette.

As I watched her devour the bread, crumbs dropping on her lap, I laughed. That was so Melody. She didn't give a fuck about smudging her lipstick. She was too busy enjoying her food and it was so damn refreshing.

It'd be easy to just sit and watch her. Get lost in her chocolate-brown eyes, salivate over the curve of her lips, the way the tendrils of hair fell around her face. But I had to keep the objective of coming here in mind.

Melody was acting like everything was normal and avoiding the elephant in the room. One of us had to step up and say what needed to be said. No matter how hard it was.

'So…' I turned to face her. 'You didn't reply to my messages…'

Melody's face froze and she put the baguette down on her lap and wiped her mouth with the back of her hand.

'Sorry. I-I was going to. I even wrote out a reply yesterday, but… I knew what you wanted and you couldn't give me what I needed, so I thought it was best to just not speak anymore.'

'What did you *think* I wanted?' I frowned.

'Sex, obviously. And it's okay. I know that's what we agreed, but…'

'No!' I put my hands on hers. 'You're wrong. That wasn't why I was messaging at all.'

'*Yeah, right!*' She rolled her eyes. 'We both know you don't do relationships. And I heard you. I heard what you said.'

'What I said? Said to who?'

'Your mum.'

'You were in the bedroom? But I checked and I didn't see you.'

'So you wanted to make sure I didn't hear the truth?'

'No! It wasn't like that. I was coming to find you and

my mum was already at my door waiting for me and when I finished, I came to your room to say goodbye, properly. And to talk. But you weren't there. And that's why I called and messaged—to speak to you.'

'What, to repeat what I'd already heard you say to your mum? That you had no interest in having children or anything serious with me? That I was just a bit of fun? Nothing I haven't heard before.' Her gaze fell to the floor.

'I need to tell you something.'

This was gonna be hard, but it was the only way. I hadn't spoken about this for years. And only two other people from my circle knew about it. But I had to make Melody understand.

'What is it?'

I exhaled. A sharp pain flashed in my chest and my pulse raced.

Melody reached over and put her hand on mine. The softness of her palm was like magic. My heart rate slowed almost instantly.

I can do this. It'll be okay.

'It… it was when I lived in America.' My eyes dropped to my trainers. It was too hard to look at Melody. 'It wasn't long after I started doing personal training there. I met a woman. She was one of my clients. An actress. She was pretty and sweet. I knew I shouldn't date someone I worked with, but I liked her. She had a kid, but it didn't put me off. Soon we were spending every day together. I grew closer and closer to them both. A month later, they both moved in with me. I loved her kid like she was my own. Kerrie was only six. I cut back my shifts so that I could take care of her and Gigi could go to more auditions. I took Kerrie to school, I picked her up. I would've done anything for her. For either of them. We were a family.'

Fuck. I pictured Kerrie's face. She was the cutest little girl I'd ever seen. She always loved wearing her thick brown hair in two ponytails. I even used to style it for her. She'd sit on the corner of the bed every morning and say 'Natey! I'm ready!' The way she said my name was adorable.

After combing her hair, I'd make a neat parting down the middle, always doing my best to make sure it was straight and even on both sides, before scooping her hair into two ponytails using her favourite pink hairbands.

The pain in my chest returned. Talking about this shit was hard.

'It's okay,' Melody said softly. 'Go on.'

I squeezed my eyes shut before inhaling and exhaling loudly. The sooner I continued, the sooner reliving this nightmare would be over.

'So, yeah. Life was good. Or so I thought. I was so happy I didn't even notice when she kept going out more and more and coming back later and later. Being an actress in LA isn't easy. You have to go to audition after audition. It's super competitive. And I wanted her to succeed and I was her man, so it was my job to support her. To be there for her. So I didn't question her. I just thought she was working hard to land a big role, y'know?'

'Sounds like you were a diamond.'

'I tried. Even though I knew it was important to build up my clients because I was starting out, I reduced my hours at the gym even more. I cooked, I cleaned... I fucking worshipped her. I even...'

Did I really need to tell Melody this part? It was so

fucking embarrassing. Even today, seven years later, I couldn't believe I was so dumb.

'You can tell me.' Melody gave my hand another squeeze. Her touch was like a shot of energy.

'I even… proposed.' I didn't know why I looked at Melody, but I did. Her eyes were wider than saucers. I didn't fucking blame her for being shocked. It was a dumb thing to do.

'Wow,' she said.

'I know.' I shook my head. 'Fucking stupid, right?'

'It's not stupid. You were in love. So what did she say?'

'She said yes. I thought she was happy. She loved the ring. I spent every fucking penny I had on that. I wanted her to have the best.'

'So what happened after that?'

'Well, I was on cloud nine, like some dumb love-struck idiot. I asked my boss for a loan to buy tickets to London. Cassie's thirtieth was coming up, so I thought it'd be a good time to introduce them to the family, and I knew how happy my mum would be that I was settling down. But I didn't tell Mum why I was coming over. I didn't even tell her about Gigi and Kerrie. Carlos knew. He was always wary of her, but it didn't matter. It was what *I* thought about her that was important. I told Dad but swore him to secrecy.'

'Did Cassie or Lily know?'

'Nope. Not even Flo or any of my friends back home. My friends in LA knew, but the plan was to announce everything properly when we all came to London. But three days before the trip, I came back to our apartment and they weren't there. They'd gone. At first I was worried. Wondering if someone had taken them. If something had happened. But then I saw Gigi had cleared out their stuff. That's when I knew it was planned. And all she left was a note with two words: "I'm sorry." That's it.'

'What? That's bollocks!'

'Tell me about it.'

A sharp pain ripped through my chest. It was like I'd opened up a wound that was healing and poured vinegar all over it.

Yeah, it didn't hurt as much now as it had at the time, but the pain was still there. Buried deep. And talking about it brought everything to the surface again.

'Did you ever find out what happened?'

'Yeah. Friends of friends found out that she'd moved in with a director of a film she'd auditioned for. She got the part, so to her, it was worth it. He was a big player in the industry and I guess she figured that it was better for her career to be with someone more powerful than just some rookie personal trainer.'

'Did you ever hear from her again?'

'Yeah. When the director traded her in for a younger actress and left her homeless, which was around the same time my career started to take off. Funny how she got in touch with me then. But I didn't reply. Which was hard. Because I missed Kerrie so much. More than her mum.'

'Shit.'

'So going back to when all the shit blew up—when she left, I still had three tickets to London.'

'Oh bollocks! And you'd borrowed money for them!'

'Right. Dad said I should still come. And I wanted to. For Cassie's birthday. But I was a mess. I tried to put on a front, but I was broken. And hurt. I was so pissed. I was never getting involved with a woman again. And definitely not a woman with a kid. The feeling of getting close to them and then that person you love being ripped away from your life was just…' I dragged my hand over my face. 'So that was why when you flirted I said I wasn't interested and why you overheard what you heard. One of my friends was trying to set me up with a woman in London who had a child. So when you heard me say that only a fool would date a woman with a kid, I wasn't talking about a friend. I was talking about myself. *I* was the fool.'

'Oh, Nate.' Melody threw her arms around me.

No way I was gonna cry.

Nope.

Oh fuck. Too late. Warm tears slipped down my cheeks.

Whatever. It wasn't the first time I'd cried and it wouldn't be the last. There was nothing wrong with expressing my feelings. I didn't buy into that bull that said *real men* didn't cry. We had emotions just like women did.

Resting my head on Melody's shoulder helped. As the scent of coconut and sherbet hit my nostrils, I inhaled it like it was oxygen.

I lifted my arms and wrapped them around her. We stayed there for a few minutes. She kissed the top of my head and rubbed my back and it felt fucking amazing.

When she pulled away, it was like being dropped in the Antarctic after spending time in the hot Caribbean sun. I missed the closeness. Feeling her warmth and her heart beating against my chest.

'Thanks for listening. And not calling me a pussy,' I laughed, wiping my cheek with the back of my hand.

'You're not a pussy. You fell in love. And someone who should've cared about you betrayed you in the worst way. Trust me. I've been there. I know exactly how you feel. Rodney, Andrea's dad, left me in a similar way.'

As Melody told me the story of how she'd returned home one day to find he'd left her alone with a tiny baby, the pain in my chest deepened. How could a man treat a woman and his own child like that? Now I understood why she hated him so much.

'We really do have things in common, then.' I attempted to smile. 'Some things better than others.'

'Yeah. I think that helps us understand each other more. I know it was painful for you to tell me your story, but I'm really glad you did. So much makes sense now. Why you don't like to date women you work with and why you don't want a relationship.'

'Why I *didn't* want a relationship,' I corrected her.

'What?'

'Past tense. I didn't want a relationship before. But I do now. With you.'

Melody's jaw dropped. She tried to close it, but it was like a vice was lodged inside her mouth.

'But…'

'That was what I wanted to talk to you about before I left the chateau. I wanted to see if you wanted to give it a try.'

'I thought you just… you said, *where you at*—like you had before, when we'd hooked up, so I thought…'

'I know what you thought. But you were wrong. I wanted you. All of you. Not just to get between your legs. I'm not interested in the sex.'

'Wow.' Melody paused again, like her brain was trying

to process everything. I knew how she felt. It was still a shock to me too. 'I don't know what to say. Other than, I feel the same. I like you, Nate. Like, a *lot*. Too much. That was why I didn't reply, because I knew I was already in too deep. That I was falling for you and I didn't want to get hurt. For as long as I can remember, I've always been the stopgap. The woman that guys used for a bit of fun before they found the woman they really wanted to settle down with. And I just couldn't go through that again. Not with you.'

'You don't have to.' I leant forward and stroked her cheek. 'You're it for me. Don't ask me how the fuck I know. But I just do. I can feel it. Here.' I patted my heart. It was fully formed again and beating like crazy.

Melody hadn't told me yet about what had happened with the French guy, but right now I didn't care. Something told me that this was different. That I could trust her. Melody wasn't like Gigi. She was the real deal.

'Are you serious?'

'Damn right I am. So what do you say? Do you want to give this a try? I haven't had much practice with the whole relationship thing, but I'm willing to give it my best shot if you're up for it?'

'Oh, trust me, I'm up for it!'

'A relationship, Mel, not sex,' I laughed.

'I know!' She cackled. 'That's what I meant. Although, there will be nookie in this relationship too, right?'

'Yeah.' I brushed her cheek again.

'Just checking, because you said you weren't interested in sex. I know it's been a couple of weeks, but I remember it being pretty good, so it would be a shame not to get jiggy if the mood took us.'

'It was more than *good*. What I mean is, I don't want sex to be the focus. I want us to start again. Do things properly. Starting tonight. If you'll let me, I'd like to take you on a date. Are you free?'

'Yeah! I'd love that.'

'Cool. I'll pick you up at seven thirty, okay?'

'Okay.'

I leant forward and kissed her on the cheek.

Every fibre in my body wanted to take her face in my hands and kiss those delicious lips like my life depended on it. But I meant what I said. This time I wanted to do things properly.

We were starting from zero. I was going to do things right. Woo her. Treat her like the queen that she was. And if that meant holding back a little on the physical stuff, I was willing to do it.

54

―――――――

MELODY

As Nate got up and walked away, I lifted my hand to my cheek, touching where he'd just kissed me.

I blinked once, then again. I needed a minute to process what had just happened. Actually, more like a few hours. A minute wasn't long enough.

Nate had just said he wanted a relationship. With *me*.

Bloody hell.

This was like the best thing. *Ever*.

Yesterday, I'd tried to pluck up the courage to message and tell him how I felt. Three times. But I'd chickened out. I'd hoped that by some miracle he'd feel the same, but even now, knowing he did, I couldn't quite believe it.

He wanted me. For *me*. Not for my body. Not for a fling. Not just for fun. For something more permanent.

And it wasn't just words. I saw it in his eyes. I felt it in my soul. He meant every word.

His actions told me it was real.

My heart broke into a million pieces when he told me how that bitch had hurt him. When I saw him crying, I wanted to hug him and never let go. Tell him that every-thing was going to be okay. Let him know that the right woman would treasure the actions that he'd done for the wrong one.

And just now. He could've kissed me. God knows I wanted him to. But even though I saw the desire in his eyes, he'd held back. Told me he wanted to do things prop-erly and take me on a date. An actual proper date.

My excitement levels might seem crazy to most people. But even at my age, I could count on one hand the amount of proper dates I'd been on. A vodka and Coke at the pub was as much as I could expect before a bloke asked me if I fancied nipping to the toilets for a quickie. So the fact that Nate wanted to wine me and dine me was mind-blowing.

I held my stomach. It felt like a million butterflies were having a rave. And it was the best feeling in the world.

Talking of my stomach, my period was due tomorrow. Normally I got pains at least a few days before, but so far, nothing. Nate said he wanted me, but how would he feel if being with me meant taking on Andrea *and* a baby of our own? Well, at least Janet would be pleased.

No. As hard as it was, I couldn't worry about that now. If it happened, I'd deal with it. Until then, I didn't want anything to spoil my happiness.

My phone chimed and I glanced at the screen. It was a voice note from Nico. I pressed the play button.

'*Salut*, Melody. Thank you for your message. However, I did not buy a dress for you. I checked this with Miriam and she confirmed. The only thing that she organ-ised was the fitting for the bridesmaid dress.'

So if Nico hadn't paid for the dress, then… who?

Cassie had been sleeping when I'd called last night but said she'd phone later, so I'd double-check it wasn't her when we spoke.

Actually, now that I thought about it, it couldn't have been her, because she would've said when she'd seen me that night.

OMG. It was Nate. *He*'d paid for it.

Nate knew I couldn't afford it, so he'd covered the cost. Wow. Just when I thought I couldn't love him anymore.

That's right. I love him.

It was pointless trying to pretend. I was crazy about him. And even though he didn't feel as much for me as I did for him, knowing that he wanted to make a go of things was good enough for me right now.

I stood up, my legs still wobbly, and walked back to my flat. The sky was perfectly blue. There wasn't a single cloud. And it reflected my mood to a T.

When Toby had told me they were considering stocking my jewellery, I'd thought the day couldn't get better. But I was chuffed to say I was wrong.

Nate turning up and surprising me took my happiness to a level I'd never experienced before.

Was it weird that I wanted to skip the rest of the way home? Screw it. I was doing it anyway. These moments didn't happen to me often, so I was going to enjoy every second.

~

I stood in front of my wardrobe. The doors were wide open and there was a pile of clothes on my bed that could rival Mount Everest.

It was so hard to know what to wear. Especially when I didn't have a clue where we were going. And I couldn't remember whether Nate had said we were meeting at seven or seven thirty. My brain was *still* processing everything he'd said.

There was only one way to find out. I looked for my phone. It was here, somewhere… eventually I found it buried under a heap of dresses.

Me
Did you say 7 or 7.30?

A few minutes later a reply popped up.
Nate
7.30.
Nate
That still okay?
Me
Yep!
Me
What should I wear?
Nate
Whatever you like.
Nate
Whatever you wear, I'm sure you'll look beautiful.

My heart fluttered for about the millionth time today. He was so sweet.

Me

In that case, I'll go with the black bin bag. I couldn't decide between that and the sexy brown potato sack.

Nate replied with a string of laughing emojis.

Nate

You'd still look hot in a bin bag. Like the sound of the potato sack too.

Nate

Can't wait to see you, Bangles.

Me

Me too!

Me

I'd better get ready.

Me

See you in a bit!

Nate

Laters.

My smile was wider than a cinema screen. I turned up the volume to the song that was playing on the radio and danced around my room.

'Someone's happy!' Andrea appeared at the door.

I wondered whether or not to tell her. It was early days. Not even *days*. It'd only been hours since Nate and I had said we'd make a go of things. So I didn't know if it was a good idea to talk about it so soon.

But when I'd come back from France, I'd encouraged Andrea to be honest with me, so I should do the same. It wasn't like she was a tiny child. She was sixteen. And I knew she'd be happy for me.

'I'm going on a date tonight.' I grinned like a sappy lovesick teenager.

'Amazing!' Andrea clapped her hands with delight. 'With the French guy that was here earlier?'

'Nope. With Nate. You remember Nate, he's—'

'Cassie and Lily's brother.'

'Yeah.'

'That's really cool, Mum! I hope he knows how lucky he is.'

My poor heart. It had fluttered more today than it had in years. That was such a sweet thing of Andrea to say.

And actually, now that I thought about it, she was right. Since we'd first hooked up in France, I'd always thought how great it was that Nate was interested. I'd been so in awe. So grateful that he would even notice *little old me*. But the fact was, I had a lot going for me too.

I was kind, loyal, hardworking, a good friend and I made nice jewellery. I knew for sure now—that was my calling. My mates told me I was fun to be around too.

No, I wasn't a supermodel and I never would be, but I had a banging pair of boobs, and since I'd returned from France, I'd been paying more attention to my arse and it wasn't as bad as I'd thought. It was a shame it'd taken me so long to start appreciating myself.

'I think he does, love. If not, I'll make sure I remind him! Now, what do you think? Green dress or the pink one?'

At seven thirty on the dot, my doorbell rang, just as I'd sat on the toilet. I think I'd weed about three times in the last hour. Must be the nerves. I heard Andrea race to the door and open it.

'Hey, Andrea.' I heard Nate's voice and my whole body tingled with excitement. I couldn't wait to see him. I wished this wee would bloody hurry up. 'How's it going?'

'Okay, thanks,' Andrea replied. 'Now, I think we should have a chat before my mum comes out.'

Oh bollocks. What was she doing? I wiped myself, then flushed the loo.

'Sure.'

'My mum's a good woman, so please don't hurt her, or you'll have *me* to deal with. I might be small, but I've taken karate lessons, so… *just saying.*'

Awww, bless.

Andrea left out the part where she'd had one karate lesson when she was twelve and hated it. She was so gentle, she couldn't hurt a fly. Such a sweetheart for sticking up for me, though.

I washed my hands, then dried them quickly before giving myself a final glance in the mirror.

For once, I didn't pick myself apart. I looked at my reflection and smiled. I looked good. Most importantly, I felt *amazing*. Like after years of challenges, setbacks and disappointments, things were finally going my way.

'I'm gonna do right by your mum, don't you worry. I like her a lot, so I promise I'll do my best to treat her like the queen that she is.'

'Too right!' Andrea said.

I stepped out in the hallway and saw them standing in front of each other. Andrea had her hands on her hips. Nate looked gorgeous as usual, dressed in a smart blue blazer, white shirt and black trousers, but he also seemed a little terrified.

'Evening!' I walked towards them. Nate's eyes widened before raking over me from head to toe and then back again.

'Wow.' His jaw dropped. 'You look fucking amazing!'

'Language!' Andrea scolded.

'Sorry.' The nervous look returned to Nate's face.

'Only joking!' Andrea burst out laughing. 'Mum swears all the time. We used to have a swear jar and she had to give me fifty pence every time she cursed, but then Mum took it away because she said I was gonna bankrupt her!'

'Yeah, thanks for that, my darling daughter!'

'*Really?*' The corner of Nate's mouth turned up into a smile. 'What else can you tell me about your mum?'

'I think it's time that we left.' I grabbed my jacket and opened the door. The last thing I needed was Andrea spilling my secrets.

'We'll talk, yeah?' Nate winked at Andrea.

'Yeah.' Andrea smiled and I'll admit, I did too. I could tell that they were going to get on well.

Nate opened the door of the taxi for me and I resisted letting out a little squeal. Such a simple gesture, but no man had ever done that for me before and it was lovely.

'So where are we going?'

'Somewhere exclusive. It's a surprise.'

'Oooh!' I liked the sound of that.

'Andrea's a cool kid.'

'She's the best.'

'How did it go with the whole, y'know, the *thing* you

found in her room before we went to France that you were shocked about?'

I paused, taking in the fact that firstly he'd remembered, second, he cared enough to ask, and third, he was being discreet about the specifics because we weren't alone in the cab.

'All sorted, thanks for asking. We had a good chat.'

I didn't want to go into too much detail. It wouldn't be right to betray Andrea's trust. I basically just told him how much better we'd been getting on and how she'd been helping me with my jewellery.

Nate sounded really interested when I filled him in about all the different pieces I'd made, how motivated I was and my plans to launch my own website.

And for some reason he seemed relieved when I told him that Toby had come around earlier this morning to give me the good news about the possibility of selling my jewellery in his stores.

Just as he congratulated me, the driver pulled up outside a house. Oh. I thought we were going *out-out* to a restaurant.

'Is this yours?'

'Yeah,' he said before getting out and running around to the other side of the car to open the door for me again. 'This way, please, m'lady.' He took my hand and led me to the front door.

If this was anyone else or even if it was a few weeks ago, I would've thought that Nate had brought me here to get his leg over. But my gut told me that wasn't true. I didn't know what he had planned, but I trusted him.

Nate put the key in the door and held it open. As I stepped inside, the hallway was lined with candles.

'Bloody hell!' My hand flew to my mouth.

'Don't worry. They're not real. I wasn't about to leave fifty candles lit whilst I went to pick you up.'

My mouth trailed along the ground as I followed the candles into the dining room. There was a larger candle in the centre of the table which lit up the room.

The table had already been laid with plates, cutlery, and thick blue napkins, and there was a bottle in a silver ice bucket.

'Oh my God, Nate. This is… amazing.'

My eyes watered and I told myself to stop being so sappy. Imagine telling someone I'd cried because a man had set up a candlelit dinner. Might sound lame to them, but to me, this was everything.

When I came to my senses, I saw Nate standing with his hand on one of the chairs, which he'd pulled out for me.

'Take a seat. Actually, let me take your jacket first.' He stepped behind me and slid off my jacket before returning to the chair and holding it, ready for me.

'Champagne?' he asked as I sat down.

'Yes, please!'

After he'd poured the bubbly, he lifted his glass towards mine.

'To us.'

'To us,' I repeated.

'So tonight is a bit of an experiment. Originally, I was going to take you to a restaurant, but then I thought I'd cook instead. I…' He paused. 'This is the first time I've invited a woman to this house. I wanted to show you how much you mean to me.'

Mind blown.

I remembered that when we drove to the castle Nate said one of his rules was never bringing a woman home. This was the real deal.

'That means a lot.' I swallowed hard. 'All of this is… just incredible.'

'Maybe save your thanks until you've tried the food. I haven't had much time to practise these dishes…'

'I'm sure whatever it is, it'll taste delicious.'

'I hope so. I thought I'd try cooking something Italian —you know, because I know how much you like pasta. And when we ordered room service in France, you said you loved pizza, so I thought, *y'know*. I called Lorenzo when I got back from meeting you this morning and he gave me some tips. Don't ask for the tiramisu recipe, though. He's sworn me to secrecy!'

I was speechless. Nate had gone to so much effort —for me.

My love for this man only intensified once I tasted his food. He'd made fresh pasta with veg for the first dish, a homemade pizza for the main and then Lorenzo's famous limoncello tiramisu, and it all tasted delicious.

'So?' he said as I scraped the bowl, trying to get every last drop of the tiramisu.

'Bloody amazing!' I gushed. 'Everything was top-notch. Better than a restaurant. Thank you so much!'

'Thank fuck!' His shoulders relaxed. 'So that's part one of the evening done. Are you ready for the next bit?'

'Eh?' I frowned. 'You mean…?'

'No!' Nate shook his head. 'Get your head out of the gutter, woman. Come here.' He stood up, held out his hand, then led me upstairs.

It was a good thing he'd clarified that he wasn't taking

me up to have his wicked way in the bedroom, because that was usually what it meant when a man led you upstairs.

But Nate wasn't like other men. It might take time for it to fully sink in, but he wanted me for more than what was in my knickers.

Nate switched on the light. It was a study, with light blue walls. On the desk there was what looked like a computer screen wrapped in shiny gold paper with a ribbon tied around it.

'I don't follow. Have you bought me a computer?'

'Ha, no!' Nate smiled. 'Touch the mouse, then unwrap the screen.'

I walked over to the desk, my chest thumping with anticipation. I had no idea what he wanted to show me, but I was excited to find out.

As I ripped open the wrapping paper and saw what was on the screen, my mouth fell through the floor and my head went fuzzy.

On the screen was a website. A website with a logo that said *Flame*. Below it read:

Exclusive designs by Melody Bailey coming soon. Click here to sign up for updates and to join our mailing list.

There was a large photo of Cassie wearing my head-piece from the wedding and then smaller close-ups of my necklaces and hair clips from the impromptu shoot that Sophia had arranged.

'How did you…? When did you…? Oh my God. Thank you!' I threw my arms around him and this time, I couldn't hold back the tears. Even with my head on his shoulder I could tell my eyes were like leaking taps.

'I hope they're happy tears?' Nate whispered into my head.

'They are,' I sobbed. 'I can't believe you did this. I'm so… it's amazing.'

To think that I was telling Nate about wanting to get a website done on the journey here, and he'd already bought the domain and set it up. This was… I had no words.

'Cassie sent me the pictures and I messaged Sophia and she recommended a great web designer. It's just a holding page for now, but when you're ready, the designer said you can chat about what you'd like to add to it. She can set up some e-commerce stuff so that you can sell your jewellery directly on there. And Sophia recommended the whole mailing list sign-up thing so that you can email potential customers when you're all set up. You've already got twenty-three subscribers. Well, twenty-four if you include me.'

The tears streamed down my cheeks and wouldn't stop. Nate led me to a small blue sofa, sat me down and handed me a tissue as I sobbed into his chest.

He had no idea what this meant to me. The fact that he'd taken the time and trouble to get the photos and set up the page, especially when he wasn't even sure if I wanted to see him again, meant the world.

And he'd listened when I'd told him the name I'd use for my company if I ever did my jewellery making again. He'd remembered and used it.

Nate had helped bring my dream to life.

'I don't know how I can ever repay you for this. Seriously. I already owe you loads for the taxi and Eurostar ticket and the *dress*.'

'How did you know?'

'Nico told me. I messaged to thank him and he had no bloody idea what I was talking about. *You* paid for it!'

'I wanted to. And I knew if I told you I was covering it you'd say no. Forget about that. You don't owe me anything. Seeing you happy is payment enough.'

'Well, know that on a happiness scale of one to ten right now, I'm at a hundred billion.'

'You know that's not possible, right?'

'Don't care!'

'Well, if you're at a hundred billion, hopefully, what I'm about to tell you will up that a little. I've got something to show you.' Nate reached in his pocket. He tapped away on his phone then showed me a photo of a shopfront. 'How do you fancy having your products sold in a cool boutique on the King's Road?'

'What?' I bolted up.

When he zoomed in, I saw one of my necklaces displayed on a pretty velvet cushion.

'One of my clients owns the boutique, so I showed her the jewellery I got from Bella and Lily and she loved them. She'd like to start selling them straight away if you have some more designs available?'

'Yes! I can't believe it!'

The King's Road was one of the fanciest streets in London. I'd never have thought I'd get my designs stocked somewhere like that.

Nate had set this up and believed in me before Toby had even arrived. My *boyfriend* was nothing short of incredible.

'You better believe it, Bangles. This is it. You're about to make it big. Your jewellery is going to take off. All of your dreams are about to come true.'

'They already are.' I looked him in the eyes, desperate to kiss him.

'Same.' He stroked my cheek.

'Why? What's happening with you?'

'Nothing much. Just met my dream woman and fell in love, that's all. No biggie.'

'You… what?' My eyes widened. 'You *love* me?'

'Yeah. You're funny, smart, kind, talented, beautiful and sexy as hell. How could I *not* love you?'

'Stop!' I fanned my face as I felt myself welling up again. 'No, continue!' I laughed.

'I fucking love you, Melody.'

'I-I love you too.'

'You don't have to say it because I have.'

'I'm not, you big numpty. I've secretly liked you for years. That's why I was gutted that you weren't interested in me. But once I got over the whole hatred thing, it wasn't much of a leap for that to turn into love.'

'It wasn't the right time. I wasn't emotionally available back then. But I am now. I want to be with you. I want to support you. I want to love you. I want to make you happy. I wanna cherish you and give you everything you deserve and more.' He kissed me softly on the lips and I melted into a puddle.

'W-wow,' was all I could say. His words and his kiss had left me speechless.

'I definitely didn't think this at the time, but now, I'm glad you picked up the wrong passport. If you hadn't, we wouldn't have been forced to spend time together and we wouldn't be together now.'

'I did it deliberately!' I said, slowly recovering. 'It was part of my evil plan to get you all to myself.'

Nate laughed and it was the sweetest sound.

'Whether it was part of your evil plan, fate or destiny, I'm glad. But you won't need any of that shit anymore. You're stuck with me. For good.'

'Poor me!' I cackled. 'I reckon I can handle being stuck with someone amazing, supportive, funny and hot like you. We're going to be great together, Nate, I just know it. I can feel it in my waters…'

MELODY
Three months later

'What's the capital of Australia?' Nate faced Andrea. 'Eight letters.'

'Er… it's not Melbourne, that's nine letters, so…' Andrea paused. 'Canberra!'

'Yes!' Nate filled in the boxes. 'Nice one, Dre!'

Andrea and Nate high-fived triumphantly and a warm feeling filled my belly.

They did crosswords together every weekend. If you'd told me four months ago that my sixteen-year-old daughter would choose to spend her Sunday mornings doing crosswords with my boyfriend, instead of sleeping in until midday, I never would've believed you.

Then again I wouldn't have believed that I'd still have a boyfriend. And I *definitely* would've rolled on the floor laughing if you'd told me that bf would be Mr Lover Man, eternal bachelor, bad boy Nate. But yet, here we were. Life was full of surprises.

'I'm going to the loo.' Andrea left.

For the past six weeks, we'd been living with Nate. When the landlord had announced he'd be putting up my rent, a month after Nate and I had become official, I'd started looking for somewhere else. I hadn't even considered asking Nate about moving our relationship to the next level. Most guys ran a mile if I suggested they stayed for breakfast. And things were going so well that I didn't want to jinx it.

So when Nate had suggested we move in, you could've knocked me over with a feather.

'It makes sense,' he'd said. 'We're always at each other's places. And I've got loads of space. It'll be cool.'

After I'd recovered from the shock, I told him I'd love that. But it wasn't just about me. I had to ask Andrea.

Andrea was totally on board. She thought it was a great idea, especially since she planned to go to uni in a couple of years and didn't want me to be alone. So that was that.

Now it was the three of us. It could've easily have been four after Nate and I had done the deed without a condom in France. My period eventually turned up—six days late, and during that time I was worried sick.

Nate noticed after just a couple of days, so I'd fessed up. I was surprised at his reaction. Rather than wanting to run a mile, he'd taken my hand and said we'd deal with it no matter what. He never failed to surprise me.

Although the idea of having a mini me or Nate running around the house sounded cute, I'd already been through so much, and now that I'd finally found a decent guy, right now I just wanted us to enjoy our time together. So being a family of three suited me just fine. But now I understood what it felt like to experience true love, I also knew never to say never. If Nate changed his mind about having children in the future, I'd be open to discussing the idea of adoption.

At first, I was nervous about moving in. Especially as Nate was a neat freak and I definitely wasn't. But I needn't have worried. Nate bought a big shed in the garden and kitted it out so I had my own jewellery workshop. There was space to store all my materials so I could work in the organised chaos that I loved and the house still stayed tidy. *Win-win.*

Even Andrea was making an effort to keep her room tidy. Maybe the fact that Nate had agreed she could paint it purple and choose her own furniture had something to do with it.

My phone chimed. I looked at the screen and smiled.

'I like that face.' Nate pulled me towards him and I snuggled up closer.

'I got another order!'

'*That's my girl!*' He leant forward and kissed me.

As our lips locked, my whole body tingled. I'd never get tired of kissing Nate. He gave me the fanny flutters every single time.

Although it was still early days, living together hadn't killed the magic in the bedroom. If anything, it'd made it better.

I was like a kid who'd been dropped into Disneyland with a ten-kilo supply of their favourite sweets. Living together just meant that I had an all-access pass to Nate's delicious body. Sex on tap. We were at it like rabbits.

Andrea had made loads of new friends at college, so she was out most afternoons and evenings during the weekend, which gave me and Nate plenty of time to enjoy each other.

But the great thing about being in a proper relationship was that there was no rush. Before, I'd always felt like I had to squeeze in as much sex as possible into one night with a man because I never knew how long he'd stick around. With Nate, there wasn't that pressure or urgency. We were able to take our time, make love slowly and savour every second.

'Mmmm.' I gazed into Nate's eyes as we came up for air. 'If you're gonna kiss me like that every time I get a new order, I might need to up the ante on my marketing!' I cackled.

'Darling, you know I don't need an excuse to kiss those damn lips. If I could, I'd kiss them every second just because you're breathing.'

'Aww, you're definitely a keeper.' I kissed him again, running my hand over his T-shirt and grazing the silver chain I'd made for him a few days after we'd got together.

The design was simple. Just with his initials on them. After we'd moved in together, he'd asked if I could change it. At first, I was worried that he didn't like it, but knew that couldn't be true because he'd worn it every day since I'd given it to him. Then he asked if I could put our initials on there instead: M&N. My heart had melted into a big puddle. This was the real deal.

As our hands roamed and our tongues collided, my whole body felt like it'd been set on fire.

'Get a room!' Andrea shouted as she walked back in.

'Go to your own bloody room!' I pulled away reluctantly, instantly missing the heat from Nate's hot lips and laughed. 'I got another order!'

'Amazing!' Andrea shouted. 'Want me to sort it out before I go?'

'Would you mind, love?'

'Course not!' She skipped to the back door and headed out to my workshop.

Andrea was just as supportive as Nate. They both did whatever they could to help me get my jewellery business off the ground: *properly*.

It was early days, but things were going great. As well as being stocked in Nate's client's boutique on the King's Road, three other shops in London were selling my pieces.

And I was *international*. I know, right? Get me!

Sophia had arranged for a couple of cool places in Italy to stock a few pieces and Toby had come through with a decent deal for his department store in Paris. It'd only been a few weeks since they'd started selling there, but it was going so well, I'd had to book a few days of unpaid leave from work to get time to make the orders.

Speaking of my job, I was still there. Even though I'd made more from my jewellery in the past month than I had in a whole year back when I'd first started, I wasn't earning enough to follow my passion full-time yet, but if it kept growing like this, I would be soon.

Nate had said I could take the leap now and he'd support us, which was so sweet, but this was something I needed to do for myself. I'd spent most of my adult life in debt, so I wanted to get myself to a good place before I quit my job for good. Knowing that I'd be able to do that in the very near future made getting through the dreaded nine-to-five much easier.

'So… as much as I'd love for you to whisk me to the bedroom and give me a good seeing-to, I'd better get started on lunch. What do you fancy? Roast lamb with potatoes and veg?'

'Yes!' Nate beamed. I knew it was one of his favourite meals, so after our workout this morning, I'd popped to the supermarket to pick up some bits.

And yeah, that was another thing that was different about my new life. Instead of just going to my legs, bums and tums class, Nate trained me twice a week. Surprisingly, I actually enjoyed it. He was great at his job. No wonder they paid him the big bucks.

My exercise and eating habits had changed, but not in the drastic way I thought. When we first got together, I was breaking my neck, trying to cook extra-healthy meals like pizza with a cauliflower base instead of normal dough. Even though Nate had said nice things about my body whilst we were in France, I still thought that once we were back in London, he'd be embarrassed to be with a bigger woman. But he loved me just the same. And he'd reassured me that if we were going to eat pizza, we could do it properly, just as an occasional treat. If he wasn't my ideal man before, his understanding of my love for pizza sealed the deal.

We ate healthy food most days, often cooking together, but sometimes we'd eat out. We tried to go out at least once a week. Either to a restaurant or clubbing—sometimes both.

We'd been on several couples dates. Lily and Carlos also loved dancing, so we'd double-dated with them a few times. We'd also had dinner parties with Bella and Mike and even gone to Paris to see Cassie and Nico.

Speaking of Cassie and Nico and couples trips, Nate and I were really looking forward to Christmas. Not just because it'd be our first one together, but also because we had a big group holiday planned.

Nico had hired a luxury cabin to mark the last holiday with Cassie as a couple before they became a family of three and invited me and Nate, Lily and Carlos, Bella and Mike to join them. Sophia and Lorenzo were even flying in from Italy too. I was so excited!

So yeah, life was good. Better than good. Life was bloody great.

I rested my head on Nate's shoulder and he kissed my hair.

'Mmm.' I smiled, my body sparking. 'I could get used to this.'

'Yeah.' Nate kissed my head again. 'I get it now. All that mushy love stuff Carlos, Lily, Cass and Nico and have been going on about for ages is fucking amazing. Part of me thinks I should've listened to them sooner. But it's a good thing I didn't—otherwise I wouldn't be with you now.'

'Too right!' I kissed him gently on the lips. 'I used to be cheesed off that guys just used me as a fanny filler. But now I'm glad none of those wankers worked out. I didn't know it at the time, but meeting the wrong men left me free to love the right one.'

'Bangles, your pussy is fine as hell, but you're no *fanny filler*. You're my lady. My friend, my lover, my motivator and my inspiration. You fulfil me. With you and Andrea, I feel like I finally have a purpose. You give my life meaning. And I never want to be without you.'

Want More?
Fancy finding out more about Melody and Nate? Join the Olivia Spring VIP Club and **receive the exclusive *My French Wedding Date* Bonus Content for FREE:** https://bookhip.com/RZSPACS

Ready For Book 6?
Want to find out what happens when Melody and Nate join Cassie, Nico, Lily, Carlos, Bella and Mike in a cabin for Christmas?

Order *My Perfect Happy Ending*, the final book in the *My Ten-Year Crush* series, from Amazon now!

The Middle-Aged Virgin

Have you read my debut novel ***The Middle-Aged Virgin****?* It includes Bella and Sophia from *My French Wedding Date* too! Here's what it's about:

Newly Single And Seeking Spine-Tingles…

Sophia seems to have it all: a high-flying job running London's coolest beauty PR agency, a long-term boyfriend and a dressing room filled with designer shoes. But money can't buy everything…

When tragedy strikes, Sophia realises she's actually an unhappy workaholic in a relationship that's about as exciting as a bikini wax. And as for her sex life, it's been so long since Sophia's had any action, her bestie has started calling her a *Middle-Aged Virgin.*

Determined to get a life and *get lucky*, Sophia hatches a plan to work less and live more. She ends her relationship and jets off on a cooking holiday in Tuscany, where she meets mysterious chef Lorenzo. Tall, dark and very handsome, this Italian stallion might be just what Sophia needs to spice things up in the bedroom…

But the dating scene has changed since Sophia was last single, and although she'd score an A+ for her career, when it comes to men, she's completely out of her comfort zone. How will Sophia, a self-confessed control freak, handle the unpredictable world of dating? And how much will she sacrifice for love?

Join Sophia today on her laugh-out-loud adventures as she

searches for happiness, enjoys passion between the sheets and experiences OMG moments along the way!

Here's what readers are saying about it:

"I couldn't put the book down. It's **one of the best romantic comedies I've read.**" Amazon reader

"Life-affirming and empowering." Chicklit Club

"Perfect holiday read." Saira Khan, TV presenter & newspaper columnist

"Olivia has an innate knack for the sex scenes, which are very hot. **This book was steamy**, but with such a huge element of humour in it that when you read it **you will certainly giggle throughout at the escapades.**" Book Mad Jo

"Absolutely hilarious! A diverse, wise and poignant novel." The Writing Garnet

Order *The Middle-Aged Virgin* by Olivia Spring from Amazon now!

AN EXTRACT FROM THE MIDDLE-AGED VIRGIN

Prologue

'It's over.'

I did it.

I said it.

Fuck.

I'd rehearsed those two words approximately ten million times in my head—whilst I was in the shower, in front of the mirror, on my way to and from work…probably even in my sleep. But saying them out loud was far more difficult than I'd imagined.

'What the fuck, Sophia?' snapped Rich, nostrils flaring. 'What do you mean, it's over?'

As I stared into his hazel eyes, I started to ask myself the same question.

How could I be ending the fifteen-year relationship with the guy I'd always considered to be the one?

I felt the beads of sweat forming on my powdered forehead and warm, salty tears trickling down my rouged cheeks, which now felt like they were on fire. This was serious. This was actually happening.

Shit. I said I'd be strong.

'Earth to Sophia!' screamed Rich, stomping his feet.

I snapped out of my thoughts. Now would probably be a good time to start explaining myself. Not least because the veins currently throbbing on Rich's forehead appeared to indicate that he was on the verge of spontaneous combustion. Easier said than done, though, as with every second that passed, I realised the enormity of what I was doing.

The man standing in front of me wasn't just a guy that came in pretty packaging. Rich was kind, intelligent, successful, financially secure, and faithful. He was a great listener and had been there for me through thick and thin. Qualities that, after numerous failed Tinder dates, my single friends had repeatedly vented, appeared to be rare in men these days.

Most women would have given their right and probably their left arm too for a man like him. So why the hell was I suddenly about to throw it all away?

Want to find out what happens next?
Buy *The Middle-Aged Virgin* by Olivia Spring
from Amazon now!

ACKNOWLEDGEMENTS

For the first time, I'm going to try and keep this page short and sweet by using bullet points. Here goes…

A HUGE thank-you goes to the following amazing people:

- Mum, Jas, Emma and Loz for being such brilliant beta readers.
- Rachel for the gorgeous cover design and illustration.
- Eliza for your first-class editing.
- Helen for your great proofreading.
- Dawn for your website wizardry.
- Meena for bidding to name a character in this book as part of the Young Lives vs Cancer Good Books campaign.
- Carey for your help and advice about jewellery making.
- My husband for patiently listening to me talk

about this book at least a hundred times a day and still showing enthusiasm.

- The brilliant bloggers, Bookstagrammers and BookTokers who read and review my books.
- And of course thank you, dear reader, for your continued support. I really appreciate you buying and reading my books and your kind messages. You're the best!

Lots of love,
Olivia x

ABOUT THE AUTHOR

Olivia Spring lives in London, England. When she's not making regular trips to Spain and Italy to indulge in paella, pasta, pizza and gelato, she can be found at her desk, writing new sexy romantic comedies.

If you'd like to say hi, email olivia@oliviaspring.com or connect on social media.

TikTok: www.tiktok.com/@oliviaspringauthor

* 9 7 8 1 7 3 9 8 6 1 4 3 8 *